THE 13TH REALITY

BOOK 3

THE BLADE OF SHATTERED HOPE

DON'T MISS THE REST OF
THE 13TH REALITY SERIES

Book 1: *The Journal of Curious Letters*
Book 2: *The Hunt for Dark Infinity*

ALSO BY JAMES DASHNER

The Maze Runner

THE 13TH REALITY

BOOK 3
THE BLADE OF SHATTERED HOPE

JAMES DASHNER

ILLUSTRATED BY
BRANDON DORMAN

ALADDIN
New York London Toronto Sydney

ALADDIN
An imprint of Simon & Schuster Children's Publishing Division
1230 Avenue of the Americas, New York, NY 10020
First Aladdin paperback edition February 2011
Text copyright © 2010 by James Dashner
Illustrations copyright © 2010 by Brandon Dorman
Originally published in 2010 by Shadow Mountain
Published by arrangement with Shadow Mountain
All rights reserved, including the right of reproduction in whole or in part in any form.
ALADDIN is a trademark of Simon & Schuster, Inc., and related logo is a registered trademark of Simon & Schuster, Inc.
For information about special discounts for bulk purchases, please contact Simon & Schuster Special Sales at 1-866-506-1949 or business@simonandschuster.com.
The Simon & Schuster Speakers Bureau can bring authors to your live event. For more information or to book an event contact the Simon & Schuster Speakers Bureau at 1-866-248-3049 or visit our website at www.simonspeakers.com.
The text of this book was set in Adobe Garamond.
Manufactured in the United States of America 0916 OFF
6 8 10 9 7 5
The Library of Congress has cataloged the hardcover edition as follows:
Dashner, James, 1972–
The Blade of Shattered Hope / James Dashner.
p. cm. — (The 13th reality ; bk 3)
Summary: Mistress Jane has tapped into the universe's darkest secret to create the Blade of Shattered Hope, and in her quest to attain a utopian reality for the future of mankind, she is ready to risk billions of lives to set her plan in motion.
ISBN 978-1-60641-239-8 (hardbound ; alk. paper)
[1. Space and time—Fiction. 2. Adventure and adventurers—Fiction. 3. Science fiction.]
I. Title.
PZ7.D2587Bl 2010   [Fic]—dc22   2009050165
ISBN 978-1-4424-0871-5 (pbk)

For Ben and the rest of the Egans.

So many memories—

most of them embarrassing,

all of them good.

CONTENTS

Acknowledgments... *xi*

Prologue: The Lake.. 1

Part 1: The Dark Basement

Chapter 1: Two Very Different Missions.............. 9

Chapter 2: The Kyoopy Quiz 19

Chapter 3: A Strange Guest 31

Chapter 4: Death by Water................................. 40

Chapter 5: A Mother's Love.............................. 48

Chapter 6: Finger on the Pulse 57

Chapter 7: Beneath 64

Chapter 8: Quite the Crowd.............................. 72

Chapter 9: Dead Ticks Everywhere................... 81

Chapter 10: Ribbons of Orange 89

Chapter 11: Latitude and Longitude 96

CONTENTS

Part 2: The Black Tree

Chapter 12: Sweet Digs.................................... 107

Chapter 13: Sleepless in the Dark 116

Chapter 14: Questions without Answers 125

Chapter 15: The Twelfth Blade 131

Chapter 16: A Diabolical Plan 139

Chapter 17: Tale of the Iron Poker 146

Chapter 18: Towers of Red................................ 154

Chapter 19: The Black Tree 163

Chapter 20: Disturbances 172

Chapter 21: The Unleashing.............................. 181

Chapter 22: Lightning and Flame..................... 191

Chapter 23: A Threat Reversed......................... 202

Chapter 24: Colored Marble Tiles 211

Chapter 25: Silver-Blue Light........................... 216

Chapter 26: Many Faces 225

Chapter 27: Soulikens....................................... 235

Chapter 28: Come Together 242

Chapter 29: The Only Hope.............................. 249

Part 3: The Fifth Army

Chapter 30: A Bowl of Debris........................... 259

Chapter 31: Making Plans 266

Chapter 32: Reunions....................................... 273

Chapter 33: Sending a Message 281

Chapter 34: The Way Station 289

Chapter 35: Darkness of the Way 297

CONTENTS

Chapter 36: The Speech 305

Chapter 37: Shivers 312

Chapter 38: Smoky Embrace 320

Chapter 39: The Surge.................................... 328

Chapter 40: Frazier's Good News 335

Chapter 41: An Interesting Gate 343

Chapter 42: Strips of Fire............................... 350

Chapter 43: The Fifth Army........................... 356

Part 4: Chi'karda's Power

Chapter 44: Talking with the Devil................. 365

Chapter 45: Splitting Up................................. 373

Chapter 46: A Very Bad Smell 381

Chapter 47: Weapons of Mass Coolness........... 388

Chapter 48: The Factory................................. 395

Chapter 49: The Miracle of Birth 401

Chapter 50: Holes in the Ground 410

Chapter 51: Flies in the Biscuits........................ 417

Chapter 52: Creatures in the Dark................... 424

Chapter 53: Eternity 431

Chapter 54: Words on a Tree........................... 438

Chapter 55: An Unearthly Shriek 446

Chapter 56: What Is Missing........................... 453

Chapter 57: From Bad to Worse...................... 459

Chapter 58: Family... 466

Chapter 59: Fists of Chi'karda........................ 469

Chapter 60: Ten Kids 475

CONTENTS

Chapter 61: Collision 482

Chapter 62: The Detour 488

Epilogue: The Mission 490

A Glossary of People, Places, and All
      Things Important 494

Discussion Questions 508

ACKNOWLEDGMENTS

I'd like to thank the following people for being really awesome:

My wife, Lynette.

My agent, Michael Bourret.

My editor, Lisa Mangum.

Chris Schoebinger and everyone else at Shadow Mountain.

Emily Lawrence and all the good people at Simon & Schuster for believing in this series enough to publish the paperbacks.

My incredibly supportive author friends: J. Scott Savage, Julie Wright, Sara Zarr, Anne Bowen, Emily Wing Smith, Bree Despain, Brandon Sanderson, Aprilynne Pike, and everyone in the Rockcanyon and Storymaker groups.

Angie Wager, for believing in my potential from the very beginning.

The people behind *Lost*. Best. Show. Ever.

The geniuses who invented cheddar cheese, potato chips, iPods, movies, books, and really soft couches. Oh, and lamps. I really love lamps.

But most of all, I want to thank you—the reader. Thank you for being here.

PROLOGUE

THE LAKE

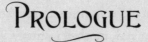

Bryan Cannon looked at the catfish—its bone-like whiskers, its slimy skin, its dark, unblinking eyes—and he saw death. For the creature, of course, not himself. Dinner would be fine and tasty tonight.

The day was beautiful. A slight coolness crisped the air, balanced perfectly by the brilliant sun shining down on Bryan's boat, sparkling off the waters that surrounded him, dancing like fairies of light. Too bad this fish wasn't enjoying things as much as he was.

Bryan had caught the fish in the little body of water in which he floated—called, quite pretentiously, *Lake* Norman. But if that tiny spit of rain-washed sludge was classified as a lake, then Bryan's toilet at home constituted a big pond. He chuckled to himself, as he often did at his own jokes, and spiked another squirmy worm onto his hook. Bryan shifted to get comfortable then he cast the line.

His small canoe rocked at the movement, sending gentle waves rippling across the lake's surface. He watched the outermost wrinkle, enjoying how it traveled along like it didn't have a care in the world. Bryan always loved it when he could keep his eyes trained on the tiny wave until it actually hit the shore. It wasn't as easy as it sounded, and his eyes watered with the effort.

There it goes, he thought, getting smaller and smaller, smaller and smaller . . . there! It hit right over by that sandy—

Splash!

A disturbance in the water, right where the lake met the shore. Then another splash, a huge one, that sprayed droplets all over the small beach. Bryan had been staring right at the spot, so he knew no one had jumped in.

Yet another splash. Then another. It looked like some kid thrashing about with his arms, trying to douse all of his friends in the face. Bryan used to love doing that when he'd been a kid.

There was only one problem. There wasn't a kid anywhere in sight. Or an adult, for that matter. Nobody.

The disturbance continued. Curious, Bryan laid

his fishing pole along the length of the canoe and reached for his paddle. Never taking his eyes off the white-water display, he lowered the tip down into the lake and began paddling his way over to check things out. He figured only one of three things was possible.

One, they had themselves a ghost right here in Lake Norman.

Two, some vicious sea monster had found itself a way to the lake from the ocean.

Or three, Bryan Cannon had finally flipped his lid and gone bonkers.

The closer he approached, the worse the splashing. Great cascades of water shot up everywhere—five, ten feet in the air. A curtain of spray unfurled next to him as he rowed along, the water soaking him and sluicing down the sides of the boat. For the first time, terror crept through Bryan's innards, and he realized it might not have been the smartest thing in the world to come so close to whatever *thing* was under the water.

He stopped paddling, slowing to a drift. As he did so, the splashing abruptly ceased. In a matter of seconds, the surface of the lake grew relatively calm, the small waves lapping against his canoe the only evidence anything had happened at all. If anything, the sudden stillness only scared Bryan more. He stared at the spot.

Something started rising out of the water.

Bryan shrieked as he saw what looked like an upside-down glass bowl break the surface of the lake like a bubble, shimmering like wet crystal. The bubble formed into the rough shape of a head, although there were no eyes or nose or mouth. Rising higher, the thing had a neck, and then shoulders, all made out of water. Up and up it rose, *forming* itself, growing out of the lake's surface like a demon rising from its grave. Before long, a human-shaped creature of water stood in front of Bryan, floating on clear feet, the sun casting spectrum-colored glimmers of light as it shone through the apparition.

Bryan sucked in a huge gulp of air, ready to let out the biggest scream of his life. But before he could do it, the watery ghost held up its arms and a sudden wave of water exploded from under its feet, crashing forward and down toward the canoe. Hundreds, maybe thousands of gallons of water, slammed on top of Bryan like a deluge from ancient and angry gods.

Bryan Cannon would never eat a catfish again.

If the waterkelt had a brain, it might've been impressed with its display of power. If the creature had a heart, it might've felt ashamed for causing the death of an innocent person. It had neither, so it simply walked its way to the shore and up into the surrounding trees, leaving behind a wet and muddy trail.

It knew where to go and what to do when it got there. So did its companion, which had been created on the other side of the lake. Their bodies sparkled and flashed in the sunlight like glistening quicksilver as they marched toward their duty.

Only their creator, Mistress Jane, understood the irony of the situation as she observed from a place very far away. Water, the basic element which sustains all human life, was about to be used for quite the opposite.

First stop, the Higginbottom house.

And then—revenge.

PART
1
~
THE DARK
BASEMENT

CHAPTER
1

TWO VERY DIFFERENT MISSIONS

Sato shivered, then grimaced. His rain-soaked clothes felt icky against his skin; it felt as if an army of leeches clung to him for dear life. He'd stood in the open for barely a minute, trying to figure out where he'd arrived exactly. Drenched already, he looked about, confused.

The air had the feel of twilight, though he knew it was almost noon in this Reality. The reason for the darkness floated above him—massive, heavy clouds of gray-black that were emptying their contents on his sopping-wet head. The clouds seemed close enough to touch. George had warned him that this Reality was a dreary, dreadful place where it rained constantly. Sato couldn't have agreed more.

But he saw no tombstones, no plaques planted in the ground to mark graves. He stood on concrete—or something like it. Hard and flat, the ground was dotted with regularly-spaced holes to drain away the water as quickly as it fell. Sato was glad for that. He didn't relish the idea of standing in a deep pool of water.

Why do I always get stuck with these jobs? Sato thought to himself. If it wasn't a windy, snow-swept mountaintop insane asylum, it was a rainy parking lot supposedly full of dead people. Fun stuff.

He noticed a small, square building about forty feet away, a scarce shadow in the wet darkness. No lights shone from any windows or outdoor fixtures. Seeing nothing else in any direction except the flat expanse of hole-dotted pavement, Sato walked toward the dark building.

As he sloshed his way across the ground, he wished he had a companion with him. Grumbling alone was no fun. Why hadn't George at least given him an umbrella? Maybe next time the red-faced geezer would send Sato to the middle of the ocean without a boat, or maybe to the desert without water, or skydiving without a parachute.

Sato shivered and kept walking, his socks soaked through from the rain. The squishy chill felt like he was smashing hundreds of iced shrimp below his feet. If no one answered at the building, he'd send the signal immediately for Rutger to wink him back. They might have found their first dead-end in Sato's latest mission.

A mission that creeped him out and left him in awe at the same time.

Oh, man, Tick, he thought. *What in the world does this all mean?*

As Sato got closer to the building, he noticed it had absolutely no markings of any kind—not a door, a window, or anything else he could see. It was made up of the same drab, no-color material of the ground, but smooth and unblemished. It was a perfect square, maybe ten feet in height and width.

He walked right up to the cube and put his hand out. Rain cascaded down the sides of the building in sheets, and when his hand made contact with the cool, hard wall, the water parted and washed across his skin, down his arm, and spilled onto the ground in tiny twin falls. Sato pulled his hand away and whipped it back and forth in a futile attempt to dry himself.

He was just about to call out the inevitable "Hello?" when he heard a loud thump and felt the ground tremble below his feet as if some giant beast from the underworld was trying to break free from its lair with a massive hammer. It happened only once, but Sato's feet tingled from the vibration of the impact. Surprisingly, he didn't feel afraid. Not yet, anyway.

There was a loud hiss, muted by the pounding rain, and then the wall directly in front of him began to move outward, toward him.

Sato felt anxiety grip his heart for the first time since arriving, and he stepped back, almost turned to run. But he quickly collected himself, reminding himself that George must have known where he'd been sending him after all. He had nothing to be afraid of.

He realized that it was only the bottom edge of the wall that was moving, swinging out and upward like an old-fashioned garage door. To his left and right, the side walls were doing the same, the groan of metallic hinges a faint squeal in the background. A soft light shone out from an unknown source, turning the thousands of raindrops into silvery sparkles. Sato could see through the cube to the other side where the fourth wall opposite him was opening up like its counterparts. Seconds later, the four walls locked into position parallel to the ground, and all movement stopped with a loud clank. Just a few feet above him, a wide shelter from the weather had formed, the doors and middle sections together now shaped like a square cross supported by four large metal pillars.

His fear gone, Sato stepped out of the rain toward the middle of what used to be a closed building and was now just a really fancy covered patio. He half-expected to see a picnic table or maybe a barbecue grill, but what he found instead surprised him greatly.

A hole.

A round hole, with a spiral set of stairs leading down into its depths and an iron handrail fastened to the wall. The light he'd noticed before was coming from somewhere at the bottom of the hole. Everything in sight was surprisingly dry. A small metal sign was bolted onto the floor right next to the first step, and several words had been stamped onto its surface:

Grace of Her Heart Cemetery

A prickle of fear raised bumps on Sato's flesh, but reason calmed his nerves soon enough. In a place where rain was the norm, it made perfect sense for the dead to be buried in some kind of vault or tomb instead of within the spongy, soaked, muddy earth. Dead people would be floating all over the place if they'd made that mistake. It was a cemetery after all—a normal, peaceful, full-of-bodies graveyard.

And over the last few weeks, Sato had become very used to graveyards.

Blowing a breath through his lips, he squeezed as much water as possible out of his clothes and hair, then set off down the stairs. With each step, an audible squish sounded, inexplicably making him want to laugh. Step by step, round and round, he descended into the hole. With every full circle he made, he saw a square light set into the wall, casting a warm glow—literally. Things heated up quickly and considerably.

After what felt like ten or so floors, Sato reached the bottom of the stairs and stepped through an open doorway. Unable to hold back a gasp of wonder, he gaped at the massive chamber in front of him. Row upon row of metal containers stretched as far as he could see, fading away into a shadowy mist in the distance. Large pillars supported the roof thirty feet or so above him, standing like iron angels guarding the dead.

For that's what filled the room. The dead. In metal caskets, stacked five high, with barely enough room between them for Sato to walk. Sato calculated there had to be thousands of deceased in the underground cemetery. Thousands upon thousands.

It took him four hours and forty-five minutes to find what he was looking for.

The casket looked like every other one in the vast tomb. Made from a dark steel, the slightest shade of silver prevented it from being utterly black. The final resting place of two other souls lay on top, two more beneath, with hundreds to either side. A dirty bronze plaque named the person whose body was inside the casket. Sato reached forward and wiped away the dust, more out of respect for the dead than anything else; he could read the words imprinted on the tarnished plaque just fine.

This was the seventh Reality in which he'd read such words.

It was the casket for Atticus Higginbottom.

⌁

Frazier Gunn had grown weary of prisons.

He'd now visited eleven of them, each one more foul than the one before it. Dirty. Grimy. Full of people with no self-control, no humanity. Full of thieves and murderers.

Now, walking down the dark, damp, smelly stone tunnel, escorted by two massively strong Brazilian guards with machine guns, he wondered how much more of this he could take. It didn't help that Mistress Jane had refused to tell him the purpose of the mission he'd undertaken, only the whats and wheres. The hows. None of the whys.

He'd long since gotten over the shock of finding his prey in prison, each and every time. Without fail, his searches had ended at some sort of jail, penitentiary, detention center, or, in three memorable cases, a hospital for the criminally insane. Always in shady institutions run by shady men and women. Always in places where the right price could buy you anything. Were there places in the Realities where this was *not* the case? He doubted it.

They came to a wooden door, heavily bolted and reinforced with a thick chain and lock. The guard to his right grunted something in Portuguese, but Frazier understood him well enough. He reached in his pocket and pulled out a thick wad of cash, obtained that morning at a local bank, in the local currency. He was amazed how easy it was to come up with money when you had someone as powerful as Mistress Jane backing the operation.

When the guard reached for the cash, Frazier pulled his hand away.

"The prisoner," he said, keeping his voice as empty of emotion as possible. "Get me the prisoner."

The man grunted again. Frazier was fully aware that these two brutes could simply take the money and leave him for dead. But he'd been sure to fill their heads with hopes of future deals, future bribes, future money-making opportunities. They'd be idiots to jeopardize such possibilities. It was, of course, a complete lie. Frazier would never, not in a million years, return to this country in this Reality, certainly not to this wretched cesspool of lowlifes. He needed one thing here, and one thing only.

After a long stare-off, the guard finally pulled out his jangly ring of keys and unlocked the chain and the three bolts of the door. He swung the door open, the hinges squealing like tortured rats, then disappeared inside, making it clear with a scowl that Frazier should wait for him to return. Frazier was more than happy to wait, having seen more than enough prisoners and jail cells in the last few weeks.

He stood next to the other fellow, a sour-faced, bearded giant of a man, who looked at the floor and never spoke a word. Frazier could only imagine what darkness lurked inside the man's brain, what memories haunted his dreams at night. For the slightest of moments, Frazier felt sorry for the man.

Several minutes passed, the only sounds that of breathing and a constant, echoing drip of water somewhere down the tunnel. Finally, the guard returned with the prisoner for which Frazier had paid handsomely. The eleventh such prisoner, the eleventh such bribe. And, according to his boss, worth every penny.

The woman stepped forward, still shackled at the wrist. Her black hair was a nest of greasy strings, her torn clothes were filthy, and her long fingernails were crusted with black dirt. For a moment, she refused to meet Frazier's eyes. Irritated, he reached forward and put his hand under her chin, tilting her face up so he could get a good look.

Despite her pale complexion, the smudges of grime, the cracked lips, and the way her skin seemed to squeeze the sharp bones of her skull, he had no doubt, none whatsoever. She was still beautiful to him.

Frazier handed the money to the guard, who then passed over the key to the chains around the prisoner's—the *former* prisoner's—wrist. Frazier nodded once, curtly, then took hold of the woman's arm.

Without saying a word, he turned and escorted the Alterant of Mistress Jane down the long and dark tunnel.

CHAPTER
2

THE KYOOPY QUIZ

Okay," Mr. Chu said, leaning both his elbows on his desk at school and staring down at the open physics book. "If you get this one right, you are The Man. That's capital T, capital M."

"Hit me," Tick responded. Even he could hear the tiredness in his own voice. He'd been studying with Mr. Chu for more than an hour, question after question. Tick was schooled at home now since Master George had insisted that it was too dangerous for Tick to be out and about with classmates and the general public every day. But enough time had passed that Tick had finally convinced his parents and Master George to let him visit Mr. Chu three times a week in the afternoons. Any break from the house was welcome, even if it did involve his former teacher grilling him with questions about physics. Mr. Chu glanced up before continuing, a grin spreading across his face. Tick faltered a moment, hating how much the man looked like his Alterant from the Fourth Reality. Like Reginald Chu. The *evil* Reginald Chu, who was stuck—uncomfortably, Tick hoped—in a place called the Nonex. Too bad Master George didn't have a clue as to where the Nonex was, or what it was, or anything else about it at all.

"Okay," Mr. Chu said, speaking slowly. "How does the wave-particle property paradox contradict the theorems related to radiation damping and nonlinearity in the pilot wave interpretation of quantum mechanics?"

Tick slumped back in his chair. He barely understood the question, much less knew the answer. Figuring his brain had finally gone to sleep, he murmured, "I give up. My head's not working right now."

Mr. Chu laughed, and any remnant of his Alterant was wiped away in a flash. "I was just kidding. I'm not sure the question even made sense, actually."

Tick couldn't help but feel relieved. He needed to understand quantum physics and all the sciences in order to figure out what was wrong with him. He had an extremely dangerous influence over Chi'karda, the force that ruled the world of quantum physics—or QP, as Mr. Chu liked to call it—and Tick had very nearly killed himself and countless others when his Chi'karda had gotten out of control just a few months ago.

Since then, he'd been careful not to get too excited or too angry. So far nothing bad had happened—except for the time he'd sent his poor dad flying across the room and through an upstairs window. If it hadn't been for that bush . . . Well, needless to say, the bush didn't survive, but his dad—whose weight was classified somewhere between pudgy and ginormous—did. Though he had complained about a hurt back for weeks, sending Tick on countless runs to the kitchen to get him cookies and milk to enjoy during their video game battles.

"Tick?" Mr. Chu asked, snapping his fingers.

Tick realized he'd been staring at the floor, completely lost in his thoughts. "Oh. Sorry. I was just thinking about something."

Mr. Chu yawned, then closed the science book with a loud thump. "Well, you've got a lot to think about. Any problems lately?"

"No." He looked into his teacher's eyes, trying to see if he could read anything there. The man had been through just as much as Tick had, and Tick worried about him. "What about you? Have you . . . gotten over it?"

"Gotten over what? Being imprisoned by a bunch of thugs, forced to torment you and your friends, almost killed? What's there to get over?"

Tick shook his head, trying not to look sad, but knowing he did. Thinking back to what had happened in the Fourth Reality, and everything that led up to it, always made him sad. He didn't even really understand why—or at least he told himself that. After all, they'd escaped. They were safe. All seemed fine in the world.

But deep down, he knew why he felt sad. He knew all too well.

It was her. It was Mistress Jane. What he'd *done* to her.

"Tick," Mr. Chu repeated, snapping his fingers again. "What's buzzing in that brain of yours?"

"I didn't mean to hurt her," Tick said, almost whispering. His heart felt like a squishy pile of mud. "I don't even know exactly what I did to her. For all we know, I killed her."

Mr. Chu stood up, shaking his head. "Enough of that." He picked up the book and slid it inside Tick's backpack, then held the pack out toward him. "Seriously. You shouldn't feel one ounce of guilt for something that happened completely out of your control."

Tick didn't respond, just reached out and took his backpack, slipping the straps over his shoulders.

"I'm not even going to talk about it with you anymore," Mr. Chu continued. "Maybe that's making your subconscious mind think it's something you *should* feel guilty about, something you should come to terms with, seek forgiveness for. Well, it's not. As soon as blame the wood for killing with fire."

"Huh?" Tick asked.

Mr. Chu shrugged. "Sorry. It was the best I could come up with."

For some reason, that made Tick feel better. "I'm fine, I guess. It's just that . . . she seemed like maybe she was starting to feel bad about being so evil. I thought maybe she was going to change, maybe even help us."

Mr. Chu put two fingers together and swiped them across his lips like pulling a zipper.

Tick rolled his eyes. "Fine. Well, thanks for helping me study. I'll see ya next week."

"Sounds like a plan. Study the chapter on natural electricity's role in physics carefully. A lot of things build off that information."

"I will. See ya."

"Take care." Mr. Chu smiled then, and he looked nothing like his diabolical twin who had almost driven billions of people permanently insane.

Tick turned and headed out the door, deciding at the last second to swing by the city library to check his e-mail before going home. He was looking forward to the best weekend ever—his sisters Lisa and Kayla had gone to stay with their cousins in Seattle until Monday night. Uncle Ben and Aunt Holly had two daughters the same ages as Tick's sisters, and the two families swapped weekends between Deer Park and Seattle about every five months.

No girls for three whole days. Well, unless you counted his mom, which he really didn't.

Peace and quiet. Books, junk food, and video games. It was gonna be great.

Mrs. Sears, the librarian, was in her usual good mood, greeting Tick with that lilting laugh of hers as the gray cleaning pad she called her hair wiggled back and forth on her head. She asked him about the pros and cons of homeschooling, the latest books he'd been reading, and how he'd been faring against his dad in the latest installment of his favorite video game, Football 4000. But every time he answered a question, he eyed the long line of computers, trying to give her a hint.

Finally she nodded toward an empty chair and said, "Well, I know why you're here. Go on, and I'll find you a good book before you head out. Deal?"

"Deal," Tick responded, already moving away.

He was logged into his e-mail in no time. Just as he'd hoped, there was a letter from Sofia and one from Paul. Jackpot. Paul's had been sent first, addressed to both Tick and Sofia, as usual. Tick opened Paul's e-mail and began reading.

Dudes,

Okay, I'm bored. When the highlight of your day is
getting an e-mail from some chick in Italy about
how she hurt her pinky toe in a vicious spaghetti
sauce can incident, you know it's time to change
things. Where in the world is Master George?
Yeah, I know we almost died and all that in the
Fourth, but better that than getting up at the
crack of dawn for school and then sitting around
all afternoon eating cheese puffs. I can't watch TV
anymore. Too boring.

Tick, how's that whole power thing of yours
working out? Melted any bad guys recently?
Dude, I was thinking we could present you to the
world as the first human microwave oven. We'd
be rich, and the ladies would swarm. Think about it.
We'll split it 50–50. You do the cooking, I'll do the
promoting.

Sofia, when you gonna bring us out to Italy?
Don't give me any junk about money. Just ask ol'
Pops to slip you a few bones to buy us airplane
tickets. I'll even bring you some hot dogs. No,
make that corn dogs. Yeah. Corn dogs and Italy.
Now that's living.

I'm out. Any time you start mentioning corn dogs,
you know it's time to end the e-mail. Later. Call us
in, Master George!

Paul

Still snickering, Tick closed the e-mail and opened
Sofia's, which had been sent soon after Paul's, despite
the time difference.

Dudes?

Did you really start that last e-mail with
"Dudes"?!?!? Promise me you'll call me a dude
next time I see you. Oh, and "chick from Italy"?
You're getting awfully brave, Rogers, what
with an entire ocean between us. Next time we
meet, you might want to wear something made
of metal.

I'm kind of bored too. Things with my parents seem
worse than ever. All my old friends just seem stupid
now. I hate how clueless they are. They have no
idea what kind of stuff is going on out there.

I wish I had a funny joke. But once Paul says
something that's actually funny, I'll try harder.

Seriously, though, I do think you guys should
come to Italy. I'll ask Frupey about it. Maybe this
summer. Of course, I hope we're doing something
as Realitants by then.

See ya.
Sofia

Tick looked at his watch and realized he should
probably get home. His mom worried her head off
every time he left the house these days. Deciding he'd
just write his friends from home later, he logged off,
checked out the book Mrs. Sears recommended, then
headed out the door.

Just a few minutes later, he was walking down the
long road toward his neighborhood, surprised that he
was already sweating.

It was almost spring, but it was still too early to
be *hot* in Deer Park, Washington. Since his escape
from the Fourth Reality, Tick had seen his birthday
come and go—he was a manly fourteen years old
now. Thanksgiving, Christmas, the New Year, and
most of the winter had passed as well; April was just
a few days away. Tick had heard less and less from

Master George in the last month or so. It gave him an uneasy feeling. He wondered if it was the calm before the storm.

He wondered about Mistress Jane, too. He'd give anything to know what had happened to her. Whether or not she was still alive. And if so, whether or not she was okay. He dreamed about her at night, reliving those terrible moments in Chu's palace when he'd sent a world of chaos at her body and attacked her with thousands of flying shards of metal.

For some reason, he'd lately had dreams where one of his sisters—sometimes Lisa, sometimes Kayla— replaced Jane and suffered the terrible onslaught instead, screaming in agony. He woke up in a sweat every time, and seeing it play out that way humanized the ordeal, made it more real. No matter what she'd done in the past, Jane was still a person, just like Lisa and Kayla.

His actions haunted him, consumed him with guilt. He wished—

Womp!

Tick stumbled to the ground, crying out as one of his elbows banged against the rock-hard dirt of the road's shoulder. He twisted onto his back, fear ripping through his body. He searched around with his eyes, tried to figure out what had happened. It'd been like a wave of hardened air had slammed against him, knocking him down with a sound like the thump of a million bass drums . . .

Womp!

He braced himself as a massive surge of energy swept across the road and past him. He expected his hair and clothes to whip in the wind, but nothing stirred. He almost felt the energy . . . *inside* his body. As if someone had injected charges of lightning into his bloodstream.

Womp!

Tick squeezed his eyes shut. He felt a surge of heat in his chest, an intense pressure that enveloped his body, then it disappeared. Terrified, he scrambled to his feet, stumbling in a circle as he searched around him. There was nothing unusual in sight, nothing out of the ordinary.

Womp!

Tick took a step backward, wrapping his arms tightly around him, tensing as the wave of force hit again. With each surge of energy, he felt heat within his heart and veins, like a raging fever. Heat. Pressure. Squeezing. But only for an instant. Then it was gone again.

Gasping for breath, he stood as still as possible, peeking through squinted eyes, waiting for it to happen again. His mind churned, trying to imagine what it could be. In some ways it felt like the attack of

Chi'karda he'd had when everything had gone crazy in Reginald Chu's research chamber.

Similar, but different.

This wasn't coming *from* him. He was feeling it coming from *somewhere else.*

A blast of panic shot through his nerves. From somewhere else . . .

Womp!

The wave hit again. Tick sprinted for home.

CHAPTER
3

A STRANGE GUEST

Lorena Higginbottom sat in the chair where she always waited for Atticus to come home from his visits with Mr. Chu at school. Her constant worrying over the boy had done strange things to her. She couldn't sleep, couldn't concentrate. She rarely laughed anymore. Sometimes—not often, but sometimes—the worry turned into utter misery, engulfing her like a horrible, *eating* cancer.

Her boy. Her one and only boy. Mixed up with the Realitants and plagued with a burden of power that no one understood yet. Something was terribly, terribly wrong with him.

She'd gone through all the usual phases. The denial,

the blame, the guilt, the despair. She'd run the whole gamut of emotions over the last few months, and it had all come to a head this morning. When her husband, Edgar, had left for work, and Atticus had disappeared into his room to study, she'd sat in her room, crying, *sobbing*, a sorry sack of gloom and grief. It had taken every ounce of willpower in her body to pull her anguish back inside and hide it away. But she did, for Atticus's sake.

With a smile on her face, she'd seen him off to his appointment with his former and favorite teacher. She'd been sitting in her chair ever since, counting down the minutes until he returned. *I should've gone with him,* she thought, just as she did every single time Atticus left the house. But she couldn't. She knew that. She and Edgar had long since agreed that they couldn't exist in a constant state of terror and fear. Atticus needed time alone, time to grow, time to learn how to bear his burden. Still, he was only a child, only fourteen . . .

A rattling sound from the back of the house snapped her mind alert.

Like a shot of pure caffeine, adrenaline rushed through her body, and she jumped out of the chair before any thought had time to form. Wondering why Atticus would come home the back way—and feeling the slightest fear that it might *not* be him—she ran out of the room and down the hallway, into the kitchen, toward the door leading to the patio behind their home.

The rattling noise continued. Someone was pulling at the knob, twisting it back and forth in vain because it was locked.

The trickle of fear turned into a gush; she pulled up just short of the patio door.

"Atticus?" she called out.

No answer. But whoever was out there quit trying to open the door.

"Atticus?" she repeated, louder.

Still no answer.

The door had a large window, currently covered by the drawn yellow curtain. Alarmed, she grabbed the side of the stiff material and pulled it back an inch, peeking outside.

The thing standing on her back patio wasn't her son.

When his house finally came into view, Tick somehow found another burst of energy and ran faster. The loud thumps and waves of energy had stopped, but he couldn't rest until he made sure everything was okay at home. A fresh spurt of panic squeezed his insides, and he picked up the pace yet again.

He was only two houses away when he noticed a car coming down the road from the other direction. His heart skipped a beat when he saw that it was his dad's.

Then his heart almost stopped beating altogether when the car suddenly accelerated, the engine screaming, the tires squealing. The car swerved off the road, over the curb, and onto his front lawn. It shot across the grass until it reached the driveway, picking up speed instead of slowing down.

Tick watched in horror as the car slammed into the garage door with a thunderous crunch, then disappeared in a pile of shredded wood and dust.

In her head, Lorena couldn't reconcile the thing she saw through the door's window with any semblance of reality she knew or felt. It looked like something out of a science fiction movie—a man-shaped, shimmering ghost made out of clear liquid, its rippled surface glistening. The face had no features, but it seemed to be looking at her all the same.

For a bare instant, she actually considered unlocking and opening the door. The creature seemed so harmless, so peaceful, the water rippling like the gentle, lapping waves of a Caribbean beach. But her hand froze halfway to the latch, and a shudder of fear snapped her out of her hypnotized state. Her mind kicked into gear, reminding her that creatures made out of water were not normal, that although she'd lived a life believing only in things that were *normal,* not supernatural, seeing this creature probably changed things forever.

The sparkling water creature she saw through the window could *not* be a good thing. And most likely, it had something to do with her son.

She stepped back, her hand rising involuntarily to her mouth as the shock of her visitor hit home. Somehow she knew that something terrible was about to happen.

The creature's watery hand reached out and grabbed the outside door handle, rattling it again. Lorena couldn't actually see the knob from her angle, and she wondered how the thing grasped objects if it was made only out of liquid. Then better sense told her that now probably wasn't the best time to figure out the physics of the situation, and that she'd better run.

But just as she took a step away from the door, the creature *melted* right in front of her, the water crashing to the pavement outside with a loud splash. It was as if a force field or an invisible membrane had been holding the thing together, and it had been abruptly taken away, leaving nothing to hold the body together. She realized she'd been holding her breath and sucked in a huge gulp of air in relief. Whatever it had been, whatever purpose . . .

Her thoughts were cut short when movement down by her feet caught her vision.

In the thin space between the door's lower edge

and the short strip of wood that kept out the wind and bugs, a three-foot wide sheet of water began pouring through and onto the kitchen floor. A puddle formed in a matter of seconds, somehow deepening into a narrow pool on the flat linoleum surface.

Before Lorena could react, a horrendous crash rocked the house, the sounds of crunched metal and shredded wood thundering through the air like a sonic boom.

Even as her hands rose to cover her ears, even as the beginnings of a scream formed somewhere in the back of her throat, Lorena saw the puddle at her feet bubble and churn, swirling, coalescing into a bulbous glob, like a huge see-through water balloon about to burst.

And then the glob rose toward the ceiling, slowly re-forming its human shape.

The scream finally escaped Lorena's mouth.

❧

"Dad!"

Tick had faltered when the car hit the house. He was too stunned to move. Of all the things he'd expected to see when he came home, it wasn't this.

He shook himself out of his daze and ran for the mangled mess of the garage. A hissing sound came from within, the engine letting out its last, dying breath. Smoke and dust billowed out, attacking Tick's lungs with a vengeance. Coughing, he kicked at the loose metal and broken boards, digging his way in to see if his dad was okay.

"Dad!" he yelled again.

He'd just moved a big chunk of something heavy when the front door to the car popped free, a horrible metal groan screeching through the air as his dad forced it open all the way.

"Dad! What's going—"

Tick's voice stuck in his throat when he saw the large body of Edgar Higginbottom stumble out of the car and fall onto the garage floor.

He was covered in . . . goo. Clear goo.

⁓

Frozen by fear. Not able to move. Your mind screaming at your legs to run, but your legs not listening. This was why Lorena had left the Realitants long ago, hoping she'd never have to experience it again.

She stared as the mysterious, impossible thing formed, water sluicing upward from the floor, defying the law of gravity in the process. Legs, then torso, then arms, finally a head. The entire process took less than twenty seconds, but it looked unnatural, like a time-lapse film of a geological event that had taken thousands of years.

When the creature finished re-forming, the watery demon stood silent for a long moment, staring at her despite the lack of eyeballs or even eye sockets.

Lorena stared back, frozen as much by stubborn disbelief as fear.

Without warning, the creature moved toward her.

CHAPTER
4

DEATH BY WATER

Tick's dad thrashed about on the garage floor, the thick layer of transparent goo that covered every part of his body bouncing and wiggling like jelly. The gel-like substance was never more than an inch thick in any one spot, but it enveloped Edgar from head to toe. Most alarming was the clear mask covering his face.

The man obviously couldn't breathe. More than a year ago, Tick had almost seen his dad die; he felt the same horrible panic now.

"Dad!" Tick yelled again. He knew screaming wasn't going to help no matter how many times he did it. He had to *do* something.

He knelt down beside his squirming dad, who kept

grabbing and tearing at the gel on his face, ripping sections away from his mouth to catch a quick breath only to have the goo be replaced almost instantly. When Tick saw his dad's hands rip at the stuff and saw the way it splashed and wavered, he realized it wasn't goo at all.

It was *water.*

Somehow, some force had captured his dad in a man-sized pool of water.

And it was killing him.

Something trembled inside Tick, fluttered, as if a raven had magically appeared inside his stomach and was trying to escape. Heat surged through his veins. Pressure built up behind his skull, pushing outward, hurting. He closed his eyes, rubbed them.

His . . . *problem.* He knew it was his problem. The stress of the situation had ignited his inexplicable reservoir of Chi'karda, causing it to erupt inside him. It was just like what had happened in Chu's palace. It was starting all over again. But he couldn't afford to lose control now.

No, he told himself. *Not this time. I have to save Dad.*

He took several long breaths and concentrated, probing his body with his thoughts, reaching out to something he didn't comprehend. Repressing it, pushing it away. Calming himself. He imagined the Chi'karda surge as a cloud of orange mist—as Mistress Jane had shown him months ago—trapped within his rib cage. Mentally, he made the cloud dissipate, weaken, flow out of him. Go somewhere else. Somewhere safe.

He had no idea what he was doing. He'd spent months trying to understand the power within him, make it a tangible thing. He'd spent months failing. But urgency won out. He felt his heart slow, felt the heat cool away, felt the pressure release.

It was gone. Tick opened his eyes, looked down, focused.

His dad's face was turning purple.

Lorena's screams were drowned out in a sickening gurgle as the cold wave of water crashed into her. The creature had leaped into the air and dove for her face, forming into a thick stream and slamming into her like a sudden burst from a fire hose. She shook her head, spitting and coughing, and grabbed at her face. Instead of washing off her and falling to the floor, the liquid seemed to stick, enveloping her head and neck in a mask of water. It crept into her mouth, into her throat. She gagged, spit again. She wiped frantically at her face, but it did no good.

The terrifying situation had created a crisp sense of clarity in her mind, and an idea formed somewhere in the dark factory of her thoughts. A very bizarre idea.

She turned and bolted for the garage. With every step,

she felt rivulets of water running down her torso, the creature capturing her inch by inch. She knew she wouldn't be able to move once the thing had control of her legs.

The garage. She had to reach the garage. She made it out of the kitchen and into the short hallway with coat hooks and shoe racks. The door was only a few feet away.

The water reached her knees. She felt herself slow a bit.

She lurched forward, reaching for the door that led to the garage. One arm had been taken completely over, and the other had only a second left before its fingers would be swallowed by the possessed water. The liquid encasing her arms made it harder to control her movements, but the creature seemed mostly focused on her head. She found the handle. She twisted the knob and pulled. An instant later, the wet monster had consumed her fully.

Lorena fell forward and toppled down the three stairs that descended into the garage. Ironically, the thick layer of water cushioned her fall.

Tick slapped at his dad's face with cupped hands, like a dog digging for a bone. Each swing caught a little pool of water and sent it flying, but more instantly sloshed back in, and the displaced splashes somehow flew back onto his dad's body like metal shavings returning to a powerful magnet. Every once in a while their combined efforts would clear just enough water for his dad to take a quick breath, but Tick knew they couldn't keep it up much longer.

The garage door that led to the inside of the house banged open.

Tick looked up and saw his mom. Fully encased in water just like his dad, she fell down the short staircase and crashed onto the floor with a wet flump.

"Mom!" Tick cried, scrambling over to her and falling on top of her. He could only hope his dad could find enough breaths to survive.

His mom clawed at the water around her nose and mouth. She kept trying to say something, but all that came out was the garbled mess you hear when someone talks to you while submerged in the swimming pool. Her eyes were open, fixed on Tick through the crystal-line, shimmering layer of water. She wasn't panicked, but definitely trying to communicate something.

Tick forced himself to stay calm. Reaching forward, he placed his hands on either side of her face. She got the message, and remained completely still. With a quick jerk, Tick slid his hands across her mouth, swiping away a huge section of water long enough for her to get one word out.

He didn't know what he'd expected, but it sure wasn't the two syllables that came out of her mouth in a gargled scream.

"Vacuum!" she yelled.

At first, confusion engulfed Tick. He thought surely his mom's mind had snapped under the pressure of being possessed by a blob of water. But then he realized it was quite the opposite. She'd been the only one to actually come up with a solution.

He turned his head to look over his shoulder, across his dad's heap of a wrecked car, and focused on the huge beast of a machine that sat next to some tools and cleaning supplies on an old wooden workbench.

The MegaVac. The thing looked like R2-D2 with a big hose.

And it could suck water out of rock.

Tick got up and ran around the front of the crashed car and over to the workbench. He reached up and grabbed the heavy, squat yellow cylinder with its thick, snaking hose attached. He dragged the vacuum toward his mom, whose face was darkening into a sick blue color.

"Mom!" he yelled. "Keep swiping at it!"

He reached her and flipped the switch on the MegaVac.

It didn't turn on.

For one agonizing second, despair crushed Tick.

But then he realized the stupid thing wasn't plugged in. He scrambled for the long black cord, found its end, then crawled over to an outlet and pushed the big plug in. A heavy roar kicked in behind him. Tick scooted back over and knelt down beside his mom, grasping the end of the vacuum hose like the mouth of a deadly cobra.

The thing worked like a beauty.

He stuck the hose on his mom's mouth and watched with elation as the vacuum sucked up the water with no problem. The MegaVac had been a birthday present for his dad two years ago, and Edgar had excitedly given a demonstration to the family on how the beast could make *anything* disappear into its glorious, hard-plastic belly, be it cereal bits or gallons of floodwater. It was the closest thing to a black hole that the Higginbottoms would ever experience, he'd said.

Tick wanted to shout in victory as he realized even a supernatural creature made of liquid couldn't resist the monstrous sucking power of a MegaVac, lord of all vacuums.

He finished cleaning the water off his mom, her soggy hair and clothes the only sign she'd been encased by a water monster just moments before. Tick's dad was only a few feet behind him, and twenty seconds later, the vacuum had sucked up his captor too.

Tick leaned back, panting as his mom and dad

gasped and spit, doing their best to recover from the ordeal. He thought of Lisa and Kayla in Seattle, and had an almost overwhelming feeling of relief that they hadn't been here. The odds of Lisa—and especially little Kayla—surviving something like this . . . Tick quenched the horrible thought before images formed that might never go away.

He looked over at the body of the MegaVac, which now contained two—what exactly were those creatures?—within its belly.

A worry hit him. He didn't want to turn off the vacuum for fear the creatures would find a way to seep back down the hose. "What should we do? Do you think we killed them?"

His dad laughed, a mere sputter between heavy breaths. "I say we flush the suckers' guts down the toilet. That oughtta do it."

And that's what they did.

CHAPTER
5

A MOTHER'S LOVE

Sofia leaned forward against the railing of the balcony outside her bedroom, resting her elbows on the smooth stone as she looked out over her family's estate toward the east, where the sun slowly rose above the horizon. The orange glow sparkled on the waters of the Adriatic Sea in the distance. A cold breeze blew past, stirring her black hair and sending chills across her arms and down her back. Though she enjoyed the cold—it was just pleasant enough to keep her awake, keep her alert and alive—she pulled her jacket tighter.

She missed Tick and Paul. She missed Sato. Master George, Mothball, all of them. Even Rutger.

Days dragged like weeks now. Their adventures in the Fourth seemed like a million years ago. She knew it was crazy to want something to happen again, considering they'd almost died, but ever since she'd returned home, returned to school, and gone through the motions of a normal life, she'd been utterly bored out of her mind.

The Realitants were her true friends now. Yes, Frupey the Butler was good to her, kind to her, ready to fulfill any command she spoke, but he was paid to do that. She had her parents, of course . . .

"Sofia?" said a soft voice.

Startled, Sofia whipped around to see her mom standing behind her—as if she'd snuck up on her. Arms crossed, her mom rubbed her shoulders through her fur coat, looking cold and miserable.

"I'm sorry if I scared you," her mom said. In Italian, of course. How Sofia missed speaking in English with Tick and Paul.

"It's okay," Sofia replied, turning back to the railing and her previous position so her mom wouldn't see the roll of her eyes. Of all the days to come up here. She couldn't remember the last time either one of her parents had stood on this balcony atop their mansion. And Sofia wasn't in the mood.

Her mom stepped up beside her and leaned forward just like Sofia, almost mockingly copying her. "I've been meaning to talk to you about something.

Ever since you . . . came back. Ever since I realized how close we came to losing you."

Not this, Sofia thought. *Please, not this.* "Mom, I'm not quitting the Realitants. I don't care what you say. It's too important."

Her mom stiffened, then relaxed. "I don't care for that tone, young lady. I'm your *mother.*"

Sofia was shocked but quickly tried to hide it. Her mom never showed the slightest hint of parenting or discipline. Almost not knowing how to respond, Sofia muttered an apology.

"In any case," her mom said, "that's not what this is about. Your father and I recognize that this . . . Realitant thing is something you will do, either with our consent or without it. Which is why I want to make sure you understand something. I think it will show you how much we care about you, despite what you may think."

Sofia couldn't help but be intrigued. It'd been years since they'd had such a conversation. "What is it?" She didn't look at her mom, but kept her eyes on the distant, brightening horizon.

"Well," her mom started, then hesitated. "It's hard to know how to say it, so please hear me out. Your father and I never intended for you to be born. I mean, we'd made a decision early on to never have children. We never meant to have you."

Sofia almost choked on the lump that blossomed in her throat. "*That's* what you came up here to tell me?"

"Now, now, I told you to hear me out," her mom quickly responded, patting Sofia's arm. "Listen to me—we never intended to have you or any child, but you came anyway. Unexpectedly. And even though it was against all of our plans, even though it hindered your father's career and made it difficult for us to travel and accomplish the goals we'd set out before getting married . . . Well, I think you can see that despite all that, we accepted it and raised you and have always provided you with whatever you needed. And, above all else, we made sure to love you."

Sofia shifted her hands so she could grip the edge of the railing, squeezing hard to prevent her arms from shaking. Something terrible formed in her chest; something bulging and hurtful and full of bad things. It seemed to reach through her heart, through her throat, grabbing her mind and soul, begging her to cry. That was it. Every piece of her wanted to bawl her eyes out, sob until she felt nothing.

But she refused. She didn't understand how she did it, but she refused to let the tears come. There was no way she would let her mom see such a thing and misinterpret it, think that she'd finally bonded with her only child. Mistake her tears for love.

Concentrating with all her might, Sofia forced the

heavy feeling away and took control of her emotions. Finally, she relaxed her hands.

"Well?" her mom said after a long few seconds. "Do you understand? Is everything okay now? Better?"

"Yes," Sofia said, pushing the word out of her mouth, praying it was over and her mom would walk away.

"That's wonderful." She patted Sofia's arm again. "You know I love you, right?"

"Yes, Mom."

"And you love me?"

"Yes, Mom." That's all Sofia could manage. Just those two words. She clung to them, hoped they'd be enough to end this conversation.

"And your father?"

"Yes, Mom."

"Great. I'm so glad we had this talk. Aren't you?"

"Yes, Mom."

"Okay, then. Your father and I are going away for a few days. We'll be leaving tonight. Bye, now."

And with that, she turned and walked away.

Sofia thought about the fact that they hadn't even hugged. She knew it should bother her as much as everything else, but it didn't. Sadly, it didn't bother her at all.

When she was absolutely sure her mom wasn't coming back, Sofia finally gave up the internal battle and decided to let the tears flow.

But nothing came.

An hour passed. Maybe more. She couldn't really tell. She felt like she was in a haze, numb to the world. Eventually the cold got to her, and she went inside, though in some ways, the house felt chillier.

For a while she wandered the large house, completely ignoring the paintings and vases and tapestries and wood paneling and plush carpet that marked it as a mansion. She wandered, dreading her afternoon lessons with Lolita the private tutor. Sofia longed for the weekend, for two full days of nothing and no one—even though she knew she'd spend it sulking and checking the computer every two minutes for e-mails from Tick or Paul.

She entered the massive kitchen, all marble tile and shiny silver appliances, hoping a snack from the fridge would jump-start her from the doldrums. Frupey—his blond hair slicked back as usual—and the head cook were there, planning meals for the few days Sofia's parents would be gone. When that was the case—which was often—Frupey and the cook schemed to make dinner a little more tasty for Sofia, a little less healthy. Sometimes they even spoiled her with hot dogs, a secret she'd never dare tell her friends back in America.

"Sofia," Frupey said when he noticed her. "I was just going to come for you. I've received word that you have a friend coming within the hour."

Sofia felt a tinge of excitement, and the dull blahs inside her vanished. A friend? Her immediate thought was it had to be a Realitant. Maybe Mothball or Rutger.

"Really?" she asked, trying not to sound too eager. "Who is it? And what do you mean you *received word?*"

"Well, it's rather strange." Frupey stood straight, arms clasped behind his back. Ever the butler. "A metal tube came flying through a window. It thoroughly shattered the glass and required quite the cleanup. Based on your stories of, well, you know, your new friends, I thought it must be from the adventurous science people."

Sofia's heart soared. It *was* them. She couldn't wait to give Master George a hard time about his less-than-apt abilities at placing his message tubes when winking them.

"What did it say?" she asked. "Where is it?"

Frupey bowed and pulled a small piece of white cardstock from his jacket pocket and handed it over to her.

She snatched it out of his hands with a quickly murmured thank you and read it:

```
Sofia, we'll be there straightaway
to pick you up. Within the hour.
It's most urgent!

MG
```

Unable to hide a grin, and now thrilled that her parents were leaving, she ran from the kitchen without another word to Frupey so she could pack a few things for her trip.

⌒‿⌒

Master George came alone.

Sofia had been standing on the large brick porch for thirty minutes, the strap of her bag digging into her shoulder, staring down the long paved drive, waiting anxiously. When she spotted the old man shuffling along with an almost comical, hurried gait, she sprinted out to meet him.

"Why didn't you just have me go to the usual cemetery?" she asked when she reached his side.

Master George stopped walking, bent over and put his hands on his knees to catch a few deep breaths.

"I don't mean to wink you back to headquarters for now," he finally responded. "Believe it or not, I've left Sally in charge of the Barrier Wands back at headquarters. I came to pick you up personally so we could travel together to our next location."

"Which is?" Sofia urged. She could hardly stand the anticipation; the desire to get away from her large and dreary house was almost overwhelming.

Master George stood straight again, fixing his gaze

on her. His ruddy face framed eyes full of concern. "Sofia, I don't quite know how to say it. We've received an . . . invitation. A very odd one, at that."

"Really? From who? For what?"

"Let's just say it frightens me greatly. Come on. We need to make our way back to the cemetery so we can wink to Florida and pick up Paul. I'll explain along the way." He turned and started down the drive.

Sofia, baffled but full of excitement, followed.

CHAPTER
6

FINGER ON THE PULSE

Tick suspected he'd probably think the whole incident hilarious a few years down the road. They'd killed two monstrous water creatures with a vacuum cleaner and a dozen toilet flushes. But that night, lying in his bed, all he could think about as he stared at the dark ceiling was how close it had been. What it was like to see his mom's face behind that deadly mask of water and his dad's big body thrash around on the floor. What it was like to see his parents—both of them—almost die.

It hurt. It haunted. And he couldn't get the images out of his mind. People always used the phrase "too close for comfort," and after all he'd been through, and more than ever tonight, he understood what that meant on a very deep level. Especially when he considered how lucky they were Lisa and Kayla had gone away for the weekend. He knew there'd be no sleep for him tonight. Even if there were, it'd be full of nightmares.

Sighing, he rolled over onto his side and looked at the closet. The door was shut. He hadn't consciously thought about it before, but he was pretty sure that door had been closed every night since the Gnat Rat had shown up and attacked him. Compared to the things happening to him now, that incident almost seemed funny. Almost silly.

Compared to his . . . problem.

That was the word he'd started using when referring to whatever was wrong with him. Somehow, for some reason, he had a natural surplus—an *extreme* surplus—of Chi'karda, that quiet force that explains and controls the world of quantum physics and therefore everything in the universe. The fact that Mistress Jane had pulled it out of him, shown it to him, burned the visual in his mind forever, only made it more terrifying.

He had enough Chi'karda inside him to power a Barrier Wand. He had enough to disintegrate a spaceship-sized weapon of metal. Enough to destroy one of the largest buildings in all of the Realities. He'd said it before, and he felt it now, for the millionth time.

He was a freak. A dangerous, out-of-control freak.

But then he felt the slightest glimmer of hope,

almost like a visible light in his shadowed room of nighttime. In the garage, when he had started to lose control, he'd been able to pull back, make it stop. The more he thought about it, the better he felt.

He'd stopped. He'd controlled the power. That was a huge thing. The realization hadn't really hit him until now—he'd been too preoccupied with the aftermath of the attack by the water creatures—but the Chi'karda had almost exploded within him, and he'd made it go away!

Tick sat up in bed, wrapping his arms around his knees. He had to tell Sofia and Paul. And Master George, of course. He looked over at the digital clock on his desk and read the time—just a few minutes before midnight. No way he could wait until morning.

Swinging his legs off the bed, he stood up and headed for the computer downstairs.

The house was dark and silent, the faint swooshing of the refrigerator the only sound. Tick knew his odds of making it downstairs without his dad hearing him were tiny, but he tried all the same, creeping along on his tiptoes, hitting all the quiet spots in the floor and on the stairs he'd scouted out long ago. If Dad did come down, surely he'd understand why Tick wanted so urgently to tell his friends about what had happened.

And to make sure nothing had attacked them.

Once in his e-mail program, and after feeling a little disappointed that he had no messages waiting for him, he created a new one for Paul and Sofia. He started typing.

Hey guys,

I don't even know where to start. Crazy day.
Horrible day. Worst day since that stuff in the
Fourth. Guess I'll just tell it how it went.

It started while I was walking home from school
after my normal visit with Mr. Chu. (Sofia, I
know you hate him, but he's not the same guy
as Reginald. He was being controlled when he
kidnapped us. Get over it!)

Anyway, I got hit by this weird feeling, like a huge
electrical charge, like some kind of invisible power,
hitting me in waves. Then things got worse.

Tick went on to tell them about the run home, finding his parents under attack by the water creatures, fighting the things, killing them with the vacuum. Flushing them down the toilet.

He winced when he typed that part, already imagining the response from Sofia. It was like handing your enemy a thousand rounds of ammo so they could shoot you with more ease. And glee. She'd have a field day with that stuff.

He paused for a moment, wishing he could make the fight sound tougher, scarier. Like it had been in real life. In an e-mail, it sounded completely stupid. Might as well write, *Hey guys, you should've seen how I wielded that vacuum cleaner! I was invincible!*

Groaning, he continued typing.

Well, it was a lot worse than it sounds. Trust me. I just wish I knew where they came from, what they were, and who sent them. And what those weird waves of power I felt were. Has anything happened to you guys? We better be extra careful, really be on the lookout.

I think we should talk again on the Internet phone-thingy Sofia's butler helped us all set up. Since tomorrow is Saturday, what about in the morning (for me)—9:00? Let me know.

Tick
Realitant First Class

Tick always signed his e-mails that way, purely for one reason: it bugged the heck out of Sofia. He clicked

SEND, then sat back and folded his arms, watching the screen as it confirmed the message had been sent on its way.

His thoughts wandered. He saw his mom, encased in water, writhing on the floor. His dad's face growing purple. Remembered the terror of those few moments in the garage, before they were safe. He felt as if his heart had turned to lead.

What if it happened again? Almost certainly, it would. Something like it. Or worse.

A yawn leaked out, almost surprising him, and he snapped out of his stupor. Stretching his arms high above his head, he stood up from the chair, then leaned forward to shut down the computer. Once finished, he turned to head up for bed, already dreading the dreams that might await him.

Womp.

Tick sucked in a breath, reaching out to grab the back of the desk chair. The burst of energy had swept across him, throwing off his balance. Once he was sure he was stable and could stand, he looked around him, searching his surroundings. All he could see were shadows draped across more shadows, a faint light coming through the windows, another small glow from a nightlight down the hall. But the house was mostly dark, and everything seemed a great hiding spot for a monster ready to spring for him.

Womp.

Again. This time he realized how much *smaller* the energy wave was than those that had hit him earlier that afternoon on the road home from school. It had only been remembering that experience that sent terror pumping his heart when he'd felt the burst of energy this time. He calmed, just a little.

Womp.

Definitely smaller. Weaker. Whatever the word was. Barely there, almost a vibration. A sound that was not quite a sound.

Womp.

A pulse. That described it better than anything else. He was feeling a pulse of energy, sweeping through the air, through his skin, rattling his insides like a tuning fork. He could sense its source, just like he'd be able to tell from which direction he heard a radio or piano playing.

Womp . . . womp . . . womp . . .

Again and again.

It was coming from the basement.

CHAPTER
7

BENEATH

Tick's racing heart eased when he realized the pulse was far less powerful this time, felt less dangerous. But having it come from the basement—the unfinished, cement-floored, dark and cold basement? That was way worse than a closet.

He had to investigate. He had no choice on the matter. He was a Realitant, and he'd brought this danger—if it *was* a danger, and it didn't take a genius to jump to that conclusion—to his family, to his home. Responsibility for that hung like a huge sack of rocks, draped with ropes across his back. Despite what he'd experienced so far with the mysterious power within him, despite what he'd done to Chu's palace and the weapon called Dark Infinity, despite what he'd done to—

He cut off the thought. The point was, he didn't *feel* powerful. Not in the least. Having a gun does you no good if it's missing the trigger.

Womp . . . womp . . . womp . . .

But none of that mattered. Something weird pulsed in his basement, and he was going down there to figure out what.

He realized his hands were clasped tightly into fists. If he'd had long nails, his palms would be bleeding like geysers. He forced himself to relax, flexing his fingers and taking several deep breaths. Then he headed out of the room, down the hall, toward the door to the basement.

He hesitated in front of it, as though the black shadows of the hallway clung to him like a gluey mass. He stared at the knob, a stub of gold that was the only spot of color in the darkness. The throbs of the unseen force continued, a small vibration in his skull.

He opened the door and stepped through it onto the landing of the stairway that led below. If he'd thought it had been dark before, the bottom of the stairs was a lightless abyss. He fumbled for the switch, found it and turned on the light, banishing the shadows. Before him lay the wooden staircase, surrounded with bare white walls with a cement floor at the bottom. He couldn't see anything else yet.

Womp . . . womp . . . womp . . .

The pulse strengthened slightly, calling to him from the basement. He had the sudden and terrifying thought that maybe he'd been hypnotized, that he was acting irrationally. He stopped before taking the first step. Was he nuts for even thinking about going down there? The first time he'd felt this energy pulse, something terrible had happened.

But he had to do it. He had to. He wondered if he should get his dad, but pushed the thought away. The hairs of his arms standing on end, he started down the stairs. Even treading lightly, each footfall still made a deadened thump. He wished the steps had carpet. He descended further, running his right hand along the wall, making a soft scraping sound, almost a swish.

Womp . . . womp . . . womp . . .

He reached the bottom, then darted toward the long string that fell from the ceiling, attached to a single lightbulb. He pulled the string, waiting in dread to see what the light would reveal. When the bulb clicked on and the room brightened, nothing seemed out of the ordinary. The single room in the half-basement was maybe twenty feet wide, and Tick couldn't see anything out of the ordinary.

The room was cluttered with boxes, bags, plastic tubs full of old clothes, a horizontal pole holding up dusty coats on hangers, a rack of shoes which hadn't been worn in years, a pile of Christmas decorations that hadn't quite been put away yet. He wondered if his mom even knew her wonderful and faithful husband had neglected that duty for months now.

But the pulsing continued, stronger now, though nothing like what he'd felt on the street. Still, it was powerful enough that the energy surrounded him, throbbing, and he couldn't tell from which direction it came.

Womp . . . womp . . . womp . . .

He slowly turned in a circle, scanning every inch of the room with his eyes. Boxes, tubs, junk. Nothing else.

The pulse stopped. Cut off.

It didn't slow, didn't fade. It stopped, abruptly. A powerful silence filled the air. Tick's skin tingled, as if it had grown used to the almost comforting vibrations of the energy waves and wanted them back. He heard his own breathing as he continued to turn, and for some reason that creeped him out. He felt stuck in one of those nightmares where you *know* you're dreaming, but you can't wake up.

His instincts came to life, telling him to get out of there. He—

"Atticus. Higginbottom."

Tick turned sharply toward the sound, stumbling backward until he hit the stairs. His knees buckled, and he sat down on the third step. He sucked in a breath, feeling as if something had been shoved down his throat, clogging it. The barely female voice that had spoken his name had been monstrous. Dry. Raspy. Painful. As if every syllable sent waves of flame through its owner's body. And it was slightly . . . muffled.

He couldn't see anyone in the basement. He swept his head back and forth but saw nothing. No one. His hands gripped the lip of the step beneath his legs.

"Two words," said the horrible voice. "A name. How different my life would be if I'd never heard them uttered."

Tick concentrated on a certain spot, a dark shadow behind a pile of boxes he hadn't noticed before. Probably another project his dad should have organized and put away months ago. But there was enough room back there for someone to stand. To hide.

"Who's there?" Tick asked, relieved his voice came out with no cracks. Relieved he could talk at all.

"An old friend," came the reply, the harsh voice softening to a bare whisper, like the crackling of dead leaves in the distance. "Someone who wanted to *be* your friend."

Tick knew his mouth was open. He knew his eyes were wide, full of terror. Every inch of him screamed that he should run. He should book it up the stairs and yell for his parents to call the police.

It was her. It was *her*.

He couldn't move his eyes away from the tall length of shadow. Something moved in the darkness. A human figure formed, then stepped into the light. A robe of dull yellow covered every inch of her body, the hood pulled up and over her head, almost hiding the face.

Except there was no face. At least, not a human face. The figure wore a red mask of metal, its features pulled into a smile that somehow looked more frightening than a scowl of anger.

"Mistress Jane," Tick whispered, his senses having turned numb. He knew it was her before she nodded ever so slightly to confirm what he'd said. So he hadn't killed her after all.

But that mask. And her voice. What *had* he done to her?

He waited for her to speak, to explain why she'd come. But she only stood there, completely still, her hands hidden within the folds of her robe. The red mask was impossibly shiny, almost as if it were molten metal. Liquid. Wet.

One of the eyebrows twitched, moving half an inch up then back down again. As he stared, the smile on the mask slowly melted into a frown, into a grimace. The eyebrows slanted with unspoken rage.

How did she do that? Tick could feel blood rushing in his temples, in his neck. What was she going to do to him?

Still, she said nothing. She didn't move.

Tick couldn't take the silence anymore. "Jane . . . Mistress Jane . . ." He was stuttering, searching for words. If his hands hadn't been firmly holding on to the stair beneath him, they'd have been trembling uncontrollably. "I promise I didn't mean to do whatever I did to you. I lost control—I don't even know what I lost control of. My mind wasn't working right. I don't know what happened."

He paused, hoping for a change on that mask. If anything, it looked angrier.

"I'm sorry," he continued. "I could tell by the way you . . . screamed, that, um . . ." He looked down at the floor. "I know I hurt you. I'm sorry. I didn't mean to."

When he lifted his eyes again, he almost cried out. She was three steps closer to him, the mask as scary as ever, the rage evident on the sparkling, deep red surface.

"I'm sorry," he said again, barely getting it out.

"Stop talking," Jane said, her raspy voice muffled but strong, creating a dry whisper of an echo in the room. "Don't say another word until I give you permission. Do you understand?"

"Ye—" Tick stopped himself. He nodded.

Mistress Jane stood still, her robe unruffled. She reminded Tick of a statue. A very angry statue with a red face. "I don't want to hear your apologies. Your excuses. Don't insult my pain by refusing to take responsibility for your actions. You know the nature of Chi'karda. You know the nature of your heart. You did this to me by your own choice. It couldn't have happened against your will. Your conscious . . . current . . . evident will." She spat out the last few syllables.

Tick felt awful. It wasn't so much the words she'd used. He felt the meaning of them more in the tone of her voice. Worse, he felt the truth of it. Shame and guilt blossomed like diseased flowers in his lungs, making it hard to breathe.

"I—" he began.

"I DIDN'T ASK YOU TO SPEAK!" she screamed, her body shaking beneath the robe, the first movement Tick had seen in several minutes. Terror pinched Tick's nerves.

Then, as if it came from another world, one in which he used to live but could barely remember, he heard footsteps upstairs. Urgent footsteps. The basement door opened above them.

No! he thought, even as he turned to look up the stairs, ready to tell his parents to run.

But when he saw who stood in the doorway, confusion and surprise almost burned away his fear. He blinked, forcing himself to swallow.

It was Sofia.

CHAPTER
8

QUITE THE CROWD

Shocked to see her, Tick stood up and fully turned around, facing the stairs, his eyes riveted on one of his best friends. He could almost forget he had the most dangerous woman in the Realities standing behind him.

"Sofia?" he asked, his voice cracking.

"Is she down there?" she responded in a whisper, gesturing with a nod.

Tick was completely baffled. "How do you . . ." He didn't know how to finish or what to ask first. What was going on?

"Is *she* down there?" Sofia repeated, her emphasis leaving no doubt who she meant.

Tick jabbed a thumb over his shoulder. "Yes!" he

snapped in a loud rasp. "She's standing right behind me!"

"Bring them down," Mistress Jane said. "They're late."

Tick wilted, hoping against hope that maybe the woman would have gone away when she realized they had company. How had she gotten to Tick's house in the first place? Only inanimate objects should be winkable to his house and its relatively low amounts of Chi'karda. And what happened to that pulsing thing? He felt completely unsettled, like the old dream where he walked into class at school dressed in nothing but his underwear.

At the top of the stairs, Sofia leaned back out the door and seemed to be talking to someone. Then she popped back in and started down the steps, each footstep a thump. To Tick's complete surprise, others followed her.

Master George, dressed in his fine, dark suit, red-faced and dry-skinned as usual, as if he'd been standing in a windy desert for hours. Behind him came Paul, an inexplicable grin on his face. Next was Tick's dad, then Tick's mom, both of them looking bleary-eyed and disheveled as if they'd just been awakened.

Tick could only stare, his mind trying to convince himself he must be dreaming. When Sofia reached the bottom step, he absently moved aside and let her pass, then Master George and Paul, both of whom patted him on the shoulder as they walked by. No one said a word, and it was impossible to read anything from the look in their eyes. There was fear there, but only a little.

His dad stopped beside him, then his mom. They both put their arms around him as Tick turned toward the middle of the basement. Everyone stood in a semi-circle, facing Mistress Jane in her yellow robe and red mask, which was now empty of expression, neither angry nor happy. For what seemed like the hundredth time, Tick felt relief that his sisters had gone to Seattle for the weekend.

The whole situation was just too bizarre, and he finally found his voice.

"What's going on here?" he asked to no one in particular. He felt like he was on one of those hidden-camera TV shows where they play pranks on people. He half-expected a cameraman to step out of the shadows any second.

"Ask her," Sofia said almost viciously as she pointed at Jane.

"Yes, my good friend," Master George added. "Ask our host."

Tick looked at Jane, surprised. She'd *arranged* this?

Jane didn't move as silence settled in the room, anticipation palpable in the air. Tick stared at the shiny surface of her red mask, trying to understand what was happening. He stood huddled with his parents in his basement, next to his two best friends and the leader of the Realitants, staring at a woman in a robe and mask, who could probably kill them all without breaking a sweat.

Time stretched as they waited for Jane to speak, to give an explanation. Tick wanted to scream, wanted to—

"I sent my waterkelts as a little opening exercise to our meeting," Jane finally said, her voice scratchy but calm and cool. "Though I'm very disappointed they didn't kill at least *one* of your parents, Atticus."

Tick said nothing, fighting the urge to run at her.

"Anyway," Jane said, "you're probably wondering why I've brought you all here."

No one replied, but Tick's thoughts ran wild. She'd brought them all to his *basement?*

The face of Jane's mask remained expressionless. "I knew Atticus would have the hardest time getting permission to leave due to his . . . unusual gift. That's why we're here. That's why I sent you the note this morning, George. I'm glad to see you're still capable of performing simple tasks. Though I wanted the boy Sato here as well."

Tick glanced at Master George, who was visibly struggling to contain his contempt for this woman. "The boy is on a mission at the moment," the old man spurted, unable to sound composed. "Be glad we came at all. I'll have you speak your mind and be done with it. Remember, you've given your word this will be a diplomatic meeting. A peaceful meeting."

Jane's mask grinned, though the lips never parted. "Frightened, George? Scared of what your old pupil may do? You can thank the boy"—she nodded at Tick—"for making your fears relevant. You should definitely *be* afraid."

"What is this nonsense?" Master George demanded.

"How did you get here?" Jane asked him.

Master George shifted on his feet. "What do you mean?"

Jane's smile vanished almost instantly, the mask frowning. "George, don't make me repeat questions a child could understand. How did you *get* here?"

"What does it matter? I fetched Paul and Sofia, then we winked to the forest a mile or so from here and walked the rest of the way. *Why?*"

"The forest?" Jane repeated. "Ah, yes, the forest. I sensed a pool of Chi'karda there. Perhaps an old cemetery, its wooden grave markers long turned to dust. I hope you walked briskly—good exercise I'm sure. Looks like you need it."

"What is your *point?*" Master George snapped.

For the first time, Jane pulled her hands from out of the folds of the robe where she'd had them hidden. No one in the room could hold back a small gasp at the sight of them, especially Tick. He felt his mom's arm tighten around his shoulders.

Jane's hands were hideously red and flaky, covered with scars. Small shards and slivers of golden metal seemed fused to her skin. She folded her fingers together delicately, then rested her hands on her midsection. When Tick finally tore his eyes away from the terrible sight and looked at her face, he saw a horrific grimace of pain. Intense, aching pain. But then it was gone, replaced once again by the expressionless mask.

Jane must have noticed Tick's own look of horror. "See something disturbing, Atticus? What, you don't like my hands? You don't think they're pretty? Wouldn't like to hold them, go for a stroll?"

Tick felt as though his insides were melting. He'd spent the last few months wondering what had happened to her, wondering if she was dead. He'd been consumed by guilt for what he'd done. Seeing Jane's hands for himself now, he made the only logical conclusion he could. She wore the robe and mask because the rest of her body looked the same as her ruined hands.

He wanted to run. He wanted to sprint up those stairs and run away forever.

Jane seemed to sense his thoughts. "No, Atticus. For what you've done to me, you will be by my side.

You'll make restitution, and you'll help me accomplish what I set out so long ago to do. That's the only way I'll forgive you."

Tick felt his mom tense again, and he couldn't stop her before she spoke.

"Now listen to me, Jane," she said. "My son isn't responsible for what happened to you any more than my left foot is. We've heard every detail of that day a million times over. He can't control what's inside him. You tried to *kill* him. What did you expect!"

Jane's mask moved fiercely to rage. "I did *not* try to kill him! He knew I was trying to release his Chi'karda. I wanted to stop Chu from driving every last person in the Realities insane. I told him that—he knew it!"

"That's a load of horse poop!" Tick's dad suddenly yelled, making Tick jump.

"You're an adult, Jane," his mom continued, surprisingly calm and collected. "You should've known what his reaction would be. Everything that happened to you was your own fault. You—"

"Shut up!" Jane screamed, her whole body trembling from the effort, the mask full of hate and anger.

Tick felt his mom and dad take a step backward. He went with them. The other Realitants did the same. A storm of emotions raced through Tick. He wanted to cheer for his dad yelling at Jane; he loved his mom more than at any other moment in his life for standing up for him, for acting so brave and leader-like. And he hated Jane. Hated her.

But laced through all the other emotions was fear. Pure, unsettling fear. Something terrible was going to happen. He knew it. And deep down within him, he felt the stirrings of his power, massing like a storm. Scared of what might happen, he forced the power away as he'd done earlier in the garage. If only he could learn how to use it . . .

After a long moment, the echo of Jane's command faded away, and silence clouded the room. When she spoke again, it was very quiet. "You'll all be coming with me. I want you to witness something."

"Coming with—?" Tick's dad began, but when Jane's arm shot out and one of her hideous fingers pointed at his face, he shut his mouth.

Jane lowered her arm and folded her hands once again. "I remember in old movies, how the villain always said, through mad laughter, that he had a dia-bolical plan. As if anyone actually *used* such a word as diabolical."

She stepped forward, the face of her mask smooth-ing back to normalcy, though Tick didn't feel the ten-sion in the room lessen, not one bit.

"But," she continued, her voice icy and soft, "it's the only word I can think of for what I have planned. My plan is, indeed, diabolical. For you, Edgar, slow-witted as you seem to be, that means terrible, horrible, awful, treacherous, and unspeakably nasty. Understand?" Her eyebrows arched.

Tick wanted to punch her for being so cruel to his dad, but did nothing. Next to him, his dad merely nodded. Tick hoped it was out of fear and not shame or embarrassment at her accusation.

"Yes," Jane said, with a slow smile. "A diabolical plan. And every one of you is going to witness it."

CHAPTER 9

DEAD TICKS EVERYWHERE

This was the eighth time Sato'd seen it now. A tomb for Tick.

Every place was unique. The wording was a little different every time, and the dates varied, but they all meant the same thing.

Tick's Alterants were dead. All of them, by the looks of it.

Sato hoped this latest discovery would finally be enough to satisfy George and let him end gallivanting all across the Realities. Tick was alive in Reality Prime, but Sato had personally witnessed his friend's grave in eight of the remaining twelve. Did George really need him to go through with making sure the other four were the same? Knowing George, Sato thought with a sigh, probably yes. Just to make sure.

Sato stood in a vast field in the Fifth Reality, dawn still a couple of hours away. He'd woken up in the middle of the night back at newly repaired Realitant headquarters in the Bermuda Triangle—Sato still missed going for walks in the Grand Canyon—and hadn't been able to go back to sleep.

So he'd made Rutger roll his round body out of bed and wink him here to the Fifth Reality. He wanted to get the trip over with and be done. He was looking forward to getting back earlier than usual and having plenty of time to rest and relax. Maybe play cards with Mothball and Sally, though those two turned vicious when the stakes got high. Especially if the pot reached a whole bag of M&Ms.

The air had winter's bite of cold—the place was far in the north with a high altitude—but he'd worn his thick coat and gloves, so he actually felt great, refreshed and full of life. Beaming his big flashlight this way and that, he'd slowly made his way across the huge cemetery, checking each and every tombstone.

It was easy to tell this was Mothball's world. Each grave was a good couple of feet longer and wider than he was used to, and the markers had an almost disturbingly humorous edge to them: "Plank, please

don't come back and haunt us—you have stinky feet."
"Toolbelt, you were a wonder in life, despite your
gigantic nose." "Snowdrift, who died with a smile on
her face, even after falling off that cliff."

The strangeness didn't completely surprise him,
knowing Mothball. She had a very unusual sense of
humor. But there was just something wrong about giggling out loud like a little kid, over and over, in the
middle of a dark graveyard.

He finally found Tick's marker after almost two
hours of searching. Standing before it, he focused his
flashlight on the large, rounded tombstone:

Here lies Atticus Higginbottom
Dead at the sad age of seven.
Atticus, you had more gas than
any normal child should,
but we still miss you terribly.
Rest in peace, our sweet, sweet son.

Sato clicked off the flashlight and stood in the dark
for several minutes, surprisingly touched by the eulogy.
It was impossible to separate these Alterants from the
people you knew—hard not to imagine that lying
beneath you was the person you'd grown to care for. In
many ways, it was the same person. Although he didn't
quite understand how it worked yet, this boy who'd died

of who-knew-what was just Tick along a different path. He'd probably been similar in personality, looked the same though much taller, had the same drive to help others—just like Tick had saved Sato's life twice now.

And even though Sato had been grumpy with George more than once about this mission, in some ways it had helped him appreciate the fact that his friends—who were few in number—were alive and well, not dead like this poor kid. But it also made him sad, imagining another version of Tick dying so young. George said they didn't quite know why these major Realities still followed the same general pedigrees and lineages despite having such vastly different histories, but there had to be a big reason for it.

It worked geographically, too. Tick's Alterants had all been born in the same place and buried in the same vicinity. And, as far as Sato knew, Tick's parents were always named Edgar and Lorena and he always had two sisters, Lisa and Kayla. Strange stuff. Interesting how it all worked. Lately George thought he was on the verge of a breakthrough.

It had something to do with soulikens, a phenomenon the old man was trying desperately to figure out. He rarely talked about it, claiming all his information would get jumbled up and confused if he tried to explain it. Once he could lay it before them piece by piece, in a rational and comprehensible discussion, he'd immediately gather the Realitants to do so—something he'd been promising for months.

Soulikens. All Sato knew was that it had something to do with the electricity that existed within the human body. Actual and real electricity. Words like *signals* and *impulses* and *imprints* were thrown around, but never enough at once to make any sense of it. The Realitants would just have to be patient and wait for George to get it all together inside his thick skull.

But Sato had learned some things on his own, and as he stood in the darkness, enjoying the cool air, the quiet, the peace he always felt in a cemetery, he thought about one of them. Electricity was an essential physical element in making the heart pump. It seemed impossible that the human body could create electricity, but it was true. And the fact that the heart—the most important organ and the symbol of so many things in life— depended so greatly on it meant . . .

Well, he didn't know what it meant. But it had something to do with soulikens, and something to do with his mission to find dead Alterants of Tick. Except every time Sato tried to put the pieces together, it got jumbled and confusing. No wonder George was so insistent that he couldn't talk about it yet.

Sato felt a headache coming on. He reached into his pocket and pushed the little button that signaled he was ready to wink back to HQ.

A nice, long morning nap. That's exactly what he needed. Folding his arms and shivering at the cold that had seeped through his thick coat and chilled his skin, he waited for Rutger to bring him home.

A minute passed, then two. To his surprise, two people appeared in front of him—one short and fat, the other tall and skinny. He didn't need to shine the light on them to know who they were, but he did anyway.

Rutger threw up one of his pudgy arms to block the brightness. He held a Barrier Wand in the other. "Point that back at your feet, Sato! I'd like my eyes to last another decade or two!"

Sato didn't budge, hoping they couldn't see the big smile that flashed across his face.

Mothball, towering over her best friend and standing like a pile of sticks thrown together at the last minute with glue and draped with loose-fitting clothes, merely squinted. "Master Sato, best be puttin' down your torch there. 'Less you're wantin' to have a nice-sized pair of fists box them sad little ears of yours."

Sato did as she said, snapping back to the reality of the situation as he did so. Why had they come? Something had to be wrong. A trickle of panic wiped his grin completely away.

"Wait," he said. "What are you guys doing here? What happened?"

Rutger, temporarily blinded by Sato's trick with

the flashlight, was making his way forward, waddling along on his short legs and reaching out with his free hand to make sure he didn't bump into anything. "Calm down, you worrywart. Everything's fine."

Mothball's eyes seemed to have already adjusted. She made it to Sato before Rutger was even halfway there. "The wee man is right, Master Sato. No need for your worries. Just come to give ya a bit of a break, we 'ave. Thought we'd come and visit me mum and dad. Let ya see what real nice folks are like here in the Fifth."

Sato felt a strong surge of relief, which made him worry that maybe he was worrying too much. *Oh shut up,* he told himself. "Serious? We're going to see your parents?" He was surprised at how much the idea lifted him.

"Right ya are," Mothball replied. "'Long as we can get our guide here to quit stumbling about like an eyeless toad. Come on, Rutger, set your dials and switches and get on with it."

Rutger grumbled something too quiet to make out, then held the Barrier Wand up, concentrating. "A light, please?"

Sato shined the flashlight on the Wand, then asked, "Where do they live? Around here?"

"No, grumpy cheeks," Rutger responded as he turned a dial or two, his tongue caught between his lips. "We're going to wink to another cemetery near them. It's a good ten thousand miles from here, so hold your hats."

"I'm not wearin' a ruddy hat," Mothball said.

"It's an *expression*," Rutger huffed. "All right, we're ready to go, and I'm locked on to all of our nano-locators. Here we go."

Without another warning, Rutger pushed the button on top of the Wand. Sato heard the metallic click and felt the familiar tingle on his neck, and then everything changed.

It was daytime, the sun above almost blinding. Sato shielded his eyes, and at first he thought that what he saw in front of him was a trick of the light on his mind. But then it came into better focus, and he had no doubt.

Several people were trying to kill each other with swords.

And they were dressed like clowns.

CHAPTER 10

RIBBONS OF ORANGE

Tick couldn't believe how quiet Paul and Sofia had been since coming down the stairs—especially Sofia. The girl could never keep her mouth shut. And Paul— he had to be terrified to stay so silent. And his face showed it. Tick thought about how many weeks he'd been dying to see these guys, and now that they were here, he'd give anything to send them safely away.

"What do you mean?" Master George asked Jane after a long period of silence, Jane seemingly content to let her pronouncement sink in. "What plan are you talking about, and why would you want us to witness it?"

Tick had been trying to look at the floor, avoiding the menacing mask on Jane's face. But his eyes kept drawing back to it, fascinated at its almost magical ability to change expressions. Upon Master George's question, it melted into compassion, almost sadness.

"You have always known my wishes," she said in a flat voice, as if beginning a long lecture. "My ways and means may have changed—certainly my abilities have—but I've never wavered from my lifetime mission, George. And that is to see the suffering of countless Alterants end. To create one and only one Reality, where the strongest of each one of us can live, and where we can stop the torturous splitting of worlds."

"I've never heard you put it quite that way before," Master George said. "I remember your talk of a Utopia, a paradise, a place where all can be happy. The way you describe it now sounds more like the wishes of an evil, insane, power-hungry monster. What's happened to you, Jane?"

She paused to let him speak, but then acted as if she hadn't heard a word he said, continuing her lecture without missing a beat. "The first step of my plan is not going to be easy. I hardly expect any of you to understand what I do or to give it your blessing. But I couldn't possibly care less. For what the lot of you have done to me, I don't expect to let most of you live long enough to see the end come to pass."

She paused, turning her head to look at each person in the room. "But you all will see what I plan for tomorrow. You'll see it, and you'll know my power once and for all."

Master George wouldn't quit pushing. "Jane, this is madness."

"Madness?" she repeated. "I tried it your way, the *Realitants'* way. And look what I got in return." She motioned to her face and robed body with her hideous hands, then held them up for everyone to see. "The irony is, that by ruining me physically, you've helped me more than you know. Not only can I channel my abilities more acutely than ever before, but I've been reminded of what I knew from the beginning. That the only way to accomplish anything is by taking the hard road, the harsh road. The sometimes cruel and hateful road. Never before has it been so true that the ends will justify the means. I'll never stray from the path again. Never."

Tick felt heat simmering inside him as she spoke, growing and intensifying with every word. Though he didn't really know the specifics of what she was talking about, he could hear the evil in her voice, the horrible intent of her words. He could almost *feel* it, just like the pulse that had brought him down here in the first place. The pulse. What had that been?

"As you can see," Jane continued, "I'm learning more each and every day about how to use the gifts that have been given to me. Take the waterkelts, for example. You'd be amazed at how easy it is to manipulate the molecules of our favorite liquid."

Tick's anger grew, heat boiling in his chest. And despite his better judgment, this time he didn't stop it. Jane had obviously noticed.

"Atticus, are we going to have a problem?" she asked coolly. But he thought he heard the slightest trace of concern, and she definitely took a small step backward. She feared him; he knew it.

"Tick," his dad said next to him, turning toward him and gripping him by the shoulders. "Are you feeling it again? Push it away, hold it back, do something." The worry creasing his face tore at Tick's heart, so he looked away, back at Jane.

His mom squeezed his arm, then whispered in his ear. "Atticus, pull it back. Go through the breathing exercises. Son, we're not going to let her hurt—"

"I won't listen to another word she says!" Tick screamed. He was losing control and felt his body trembling. He had to *do* something. "We can't just let her talk like this to us!" His skin burned. He looked at his arms, half-expecting to see blisters and smoke. But all was normal.

"Atticus—" his mom said.

She stepped away from him, as did his dad. Tick looked over at Sofia and Paul, their eyes wide. They were scared of him. They were *all* scared of him. He noticed Master George's hand had slipped into his pocket, fingering something there. Tick knew it had to be another shot of whatever Sofia had used to knock him out in Chu's mountain office building.

Tick didn't know what to do. He felt the heat inside him, the power, weaken a little. He looked back at Jane, hoping to reignite it. She hadn't moved, but her mask was pulled back in fury.

"You can't stand against me," Jane said. "Not now, not after what you did to me. Stop now, or you'll spend the rest of your short life regretting it."

"What did I do to you?" Tick spat back at her. "You tried to kill me!"

"What did you do? What did you *do?*" Jane stepped forward, closer than before, regaining her ground. "You took the strongest parts of the most powerful weapon ever created by man and melded them with a woman already equipped with a control over Chi'karda never seen before. That's what you *did,* Atticus. Your selfish, cowardly act will end up being the very thing that will allow me to win."

"It . . . will . . . not," Tick said, concentrating with every ounce of brain power he could muster, trying to sense, to feel, to grasp the boiling Chi'karda within him. He remembered last year when Jane had pulled it out of him in a cloud of orange sparkles, a mist of tangible power. He tried to visualize it the same way, tried to *touch* it.

"Stop it," Jane warned. "Stop it *now!*"

"Atticus," his mom pleaded. "She's right. Now's not the time!"

"Tick, pull it back before you kill yourself!" Sofia yelled.

The others shouted similar words at him. Master George pulled what looked like an ordinary pen from his pocket. But Tick couldn't stop. He couldn't let Jane do anything to harm his friends and family.

He turned his attention back to her, focusing again on the burning power within him, holding on to it in a way he could've never described to anyone. Then he threw it at Jane. Screaming, he leaned forward and threw the power at her, pushing it away from him in a rush of energy and invisible flame.

A thunderclap shook the room as Jane stumbled backward, fiery sparks exploding all around her. Boxes tumbled, people fell to the ground. There was shouting and yelling. Somewhere, glass shattered. Another thunderclap, a thump of booming sound, shook the whole house. Streaks of orange mist swirled throughout the basement like ribbons of sunset, slashing this way and that. Tick felt as if lava flowed in his veins and thought his head might explode from the pressure.

Still, he kept *pushing,* kept aiming every bit of his strength at Jane.

She didn't fall. She planted her feet against the

onslaught. Her red mask raged. Thunder continued to blast the air in repeated bursts, filling the world full of noise. A loud, piercing, terrible *noise* that only fed Tick's fire.

But then, somehow, through all that sound, he heard Jane's voice, as crystal clear as if she'd spoken directly into his ear in a silent room. It took a moment for her words to register, for him to comprehend exactly what she was saying, but when it clicked, when he realized what he was jeopardizing, what he was risking, he immediately pulled it all back, all of it. He had no idea how he did it, but in an instant the power vanished, sucked back into him and quenched like a candle in a rainstorm.

Jane had said four words.

"I have your sisters."

CHAPTER
11

LATITUDE AND LONGITUDE

Frazier Gunn walked through the thick forest, trying his hardest to ignore the humidity that tried to suck the life out of him and fill his lungs with heavy water. Every breath seemed an effort, and every inch of clothing clung to his skin. He was miserably uncomfortable.

And then there were the insects: almost microscopic gnats that swarmed in small packs around his nose and eyes, tiny dragonflies that appeared to love the darkness and warmth of the human inner ear—at least that's where they kept trying to get to, wasps and bees. But the mosquitoes were the worst—big as moths and drinking up his blood like miniature vampires. With his free hand, he swatted the latest one to land on his neck, then looked at the greasy dark smear on his palm. Disgusting.

His other hand was occupied, gripping a makeshift handle on the end of a thick rope, which dangled away behind him to its other end, tied loosely around the neck of a woman. He didn't want to hurt her, but he couldn't have her running away, either. Her long, black hair was matted against her face and head, and her clothes were soaked with sweat, but she kept Frazier's pace, never uttering a word of complaint.

Yes, she was a criminal, but she was also an Alterant of Mistress Jane. She looked just like her except for the long mane of hair. But it was the same face, the same—

Frazier faltered in his steps, almost tripping over a big root. He'd forgotten—just for the barest of moments— that his boss no longer had the beauty and grace that had distinguished her for so many years. She'd yet to show him her face, but he'd seen enough—just her *hands* were enough—to know that the Higginbottom kid had done something truly horrific to her body. The poor woman Frazier dragged along behind him was a goddess compared to Mistress Jane now.

The thought saddened and angered him in equal parts, and when they rounded a massively thick oak tree, he accidentally jerked on the rope. The Alterant yelped behind him and stumbled to the ground, gurgling out a choke as the noose tightened. Frazier quickly got her back on her feet and apologized, though he knew it was empty and cold. He kept thinking of her as his boss, and he had to stop it.

On they went, hiking their way through the hot, wilted, miserable forest.

Frazier was exhausted. The only other person in the Realities to whom he'd dare entrust this assignment was Mistress Jane herself, and she obviously couldn't do it. If two Alterants met face to face, bad things happened. Reginald Chu had discovered that little gem of information himself, and now he was stuck in some place Frazier hoped he'd never see. The Nonex. What a stupid name.

It wasn't just the humidity and the heat that had Frazier so tired. It was more the fact that he had to do the same thing twelve times—taking each Alterant to the exact same location in each of their respective Realities, leaving them chained and secure, but with enough food and water to survive until the plans were complete. He'd already finished with ten; two more to go. But only a handful of Realities had GPS equipment in the air, so most of the time he had to use maps and human guides to find the latitude and longitude coordinates. It was a real pain in the bahoonkas.

This world had the satellites and the technology, for which he was extremely grateful. Having a group of jabbering guides and a backpack full of maps didn't sound like something he could handle right now, trudging through the dense, suffocating woods. The Blade component strapped across his shoulders was plenty heavy enough, and sweat poured down his body in streams. He looked at his GPS navigation watch— the one he'd, um, taken for free from a poor sucker back in Carson City, the closest patch of civilization to this wretched place. They were close to the destination now.

Frazier squeezed his way through a clump of thin, gangly trees into a wide patch of vegetation. His spirits lifted slightly. Maybe they were past the thickest part of the forest. Kicking and pounding down with his foot, he pushed his way through the thick, clinging growth, leading the Alterant and moving ever closer toward the exact latitude and longitude of the Blade location. By the time he saw another grove of gigantic trees looming up ahead, his watch beeped, once, long and loud.

They'd reached the fifty-foot radius point.

If he hadn't had a prisoner behind him, tied and bound to him and watching his every move, he would have dropped to his knees and howled at the sky in delirious joy. Of the now eleven times he'd made this journey, this one had been the most difficult. It was the heat; it had to be the heat. He felt utter dread knowing he still had one more Reality ahead of him. But, for now, he allowed himself some elation, at least a little. Even if he did keep it on the inside.

he said, making sure he didn't allow
trickle into his voice. "I need a minute to
on't try anything. Or, um, I'll have to, um,
a." Of course, not in a million years would he do
that—the Blade operation was way too important, and
it couldn't happen if even one of the Alterants died—
but *she* didn't know that.

"Where's here?" the woman asked, her voice hoarse
and scratchy. "Why won't you tell me anything?"

"Because you don't need to know." Frazier walked
a little way farther until they were in the rough middle
of the designated area. He let go of the rope, giving the
prisoner the evil eye as he did so, knowing she'd get the
message. He swung the Blade component off his shoulders, unhooked the leather straps, and let it thump to
the ground in front of him.

"I've dealt with people a lot worse than you," she
said in a raw whisper.

Frazier barely heard her. He was down on his knees,
studying the Blade. Or, more accurately, a *part* of the
Blade. One of thirteen parts, it was a beautiful piece of
work. Made of the blackest stone—a substance that did
not even *exist* in any Reality, at least not naturally—it
had no measurable shape or dimensions. Twisty, curvy,
and slightly elongated, it was like a beautiful, abstract
sculpture, with dozens of thin strands connecting two
bulky end pieces, all of it harder and stronger than the

toughest metal or stone. And blacker than the deepest, starless night.

Jane had *made* this. She'd created it. He'd begged her to explain how she'd done it, explain what the material was, explain the science behind it. But she always refused, saying it was on such a deep and complex level he'd never understand. A lot of it, she finally told him, came about purely on instinct, a result of her digging through the wonders of quantum physics and spacetime. But on several occasions, when she otherwise seemed asleep or lost in thought, he'd heard her whisper two words:

Dark matter.

He was sure of it. She'd said *dark matter.* Whether or not it had anything to do with the Blade, he couldn't be sure. He certainly had no idea if what lay in front of him now was made of dark matter or contained it somehow. But his gut told him that his boss had stumbled upon a discovery that would alter the Realities forever if she ever chose to share it with her fellow scientists. But that, he knew, would never happen.

Dark matter.

He shivered, and feeling the chill in the brutal heat ripped him out of his wandering thoughts. He snapped his head up to look at the Alterant, who stood quietly, everything from her face to her hands to her clothes seeming to wilt toward the ground, a display of misery.

He felt truly sorry for her, and knew it was because of how much she looked like Mistress Jane.

"I'm sorry this has been so rough on you," he said, positive she'd think he was up to something and not being sincere. He didn't care. "Sometimes I lose myself in the amazing things we're trying to accomplish. Sometimes I . . . forget that the people we hurt along the way are human."

The woman stared at him, disgust wrinkling up her face. Then she spat on the twisted black stone. "You can take your sick voodoo toys and shove 'em up your nose. Go ahead and kill me. Do whatever. I don't care."

Frazier couldn't take his eyes off her for a long moment. She looked so much like his boss, it hurt his heart to hear her say such things. He felt a sudden surge of something between pain and love. He wanted to go to the woman, hold her, kiss her. In that instant, he didn't want to hurt her like this.

"Get your ugly eyes off me," she said. "I've seen rats who look more intelligent than you."

That ended his brief flare of weakness. He reached out and grabbed the rope around her neck. He stood up and made her sit on the roughly flat surface of the Blade's top bulky section. The thin strands of hard, black stone twisted and curved their way down until they connected with the bottom section. They looked like a clump of wires. Maybe, he thought, somehow that's what they were.

"Sit there and don't say another word," he said as he wrapped the rope around her body twice and then strung the rope through the tight spaces between those strings of dark rock. Once he'd tied that off, he took a set of metal shackles from his pack and clamped them around the Alterant's ankles, securing them to a couple of strands that bent out more than the others. There was no way she could get away, and the stone was far too heavy for her to drag and shuffle along in tiny steps.

Everything was set.

"Are you going to leave me here?" she asked, having lost her bravery from a minute before. "Let me die?"

"Yes and no." He loved giving that answer, loved seeing the perplexed look that came over the Alterant's face when he said it.

"What's that supposed to mean?" she responded.

Frazier placed the prepared sack of food and water next to her feet. "Just answering your question." He stood up, then turned and started to walk away.

"*Wait!*" she screamed. "Please! I can help you. I'm the best of the best! Please don't leave me here! *Please!*"

Frazier didn't respond. He found it was better that way. He just kept walking, knowing it'd be easier to make it to the winking point without a huge block of stone on his back and dragging a prisoner behind him. Ignoring her desperate pleas, he reached the end of the swatch of vegetation and reentered the vast forest.

The Blade of Shattered Hope was almost complete.

PART
2

THE BLACK
TREE

CHAPTER 12

SWEET DIGS

Mothball had to grab Sato and physically pull him away from the spectacle. The sight was just too hard to believe and had put him in a daze. Luckily the fighting clowns didn't seem to notice them.

"Come on," she yelled at him, dragging him across the field as easily as a sack of raked leaves. "Soon as those lugs take notice we've got one the likes of you, we'll be the ones they be fightin', not themselves—bet your buttons. Come *on!*"

Sato finally got his feet under him and regained his composure, walking quickly alongside Mothball as Rutger struggled to keep up. "What *was* that? Who are those people?"

"Bugaboo soldiers," she replied. "Nasty people, they are. Completely insane."

Sato forced out a chuckle. "They're dressed like *clowns* and trying to stab each other with sharp swords. What makes you think they're crazy?"

Mothball seemed to miss his sarcasm. "Not right in the head. Been crazy ever since the war ended, not knowing what to do when there's no one to fight. Rutger, chop-chop, little man!"

Sato turned to see Rutger a good twenty feet behind them, pumping his short little arms as he tried his best to run. "Slow *down!*" the short man yelled. "Before I croak!"

They topped a small, sparsely wooded rise and headed down the other side. Once they were out of sight from the odd group of battling clowns, Mothball finally stopped and allowed Rutger to catch up. The poor man's face was bloodred—a cherry on top of a black ball. Sato expected a blur of insults and smart remarks from Rutger, but it was all the guy could do to breathe, heaving air in and out.

"I still don't get it," Sato said. "Who *are* those people?"

Mothball rolled her eyes, in a rare bad mood. "'Tis a long story and no time to tell it. Once we make it to me mum's house, you can ask your questions. Can we go now?" She loomed over Rutger with her hands on her hips.

The robust little man looked up at her. "How far?"

"Just 'round the bend up yonder," she answered, pointing toward a small paved lane that came out of a forest to their right and went over the next hill. "We can stop runnin', we can. I 'spect them Bugaboos'll be quite occupied for a spell. Come on." She headed off for the road.

Sato looked at Rutger. "Do *you* know anything about these Bugaboo soldiers?"

Rutger shrugged, a movement that shook his whole body. "Enough not to bug Mothball about it. She has a *long* history with those nutsos. Let's just get to her house and then we can talk about it."

"Whatever," Sato muttered, consumed with curiosity. Sword-fighting clowns were bad enough, and the fact that Mothball was scared of them only made it worse. He felt a disturbing chill that made him shudder. "Let's go."

Rutger started off down the hill, and Sato followed.

The road led to a cluster of homes surrounded by an enormously tall wall of roughly mortared stones. In fact, everything about the neighborhood was tall: the houses, the trees, the carriages and their horses. And once he got past the sheer size of it all, Sato was amazed at how medieval everything looked.

What kind of a world had Mothball grown up in?

She seemed to sense his thoughts. "Don't ya worry, Master Sato. Plenty of fancy things in this Reality—cars and tellies and the like. We just enjoy livin' the old-fashioned way 'round these parts."

"Just be glad they have fridges and real toilets," Rutger muttered.

They made it to the wide opening of the border wall, where a massive iron gate was closed and locked to prevent anyone from entering.

"Can't be lettin' in the Bugaboos," Mothball said. "Gate stays closed every minute, 'less you say the password." She took a deep breath, then yelled in a slow, booming voice, "Donkey hoe tea!"

Sato wasn't sure he'd heard right. "Did you just say *Don Quixote?* Like the book?"

Groans and creaks of metal filled the air as the gate swung inward.

"No, never 'eard of that one," Mothball responded as she stepped forward to enter. "I said *donkey . . . hoe . . . tea.* Chooses three random words, it does, and every day's different."

Sato hurried to keep up with her, Rutger hustling along right behind him. "It? What is *it?*" A loud clang announced the gate had closed again.

"Old Billy's fancy 'puter that runs the place. The gate, the lights, the whole bit."

Sato couldn't help but be fascinated by this Reality.

Up until now, he'd seen only the cemeteries of Tick's Alterants, and he was excited to have a break and meet more people, see if they were a lot like Mothball.

A gravel path led them from the entrance through a greener than green patch of grass, speckled with red and yellow and purple wildflowers. A slight breeze picked up, running across the grass in waves, bringing a sweet scent along with it. It hit Sato that the temperature was perfect here—not too cold and not too hot. For the first time in a while, he had the urge to kick back and relax, take a long vacation. And right here in his tall friend's neighborhood seemed like the perfect place.

With a deep sigh, surprised at his sudden good mood, he followed Mothball as the path intersected a wide, cobblestone road, running away from them for at least half a mile, both sides of the road lined with those ancient-styled houses. Made of large rocks and roughly hewn brick, the homes would have looked almost like natural formations that had stood for a thousand years, except for the countless boxes of flowers hanging here and there, the roofs thatched with bundles of long grasses, the multicolored windows, and the brightly painted wooden doors—mostly reds and yellows.

And the yards. Sato was used to his home country of Japan, where the small homes sat almost on top of the streets and had maybe just enough room for a tiny tree and a single bush. But these houses had huge yards, filled with green grass and finely groomed bushes and majestic trees. And gardens. Lots and lots of gardens, growing every veggie and fruit known to man, by the looks of it.

As they walked down the street in silence, Sato had the feeling that if he'd been born in this Reality instead of his own, he would've grown up the happiest person ever. How could anyone be grumpy in a place like this?

Then he remembered those psycho people dressed up like clowns and fighting each other with swords. The big stone wall and locked iron gate. Maybe life here wasn't so blissful after all.

"Which one's yours?" Sato asked. "And where is everybody?" He'd yet to see one other person.

Mothball absently pointed somewhere up ahead. "Just a bit farther. And most folks are off to town, doin' their jobs and such. Thems that ain't are havin' after-noon tea in their parlor, I 'spect."

"I don't think my feet will ever forgive you," Rutger said through heavy breaths. "We need to bury a bunch of dead people in your backyard so we can wink straight there next time."

"Mayhaps we'll start with you," Mothball replied.

Rutger barked a fake laugh. "Well, the way my heart's beating, you just might be right! I've probably lost ten pounds already."

"Walk another few weeks straight, and maybe you

can fit through me mum's door without me kickin' ya in the ruddy bottoms." She laughed, a rolling stutter of thunder that lifted Sato's spirits even more.

"You guys are the weirdest best friends I've ever met," Sato said. "Maybe you should just go ahead and get married."

"Married?" Mothball roared. "What, and have little monster babies with my ugly face on little balls of fat? Methinks I'd rather marry a horse."

"Feeling's mutual!" Rutger countered.

"Would eat a lot less, that's for sure," Mothball murmured.

"And wouldn't complain at your incessant gibbering!"

"Smell better, too."

"You know what they say—sometimes a husband and wife look like brother and sister. You and a horse— well, perfect!"

Mothball scratched her chin, acting like she couldn't hear him. "There'd be horse patties lyin' 'round about me flat. Might get a bit messy."

"Okay, this is getting creepy," Sato interjected. "Where's your house?"

Mothball stopped, then threw her arms up and clapped once as she looked at the large home to their right. "Well, bite me buttons, here we are!"

The house and yard looked a lot like the others,

though the front door was pink. Mothball's proclamation had barely ended when the door swung open and a gigantic woman with a huge mop of curly black hair on her head came rushing out to greet them. Her clothes were the same style as Mothball's—loose, dull colors, hanging off her skin-and-bones body like drying laundry. Or maybe *dying* laundry.

"Me love!" the lady yelled as she ran down the stone steps, all gangly legs and arms making her look as if she might collapse into a heap of sticks at any second. "Oh, me sweet, sweet love! Been 'specting you, we 'ave!"

She reached Mothball, and they squeezed each other tightly, circling around, both of them crying. Sato looked away, uncomfortable at intruding on something intimate and personal. When they finally let go of each other, Mothball pointed straight at him.

"This here's Master Sato," she said proudly. "And, of course you know Rutger, me best friend."

"Ah, yes, yes," her tall mom replied, the enormous smile she'd worn since opening the door still there. Sato noticed her teeth were just as crooked as her daughter's, but much whiter. "So good to see you again, Rutger. And you, Sato, welcome. My name is Windasill, and I'm so happy to say we've finally met. I've been waiting for months."

"Really?" Sato said, surprised.

"Of course." She looked at Mothball, a slight look

of confusion on her face. "You didn't tell him?"

Mothball shrugged, clearly embarrassed.

Sato couldn't imagine what was going on. "Tell me? What didn't you tell me?"

Instead of answering, Mothball nodded at her mom.

Windasill grinned again and curtsied—quite the display from someone so big. "You do look just like him, I must say. A wee bit shorter's all." Then, inexplicably, she started crying, the stifled sobs accompanied by tears streaming out of her eyes.

Now he was beyond confused. "What are you *talking* about? What's going on?"

Rutger answered for them. "Sato, you're the Alterant of Grand Minister Sato Tadashi, who was the supreme ruler of this entire world—in this Reality anyway."

"*Was?*" Sato repeated, not knowing how to react to the strange revelation.

Mothball's mom answered, right after spitting on the ground. "Bugaboos killed him last month, they did, just weeks after he took office. Sacrificed hundreds of blokes to break through security and get to him. He was the most respected leader we've had in ages, despite being so young. Gone and dead now."

"Why . . . why'd they kill him?" Sato asked. He had an uncomfortable feeling this was leading somewhere he wouldn't like. Mothball's answer confirmed it.

"They thought he was you."

CHAPTER 13

SLEEPLESS IN THE DARK

rip.

Drip.

Drip.

That was all Tick could hear, and it was driving him crazy. The others were asleep, and even though the soft sighs and snores of their slumber floated through the air, all his mind could focus on was that stupid dripping water.

Drip.

Drip.

Drip.

Everything had happened so fast after Jane revealed that she'd kidnapped his sisters, Lisa and Kayla. The news shocked every bit of surging power out of him, and he'd collapsed to the floor in defeat, knowing he couldn't take the risk she might be lying. He couldn't risk their lives. Not them.

As soon as he'd given up, Jane had winked them all away. He didn't know how she did it, or who helped her, but one instant they'd been in his basement, and the next they were here, in some kind of cell made of gray stone, damp and cold and dark, with that maddening drip of water as a constant companion. The only light was faint, coming from somewhere down a long hallway outside the bars of their prison.

They'd been there for hours and hours. Every question in the world had been asked, every nook and cranny of the room examined, and they had shouted and screamed for help until their voices went hoarse. Then exhaustion crept in, and now everyone was asleep.

Except Tick. He huddled with his back against the hard, cold wall, his arms wrapped around his knees, his hands clasped in front of him. He felt empty, like his mind and heart had become a complete void of space, sucking every last bit of strength and will away. Jane had his sisters—but who knew where or how or why. And he was here, with his mom and dad, his two best friends, and the leader of the Realitants, all of them captured and helpless.

He'd tried several times to summon even the smallest trace of the power he'd felt against Jane in the basement of his house, but nothing came. Just emptiness. He floated in a void. A yucky, blecky, hopeless void.

"Tick?"

The voice startled him. He put his hands down to the ground, ready to spring to his feet. But a second later he realized it was Sofia, just a few feet from him, lying down with her head resting on her folded arms. She pushed herself into a sitting position and looked at him. He could barely see the features of her face, but they didn't look as sad as he would've expected.

"Still here," he replied. "Did you actually fall asleep?"

She yawned in response. "Think so. Had a bad dream."

"I wish *this* were a bad dream."

"Yeah."

"Dude, I finally snooze and you guys wake me up." Paul was getting to his feet, rubbing his eyes. He made his way over to sit next to Tick and Sofia. "You think the geezer and your mom and dad are actually sleeping?"

"I hope so," Tick said. "They're old—they need it."

"Actually," Sofia whispered, "the younger you are, the more sleep you need. Just for the record."

Tick wasn't in the mood for her smarts. "Whatever."

"So what do you think she's up to?" Paul asked. "Jane the Beast, I mean. And what's the deal with that robe and mask, the scratchy voice? Tick, you're the only one who's met her before—did she talk like that? Did she have that mask?"

Tick shook his head and was happy to realize he didn't feel any guilt at what Paul had just said. In fact, he wished she'd died. "Remember when I broke apart Dark Infinity and attacked her with it? I think it burned her and melted stuff all over her. Kind of like it . . . fused them together."

"And maybe it made her more powerful, too," Sofia added. "Maybe she somehow kept the powers of Chu's weapon. How else could she have winked into your basement *and* winked us all here?"

"Huh?" Tick asked. "How do you know *she* did it? Not someone with a Barrier Wand?"

Sofia pointed in front of her as if Jane were standing there. "Because I was staring at her the whole time. As soon as you quit trying to do whatever you were doing with your orange hocus-pocus stuff, she reached out with her hands and swept them through the air, like she was picking up a big pile of leaves and throwing them. Then I felt the tingle, and next thing I know, we're here."

"What *were* you doing to her, anyway?" Paul asked.

The question hit Tick like a thump in his chest. He hesitated, not knowing what to say.

"Hello?" Paul pushed. "Earth calling Atticus Higgin-bottom."

Tick shifted to get more comfortable. "I don't know, man. It's hard enough to understand it in my brain, much less explain it to you guys."

"Well, try," Sofia said. "If we can help you figure out these freaky powers of yours, we might get out of here someday."

Freaky powers, Tick thought. Did she have to say it that way? After a long pause, he cleared his throat and resolved to tell them everything. "Every time I've had an . . . episode, I feel this heat in my chest and gut, something burning inside me. I've been able to push it down a couple times recently and make it go away."

"Hey," Paul said, "at least that's progress over what you did at Chu's shack. Maybe you're learning to control it."

Tick nodded. "Maybe. Anyway, in my basement, I kind of panicked when Jane started talking, and when the heat came, I didn't stop it. I . . . encouraged it, tried to hold on to it, make it grow. It was like I had these mental hands, trying to clasp invisible fingers around an invisible . . . something. I don't know—I can't describe it. It took a lot of focus and concentration. Then, I just mentally threw it at her. I guess I attacked her just by thinking it and wanting it."

Paul and Sofia stared at him, apparently at a loss for words, a minor miracle with those two.

"Anyway," Tick continued, "it felt really good. I

still think I'm a long way from controlling it anytime I
want to, but this was about a billion times be— what
what happened a few months ago. Back then it was like
somebody had ripped my spirit out of my body and I
couldn't do anything about it."

"What *is* the power?" Paul asked. "I mean, you're
doing some crazy stuff here, dude."

"It's Chi'karda, brainiac," Sofia answered. "We
know that much. For some reason Tick has a ton of it."

Paul shook his head. "I know it's Chi'karda—
at least, that's what Master Georgie boy over there
thinks." He pointed to the snoozing man, who looked
a little ridiculous all dressed up in a prison cell. "But
what does that *mean?*"

"What do you mean, what does it mean?" Sofia said.

"I mean, what does it mean?"

Sofia blew out a loud breath. "I don't know what
it means."

"Man," Tick said, "we are really making progress
here."

They stayed quiet for a while, and then Sofia broke
the silence. "Well, we can leave the science side of it
to Master George and the Realitants. We just need to
help you learn how to control it so we can use it. As a
weapon."

"Yeah," Paul agreed. "How about right now? I don't
think I'm up for hanging around here much longer."

Weapon. For some reason that word gave Tick the chills. He didn't want to think of himself as a potential killing device. "It doesn't matter right now. I can't feel anything, not even a flicker."

"Maybe you need to be ticked off," Paul said. "Here, let me kick you in the—"

"I'm good, thanks." Tick scooted away.

"Just start thinking about stuff," Sofia suggested. "Think about Jane and what she's done to us and how we're sitting in this prison. Think about your . . ." She didn't finish, looking at the ground as if she'd just confessed something horrible.

Tick felt tears glisten his eyes. "You were going to say *sisters*. Think about my sisters."

Sofia looked up at him, then nodded.

"Maybe that's why I'm so empty," Tick said, hearing the gloom in his own voice. "She threatened to hurt them if I try anything, so my subconscious won't even let me get close to trying."

"Man," Paul said, "guess we shouldn't expect you to, then. Too risky."

"What *are* we going to do?" Sofia pleaded.

Master George stirred to their right, grunting as he rolled over and pushed himself into a sitting position. He let out a huge yawn while rubbing his eyes. "Goodness gracious me, how long have I been sleeping?"

"Couple hours," Tick said.

"I had the strangest dream," the leader of the Realitants said in a groggy voice. "I was in your basement, Master Atticus, and I saw a person in a big rabbit suit. It was a very creepy bunny. Quite disturbing. I woke up just as the person started to take off his head. What I would give to have seen the face beneath the mask."

"It's symbolic," Sofia said. "Jane wears a mask now. I'm sure it's her you would've seen."

"Uh, what about the whole bunny thing?" Paul asked with a slight snicker.

"Well," Master George began, clearing his throat, embarrassed. "I was, er, a bit frightened of bunnies as a child."

Tick shocked himself when he laughed out loud. So did Paul.

"Poke fun if you must," Master George countered, though he had a smile on his face. "You try falling into a cage filled with a dozen hungry rabbits and see how—"

A loud metal clang cut him off, and they all turned to see the iron-grilled door to their cell swing open. Standing behind it in the hallway was Mistress Jane, still dressed in her yellow robe and her expressionless red mask. There was a cart next to her, loaded with several plates of steaming food.

"My, you all look cozy," she said. "I've brought you

something to eat. I can't have you starving to death before our big plans come to fruition." She pushed the cart into the cell then swung the heavy door shut again. Its clanking ring echoed like some haunted musical instrument.

She turned to walk away, apparently done with them.

"Where are we?" Master George shouted at her.

Jane stopped, but did not look at them. "You're in the Thirteenth Reality, George. Though it won't be called that much longer."

She started walking again, and soon was out of sight.

CHAPTER
14

QUESTIONS WITHOUT ANSWERS

Mothball's dad was actually shorter than his wife, and, impossibly, even nicer. His dark hair and the angled features of his face would have looked hard and cold except for the permanent smile breaking it all up. He ushered Sato and the others into the huge living room, where they all sat down with cups of steaming hot tea. His name was Tollaseat, and he wore a bright red sweater with his drab-colored pants. He looked about as unfashionable as a person could possibly get.

As for the inside of the house, it was finely decorated. Bookshelves made of a dark and shiny wood were everywhere, some of them stocked with leather-bound books, others with various porcelain sculptures, dishes, and other knickknacks. The furniture all seemed a little fancy, with frilly carvings and flower prints and lacy stuff here and there. But at least the chairs were comfortable, and the soft carpet was easily three inches thick. Over a huge fireplace—which looked like it could burn an entire forest in no time—hung a portrait of an old woman just as tall and awkward-looking as Mothball and her mother.

"So," Tollaseat said, his voice like a massive tolling bell, "Sato, my friend, I can't tell you how nice it is to finally meet you."

"Thanks," Sato said, nodding with a curt smile. He couldn't quite settle down, trying desperately to come to terms with his connection to the recently murdered ruler of the Fifth Reality. Why would a fifteen-year-old kid be the leader of an entire planet? It was just too bizarre. And if those Bugaboo soldiers—what a ridiculous name!—really wanted him dead . . .

Rutger cleared his throat. He was perched on a chair, his short legs dangling like a little kid's. He glanced sidelong at Sato. "You'll have to excuse our new Realitant friend. He's not one for a lot of words. I'm sure he's very happy to meet you too."

"Ah," Tollaseat scoffed, waving at the air with both hands. "No bother, really, no bother at all. We're simply thrilled to have the lot of you come and sit a spell. No need for jabbering and such."

Sato had to figure this out. "Could someone please explain to me about my Alterant? How could these psycho clown soldiers possibly think I'd come to this world and become the . . . what did you call it?"

"Grand Minister," Windasill said quietly, as if indulging a child taking a quiz.

Sato snapped his fingers. "Yeah, that. How could they think I'd become the Grand Minister of the Fifth Reality? And why would they want to kill me in the first place?"

Mothball was sitting directly across from him. She leaned forward and put her elbows on her knees. "We think the Bugs and Mistress Jane have gone off and made some type of nasty arrangement. Mayhaps done it quite some time ago. And we reckon old Jane put out the scoop on you and your friends. Looking for revenge, she was. Just happens that your Alterant became our Minister, and the Bugs thought maybe we'd planted you. Replaced Sato Tadashi in a swap. Like we'd wanna ruddy take over the Reality or some such nonsense."

"They must be the dumbest people in the universe," Rutger muttered.

"No, no, my friend," Tollaseat said, shaking his head. "Crazy, vicious, bloodsucking tyrants, maybe. But not dumb. That I can promise ya."

Sato ran a hand through his hair, not sure which bothered him more: that his Alterant just happened to be the ruler of an entire planet, or that a group of crazy clown soldiers wanted him dead. Scratch that, he thought. The second one was definitely worse.

"Wait a minute," he said, just realizing something that should've been obvious from the start. "How could they possibly think that guy was me? Wouldn't he have been way taller?"

"Not really," Tollaseat answered. "Most of us chaps here in the Fifth don't hit our growth spurts 'til we hit drinkin' age. That not the same in your neck of the woods?"

Sato shrugged his shoulders wearily. "This is weird," he said, as if those three words summed up everything. Maybe they did. "I really feel like I'm missing something. And why'd you guys bring me here if you knew all this?"

Mothball's face scrunched up into a look of apology. "Sorry 'bout that. Really I am. Never thought we'd run into the Bugs. They 'aven't been about much lately, according to me parents. Thought their troubles with these parts was quite well and over."

"Quite true," Tollaseat added. "Had our wars with 'em blokes back when Mothball was a wee one, but not seen 'em much since. No idea why they're up in the deadie fields today. Strange, really."

Sato folded his arms and stared at the floor. Staying here much longer didn't sound like a good idea. "Well, maybe we should go back to headquarters. If those clowns want to kill me, I'd just as soon not be hanging out a couple of miles from them."

"Leave before supper?" Tollaseat exclaimed, shooting up from his seat. "Not a chance. I've got all three ovens runnin' top heat, cookin' a feast like you've never seen before, young man. Bugs 'ave no idea you're 'ere, I'd bet me left shoe. You just sit there and enjoy yourself with me wife and daughter while I go ready things up."

Windasill reached out and patted Sato on the knee. "I married the best cook in the entire valley, I did. Good thing me blood runs fast and hot, or I'd look like poor Rutger sitting over there."

Sato felt his eyes widen. He glanced quickly over at Rutger, who didn't seem fazed in the least by the rude comment.

"I'd rather be down close to the ground," the man said. "Safe and balanced, fat and happy. Lot better than looking like a bunch of dusty bones with clothes."

Windasill laughed, the nicest sound Sato remembered hearing in a long time. "Oh, Rutger, we do love you so. Every last inch of you—and that's saying quite a lot." Giggling, she left the room, presumably to help her husband in the kitchen.

Once she was gone, Sato sat up straighter and glared first at Rutger, then Mothball. "This is crazy. Is all that stuff true?"

"Right as rain," Mothball replied. "What's all the fuss? We'll have our dinner and be on our way, we will."

Rutger rolled forward until he plopped off the chair and onto his feet. "If anything, you're safer than ever. They think they killed you, remember? Calm down, and let's go eat. I'm—"

"Let me guess," Sato interrupted. "Starving."

"How'd you know?"

"Come on, funny bunnies," Mothball said, standing up on her tall legs. "I could use a bite to eat myself." She reached down and swatted Rutger on the back before moving toward the kitchen, her best friend right on her heels.

Sato stared at their backs until they disappeared out of the room. How weird had his life become? He was standing in a house that made him feel like he was four feet tall, in an entirely different world, about to eat dinner with three giants and a man shaped like a big beach ball, in a place where his twin had been the leader of the entire planet and had been assassinated by insane men dressed like clowns.

Could it get any stranger?

Refusing to answer that question, he walked quickly out of the room and toward the wonderful smells wafting from the kitchen.

CHAPTER
15

THE TWELFTH BLADE

Frazier Gunn stared down at the twelfth Alterant of Mistress Jane.

She was huge. And she was the last of them.

This one had been living a normal life in a small village in the Fifth Reality, where quirks of evolution, diet, and climatic factors had led to an unusually large race of humans. He guessed the woman sitting in front of him, now safely chained to the twisty black stone of the twelfth Blade component, had to be almost eight feet tall, and skinny— like she'd eaten nothing but lettuce her whole life. Crooked teeth, no makeup, stringy black hair.

And yet, even then, she was beautiful. Despite the tears streaming down her face, despite the constant begging, despite the disgusting way she wrung her hands and wiped snot from her nose with her fingers, she was beautiful to him. Maybe it was just the resemblance to Jane. He hadn't seen her in days and missed her terribly. Maybe it was his longing for how she'd looked before the terrible Atticus Higginbottom incident. Maybe it was a lot of things.

But he was wasting time. He had to get back to the Thirteenth.

"Please," the woman whimpered for the thousandth time since being dragged from her garden. With her size and surprising strength, Frazier had been forced to use the Stunning Rod Jane had created for him, jolting the Alterant every so often to remind her to cooperate. It'd been a long and grueling trip. But nothing could dampen his spirits now—it was over. The hardest mission of his life was finally over.

Now the exciting part would begin.

"Please don't leave me here," the Alterant said between loud sniffs. "I 'ave children, I do. Me husband's away. None to take care of the wee ones."

Frazier leaned over, looking her square in the eyes. "Please be quiet." He dropped a pack of food and water at her feet then straightened and turned to walk away, moving as quickly as he could so he wouldn't have to hear her wailing pleas for help. He knew he should've told her what a good cause she was participating in, how eventually great things would come from Jane's plan with the Blade of Shattered Hope. But he couldn't bring himself to do it. He was too tired to speak anymore.

He topped a rise and quickly went down the deep slope. The woman's screeching, painful cries finally faded into the background. Capturing her had been the worst by far, maybe because she was the only one who hadn't had some kind of criminal or shady background. Of course, the pitiful lady didn't know this, but she had very good reason to feel such hopeless desperation.

Of the twelve Alterants of Mistress Jane, this one in the Fifth would be the only one to die. Well, this time around, anyway.

Mistress Jane stood at her favorite spot in the entire Lemon Fortress—maybe her favorite spot in all of the Realities. The open window of her room overlooked countless miles of forests, fields of green grass and wildflowers, and the snowcapped mountains in the distance. The beauty of it was overwhelming, even as seen through the eyeholes of her mask.

Normally she'd take it off, but she expected Frazier to report at any minute. And despite several months having passed since her entire body had been scorched and mutilated by Higginbottom, she had yet to let anyone see her true self—only her hands, so they'd know something horrible had happened. But she was still too ashamed, too embarrassed to reveal any other part of her now-hideous body. *Especially* her face. A face that had once, she thought proudly, been very, very beautiful.

A face that now looked like the scarred surface of a planet too close to a boiling sun.

At least the pain had subsided somewhat. With her increased powers over Chi'karda, she'd spent many days experimenting until she'd finally been able to manipulate her nervous system, a complex network of seemingly infinite human "wires." In the beginning she could only reduce the pain when she concentrated, focusing in deep meditation. But as the weeks passed, she'd come to learn to do it on instinct, and life had become much sweeter. More conducive to fulfilling her long-awaited plans.

But, unfortunately, she was still a long way from changing her appearance. For now, she had to settle for the robe and the mask to hide herself from the world, even from her closest friends.

Friends, with an "s" at the end? She was being far too generous. Only one person in all the Realities considered her a friend—Frazier.

Speaking of the devil, she heard a knock at the door.

"Come in," she said, sending out a wave of Chi'karda to dissolve the door, something she'd done a thousand times—much more satisfying than merely pulling it open, and a task that was much easier now with her supercharged abilities over the realm of physics.

She looked over from where she stood next to the window, and after Frazier had stepped through, she imagined the billions of tiny particles that made up the wood of the door coming back together. She *pushed* a mental surge in that direction, and with a buzzing swoosh, the door appeared as it had seconds before, unblemished and whole.

With another mere thought, she made one of the eyebrows on her red metal mask arch upward. "Is it finished?"

Frazier walked over, obviously trying his hardest not to smile, but it was there anyway, especially in his eyes. "Yes, Mistress. The twelfth one is in place, secured in the Fifth. All of them have nanolocators and monitoring devices injected within their bodies. The observation area is alive and chirping as we speak. All we need now is—"

"I know what we need!" Jane snapped, flowing her mask into anger. "Honestly, Frazier, sometimes you act as if all this were your idea, your plan. Keep speaking to me like I'm some lowly wretch, and I'll end your service to me—swiftly and painfully, I assure you. I don't care who you are or what you've done for me."

She regretted the words even as they flew out of her

mouth, hating the look of sincere and utter hurt that melted the poor man's face. But they had to be said. Once again, Frazier had shown traces of . . . confidence. Too much of it. She couldn't allow it. Confidence led to insubordination and betrayal. Always.

"I'm sorry, Mistress," Frazier muttered, his eyes downcast, his hands folded in front of him. "I'm only excited to see our—um, I mean, *your* plan—come to fruition."

There it was again, even after she'd rebuked him. *Our* plan—he'd actually said it! As much as it would hurt her, and as much as it would cause even more loneliness for her, she had to distance herself from him. Now more than ever.

"Very well, Frazier. Have a seat." She gestured toward the couch by the fireplace, then followed behind him until he sat down. She sat in the armchair directly across from him. The stone hearth to their right was dark and cold.

Bringing her mask back to a smooth, calm expression, she crossed her legs under the loose folds of her robe, instinctively suppressing the pain with her power the instant she felt it. "Let's be clear. All twelve of my Alterants are currently chained to the Blade devices, in each Reality, including Prime, within the specified ranges of the needed coordinates?"

Frazier nodded, his face now pale. *Ah,* she thought.

She *had* gone too far. When the man got too frightened, he became useless. Somehow she needed to learn how to hold back.

"Are you certain they're undisturbed?" she asked, trying to speak with a soothing voice. For all his tendency to fear her, he usually melted back to stupefied worship easily enough. "They're all alive and well?"

He only nodded again, but some of the color had returned to his face.

"Any potential problems?"

"Well, Mistress," he said, croaking a bit on the last syllable. He cleared his throat. "The coordinates in each Reality were in pretty remote areas, except for two. Your Alterant in Prime is in a basement, and in the Seventh, in the bottom floor of a parking garage. I left a couple of Sleeks in each of those locations to guard against potential intruders. As long as we stay on schedule, we should be okay."

Mistress Jane nodded slowly, pleased. If Frazier was correct, all the pieces were in place and everything else was up to her. All she needed was the Blade Tree, her witnesses, a quick wink to where she needed to go, and a few minutes of the most intense concentration she would ever embark upon.

She stood from the chair and held a hand out to Frazier. "Then I think we're ready to induce the Blade of Shattered Hope."

Frazier took her hand without the slightest hesitation, even though the hideous scars and melded chunks of gold were plainly evident. His touch warmed her, and the fact that he had no reservations or prejudice against her new nature . . .

That meant something. She felt ashamed of how she'd treated him earlier.

"Frazier," she said, pulling him up from the couch so he stood in front of her, just inches away. Her mask flowed into the most sincere smile she could conjure up in her mind. "You'll be by my side when we do this. Agreed?"

A trickle of . . . something pricked her heart when she saw tears glisten his eyes.

"Yes, Mistress," he said. "I'd be more honored than words can say."

"Good. Then let's go change the Realities once and for all."

CHAPTER
16

A DIABOLICAL PLAN

When Tick woke up, his parents had disappeared from the prison cell.

At first, he didn't quite notice, his mind still numb from sleep. Almost absently, he scanned the dimly lit room from left to right, expecting them to be *somewhere*. Huddled in a corner, maybe. Or hidden behind Master George, Paul, or Sofia, still dozing. Veiled in a shadow to which his eyes hadn't adjusted quite yet.

But then it hit him. They were gone.

His body jerked to full awareness like a bucket of water had been dumped on his head, and he jumped to his feet. "Where's my mom and dad? Where's my mom and dad!"

The others stirred, his shouts waking them.

"Huh?" Paul said groggily.

Sofia was looking around the room, much like he'd done just moments earlier. Master George grunted as he got to his feet, also searching with his eyes.

"Goodness gracious me," he said. "Where could they have gone off to?"

"We would've heard the door open," Sofia said. "No way we could've missed that."

That familiar panicky feeling threatened to consume Tick. "Where could they be?" He ran over to the bars of the cell, gripped his hands around the cold iron. "Mom! Dad! *Mooooom! Daaaaad!*"

First his sisters were taken, hidden in any one of who-knew-how-many horrible places. Now his parents were gone. "This can't be happening," he murmured, whispering it over and over. Then, "I'm gonna stop her. Once and for all, I'm gonna stop her."

"Calm down, Atticus," Master George said, hurrying to his side and placing a hand on his shoulder. "Remember the whole point of why Jane took your sisters. To *prevent* you from doing anything reckless."

For the first time since they'd left the basement of his house, Tick felt the surging boil of Chi'karda within him, burning and growing. But he also knew that Master George was right—he couldn't take a risk. Not now, not yet. Closing his eyes and concentrating with all his might, he pushed the power away, urged it to cool and dissolve.

"Why would she have taken my parents?" he asked when he felt the episode was safely over. "Why now?"

"I'm sure we'll find out soon enough," Paul said. He stepped up next to Tick and squeezed his arm. "Sorry, dude. Seriously, though, we'll figure this out. We've been in worse shape, haven't we? We're like superheroes, man—we'll win this time, too."

Sofia walked over and hugged Tick, squeezing him tightly. Surprised, it took him a second before he squeezed back.

"Paul's an idiot," she said as she let go and stepped back. "And he never knows how to say anything. But he's right. We'll get your family back, don't worry. There's no way she'll . . . hurt them. Then she'd have nothing to threaten you with. I think she's terrified of you."

"Terrified?" a voice asked behind him.

Tick spun around to see Mistress Jane standing in the hallway, her red mask glaring at them with eyebrows raised.

"Where are they?" he shouted at her.

"They are safe for now," she replied, her face melting back into that non-expression she wore most of the time. "I decided there were too many of you to keep track of. Plus, your parents have been winked to a different location than where your sisters are. I now have double collateral to hang over your head. I sense even a spark of Chi'karda surge out of you, and one of them dies. On and on until they're all dead. If something bad happens to me, they all die at once. I trust you'll not test me on this."

Tick fumed more with every word that popped out of her mouth. It took all his concentration to keep the warmth from igniting to pure heat inside his chest. But he also felt a slight glimmer of hope. Based on what she'd said, it seemed like she couldn't sense his surges of Chi'karda as long as he kept them at bay. Maybe, when the time was right, he could let the power build and build, unleashing it all in one powerful explosion before she could react or send a message to anyone.

What am I thinking? he thought. *I don't even know what I'm talking about. I can't control this stuff.* It was just as likely he'd kill himself and his friends as it was he'd kill Jane.

"I'll take your silence as a sign that you understand the situation." Jane's arm shifted slightly, and the lock on the door sprung open with a loud click. The metal hinges groaned and squealed, and the door swung open. "And the same goes for any one of you. Try anything, and Tick's family will suffer the consequences. If we run out of Higginbottoms, we'll just have to do some hunting for Pacinis and Rogers. Or perhaps the tall ugly woman and her little pet, the ball of fat named Rutger. Do we all understand one another?"

When no one responded, Jane's scream pierced the air like a burst of thunder. *"Answer me!"*

"Yes," Tick said quickly, as did Paul and Sofia. The best she got out of Master George was a firm nod.

Jane stepped through the door and into the cell, standing very close to Tick. "We will be winking to a specific location here in the Thirteenth. Frazier has set up several spinners and monitors so all of you can best witness what happens today. When it's over, you'll spread the word, and we can begin the process of my taking over the Realities and putting the Utopia Initiative into full swing."

Master George laughed, a slow, condescending chuckle. Tick braced himself for Jane's reaction. He didn't see what was funny. Though he didn't know what she was talking about, her words had been like icy daggers scraping down his spine. She had something terrible planned, no doubt about it.

But Jane didn't explode with her usual anger. "Laugh all you want, George. Giggle, chortle, snicker, whatever pleases you most. A couple of hours from now, when you see what I do, you may never make such jolly sounds ever again. The Blade of Shattered Hope, George. Soulikens. Dark Matter. These are things you aren't even close to understanding yet."

Master George's face now showed no humor whatsoever. It burned red, almost as if he wore his own mask. "Words, Jane. Anyone can say fancy words, trying their best to sound smarter than others. You keep telling us you have this *diabolical* plan. Well, then, what is it?"

Jane paused before answering, the corners of her metallic lips curving upward slightly. "I'm going to destroy the Fifth Reality."

Master George huffed. "Destroy it? What kind of nonsense is this? A mess of atomic bombs come across your path recently?"

Jane's mask turned a darker shade of red, something Tick hadn't thought possible. However, her expression didn't change. It was still set in that mocking half-smile. For a long time, she just stared at Master George.

"Jane," he finally said, "I worry your mind has slipped down a slope from which it can't be saved."

"You mistake my silence, George," Jane replied. "I'm surprised, actually. I'm baffled that you could be so short-sighted. So . . . *stupid*."

"What exactly is *that* supposed to mean?"

"Do you really not understand my power over Chi'karda? Even before my . . . *union* with the core of Dark Infinity, I almost had the ability to do what I plan for today. Now, it will be done with absolute certainty."

"Well," Sofia chimed in, "quit talking about it and tell us what your big bad plan is."

Tick winced. She and Master George weren't being smart about this. Couldn't they see that Jane was deadly serious? Ticking her off even more was a very, very bad idea. But when Jane responded, her voice was as calm and collected as anything Tick had ever heard come out of her mouth.

"The Blade of Shattered Hope will collect every souliken from my Alterants, channel them into the necessary components, and ignite the dark matter within. The Blade will then *slice* the Fifth Reality from existence. Forever." She paused, then took a step forward. "Let me say it slowly for you, George. The Fifth will . . . be . . . no . . . more."

CHAPTER
17

TALE OF THE IRON POKER

As Sato devoured his third helping of the duck dumpling stew, he realized he'd gone at least five minutes without thinking about the whole nonsense of his Alterant being the ruler of a Reality before being murdered. There is something about tasty food that tends to wash your troubles away. And Tollaseat's food was, without hesitation or doubt, the most excellent stuff Sato had ever put in his mouth.

"This is good," he mumbled between bites, probably having said those three words a dozen times by now. "This is really good."

"Glad ya like it, I am." Tollaseat leaned back in his chair and puffed on his pipe. He'd lit it after eating only one helping, and seemed to be enjoying every second of watching Sato eat like a starved hyena.

"Quite good, it was," Mothball pitched in, folding her arms and looking very satisfied.

Surprisingly, even Rutger—who was propped up on at least three pillows and a very large book—was finished, wiping his mouth and laying the napkin on his bowl. "Sato, I had no idea you could stuff your face like that. You'd make my mama proud."

Windasill grinned as she leaned forward and reached for the ladle in the big pot of stew. "Care for another helping, Master Sato?"

Suddenly, as if a switch had been flicked inside of him, Sato realized he was terribly, horribly, awfully full. He dropped his spoon and looked up, hoping the feeling that he might explode at any second didn't show on his face. "No, thanks. I think I might've taken one bite too many."

"Oh, rubbish," she said through an exaggerated frown. "There's always room for more duck dumpling stew. Isn't there, my sweet?" She glanced over at Tollaseat.

Mothball's dad puffed out a big cloud of wispy smoke. "Methinks the lad's proven himself quite nicely, me love. Let him rest up an hour or two. Then we'll bring out the *desserts*." He emphasized the last word in a roar with his wide eyes twinkling. He put the pipe back into his mouth and chuckled lightly.

The thought of dessert almost put Sato over the edge. "Sounds great," he managed to get out.

"Tell us a story," Mothball said, looking at her dad. "Been quite some time since we've 'eard you make somethin' up 'bout the war years, it 'as. Sato 'ere might enjoy your boastin' for a while." She looked over at Sato and winked. "Won't quite know what's true and what's not, but it's fun to listen to, ya can trust me on that one."

Rutger pounded the table. "I second the motion. After a meal like that, a body needs to hear a good tale or two."

Tollaseat scrunched up his face into something very serious, looking around the room at each person in turn. "Wanna hear a story, do ya?"

"Yeah," Sato said at the same time as everyone else. He was surprised at himself, but he suddenly wanted nothing more than to hear this tall, kind man tell stories about the old days, even though those old days would be very different from days in Reality Prime.

Tollaseat leaned back, his chair creaking, and shifted so that the elbow supporting his pipe-holding hand rested on the other arm. He took a puff or two then started talking, swirls of wispy smoke slowly drifting toward the ceiling.

"Back when I was a wee lad, barely ten and six— that's sixteen to you, Master Sato—just when the growin' pains started stretching me arms and legs, life was sweet and terrible. Sweet in that me mum and dad were alive and well, the crops were growin' right sprightly, and I'd just met me future love"—he nodded toward Windasill—"at the August Festie. But it was terrible, too, yes indeed. That ruddy summer marked the worst we'd had yet with the Bugs, it did."

He coughed and reached out for a sip of water before taking another puff from his pipe. "Late one night, I was sleepin' nice and cozy in me bed, dreamin' of good days to come. Mayhaps dreamin' about Windasill, even. Most of the fightin' with them nasty Bugs was off in the far country, ya see—just frightenin' tales and rumors to the likes of us, it was. But we knew things were quite bad, and that blokes like myself might have to run off and get to soldierin' and whatnot. But that night, all was well when I put on me long johns and dozed to the soft sounds of the breeze and the stream out back.

"But then came the knock on the door." He leaned forward, putting his elbows on the table. "Woke me right up, it did. I remember sittin' up, perkin' me ears. Heard the footsteps of me dad, heard the door creak as it swung open, heard the murmurs of conversation, though I couldn't make out any words. Then . . ."

He trailed off, a glazed look coming over his face. Sato felt his own face redden in embarrassment. Maybe the old man—

Tollaseat slammed his hand against the table. Dishes rattled and his pipe went skittering across the floor. Windasill quickly jumped up to retrieve it and returned it to her husband. As she sat down again, Sato waited breathlessly for what Tollaseat might say next.

"Can't quite say what sound it was I 'eard next," Mothball's dad continued. "A groan. A sigh. Maybe a bit of a whimper. But for some reason, it sent me brain spinnin' with alarm. I jumped from me bed and scrambled out to the main room. Right there in front of me, a ruddy Bugaboo was on top of me dad, his hands raised, claspin' the biggest sword you ever did see. Mum came in right then and screamed a sound you'd never believe 'less your own ears were there to 'ear it. If I'm honest with ya, which I am, 'twas that sound— me mum splinterin' the air with all the anguish in the world—that made me move. Even more than seein' me dad 'bout to meet the pointy end of a sword."

Sato leaned forward, sure he'd never been so capti-vated in his life.

Tollaseat barely paused between sentences now. "Acted, I did. Ran straight for the hearth—the ashes still glowin' hot—grabbed the iron poker me own Uncle Kent forged, gripped it with both of me ruddy hands, swung it up, and charged that Bug. Saw the fear in that loonie's eyes. Saw them widen and turn into pools of pure white. He started to say somethin', started to move, started to swing down with his arms and his sword. I screamed and swung that blessed iron poker. I swung it with every bit of strength cloggin' me pores and joints. I swung it straight for the Bug's face."

He paused then and took a long pull on his pipe. Scanning Sato and the others at the table, he finally blew out a stream of smoke. He looked down at the table, his eyes full of shadowy memories.

"What happened?" Sato whispered, unable to help himself.

Tollaseat, still staring at the empty plate in front of him, answered in a haunted voice. "I missed him. Completely missed the ruddy buzzard."

Sato swallowed heavily, slumping in his chair.

"Killed me dad, the Bug did." Tollaseat finally glanced up, his gaze resting on Sato. "But I saved me mum. I was able to run off the Bug. Swore the rest of me life to hunt them down, one by one, 'til every last one of them buggers was dead and rottin'."

The pipe went back into his mouth, and complete silence settled on the room. After a long minute, Sato looked at Mothball, her eyes moistened with tears, and then at Rutger, who was probably unaware he was still nibbling a biscuit. Both of them were staring at Tollaseat. After a moment, it became evident the story was over.

"Thank you for sharing, dear," Windasill said,

patting her husband on the arm. "'Eard it a thousand times, I 'ave, but I marvel at your courage every time. Never forget you saved your mum that day, dear. Never forget."

"Wish I could've met Grandpa," Mothball said, a choking clog in her voice. "But 'tweren't for you, Daddy, I wouldn't've spent me whole childhood with Grandma. Thanks be to ya, Daddy. Thanks be to ya very much."

Sato was stunned. He'd expected a story more along the lines of a fairy tale, maybe a funny or an embarrassing moment. But Tollaseat had just shared probably the most terrifying, pivotal moment of his life. And Sato had absolutely no idea what to say. He stared at his plate, feeling the heavy weight of all the food he'd eaten.

"Right cheerful, don't ya think?" Tollaseat said, a smile breaking through the gloom on his face. "Not quite sure why I told that story. Meant to tell somethin' else, I did. But it just popped out of me mouth."

"Important we remember," Mothball offered, giving her mom an uncomfortable look.

"Yes, me sweet," Tollaseat replied. "Reckon I wanted Master Sato 'ere to understand why them Bugs aren't just a joke, even though they look it. Crazy, they are. Vicious little rats. But underestimate 'em, and you'll be lookin' up at ten feet of dirt soon, you will. Be wary while you're about these parts, is all I'm sayin'."

Sato merely nodded, still unable to speak. He didn't know why, exactly, but that story had touched him, made his heart ache with sorrow. And then it hit him why.

Sato, too, had seen his father killed right in front of him. Burned to death by Mistress Jane's flying flames. Maybe that was worse than seeing your dad stabbed by a sword. Maybe not. It didn't matter. Something came over him in that moment.

He stood up. "Mister, um, Master . . . Tollaseat?"

Mothball's dad lowered his pipe, looked at Sato with dark eyes, and Sato somehow knew the old man had already figured out what he was about to say.

"I want to help," Sato said, trying to sound like an adult and hoping no one laughed. "I want to help your people fight the Bugs."

CHAPTER
18

TOWERS OF RED

Tick," Master George whispered. "I need you to listen to me very carefully. And do me a favor."

Jane had brought them to a room several levels above the prison cell in which they'd been held captive. She'd left a couple of guards at the door. The creatures in full armor were human in shape but all comparisons ended there. Tick hadn't gotten a good look, but he swore he saw horns or tusks coming out of their shadow-hidden faces and large bulges on their backs.

"What?" Tick asked.

In response, Master George handed him a small, metal tube.

"What's this?"

"What do you *think?*"

Tick looked over at Paul and Sofia, hoping they were listening. But both of them were trying to look through a grime-covered window. "Is it a message for somebody?"

"Precisely," George whispered.

"For who?" Tick asked. "And what do you want me to do?"

"It's a message for Sally. It's short, but he should get the point. I want him to gather the Realitants so they'll be ready on a moment's notice. For what, I have no idea—but he needs to get them to headquarters straightaway."

That made perfect sense to Tick, but he had a bad feeling about this all the same. "And . . . what does that have to do with me?"

Master George looked at him, his eyes shifting slightly back and forth. "Well, er, well, I need you to . . . wink it to Sally."

"What?" Tick rasped, way too loudly.

Sofia noticed. "What are you guys talking about over there?"

"Never you mind," Master George answered, surprisingly harsh.

Sofia, of course, completely ignored him and walked over, dragging Paul with her. "No secrets, boss. What's going on?"

Tick couldn't remember the last time he'd seen

Master George look so perplexed. His face was red, eyes darting around the room, sweat trickling down his temples. "Someone's going to *hear* us!" he exclaimed in a half-shout, half-whisper.

Tick didn't like it that Master George had asked him to use his power in the first place. Only a half an hour ago, Jane had threatened to kill his family one by one if she sensed him using Chi'karda. "How am I supposed to wink the message? Even if I could, even if I had a clue how to do it, I can't risk Jane finding out."

"Yes, yes, I *know*," Master George said, throwing all the frustration he could into the last word. "But perhaps you can risk it when she's . . . occupied with whatever she has planned. If we don't gather the other Realitants to help us, it may all be quite moot anyway."

Tick slid the message tube into his pocket. The old Brit was being coy, but Tick knew exactly what he was *really* trying to say. "So you think it's okay to sacrifice my family for the greater good. Let them die if it'll save the world. Worlds. Whatever." Tick couldn't believe how bitter he sounded. To make it worse, Master George had a *point*. But not one Tick could accept.

For the hundredth time, he felt an overwhelming, gloomy sorrow squeeze his chest and lungs. His sisters. His mom and dad. Jane had them. No matter what, he had to save them. No matter what.

But how?

"Tick?" Sofia asked, jolting him back to reality. "You okay? What does he want you to do?"

"We need to stop talking about this," Master George said. "Right now!"

"Dude," Paul said, "what are you two freaks talking about?"

Tick looked at him and shook his head. "It's nothing—George just wants to get a message to Sally." He turned his attention back to Master George. "Don't you have a way of talking to him? Through your nanolocator or something?"

Master George shook his head. "I think she's done something to us. Shielded us somehow. I've tried making contact several times. Nothing."

"Since when is Sally in charge?" Paul asked. "Rutger finally explode or something?"

"Maybe he ate one of his own Ragers," Sofia added.

By the looks of it, Master George was not amused. He turned his back to the three of them and walked over to a corner.

Sofia elbowed Paul in the arm. "Way to go, smarty."

"You, too, Godzilla," he replied. "Your comment was worse than mine."

Tick couldn't remember a time when he'd been *less* in the mood to listen to his friends fight. "Guys! You think this is all some kind of stupid joke?" As soon as the words were out, he regretted them. Especially when he saw the look on their faces—shock, mixed with a little hurt.

"What crawled up your pants and started biting?" Paul asked.

"Tick's right," Sofia said, her eyes never leaving Tick's. "His family's been taken. I can't imagine . . . what that must be like. We need to take things more seriously."

She looked away, and Tick saw an expression he couldn't quite identify come over her face. Regret? Longing? Whatever it was, it was something to do with *her,* not him. He thought about all her comments in the past, the subtle remarks here and there about her family—none of them very nice. Maybe she was wishing she had parents and siblings whom, if taken, she'd worry about as much as he was worried about his. The twisted thought added to his sadness.

"Well, we still have to be ourselves," Paul said. "Tick, dude, sorry, but if we get all mopey, then we might as well just give up and die. You know I don't think this is all a joke, man. Give me a break."

Tick looked at him, surprised at the angry tone of his voice. Paul was always laid back, taking what came at him. Even his sparring words with Sofia were always filled with obvious jest.

Tick shook his head. "Okay, whatever. This is all stupid anyway. We're sitting here in a soap opera while

Jane's planning something *diabolical*. What are we gonna do?"

Master George was still in the corner, but he turned around to face them. "We need to stay on our guard and look for the first opportunity that comes along. I've no idea what that may be, and I've no idea what we'll do. But something will come along, and we *must* be ready."

"What about Tick's family?" Sofia asked.

Tick had been wondering the same thing, but reality hit him then. He didn't know what it was—maybe it was the distressed look on Master George's face, maybe it was something in what he'd said. Either way, Tick realized a heavy truth. This wasn't just about him and his parents and his sisters. Jane was planning the single worst thing to ever happen to humans in the history of the universe. At least, that's what it sounded like. Her plan involved destroying an entire world full of people.

Could he really put his family above that? If it really came down to choosing between them and dozens, hundreds, thousands, even millions of lives, what would he do? What *should* he do?

He wanted to scream. No one should have to make decisions like this, especially not a fourteen-year-old kid. In that instant, his hatred for Jane changed into something more powerful, more acute. Every single molecule in his body wanted her dead.

"Tick?" Paul asked. "What are you staring at?"

Tick realized his eyes were focused on a greasy, dark smear on the stone on the opposite wall. He shook his head, scrambling the thoughts in his mind. "Sorry. Just thinking."

Master George walked back to him and the others. He held a hand out and squeezed Tick's shoulder. "Master Atticus. I give you my word that I will do everything in my power to help save your family. I will give my life, if necessary. But in return, you must promise me that you'll look at the bigger picture and do whatever it takes to stop Jane before she does something apocalyptic. I know her, my good man, and when she says she'll destroy the Fifth Reality, she means it. She has no reason to boast with lies. We're talking about billions of lives, Atticus. Billions."

Tick couldn't meet his gaze. He couldn't promise himself or anyone else that he'd be able to make the right choice if it came down to that. All he could see in his mind were his parents, Lisa, and . . .

Kayla. Thinking of little Kayla just about shattered his heart.

Unable to do anything else, he nodded.

"Very well," Master George said. "We can only take things step by—"

tingle

"—step."

In the small blip of time between his last two words, everything changed. As Tick was looking at their leader and listening to him speak, he felt the familiar tingle shoot down the back of his neck. The room around them disappeared, replaced by red rock.

He noticed the others spin around, just as he did, to see where Jane had brought them with her strange winking powers. They were in the middle of a desert, towering spires of stone standing all around them, jutting up from a natural rock wall that more or less encircled them. Tick couldn't see one plant, not one weed, or anything close to the color green or even brown. Everything was reddish-orange, jagged and rough, all sharp corners and cracks and crevices. Desolation.

The sun was behind a massive tower of stone, but the heat was suffocating. Tick already felt himself sweating.

"I don't see any tombstones," Paul muttered, and Tick couldn't tell if he was being sarcastic or making a very good point.

"Realities help us," Master George said. "If she can wink people to anywhere she wants so easily . . . Let's hope a lot of poor saps were killed here at some point in history."

"That's a cheerful thought," Sofia said.

Just then, Mistress Jane appeared in front of them. As always with winking, there was no puff of smoke, no flash of light or sound. One second she wasn't there, and the next second she was, dressed in her usual yellow garb and her shiny red mask. Her face was pulled into a genuine smile. It gave Tick the creeps.

"Looks like I miscalculated a bit," she said. "Guess I'm not perfect after all. We need to be on the other side of that."

She pointed at the stone face to their right. The wall was maybe forty feet high, with several spires of rock stretching toward the sky from its top edge. Though it had a menacing feel to it, the slope didn't seem too steep, and Tick thought they could probably climb it pretty easily.

"Follow me," Jane said as she headed in that direction, lifting up the bottom folds of her robe as she walked and carefully avoiding chunks of rock strewn about the desert floor. "And remember, Atticus—don't try anything."

When neither Tick nor anyone else made a move, Jane stopped. Her body stiffened, and some kind of unspoken warning seemed to flow from her, back at them like a misty spray of poison. She didn't need to say a word.

As one, Tick and his friends stepped forward and followed her.

CHAPTER
19

THE BLACK TREE

The heat was stifling, an invisible fire that suffused the air of the world, filling Tick's lungs with every breath he took. Once they reached the slope of the red wall, he realized it was much steeper than it had originally looked. Amazed at how easily Jane scooted up its face, he determined to do just as well.

Grabbing rocks that blistered with heat and finding footholds aplenty in the cracked and creviced stone, he found climbing wasn't so bad. About halfway up the wall, he looked down to see Paul and Sofia right below him. Master George was struggling a little, mainly because he was trying to keep his suit from getting dirty, but the darker patches of sweat under his arms revealed that his suit would need a good wash anyway—though Tick doubted they'd be seeing a Laundromat on the other side of this wall.

What am I thinking about? Tick asked himself as he continued to climb. Laundry? Sweaty armpits? He needed to stay focused.

Jane reached the top ridge above him and disappeared from sight, kicking a trickle of rocks down the slope with her last steps. Tick squeezed his eyes shut until the rocks passed; a couple of pebbles nicked his forehead. He pulled himself up the last few feet and stood on the top edge of the wall, taking in the sight before him. Sofia thumped the back of his leg.

"Scoot over, Tick," she said. "Give us some room here."

Tick stepped forward, too focused on the strange setting below him to respond to Sofia. The ground slowly sloped from where he stood, leading to a wide depression surrounded by squat, scraggly trees that barely clung to life, their sparse leaves more brown than green. Scattered across the dusty ground of the natural bowl formation were several groups of people, each group focusing and working on various stations that couldn't possibly have looked more out of place.

Computers and monitors covered tables scattered around the ground. Other platforms held large, silver machines he'd never seen before, each one loaded with odd appendages and dials and switches. Several viewing screens had been set up, tall and square and white, perched precariously on metal stands. Tick feared the slightest wind would topple them over. In the middle of each screen, Tick saw something he recognized: a small metal rod attached with a suction cup.

Spinners. Devices from the Fourth Reality, spinners used some kind of laser technology to project pictures and video. Jane had said she wanted them to witness something, but Tick hadn't thought they'd be watching it like *that*.

Sofia and Paul were standing next to him now, scanning the area as he was. Master George finally made it to the ridge as well. Tick heard him grunting and gasping for breath behind them.

"What's that in the middle?" Paul asked, pointing.

Tick looked, and when he saw what Paul was pointing at, he couldn't believe he'd missed it before.

It was a statue of a tree, maybe four feet tall, and made of the blackest material Tick had ever seen. There was no blemish to its darkness, no dust, no flash of light or reflection. Every inch of it was pure black. The trunk of the tree was about a foot thick, and its limbs shot off starting halfway up, branching out over and over until the outermost tips were as thin as toothpicks.

"That's plain weird," Sofia said.

"What could she possibly be doing with all this

junk?" Paul asked. "Especially a stupid sculpture of a tree?"

Master George had finally caught his breath. "Whatever that tree is, I suspect it's the most important thing down there. It gives me a very bad feeling."

"It's so black it doesn't seem real," Sofia said.

Tick noticed Jane had walked all the way down to the outermost group of people next to a row of computers but was now coming back. Her red mask still had that creepy smile, like she was a kid at Disneyland and having the time of her life.

"Come down!" she called. "I've got chairs for you!"

Tick exchanged looks with Paul and Sofia. Jane sounded way too cheerful, way too nice. That scared Tick almost more than when she screamed at the top of her lungs.

"Off we go," Master George whispered, giving the three of them a gentle push from behind.

When they made it to the bottom, Jane gestured toward a man holding four folding chairs in his hands, two in each. He had black hair and unusually thin eyebrows, and he wore a faded red T-shirt and jeans. As he started setting up the chairs, Jane introduced him.

"This is Frazier Gunn, my most loyal servant. He'll be in charge of ensuring you all witness today's events. I'll be too busy to see to it myself. But let me make this clear—if you cooperate, no harm will come to you or the

Higginbottom family. However, one sign of trouble, and Frazier . . . has his orders."

Tick's hatred for her burned inside him, and he had to suppress a rising tide of Chi'karda. He pushed it away, feeling an icy chill settle in his gut. Completely dejected, he numbly walked to one of the chairs and sat down, saying nothing, ignoring everybody. All he could see in his mind were images of his family.

"That's the spirit," Jane said. "The rest of you sit down. The show will begin shortly."

"What *is* the show?" Master George asked, not having moved an inch at her command.

"Sit, George," Jane replied. "You'll see soon enough."

Paul and Sofia sat down on either side of Tick, their faces looking half confused and half angry, and maybe a little curious as well. Tick couldn't help but wonder what they were thinking. If the roles were reversed, would he think them selfish if they refused to fight Jane because they didn't want to risk the lives of their families? He hoped not.

"Hey," Paul whispered as he leaned toward him. "Look at that tree. It almost looks like it's made of liquid or something. Does funny things to my eyes when I stare at it."

Tick moved his eyes in that direction. The black sculpture was fascinating this close up. The tree was deeply dark, its details crisp, the edges finer than they naturally should be. Every branch, from the thick parts where they connected to the trunk to the needle-thin tips, which looked sharp enough to impale rock, almost seemed to move in an unseen breeze, tricking his vision as he scanned the sculpture from top to bottom, side to side.

"It *is* weird," he finally said to Paul.

He felt like he wasn't looking at something in the real world. It reminded him more of animation, something done with the most advanced computer technology available. It made him queasy; he finally looked away. Jane's workers bustled about the area, checking dials and switches, typing on keyboards, adjusting the screens. But no one came within a few feet of the black tree. No one even appeared to look at it.

Maybe they are as terrified of it as we are, Tick thought. What could it possibly be?

Actually, one person *was* looking at it. Jane stood on the edge of the temporary complex, almost hidden from his sight by one of those movie screens. Arms folded, her mask showing that unreadable expression, she seemed to be concentrating on the tree. Tick would've given anything to see her real face at that moment, or better yet, to read her thoughts. What was going on here?

"Tick," Sofia said quietly.

"What?" He cringed—he hadn't meant to sound so harsh.

Sofia's head snapped around to glare at him. "Okay, you know what, *Atticus?* I know they have your family, and I know you're stressed to the max. But being rude to us isn't gonna help anybody."

Tick knew she was right, and for about three seconds hated her for it. "Sorry," he finally muttered.

"It's fine. Listen, what can you do with this power of yours? The Chi'karda. We haven't really had much chance to talk about it."

Paul leaned forward to put his elbows on his knees, looking their way. "Yeah, man, it seems like you learned a lot more about it since last time you gave us an update on e-mail."

Tick shook his head. He didn't really want to talk about it, but he forced himself to do it, hoping he could get his mind off his family. "It's crazy. I feel this really warm burning in my chest, like hot air is swirling around in there. In my basement, I concentrated on it, tried to picture things in my mind. Like it was something I could grab with my hands—my pretend hands, I guess. Then I threw it at her. It was all mental—just like acting out images in my head."

"I couldn't really tell what was happening," Sofia said. "I felt something, like a big surge of energy or electricity. And I could tell Jane was struggling against an invisible wall of whatever. But it wasn't like you were shooting balls of fire."

"Yeah," Paul added. "Why can't you just shoot balls of fire? That'd be nice."

Tick ignored that, trying to decide if he dared say what he'd just thought. "Well, there might be something."

Sofia gave him a puzzled look. "What?"

"You know how she keeps saying she can sense when I use the Chi'karda?"

Sofia and Paul both nodded.

"I think she might be bluffing."

"Really?" Paul asked. "Why?"

Tick tapped his chest. "There have been a few times when it swelled up inside me, and I had to fight it off. She never said a word about it."

"Maybe she can't sense it unless you actually use it," Sofia suggested. "Or throw it, or whatever it is you do."

"Yeah," Tick said. "Still, maybe I can play with it a little bit. Test it out a little and see if she says anything. I bet she'd give me a warning before she actually did something to my family."

Paul grunted. "Dude, you sure you wanna risk that?"

Tick looked at him, surprised at how glad he was Paul had asked that. He hoped Sofia felt the same. He hoped they understood how careful he had to be.

"No, but I think I have to try. Next time I can trigger

something in here"—he tapped his chest again—"I'll try it a little."

Sofia looked like she was about to respond when a loud humming sound cut her off.

Tick's hands instinctively covered his ears. It wasn't so much the volume of the sound as the *vibration* of it. A deep, thrumming toll, like a massive bell had been struck just feet away. The noise had an underlying buzz, too, as if the same bell had upset a nest of gigantic wasps.

"What is that?" Paul shouted.

Tick didn't know for sure, but it seemed like the source of the horrible sound was coming from . . .

He saw dust and pebbles bouncing on the ground. He had no doubt.

It was coming from the black tree.

CHAPTER
20

DISTURBANCES

It took a lot of persuading, but Sato finally convinced Mothball and Rutger to accept Tollaseat's offer to stay overnight and return to headquarters the next morning. They were anxious to get back and hear about the results of some secret meeting Master George had run off to, but agreed that one night wouldn't hurt.

But the promise of a warm fire in a cozy house, and the promise of more desserts from Tollaseat—maybe even a story or two—sealed the deal. And Sato loved the idea of sleeping in one of the gigantic—and soft—beds upstairs. His cot back in the Bermuda Triangle always made him feel like he'd slept on a concrete floor.

They'd just sat down in the living room, plates

of cheesecake balanced on their laps, cups of hot tea steaming on the end tables, and a large fire crackling in the brick hearth, when Rutger brought up for the tenth time what Sato had said earlier about wanting to help in the fight against the Bugaboo soldiers.

"What made you say that?" Rutger asked, not caring that his mouth was full of cake. "You were just being nice, right?"

"I thought it a very kind gesture, indeed," Windasill said. She held her cup right below her lips and blew across the hot tea.

"Why do you keep asking me about it?" Sato turned to Rutger. "It just ticks me off that they've done so many bad things. I want to help. Why is that so hard for you to get?"

"I just meant—"

"Isn't that what we're about?" Sato snapped. "The Realitants? Aren't we supposed to help people?"

Rutger's eyes widened in surprise. "Well, yes. Of course it is."

"Then quit asking." Sato forked a bite of cheesecake into his mouth, then took a sip from his cup.

He had no idea why he felt so edgy and irritated. He shouldn't feel embarrassed that the real reason he wanted to help was because of Tollaseat's story about watching his own father be killed. No one had been there to help Sato when the same tragedy had happened to him. He felt obligated, but not in a forceful, guilty way. It was more that he felt a connection to Tollaseat that wouldn't go away.

For the first time, his feelings solidified into one easy statement in his mind: He wanted revenge. And by fighting the Bugs who had killed Tollaseat's father and were connected with the woman who had killed his own father, maybe he could find it.

"Sorry, Sato," Rutger said. "I didn't mean it as an insult. The opposite, actually. I was impressed, and that made me curious as to what was behind it. I'll shut up now."

"That'd be perfect," Sato said, trying to soften his words with a smile, trying to return to the good mood of his earlier determination to fight the Bugs and his excitement at spending the night in the Fifth Reality. "Seriously, I mean it, though. Tollaseat, I'm going to get permission from George to come back and help. Whatever I can do."

Tollaseat bowed his head in a deep nod. "I'm quite honored, Master Sato. I'll ask around town for ways you . . ."

He trailed off, slowly lowering his cup back to the small table next to his chair. He looked confused.

"What is it, dear?" Windasill asked.

"What?" He focused on her. "Oh, well, I just had a thought. People will see that Sato here is a dead ringer for our deceased leader. Don't know how we can get around that."

"Makes a good point, he does," Mothball said. "Sato, not sure we can be doin' that. Quite risky. Might make folks talk and wonder."

Sato couldn't believe he hadn't thought of that very problem. How would that work to have someone come along who was the Alterant of your dead leader? He felt a pit of disappointment open up in his stomach.

"No matter," Tollaseat said, waving his hand in the air. "Think on it, no rush. Things have been quite cool of late, not too many problems with the ruddy Bugs. Mayhaps when you get a bit older, look a bit different, when it's . . . less obvious you're not from these parts and couldn't be him."

Rutger suddenly chuckled.

"What's so funny?" Mothball asked.

Rutger shrugged. "Could be quite a sight. Those clowns seeing their victim come back from the dead. Maybe they'd—"

A loud, horrible crash and the crunch of shattered glass cut him off. Sato jumped up, looking over in time to see hundreds of shards from the big window that overlooked the front yard blow inward, the glass bouncing and clinking off furniture as it fell to the floor.

Mothball's mom yelped; Tollaseat called out something, but Sato couldn't tell what he'd said. Rutger, who had been the closest to the window, seemed too shocked to move. Pieces of glass glittered in his hair and on his shoulders.

Everyone stared at the empty window as if waiting for someone to jump up and explain what had happened. In the silence, Sato heard the distant sounds of glass breaking in other parts of the house. Then, from outside, came a low, repeating pulse of noise, some kind of deep buzz or static, surging in short waves. He almost *felt* it more than heard it with his ears.

"What's going on?" Sato asked. "What is that noise?"

"No ruddy idea," Mothball answered.

The sound grew and intensified, making Sato's head hurt. "What shou—"

He fell to the floor as the whole house started to shake and tremble.

Tick sat still, transfixed by the humming, throbbing black tree. Its waves of energy were almost visible to some sixth sense he didn't quite understand. Since the noise had started, none of his friends had said a word, and Tick was sure they were as mesmerized and scared as he was.

The man Jane had called Frazier Gunn was walking from screen to screen, flicking the thin metal bar of each spinner that was attached to the exact center. He moved on without even waiting to make sure the spinner worked. As if by magic, and certainly by a technology Tick didn't understand, the metal rods spun faster and faster, despite the seeming lack of any motor.

A shimmering silver disk, maybe four inches wide, appeared. Once the spinner hit full speed, a much larger, red-tinted projection shot out, creating a wide, hazy circle that covered most of the screen behind it. Only the white corners of the squares were visible. Tick knew that soon those red circles would turn into video feeds, as clear in quality as any movie he'd ever seen.

Just as Frazier flicked the last spinner, Mistress Jane came over to Tick and the others, seemingly done with whatever she'd been doing to make the menacing black tree hum as it did. She stopped a few feet in front of their line of chairs, her red mask looking somewhat weary. She stared directly at Tick.

"I'm going to explain everything to you," she said, her voice tight. Strained. "And this isn't some example of the bad guys telling the good guys the whole *diabolical* plan just in time for them to escape and save the day. No, I *want* you to know. Every last detail. Once you do, and once you witness the extent of my power, I'll set you free so you can tell the other Realitants and spread the word throughout each world. Everyone must know what I'm capable of, and the reasons why it must happen."

She paused, and the eyes of her mask, dark and deep, never wavered from Tick. "Correction. I'm going to set *most* of you free to spread the word. Atticus stays with me."

Tick stood up, not sure where the courage came from. "What? Why? You promised you'd let me and my family go if I didn't try to stop you."

Jane's scarred hand shot out from beneath the folds of her robe, her palm outward. At the same instant, Tick flew backward, hit by an unseen force that thumped him in the chest. He fell into his chair and toppled over, banging his head against the dusty, hard ground. Shaking it off, he scrambled to his feet and picked up his chair. Glaring at Jane, he took a seat, hating himself for being such a wimp. Not an ounce of Chi'karda flickered inside him.

Jane's mask was a sneer. "I never made any such promise of letting *you* free, Atticus. Only your family. Now stay silent, or I'll get rid of one of your sisters."

Tick gripped the sides of his chair to stop his hands from shaking. He had to do something. This wasn't right, letting this woman treat them this way. He had to do something!

Jane continued with her speech as if nothing had happened. "What you'll be witnessing today is the first fully functional use of the most mysterious substance in the universe. Most scientists throughout the Realities don't even know what it *is,* much less how to use it."

"What are you talking about?" Master George said.

Jane didn't take her eyes off Tick, answering her former boss without so much as the courtesy of a glance. "George, as usual, you speak to me with your condescending, I-know-more-than-you-do arrogance. Now shut up."

Tick looked over at Master George, shocked at how childishly rude Jane's command had been. The old man glowered, his face redder than ever, his lips quivering despite being pressed together so hard they were almost white. But he didn't say anything.

"The Blade Tree before you," Jane continued, her expression still angry, "is made from the substance I was trying to tell you about before being so rudely interrupted. No tool of modern science could've accomplished such a thing as creating this object, I assure you. It took my ever-growing skills—fostered from my connection with the Thirteenth Reality—along with the additional powers granted to me by being unified with Chu's Dark Infinity, and an understanding of physics only my innate brilliance combined with a lifetime of study could accomplish."

She leaned closer to Tick. "Think on this, Atticus. As great as my gifts over Chi'karda have become, I could not have done this without the catalyst and boosting power of Chu's failed mechanism. In many ways, you are my partner. Think on that as you see what's about to happen."

She knelt down before him, reached out her disgusting right hand, and placed it on Tick's knee. Even through his jeans, he could feel the roughness of her palm, the tiny pricks of metal jutting out from her skin. Though every instinct told him to get up, scream, and run as far away as possible, he refused to cower away from her.

Jane's mask melted and flowed into an evil grin.

"Yes, Atticus," she said in a mockingly gentle voice. "Think on what you did to me as you watch billions of people in the Fifth Reality die."

Tick had hoped deep down that she hadn't meant it when she'd said her plan was to destroy an entire planet. But the demented tone of her next statement erased all doubt—and hope.

"Billions, Atticus. Billions."

CHAPTER
21

THE UNLEASHING

The constant, terrible, pulsing waves of sound increased in volume, rattling Sato's skull as the earthquake's intensity slowly escalated.

He crawled toward Windasill, unable to get back to his feet. The house shook like a ship at sea, thrown about by massive waves and wind. Things crashed all around them: lamps, dishes, picture frames, decorative trinkets of glass. Their remains littered the floor, sharp and vicious. Sato picked through the wreckage, ignoring the pricks of pain, the feel of moistness on his palms. He refused to look down, hoping it was sweat, not blood.

He'd seen Windasill fall but hadn't heard a peep from her since. With no idea where Mothball, Rutger, and Tollaseat had gone off to, Sato could only think to try to help where he could. Windasill.

He rounded an overturned cabinet, the large wooden drawers spilling out. Windasill was on the floor, lying on her side, a trickle of blood running from her mouth. Her eyes were closed, but her chest rose and fell with deep breaths.

"Windasill!" he yelled. When she didn't respond, he lurched forward. He felt like he was trying to move with three extra arms and legs. Thumping to the floor next to her, he smashed his nose against the ground. Somehow, despite the world shaking all around him, he got his arms around her and lifted her head into his lap as he sat up.

"Windasill!" he shouted again.

A moan escaped her, and her eyes flickered open. "What's happening?" she whispered.

Sato wouldn't have understood if he hadn't been able to see her lips mouth the words. "I don't know!" he shouted back. "I—"

"Sato!"

Mothball's voice. He turned his head to see her and Rutger at the front door, the two of them clutching the doorframe as their bodies swayed back and forth, constantly bumping into each other. He could see past them to the trees whipping in the wind. The sky was dark, only a few stars barely bright enough to flicker.

How had he gotten here? He thought he'd been moving toward the kitchen, toward the back of the house. "Where's your dad?" he yelled, completely disoriented.

"Out in the yard! Come on!" Mothball let go of the doorframe and stumbled toward him, her tall body losing the balance battle as she toppled to the floor, almost on top of her mom. She quickly got her hands and feet under her and began helping him with Windasill.

Like three drunken sailors, they got up, shuffled to the door, glass crunching under their feet with every heavy step. Rutger did what he could, reaching out and holding on to clothes, pulling, pushing. Soon they were all outside, where at least the danger of a house falling down on top of them was eliminated.

Sato drew in ragged breaths, his chest heaving as he released Windasill into Mothball's care. He spread his feet in the grass of the front yard, putting his hands on his knees to keep his balance as best he could. The earthquake rumbled on, distant sounds of destruction wafting through the night: crunching wood and breaking glass, alarms blaring and people screaming.

Sato couldn't believe what he was seeing. The trees seemed to be jumping up and down. The yard looked like a bed of thin grass growing on a lake, rippling in waves that made him queasy. The road and driveway did the same, cracking and crumpling.

Through it all, suffusing it all, was that sound, thrumming and humming and buzzing, like horns and bees and gongs amplified a thousandfold. Sato's head felt split in two, pain lancing into his eyeballs. He'd lived in Japan most of his life and endured a dozen or so earthquakes. But nothing like this. Not even close.

All he could think was that the world was coming to an end.

⁓

"Dark Matter," Jane said after letting her statement about killing billions of people sink in. She was acting as though she'd merely announced she was having layoffs at the fangen factory. Tick realized he was more scared of Jane's insanity than he was of her powers over Chi'karda.

"What do you mean, *dark matter?*" Master George asked. "You can't possibly expect me to believe your fancy tree statue is made of dark matter. Impossible. Utterly impossible, and you've now proven yourself quite mad. As if we needed any further proof on the matter."

"Dark matter," Jane repeated, as if she hadn't heard Master George. "It makes up more than seventy percent of the universe and yet, until recently, no one could determine its nature. I'll spare you hours of lecture and say this—by combining the powers of Chi'karda with the non-baryonic dark energy, I can eliminate the electromagnetic forces holding the Fifth Reality together. I can ignite extreme entropy. In other words, I can dissolve it into floating atomic gunk."

Tick knew a little about dark matter, mostly from a couple of books he'd read. But they had been science fiction stories that didn't really explain what it *was* exactly, just made up some cool uses for it. Destructive uses. Cataclysmic destruction. If Jane was serious about what she could do with it . . .

"The connections between my dark matter components are already strengthening, channeling through the hub of the black tree, magnified by my Alterants, each one of whom is set up in her own Reality, in these same coordinates. The soulikens are strong in these Alterants of mine, just as I knew they would be. Our genetic makeup is almost perfectly compatible. Any one of them could have done what I have done in the Thirteenth, if only they'd been given the opportunity."

Her voice grew quiet. "The Chi'karda is flowing, my friends, flowing on a scale I doubt you could scarcely comprehend. Soon the dark matter will be linked, and the Blade will do its slicing."

Dark matter. Alterants. Soulikens. Chi'karda. Blade. Jane's words bounced around inside Tick's mind, trying to sort themselves into something that made sense. But it wasn't working. He felt completely confused and out of his league. Jane was up to something monstrous.

Mistress Jane finally looked away from Tick, taking in each of his friends one by one with her mad gaze. Then she settled back on him. "I don't expect you to comprehend the workings of the Blade of Shattered Hope. Just know this, and know it well so you can spread the word: the Blade is a series of dark matter components, linked by my Alterants to create the greatest flow of Chi'karda since the beginning of time and space. And when I tap into that power and give the order to *sever* the Fifth Reality, the dark matter will consume the Fifth like a black hole. The Fifth will cease to exist—along with every man, woman, child, beast, insect, and plant living there. *That* is what you are about to witness."

Tick couldn't hold back anymore. "How can you do something like this? You're always spewing this garbage about wanting to do good, but now you suddenly think it's okay to kill billions of people?"

"Yes, Atticus, you're absolutely correct."

She turned and motioned to the closest screen, where moving images had now appeared in the spinner's projected circle. A woman sat huddled on another odd black sculpture—this one had a solid top and bottom connected by dozens of curved, twisty rods. The lady was dirty and appeared to be terrified and hungry, but Tick could tell she was an Alterant of Jane. He remembered his time with the "real" Jane at Chu's mountainous palace. This lady had the same black hair, the same eyes, the same face.

Tick looked at the other screens and saw similar video feeds. More Alterants, more black sculptures. Each woman had her own unique attributes, but there was enough there to see that all of them were Jane's inter-Reality twins. In one of the video feeds, the image shook, as if the person holding the camera was doing some kind of jig. The Alterant was screaming uncontrollably, trying to free herself from the chains binding her to the dark black object below her. Then the other video feeds started to shake as well, one by one, worsening every time Tick looked at a new screen.

"I've learned my lesson," Jane said, "about walking softly and kindly as I try to achieve my dream of a Utopian Reality. I'll tread lightly no longer. The people of the Fifth will die, yes, but it is for the good of mankind. In the long run, we will all be eternally grateful for their sacrifice."

Master George's whole body trembled with rage. "How could even your twisted, sickened mind stretch a tragedy of such proportions to something that will achieve good? You've lost your soul, Jane."

Jane's hand whipped out again, her palm facing George. But she paused, then slowly withdrew it back into her robe. "Yes, you may be right. But if I'm willing to sacrifice billions of lives, wouldn't it be logical for me to also be willing to sacrifice my soul? I don't care what guilt I must endure, what internal torment I must suffer for the rest of my life. Only one thing matters, and I *will* see it achieved."

"Why are those places shaking?" Paul blurted out, pointing to the screens. Every image now showed a world that seemed to be suffering from massive earthquakes. The Jane Alterants jerked about, still chained to the black sculptures that had toppled over on their sides.

"The Chi'karda is building, that's why," Jane answered, her voice so calm it made Tick mad. "Each Reality will see its own effects from the Blade's purge of the Fifth, but in the end, they'll suffer minimal damage. And all of my Alterants will survive to move on to the next phase of my plan. All except for the one in the Fifth, of course."

Tick was filled with turmoil. Though he didn't entirely understand what was going on, he felt an overwhelming responsibility to do something, to at least *try* something. He looked down into his lap, where his hands were clasped, squeezing them together so hard his fingers drained of blood. Maybe, if he could just reach for a trickle of Chi'karda . . . experiment a little . . .

"It's time for me to bend the Blade to my will," Jane announced. "Move from your chairs and die, as will Atticus's family. Frazier's watching. Remember to keep your eyes on the spinners. If your abilities to spread the message of what you witness today aren't sufficient, there'll be no reason for me to keep you alive."

Without waiting for an answer, she turned sharply and walked away, back to a spot before the black tree.

Tick barely saw her go. He was still looking down, concentrating on his hands. He didn't know exactly why, but it helped to have a spot for his eyes to focus on as he mentally probed his mind and heart and body, searching for a spark of Chi'karda. Something small, he told himself, something Jane won't be able to sense . . .

"This can't be for real," Sofia said next to him, though he barely heard her over the sounds of the humming tree and through his efforts to think. "She can't possibly do something like this."

"She's doing it," Paul said. "Look at her. She's a nut job."

Tick finally closed his eyes, squeezing his mind as he tried to latch on to that mysterious something within him. He pictured Jane, focusing on his hatred of her. He pictured his family. He tried to think about what his heart must look like, pumping blood to his veins. It always started there, the warmth—

There. He could feel it. A spark. A little surge of heat. Like a flickering flame.

Just as he'd done before in his basement, Tick reached for the warmth, mentally grasping it with unseen hands.

He didn't fully comprehend how he was doing it, but he threw all his energy into doing it anyway.

But then Master George said something, and even though Tick heard it only from a distance, as though it had been spoken through a thick wall, the words sliced through his concentration. The flame of Chi'karda, small to begin with, went out completely.

Tick opened his eyes and looked at Master George. "What did you say?" he asked, practically shouting to be heard over the thrumming of the tree.

The old man hung his head sadly. "It's true, I'm afraid. I believe Sato, Mothball, and Rutger are in the Fifth Reality even as we speak."

CHAPTER 22

LIGHTNING AND FLAME

Terror. Panic. Fear.

Those were words Lisa associated with disaster movies and scary books. News stories of dangerous lands thousands of miles away. History lessons of wars past. In her sixteen-and-a-half years of life, she'd never considered that one day those words might describe part of her own life, her own experience. Though she tried to be brave for her sister, she couldn't keep herself from crying every few minutes. Kayla's tears were a constant.

They'd been in the small room for at least a full day, maybe longer. Sparsely decorated, it held only two hard wooden chairs and a small bed with a table and lamp next to it. Drab wallpaper covered the walls, and ugly brown carpet covered the floor. There were no windows.

She had no idea how they'd gotten there. She'd been sleeping in her bed, dreaming about something icy crawling down her back, and then she woke up in this room, lying on the floor with Kayla right next to her. Since then, food had been brought to them by cruel ladies who refused to answer any of her questions and who glared at the two girls as if she and Kayla were hardened criminals.

Kidnapped, imprisoned, hated for no reason. It was all terrifying. The worst part was not knowing anything. She and Kayla mostly huddled together on the bed, hugging and consoling, sharing their tears. Lisa had no idea how many times she'd said the words, "It'll be okay," but it had to be at least one hundred.

She knew this had something to do with her brother. No one had told Lisa anything directly, but she knew about the Realitants and how Tick was special to them, helping them in some way. And somehow it had all led to this.

Come save us, Tick, she thought. *I know you got us into this mess. Now come get us out!*

Someone knocked hard on the door, just once, then opened it. Lisa had already started scooting as far away from the door as possible, dragging Kayla with her to the other side of the bed.

It was the older of the two ladies, her gray hair

pulled into a tight bun, her pale face full of hard-lined wrinkles. "Might wanna see this," she said gruffly. Then she opened the door wider and stepped to the side, nodding toward the hallway.

"See what?" Lisa asked warily. "You want us to come out there?"

The old woman let out an exasperated sigh. "Yes. Come on, I'm trying to be nice, you little ingrate. Such a historic moment—wouldn't want you to miss it."

Lisa squeezed Kayla's arms, then moved to get up from the bed.

"No!" Kayla shouted.

"It'll be okay," Lisa said softly, taking her sister by the hand. She hated saying those words again. "Come on."

Kayla looked up at her with moist eyes, then slowly slid off the bed and followed Lisa, their hands still clasped. They walked to the doorway and into the hall. From there, the woman led them down a set of stairs and into a living room that was as ugly as the rest of the house, all dull colors and boring furniture. Several other ladies were sitting on chairs and a worn-out sofa. Every pair of eyes was glued to a television set on a small table.

When Lisa saw and heard what was coming from the TV, she almost forgot how terrified she'd been just moments earlier. It was a news program, a man's tight voice narrating as the view switched from one scene of destruction to the next.

Fires. People trapped under cement, bloody and crying. Sirens. Shaky film of a large building, the horrendous crashing sounds booming from the television speakers when the structure crumbled to the ground. A massive car wreck. Smoke everywhere.

At first, Lisa was too shocked to read the words flashing across the bottom of the screen or hear exactly what the reporter was saying. But then she focused. The scrolling words accompanying the images made it clear the disasters were happening in different parts of the world. Paris. London. Berlin. Moscow.

Wait, she thought. Those cities were all in Europe and spread apart by hundreds and hundreds of miles. What could possibly be happening?

"The earthquakes are still rumbling as we speak," the reporter was saying. "They've already shattered all known records in terms of length of time, and they still continue, as you can tell from the shaky video footage. All of Europe and Asia seem to be affected by these quakes. Mass panic is spreading out of control."

Lisa felt an entirely new fear grip her. It made what she'd been feeling back in that prison of a room seem silly. That fear had been about just her and Kayla, trapped in a room, but otherwise safe and sound. This was something else. And whatever it was that was happening, Lisa knew the world would never be the same.

"What's going on?" Kayla asked, her small voice breaking Lisa's heart.

"I don't know, sweetie. I don't know."

The last word had barely left her mouth when the lights suddenly went out. The TV made a popping sound as the screen went black. Kayla screamed, and the ladies in the room started bustling about in the darkness, each of them calling out things that jumbled into a chorus of panicked nonsense.

The room started to vibrate.

The floor trembled.

And then the house shook like someone had picked it up and thrown it.

⁓

Tick couldn't take it anymore. He had to do something.

As the black tree hummed and throbbed its pulses of energy, as people ran about adjusting computers, as Mistress Jane stood completely still, her expressionless mask pointed at the tree, as Paul and Sofia and Master George fidgeted in their chairs, Tick leaned forward, closed his eyes, and searched once again for the flame of his Chi'karda.

With mental hands, he probed and picked and prodded.

There it was—a puff of heat.

He found it much more quickly this time. Encouraged, he threw all his thought and concentration into the warmth, grasping it, tensing his body as he imagined himself enveloped in the heat, consumed by it. Once again, he had no real clue what he was doing, but he did it anyway. Somehow, with his mind and heart, he became one with the Chi'karda. He felt it spread through his organs and veins and skin. Felt himself burn.

Ordering the power to stay, to wait, to hold, he opened his eyes.

Everything was as it was before, except for one small change. He saw things more clearly, more crisply. He heard sounds more distinctly, each one somehow separated from the other, each one crystal clear. He sensed vibrations in the air, particularly from the black tree, its power tickling across his skin with every throb.

He looked at Jane standing in front of the tree, probably throwing her powers into the Blade of Shattered Hope, maybe even close to flicking the final switch and severing the Fifth Reality. Tick turned his gaze back to the black tree. Its darkness was so deep, its edges so finely detailed, he had a hard time believing his own eyes. His vision had gone beyond anything he thought possible— maybe this was what they called four-dimensional sight. Maybe five or six. Maybe infinity.

None of it mattered. He had to act. He'd convinced himself of this without realizing when or how, but he had to try. His family would be safe. He'd make sure of it. He'd do whatever it took.

Focusing as deeply as possible on the trunk of the black tree, he imagined a pinhole in the imaginary barrier he'd created within him. With his eyes wide and his hands gripping his knees, he released the slightest bit of pent-up Chi'karda. He felt an almost untraceable amount of heat leave his body.

A trickle, nothing more.

And not knowing what else to do, he focused all of his thoughts into one distinct line of words, saying them over and over in his mind, projecting them at the same spot where he'd aimed the Chi'karda.

Stop the Blade. Stop the Blade. Stop the Blade.

◦───◦

Sato ran, though he fell down with every fourth or fifth lunging leap forward.

The others did the same, stumbling and bumbling about like they'd just been granted the gifts of legs and were trying to figure out how to make them work. Rutger was having the hardest time of it. Sato swore he actually saw Rutger *roll* forward like a ball a few times.

Mothball stayed by her friend's side, helping him

along as best she could. Tollaseat and Windasill worked together, pushing and pulling and balancing each other. Sato was on his own. He kept his head down and ran.

The earthquake continued to rage, shaking the entire world and everything on it. Crashes and clangs and breaking glass sounded like small explosions. The air reeked of sulfur and gas and burning wood. Screams came from every direction, from young and old, male and female.

And even though neither Sato nor anyone else knew where they were running to, there didn't seem to be any choice. You ran from terror, and that was that.

A booming crackle sounded to his left, splitting the air just as he caught a flash of bright light on the edge of his vision. He snapped his head around, but it was too late. The light was gone. It had been like a bolt of lightning.

Another one exploded in front of him. He barely had time to register the jagged line of brilliant white before he closed his eyes, hoping he wasn't blinded for life. Electric thunder rocked the air and shook the ground. Sato fell on his face and rolled three times, feeling rocks bruise and batter his body.

Another lightning strike, somewhere to his right. Another one way behind him. Each one was an explosion of light and energy and sound.

He got to his hands and knees, searching the area

He caught sight of Mothball sprawled scrambling to get up. No sign of her

stood up, lurching back and forth as the land continued to shake and tremble violently. Lightning was striking everywhere, long, crooked bolts of white fire hitting the ground in quick flashes instantaneously with the world-crushing sound. He held his hands up to his ears, wondering if he'd ever be able to see *or* hear again.

A brief pause in the lightning storm was as sudden as it was welcome. Sato squinted against the bright blurs of afterimages obscuring his vision as he headed toward Mothball. He had taken a few steps before he realized something very strange. The screams had stopped. So had the yelling and crying.

In disbelief, he scanned the area, shocked that he couldn't see anyone. Nobody. Nowhere. Only Mothball and Rutger. Where had everyone else gone?

He cupped his hands around his mouth to yell something to Mothball. "What's—"

A massive bolt of lightning shot from the sky, landing exactly on top of his two friends.

Sato threw his arm up to block the light, then looked as soon as it was gone. Barely able to see, he ran desperately toward the spot.

But even with his burned-out vision, he could tell

Mothball and Rutger weren't there. They were gone. Completely gone.

Not even charred remains or blackened, smoking skeletons were left behind. And, oddly enough, the grass wasn't burning or even disturbed as far as he could tell. It was as if his two friends had just disappeared.

Maybe they've been winked away, he thought with an unexpected rise of jubilation. Maybe someone had saved them at the last second. In his present state of shock and panic, the idea didn't seem so far-fetched. Anything was possible, right?

As if in answer to his question, the world around him suddenly turned white, a blanketing sea of complete and utter brilliance that engulfed his body even as the air singed with burning heat.

Sato felt his body erupt in flames.

CHAPTER 23

A THREAT REVERSED

Lisa's only thought was to find Kayla and keep her safe.

The house shook and rattled around her, the echoes of wood groaning and cracking, glass breaking, and the terrible ladies screaming. Darkness pressed in, and the air filled with a choking dust. Something smelled burnt.

Lisa crawled forward on her knees, fighting to keep her balance. She didn't understand why Kayla wasn't crying or yelling for her. They'd been standing close together when the earthquake began, but lost each other in the first chaotic seconds.

"Kayla!" she shouted. "Kayla!"

No one answered, but Lisa heard a distinct whimper to her left, a miracle considering the sounds of destruction surrounding them. She shuffled in that direction and bumped into the small body of her sister, who was curled up into a ball, shaking with sobs.

"Kayla," Lisa whispered. "It's okay, sweetie, it's okay. Come on. We need to get out of the house."

"No, no, no," Kayla murmured.

Scared the house might collapse on them at any second, Lisa put her arms around Kayla's body and lifted, grunting with the effort. She staggered to the right, running into a table, then to the left, hitting a wall. Squeezing Kayla tightly to her body, she moved forward, taking heavy and careful steps so as not to fall down. The light was dim, but she could see a hallway leading to the front door, which was open and hanging crookedly on one hinge. The whole house jumped as if it had grown legs.

"Let's get out of here!" she yelled as she decided to go for broke and sprinted for the door.

With a wobbly run, she made it to the opening and stumbled outside, falling into a clump of bushes. Tiny, sharp branches scratched her as she squeezed her arms even tighter around Kayla, trying to protect her. She kicked with her legs and used her elbows to maneuver their way out of the bushes and onto the front lawn.

The sounds of things breaking inside the house had been replaced with horrible, world-shattering cracks of thunder. Constant flashes of light illuminated their surroundings. Lisa saw people running, more people falling. The air smelled like burning plastic and tasted like . . . electricity. That was the only word she could think of.

Then, forty feet away, a bolt of lightning arrowed down from the sky and exploded around a woman in a bulb of pure incandescence. Lisa squeezed her eyes shut, though it was too late. When she opened them, she was completely blind, seeing only blurs of white in front of her.

Not knowing what else to do, she hugged Kayla and smoothed her hair, crushed by how the little girl's body shook with sobs and terror. How could this be happening? *What* was happening?

The air around them exploded with heat and electricity. Pain ripped through Lisa's body, and her arms suddenly closed on empty air.

Kayla was gone.

~~~~~~

Tick didn't know what he'd done.

He felt as though a chunk of his insides had somehow been squeezed through his skin and catapulted toward the black tree, engulfed by the pure darkness.

He fell from the chair, gasping for breath. His link to Chi'karda had vanished, replaced by a cold emptiness.

"Tick!" Sofia shouted, jumping out of her chair to kneel next to him. "Are you okay?"

Tick rolled over onto his back, looking up at her. "Yeah. I'm fine."

Paul stood and reached down to grab Tick's arm, then heaved him to his feet. "What happened?"

Tick shook his head. He couldn't have answered even if he felt like talking. He had no idea what had happened and began to worry that he'd done something really stupid.

"Take your seats," Master George snapped in a tight whisper. "She's coming."

Tick quickly sat down, as did Paul and Sofia. Sure enough, Mistress Jane was almost to them, marching with determined steps, her red mask showing an anger that made Tick's heart want to stop.

"What did you do?" she screamed into Tick's face. "What did you put in the Blade?"

Tick leaned back in his chair and looked up at her, embarrassed and terrified. "I don't know," was all he could get out.

Jane's chest heaved up and down beneath her robe. "You . . . don't . . . know?"

Tick shook his head, dread exploding within him. What had he done? What had he been *thinking?* She was going to kill his family. He knew it. She was going to kill them!

"I felt a surge of Chi'karda slice into the Blade," Jane said, her breath still quick. "It had to come from you. What did you do? If I have to repeat the question again, your youngest sister will be killed. Then the other one. Speak."

Tick fought the panic thrusting up his throat, threatening to choke him. He had to have lost his mind. How could he have been so stupid to try something when he didn't even know how to control it or what he was doing?

"What did—" Jane began.

"Wait!" Tick shouted. "I . . . I just . . . I tried to use my Chi'karda. I don't know what I was thinking. . . . I'm sure it didn't do anything!"

"What did you expect?" Master George said, coming to Tick's defense. "You tell us you're about to kill billions of people, and you expect the boy will sit there quietly? He has something you don't, Jane. Morals!"

Jane's head slowly swiveled around until her eyes paused on Master George. "Enough talk. Frazier!"

The man was at her side before the ring of her shout had faded away. "Yes, Mistress?"

Jane returned her gaze to Tick, the features of her mask melting into a void of expression. "Order the Ladies of Blood and Sorrow to kill the younger girl. Now."

"No!" Tick screamed, vaulting to his feet as Frazier walked away. He felt like an arrow had just sliced through his chest, tearing a jagged rip across his heart.

Jane's hand shot out from her robe, her palm flat and facing Tick. A thump of solid air slammed into his body, throwing him into the air. He flipped backward and landed on the ground behind the row of chairs. Jolts of pain made him shudder as he turned his head to look back toward Jane.

"Stop it!" Sofia yelled. She stood up as well, her hands clenched into fists at her side. She rocked back and forth on her feet as if contemplating whether or not to attack Jane. "How can you be such an evil—"

Jane's hand flicked toward Sofia and sent her body shooting through the air to ram into one of the screens that currently showed a burning building. Sofia and the screen crashed to the ground with a clatter of clanging metal rods and ripping cloth.

Tick pushed himself off the ground, groaning from soreness. Anger lit his insides like liquid flame, and he knew his Chi'karda was welling up again, threatening to explode out of him. Kayla. All he could think about was Kayla. What could he do . . .

Movement by the chairs grabbed his attention. Paul had been sitting still, obviously waiting for the right moment. Just as Jane turned away from Sofia, Paul leaped from his chair and tackled Jane. He grabbed her around the waist and pushed her to the ground, falling on top of her. They'd barely landed when Paul suddenly shot straight up into the air, hovering ten feet above Jane. Then his body flew away until he slammed into another screen, with the same result as Sofia's unwanted flight.

Jane got to her feet, brushed the dust and dirt from her robe, then looked at Master George. "You want to try something, George? Here, let me go ahead and save you the trouble."

She pushed her hand toward the old man. He flew up and backward over the chairs, landing on his stomach just a few feet from Tick. He didn't move, lying flat with his arms and legs twisted at awkward angles, his face on a rock. There was blood.

Tick couldn't take it anymore. This woman was evil. She was too evil.

He got to his feet, staggering a little until he caught his balance. Then he held up a hand and pointed a finger at Jane.

"Listen to me," he said, his voice straining from the internal effort of holding back the Chi'karda burning within him. "If you kill my sister—"

"What?" Jane snapped, taking a step forward. "What, Atticus? What will you do?"

"Then I won't care what happens anymore," Tick said. "If you kill Kayla, I won't care about anything. I'll build up this Chi'karda until it's a million times stronger than it was back at Chu's mountain. I'll build and build, and then I'll let it all out. I'll throw it all at you."

Jane shook her head. "So selfish, so . . . *weak*. You can still save your other sister and your parents. And you can help me achieve great things in the Realities, if you'd just grow up and see things with a bigger perspective."

Tick hated her. Oh, how he hated her. "Don't say another word to me! Tell him not to kill my sister. Now!"

"No."

She said it so simply, so nonchalantly. But Tick couldn't back down—he had to reverse the threat here. The power burned and boiled inside his chest. "I'll count to three. Stop Frazier, or I'll throw it all at you. Every ounce of it. Even if it kills me."

"No," she said again.

The Chi'karda was starting to overpower him. He felt his hands begin to shake. He quickly stepped forward and gripped the back of a chair to steady himself. "One," he said as calmly as he could.

Jane did nothing, just kept staring at him with a blank expression on her mask.

"Two," Tick said. Fear filled him. He didn't know if he had the courage to go through with his threat.

"Three," Jane said for him.

Tick's fingers tightened on the chair. He looked down to see that they'd actually sunk into the metal, warping it. He had to do this. He had to—

"Mistress Jane!" a man's voice yelled.

Tick's head snapped up to see Frazier run frantically around the computer tables, heading straight for them.

"Mistress!" the man shouted again. "Something's wrong!" He pulled up, panting with deep breaths.

"Speak!" Jane yelled back at him.

Frazier held his hands up to his ears as if his head were about to explode. His eyes were lit with panic. "They're all gone—all of them. Everything's gone crazy with the earthquakes and lightning . . . but there's no doubt. I can't find them anywhere. None of them!"

"What are you saying?" Jane insisted.

Frazier turned to look at Tick. "His sisters. His parents. They've all disappeared."

CHAPTER
24

COLORED MARBLE TILES

The scream had barely escaped Sato's mouth before the excruciating pain vanished, gone in an instant. It didn't fade or slowly feel better. One second he felt like his entire body was on fire, horrible burns eating away at his skin, the next second he was perfectly fine. He collapsed to the rock-hard ground anyway, the mental shock of the pain bad enough. The air around him was gray and dull, twilight's last moments before full night.

On his back, he held up his hands even though he dreaded what he might see. Blood and red blisters at best. Black, charred flesh at worst. But instead, in the faint glow of the light around him, he saw smooth, healthy skin, not a blemish or a scrape or a bruise.

What had happened? He remembered the earthquake, then bolts of lightning striking everywhere, and people disappearing when struck. Then the world had lit up, exploded in fire, as if he himself had been . . .

Sucking in a gasp, he sat up, then scrambled to his feet. He turned in a slow circle, looking all around him. With each second, with each revolution, his eyes grew wider and wider. He saw no sign of the homes and trees and stone walls of the Fifth Reality. He'd been taken to another place. Even though the light was dim, he had no doubt of it.

He stood on a vast, flat ground made of a hard substance and checkered with large squares of differing colors. It seemed to stretch in every direction as far as he could see, with no breaks of any kind. He knelt down and felt the floor. It was cool to the touch. Marble, maybe. The light wasn't strong enough for him to see if the floor had the familiar pattern of that stone.

He stood back up and looked above him. Though the marble floor beneath him would suggest that he was inside a building of some sort, no other evidence supported it. No roof hung above him—just blank, unblemished air. No stars, no clouds, no planes in the sky. The perimeter around him was just as gray and lifeless. The floor went on forever, with no walls or fences or trees. No mountains in the distance. No furniture.

That was all; a marble floor with countless squares of color, stretching to infinity in every direction and a lifeless sky that seemed the definition of *nothing*.

I'm dreaming, he thought. Or maybe he was dead. Though he'd never learned much about religion and the afterlife, he couldn't help but think of the possibility that he'd died and was in some sort of waiting room for souls. Certainly no place like this existed in the real world, no matter which Reality.

He heard a humming sound behind him and turned quickly to check it out.

Twenty or thirty feet away, a figure lay crumpled on the floor. It was a girl with curly blonde hair, her clothes filthy and torn. She had black smudges on her bare skin. She looked to be about his same age. She twitched a little and let out a low groan.

"Hey!" Sato yelled, cringing when it came out so harshly. "Are you okay? Do you know where we are?"

The girl glanced at him when she heard his voice, her eyes filled with fear. "Hello?" she called back weakly.

Sato ran to her, sure he must be in a dream after all. He approached her and knelt on the ground, putting a hand out to touch her shoulder softly.

"You okay?" he asked again. "I don't know how we got here."

He looked around again, scanning their surroundings to see if anything had changed. Still nothing but colored marble tiles going forever and a sky of dead air. He returned his attention to the girl.

"My name's Sato," he said, hoping the girl would snap out of her daze and help him understand what was going on. She looked up, and he saw tears streaking down her cheeks.

"I'm Lisa," she said, stifling a sob. "Have you seen my sister?"

At first, Tick felt the slightest hint of hope at Frazier's words, but it didn't last long. He remembered the horrible images of destruction on the screens, recognizing that the man had said his sisters and parents had vanished *after* mentioning earthquakes and lightning.

There was nothing good about that. Maybe they'd been trapped under rubble. Maybe they'd been struck by lightning. Maybe no one could find them because they were dead.

No! he shouted in his mind. His insides still boiled, the heat of his Chi'karda flaring up even stronger at the depressing thoughts of what might have happened. He didn't know if he'd ever felt so scared and completely hopeless. Useless.

Jane had stayed quiet for a long moment after Frazier's pronouncement, staring at the man with a blank expression. Then she turned to Tick.

"Then they're probably dead already," she said coolly. "How fitting it would be if it was *your* disobedience, Atticus, your arrogant, reckless use of Chi'karda that ended up killing your family. I hope you can live with that."

Tick barely heard the words. He couldn't hold back the Chi'karda anymore. He'd let it go too far, and now it was too late to stop it. His insides had become a roaring inferno.

Something seemed to rip deep inside of him, and he screamed from the pain. He fell to his knees, wrapping his arms around himself. Trying to escape it, he curled into a ball and screamed again, as loudly as he could.

Everything *changed*.

The dusty desert around him vanished, replaced by trees.

The power and burning disappeared, as did the pain, and everything was perfectly silent, except for his quick and heavy breaths.

He was in the middle of a forest. And he was alone.

CHAPTER
25

SILVER-BLUE LIGHT

Tick didn't move for a long time.

The forest was dark, only the slightest traces of moonlight seeping through the thick canopy of branches above him, dappled here and there on the ground. He heard nothing but a few insects and the very distant sound of a dog barking. The woods smelled fresh and pungent, the scent of the pine trees closest to him by far the strongest. It made him think of Christmas.

Which made him think of his family, which pulled at his heart like a huge rock had been tied to it and dropped to his stomach. He ached for them, and he didn't know how he could survive if they'd been hurt or killed. For now, not knowing anything for certain, his mind only allowed him to hold on to hope. He didn't let anything too dark settle on his thoughts. They *could* be alive. There were a million possibilities for such a thing, and he held on to that.

He had to get going. He had to figure out where he'd been sent. Had he actually winked himself? That seemed the only logical explanation, but the instant he'd arrived in the forest, the flames of Chi'karda had burned out, leaving him empty. He was cold, and not just because the air in the forest was cool and wetly crisp, as if a storm might be coming. He also felt the chill of fear.

He stood up and turned in a slow circle, scanning the woods. He saw only trees, some thin, some thick, all of them crowded one after the other until they faded into obscure shadows. He closed his eyes to focus, but again, he heard only the insects and that frantic dog, still in the distance. Unless some super spy was nearby, watching him in silence, he was alone.

What *had* happened? His experience with winking kept the situation from being completely bizarre, but had he really done it to himself? Or had it been Sally back at headquarters? He doubted that since no one else came with him; also, it would have made much more sense to wink him to Master George's compound in the Bermuda Triangle, not to the middle of the woods.

A lot of questions, no answers, and it was cold. He shivered, rubbed his arms, and told himself once again that he needed to get going. But the worry that he'd go in the wrong direction kept his feet glued to the forest floor.

Go, he thought. *Just go. That way.*

He stepped forward, but stopped when the sound of crunching ground cover startled him. He took another quick look around him. Nothing.

Shaking off his childish worries, he walked forward resolutely, moving aside tree branches and stomping down weeds. The crick-crash with every step filled the air with echoes until it almost seemed like someone *was* following him. He realized he was acting a little ridiculous and feeling way too paranoid. Refusing to slow again for another look, he kept going through the trees.

He'd just squeezed through two big oaks when he definitely heard something behind him: a quick but loud moan, as if some giant had awakened with a stomachache. Sucking in a breath, Tick spun around, throwing his arms out to catch his balance on the thick trees. There'd been an odd glimmer of light behind him, he was certain. But it disappeared the instant he saw it.

Silence returned, thicker than before. The moan must have spooked the insects, because they'd quieted as well. Tick felt a sudden burst of claustrophobia, there in the darkness with the trees pressing in around him.

Childish or not, he was officially scared. That stifled groan had sounded otherworldly, like a . . .

Well, like a ghost.

He turned and ran, not taking the time to be careful anymore. Branches slapped his face, and twigs and leaves scratched his skin. He didn't stop, dodging the obstacles as best he could.

Ooooooohhhhhhhhhhnnnnnnnnnnn . . .

There it was again—the low moan. It was still behind him, but this time it lasted much longer. A flicker of terror, like icy water shooting up his throat, made him cough and wheeze. He wanted to look back. Every instinct *screamed* for him to look back, but he knew he'd have to slow down to do that, or he'd run right smack into a tree. Weaving, dodging, ducking, he ran on.

A flash of silvery light gleamed from behind him, illuminating the woods. Unable to fight the urge to look, Tick stopped, put his hand against a pine tree, and turned around. Once again the strange glow vanished as soon as he saw it, but he'd caught a glimpse of wispy brilliance, as if streamers of fog had magically transformed into a cloud of almost blue light.

Ooooooohhhhhhhhhhnnnnnnnnnnn . . .

The sound came again, along with another few flashes of the silver, misty beams. There was something oddly *metallic* about the light, making Tick think of aluminum or steel. And then it was gone.

Tick turned and ran again, swearing to himself he

wouldn't stop again until he found a person, a building, something. A policeman or a ghost hunter would be great.

Because of the darkness, he had no idea he was at the edge of the forest until he broke through the last line of trees. A sharp but short hill sloped up, and he stumbled and fell before he could slow down. His face smacked into a clod of dirt. He spit the gritty stuff out of his mouth as he scrambled with his hands and feet to move up the hill.

He reached the top, pumping his legs and flailing his arms until he found his balance and could run again. His feet slapped pavement—a road. It took another few seconds for Tick to realize where he'd been sent. Or where he had sent himself. A mixture of relief and confusion consumed him, almost making him stop again.

But he didn't stop; he didn't even slow down. He knew exactly where to go, and a fresh surge of adrenaline lifted his energy and spirits.

He was in Deer Park, Washington, on the road leading to his neighborhood, a path he'd walked thousands of times in his life. The why and how ceased to matter in his mind. Something creepy was behind him, and his house was in front of him.

He ran for home.

As Tick rounded his mailbox and shot up the driveway, he couldn't help but feel a trace of déjà vu. His thoughts went back to his very first wink, when he'd gone to the cemetery as instructed and performed the strange initiation ritual he'd had to figure out from the twelve clues sent to him by Master George.

When he'd winked that night and felt that cool tingle down the back of his neck, the first of many more to come, he thought it hadn't worked. Sullen and heartbroken, he'd headed for home only to discover he'd been sent to an alternate Reality, one in which a strange, nasty old man lived in Tick's house.

What if that old man was there again? Or another one?

What if Tick had been winked to another Reality, and his Alterant was in the house, sleeping or sitting at the computer or about to come outside? Though he'd been totally unconscious in the Fourth Reality, Sofia and Paul had told him about what happened when the two versions of Reginald Chu met. There had been an earthquake, a wave of air, and the Reginald from the Fourth had disappeared, gone to some place Master George called the Nonex.

What if that happened to Tick when he opened the door?

Then, despite the darkness, he noticed the crashed garage door from when the water creatures had attacked his parents. His doubts washed away, and he ran up to the bushes lining the house and dropped to his knees, searching for the fake rock that contained a spare key. The key had been missing before when he'd unknowingly been winked to an alternate reality. This time he found it, and, pulling the key from the rock, he ran up the porch steps and unlocked the front door. He went inside and flicked the light switch in the hallway. Nothing happened.

He walked into the kitchen, the moonlight seeping through the windows just enough to aid his way. The lights there didn't work either. He paused and listened for a minute. Nothing, not even the sound of the fridge or the heater.

So the power was out. Maybe nearby areas had been hit by the same devastation he'd witnessed on the screens back in the Thirteenth.

Based on what little he could see, he no longer had any doubt this was Reality Prime, and that this was his very own house. Just to make absolutely sure, he made his way back to the stairs and went up them to his room, feeling carefully along the wall in the dark. Every bit of furniture, the blankets on the bed, the wall decorations—everything was exactly as he last remembered seeing them.

He felt a little disappointed. Deep down he'd been hoping to find his family here, even though he knew it was a long shot. Jane had taken them, but then Frazier had said they'd disappeared. Tick had hoped the same thing might have happened to them as what had happened to him. He'd hoped they had been sent back home too.

Bad thoughts drifted through his mind, images of all the terrible things their vanishing from Jane's captors might mean.

To get his mind off it, he knelt down on the floor and reached under his mattress. After feeling about, he found what he'd been looking for and pulled it out, then sat on the bed. Though he couldn't see it very well in the pale light coming through the window, he knew every detail of the object anyway. His *Journal of Curious Letters.*

Yes. Unless this was a Reality that had split from Prime very recently, he at least knew he was in the right place. But what in the world was he supposed to do now?

He set the book on the table by his bed and kicked up his legs onto the bed, not bothering to take off his shoes. He lay back on to his pillow, hands clasped behind his head, and stared at the ceiling. Odd-shaped shadows from the moonlight slanted from corner to corner, dark and menacing. He closed his eyes.

Sleep. Could he really sleep despite all the terrible things going on that very instant? He didn't know, but he needed it for sure. Surprising himself, he relaxed, feeling the first trickles of sleep edge his mind.

A minute passed. Two. The darkness was deep. No sound except a slight breeze pushing branches against the outside of the house. Something smelled good, like the fresh scent of laundry detergent and dryer sheets. All of it seemed to pull him down into the bed, as comfortable as he ever remembered being. Almost feeling guilty, he sank into the welcome pool of slumber.

Oooooohhhhhhhhhhnnnnnnnnnnn . . .

This time the sound came from the hallway right outside his room, a miserably haunted, ghostly moan. Tick shot up in bed, his feet swinging to the floor. A silver-blue light glowed through the space under the door.

So much for sleep.

CHAPTER 26

MANY FACES

He heard the sound again. Then again. And again. Each time it was only a few seconds apart. The moan had such a creepy, deathly feel to it that prickles of goose bumps shot up all over his body, and he felt like every hair on his head reached for the ceiling. This was a new kind of terror—something very different from the constant worry of being killed or hurt, something he'd almost become accustomed to.

No, this was like a real-life ghost story. He was in a horror movie.

He quietly stood up and walked over to the window, carefully stepping on the non-creaking spots of his bedroom floor. He looked through the glass, wondering if he'd have the courage to jump out. The moon cast its pale glow on the yard outside, making the trees look dark blue and creating shadows in which he could imagine every monster from his every nightmare hiding, waiting.

Ooooooohhhhhhhhhhnnnnnnnnnnn . . .

Tick turned around to face the door. His mind felt hollowed out. How had it come to this? An hour ago he'd been in the middle of a desert in the Thirteenth Reality, watching Mistress Jane destroy an entire world. Now he was back in his house, in the dark, staring at a sheet of silver-blue light panning across his floor. He saw that it wavered with flashes and glimmers of shadow as though the source of the light was a gigantic TV out in the hallway, showing an old black-and-white film.

He didn't want to face whatever was out there. He turned back to the window and unlatched the lock. After pulling up the window, he unhooked the screen. He stuck his head out to look at the ground twenty feet below. If he could land in that clump of bushes . . .

Behind him, the moan took on a different pitch, stuttered. Then something sounded almost like a cough, followed by an odd crackle. Tick couldn't help but look back at this new noise.

Tendrils of bright white electricity danced around the doorknob, sparking and zigzagging like small bolts of lightning. It had a charged sound to it, like the monster-making machines in the old Frankenstein movies. There were dozens of small sparks casting flashes of light all over the room.

Tick was pretty sure he had stopped breathing and didn't know if he would ever start again.

The lightning and electricity intensified, spreading out and growing larger until they covered the entire door and the walls around it. A glow of silvery light formed in the middle, growing brighter and brighter until Tick couldn't see the features of the door or his wallpaper. Just a globe of metallic blue.

He realized he was in some sort of a trance. He was about to turn away and jump out the window—he'd take the broken leg or arm instead of whatever this was—when the entire display in front of him collapsed into an oblong and upright shape, standing maybe six feet tall. Crackles of electricity still danced along the surface, but they seemed more controlled, swirling around the oval body of light.

Then, to Tick's shock, a large face appeared in the middle of the light. It was a young woman, her features shimmering but smooth, and her expression showing a small struggle, as if she was concentrating on a difficult task. But then she was gone, replaced by another face. This time it was a man, his features rigid and angled. Then another face formed—a young boy. Then another one—an old woman, her wrinkles lines of blue against silver. A second later, a younger woman appeared, this one with a round face and eyes.

More faces appeared, each one lasting only a few moments before another took its place. Boys and girls, men and women, all ages and all races. They all had that same look of intense effort, their eyes focused on Tick, sometimes with their tongue bit between their lips.

Tick realized he'd relaxed. He was breathing normally and no longer felt the urge to jump out the window. If this thing was a ghost, it didn't seem very scary. After all the studying and intense reading of science and its inner workings he'd done over the past months, his rational mind had finally taken over. What he saw before him had to be some kind of explainable phenomenon, and his fear had been replaced by excitement to find out what it was.

The faces continued to change, one after the other, all types and ages. The light cast from the glowing oval shimmered and danced in the room, which had an even more relaxing effect on Tick. He stepped over to his desk, pulled out the chair, and sat down, never taking his eyes off the apparition.

The morphing faces seemed to relax a bit. When a young Asian man appeared, the lips of his mouth parted. He transformed into an African-American woman, and her lips began to form a word. When the sound finally came out, traveling across the room for a very shocked Tick to hear, it came from a teenage

boy. Then a fat man. Then a beautiful woman. Then an old man. Face after face, image after image, their lips remained in sync as the odd phenomenon began to speak. The voice never changed, however; it was deep and charged with energy, laced with crackles of electricity.

"Atticus Higginbottom," it said. *They* said. "We need to have a very serious talk."

⌒

Sato had learned a lot about Tick's sister. There wasn't much else to do when you were stuck in a place that stretched to infinity in every direction with nothing to see but colored marble squares. They'd walked for a while as they talked, but eventually had given up, deciding they were just as well off sitting and waiting for something to happen as they were wandering about aimlessly.

"I'm sure your sister is safe," he said after a long lull in their conversation. "Somehow those bolts of lightning sent us somewhere else. Here. Maybe other places. Maybe totally random, I don't know. But the more I think about it, the more I think it has to be something like that. If the lightning had been killing people, it would've left behind charred bodies."

Lisa nodded absently, staring down at her finger as

she traced the lines in the red marble square on which she sat cross-legged. "Charred bodies. Pleasant."

"How much do you know about the Realitants?" Sato asked.

"Most of it," she replied, looking up at him. She'd stopped crying, but her eyes were still puffy and red. "I tried to keep living my normal life and pretend it was just something for Tick, something I didn't have to worry about. I have my friends, you know? I have my own life. My mom and dad tried hard not to put all their attention on Tick and his fancy Realitant stuff, but they couldn't help it. I don't really blame them. I was happy to kind of ignore it all. Guess I have no choice now."

She pulled up her legs to wrap her arms around her knees. "This has something to do with Tick, right? It can't be a coincidence that I'm his sister and was kidnapped and then sent here by a bolt of lightning."

"I'm sure it has something to do with Tick and Mistress Jane," Sato said. "Our boss had a meeting scheduled with her, and I'm sure it all went to pot right about then."

"What's really happening? I've never been in an earthquake before, but I'm pretty sure what I just went through wasn't normal. Especially with all the lightning."

Sato shook his head. "I don't know. We're not sure what happened to Jane after the crazy stuff in the

Fourth Reality, but if she survived, I'm guessing she's one ticked-off lady. And she has weird powers. She can do things with Chi'karda. For all we know, she's messing things up pretty bad out there."

"Yeah," Lisa replied, her eyes staring at a spot in the distance. She looked slightly dazed. Sato had to remind himself that all of this was new to her, no matter how many times she'd heard about it. To really understand it, to really *know*, you had to experience stuff like this yourself.

They sat in silence for a while. Then Lisa said, "I can't imagine how scared Kayla is." A tear trickled down her cheek. She sniffed and squeezed her nose with her thumb and forefinger. "I won't be able to live if something bad happens to her."

Sato couldn't help but feel her sorrow. It made him think of the days and weeks and months he'd spent bawling his eyes out after Jane killed his parents. Why did there have to be so much evil in the world? Why couldn't people like Jane realize the pain they inflicted or understand the end results on everyday lives? How was it possible to have such a complete absence of compassion? He couldn't possibly hate Jane any more than he already did, but he felt his rage and thirst for revenge spring up anew.

"We'll find your sister," he said, hoping the promise didn't sound too empty. "We'll find your whole family, and we'll make Jane pay for whatever she's done. It's the only thing I live for now."

Lisa looked at him, her eyes red and wet and surrounded by dark, hollow circles on her face. "Thanks."

Something hummed deeply behind Sato, and he noticed Lisa look sharply over his shoulder, surprise transforming her face. The floor vibrated slightly as well.

He spun around to see what had happened.

Mothball was standing there, looking as surprised as Sato felt.

It took a minute or so for Tick to gather himself, remembering that he'd seen many strange things since receiving his very first letter from Master George and that this was just the next in a long line of oddities. He pushed away the shock he felt, ignoring the impossibility of what he saw before him. So a big oval of silver-blue light was talking to him with hundreds of different faces mouthing the words. Big deal. He had to respond.

"How do you know my name?" he asked, proud that the words came out with no squeaks or stutters.

When the entity responded, its face started out as a teenage girl with long hair but had morphed into an old man by the time the short phrase was finished. "We have been observing you and your Realitant friends."

"Really?"

"Yes," said a woman who changed into a man.

Tick was completely fascinated. "What are you? I mean . . . *who* are you?"

The glowing apparition was quiet for a moment, though the faces continued to change at the same rapid pace. Finally, a wise-looking, ancient woman appeared to speak the words, "They call us the Haunce."

CHAPTER 27

SOULIKENS

The entity paused after revealing its name, as if it wanted Tick to respond. But Tick had questions buzzing around his head like flies swarming a lightbulb, and he couldn't settle on just one. So he sat there, slack-jawed and silent.

"Do not be afraid," the many-faced apparition said. "We are as close a thing to a ghost as you will ever see, but we are much kinder than the storybooks make us out to be. It takes considerable effort to gather ourselves into something strong enough to appear visually to those still alive. We would never do it simply to scare someone. It would be ridiculous."

If Tick had flies buzzing a moment earlier, now

they had become an army of bees. *A ghost? Appear visually to those still alive?* What was this thing?

He decided to make a statement that encompassed all of his confusion in three short words. "I don't understand."

A smile appeared on a girl's face, glowing silvery blue. When the face transformed into a middle-aged man, the smile was still there. "We would not expect you to. Sit and listen. We will explain."

Tick had never heard a better idea in his life. He nodded his head emphatically.

"Good." The Haunce's orb of light expanded then retracted, as if it had taken a deep breath. The ever-changing faces spoke. "We are here because terrible things have happened in the Realities over the last few hours. When it became apparent that we must reveal ourselves, we chose you. The reason for that choice is something we may not have time to explain, but we shall see."

Tick didn't say anything, but he scrunched up his face in confusion, hoping the entity would change its mind. Whatever this ghostly visage was, why would it have chosen *him* of all people to appear to? Tick wanted to know the answer to that question very badly, but he forced himself to remain silent and listen intently as the Haunce continued speaking.

"We come to you now because enormous and catastrophic disturbances have shattered the barriers of the Realities. We know this because we are *part* of the barriers, interwoven into the Chi'karda that has served to bind the Realities together and build the wall to keep them apart. If we had not acted quickly, we might have been destroyed and the memories of billions upon billions of lives would have been obliterated. But we escaped before the worst of it happened."

The Haunce paused, flashing three different faces before a weary-eyed man with a short-cropped beard appeared and spoke. "We never would have thought it possible that someone could harness, much less control, the dark matter as the woman named Mistress Jane has done. Even we do not understand its properties to the fullest. And yet, she has unleashed it, annihilating the bonds between the Realities and sending them to drift apart from one another. What she does not understand is that soon the fragmenting will begin. In *every* Reality. A human body cannot survive when separated into pieces; the Realities are no different. What she has done will lead to the end of everything as we know it. The end of existence."

Tick felt a leprous lump growing in his belly. Although he didn't understand the nitty-gritty details, not to mention any of the logistics or complex science of what the Haunce was describing, he was smart enough to connect the dots. Mistress Jane had said from the start that she was going to sever the Fifth Reality and destroy it. From what the Haunce had just said, Tick suspected Jane must have accidentally enacted her diabolical plan on every last Reality.

And then Tick had another thought, perhaps the worst thought to ever cross the pathways of his mind. What if *he* had done this? What if his little exercise in throwing a trickle of Chi'karda into the black tree, into the dark matter that made up the Blade of Shattered Hope, had somehow disrupted Jane's plan? What if, by trying to help, he'd made it worse—infinitely worse? His more rational side had told him he wasn't ready to try something so foolish. Why hadn't he listened?

The lump inside him grew, filling his body with acid. He'd spent the last few months trying to ensure he never repeated anything like what he'd done in Chu's mountain palace. But if he'd just helped destroy every last Reality, that made the fiasco with Chu's Dark Infinity and Mistress Jane look like a food fight. Panic and worry consumed him.

"Atticus," the Haunce said. "We can feel your thoughts. We can feel your mind and see this dark path which you choose to walk. You must stop. Immediately. You do not understand even the slightest parcel of the whole."

Tick was staring at the floor. He didn't remember looking away from the Haunce, but he returned his gaze to the glowing entity at its words. He sensed some hope, maybe some redemption, in what it had said.

A young woman stared back at him, her face full of compassion. Tick wished desperately she could stay, that her face not change. But a few seconds later it slipped into an older man, the kind look not as reassuring on him.

"We are soulikens, Atticus," the Haunce said. "Do you know what that means?"

Tick shook his head.

"We sense in your memories that you have recently come to understand the heart of the human body and how the power of electricity is vital to its life-giving properties. Without electricity, the heart would not pump. If the heart did not pump, blood would not flow. And if the blood did not flow, there would be no life."

Tick nodded, surprised by this turn in the conversation, but intrigued.

"Most people do not understand that electricity is a natural phenomenon," the Haunce continued. "Much of its uses are unknown and immeasurable to scientists. Similar to how Chi'karda is not understood by most quantum physicists in the Realities, except for those who have joined ranks with the Realitants. Electricity is the key. Electronic pulses. Electronic imprints. They intertwine with almost every function of your mind and body, creating permanent stamps in the fabric of

Reality—of time and space—that represent the person from whence they came."

The Haunce paused, and Tick realized if he moved one more inch forward, he'd fall out of his chair. After an interminable few seconds, the glowing pool of faces continued.

"*That* is what soulikens are, Atticus. They are your imprints on the universe, and they can never be erased. They pool together every second of your life, collecting and gathering and forming into something that is undeniably as much you as . . . you. That is what we are. We are the soulikens of billions of people, a bank of memories and thoughts and feelings. We give life to the spaces between the atoms and neutrons and electrons. We give life to the universe of quantum physics. We give life to Chi'karda."

Tick stared at the morphing faces, completely and utterly engrossed in every word.

But then the faces frowned, the endless eyes filled with a deep sadness.

"What's wrong?" Tick asked quickly.

The Haunce wiped away the frown, but it still looked unhappy. "It works both ways, Atticus. The Chi'karda also gives us life. One cannot exist without the other. Mistress Jane has severed the Realities from one another, destroying the bonds between them. And when the fragmenting begins, when all of Reality begins to fall to the lasting and eternal grip of entropy, so will we. Everything will end. Everything."

Tick didn't know how to respond. Impossibly, he almost felt as if his grief and worry for this collection of ghosts was as strong as his concern for his family. He was starting to understand that what Jane had done would not only kill all those living today, but also all those who had lived in the past. It would be a holocaust of all time and of all people, of all thoughts and ideas and memories. Everything would be wiped away into the oblivion of dark matter.

The Haunce spoke again, snapping him back to attention.

"But not all is lost."

"What do you mean?" Tick asked.

"We believe there is someone who can save us. Save the Realities."

Tick had the horrible feeling he already knew the answer, but he asked anyway. "Who?"

The Haunce glowed brightly. "You."

CHAPTER
28

COME TOGETHER

Sato and Mothball stared at each other for what seemed like a full hour, eyes locked, eyebrows raised. She was filthy from head to toe, her hair hanging in ratty strings to her shoulders. Sato kept thinking she'd disappear any second, sure that he was having a hallucination. The staring became almost comical. Especially when she broke into a grin and simply said, "'Ello."

Hearing her speak snapped Sato from his trance. "Mothball! What are you doing here? Where are we? What happened to everyone else?"

Mothball limped forward, eyeing Lisa as if she'd just noticed Tick's sister was there. "No idea what's 'appened. Felt like I've been nappin' for a full week, just woke up, and 'ere I am in a ruddy place that can't possibly exist. How long you been 'ere?"

Sato realized he had no clue. "I . . . don't know. Maybe an hour? I wasn't here very long before Lisa showed up. By the way, this is Tick's sister."

Mothball couldn't hide her surprise. "What in the name of the Grand Minister is Tick's wee little sis doin' 'ere?"

"Nice to meet you too," Lisa said in a deadpan voice.

"So sorry," she said quickly, holding out one of her gigantic hands. After Lisa shook it, Mothball continued. "Just surprised, is all. What are the ruddy chances of us meetin' 'ere with you?"

Lisa shook her head. "You think you're confused? Guess how I feel."

Sato felt it too. Everything seemed to have gone completely insane. He turned in a circle, throwing his arms up to gesture at their strange surroundings. "Where could this possibly be? What is it? Why would the three of us—"

Before he could finish, that same humming noise vibrated through the air, this time coming from a spot directly in front of him. At the same time, a dark blue square of marble rotated on an unseen axis, completely turning over until what had been the bottom was now the top, though with dark-red squiggly lines scratched across its surface. As soon as the tile settled into place, a person appeared on the marble square, instantly flashing into existence.

It was Mothball's mom, Windasill.

Sato swore right then he was done being surprised.

Mothball ran to her mom and pulled her into a massive hug as Windasill looked about in confusion.

"Don't worry," Mothball said after stepping back. "None of us know a ruddy thing, but thank the heavens we're together. Mayhaps the old man'll show up soon, he will."

"It was so dreadful," Windasill said after giving her daughter the kindest smile Sato thought he'd ever seen. "The shaking, the lightning. Last thing I remember, a bolt of energy came straight down on me head. Burned like the dickens, it did. Then it was dark, like sleep. I was barely aware. Next thing I know, I'm 'ere. Mothball, what's going on, dear?"

"Don't know." She shrugged and looked at Sato.

"Me, neither," Sato murmured.

"Does anyone at least have a guess?" Lisa asked. "Come on. You guys are Realitants, right? At least take a wild stab at it."

Sato was impressed with Tick's sister. She was no-nonsense, levelheaded. Brave. Tick had once made her out to be a smart-aleck pain in the rear. Maybe hard times had brought out her inner strength.

"Well?" Lisa said.

"If I 'ad to make a guess," Mothball said, folding her arms as her eyes revealed she was frantically trying to come up with an answer. "I reckon I'd say that . . . well, me instincts tell me that . . . if that lightning was . . . mayhaps it could've been . . . if you think about it . . ."

Luckily, another humming sound saved her. Sato looked to his right just in time to see a light green, marble square settle into place after rotating. An instant later, Rutger appeared, sitting on his bum in his black pants and black shirt, looking as frightened as Sato had ever seen him.

"What happened?" he yelled, scrambling to get his short legs under him. He looked so much like a huge ball pitching back and forth on two sticks that Sato worried what Lisa would think. He'd grown quite fond of Rutger, despite the constant teasing, and he always worried when the short man met new people. But Lisa seemed completely at ease, and his esteem for her went up another notch.

Before anyone could answer Rutger's inquiry, another humming sounded. Sato didn't look around in time to see the marble rotate, but about forty feet behind him, Tollaseat had appeared.

Windasill's shriek of delight had barely pierced the air when there came another humming. Then another. Then another. Sato was spinning in circles trying to catch sight of all the flipping tiles. People appeared each time, people he didn't know. Most of them were tall like Mothball and obviously from the Fifth. Hum, hum, hum—the sound blended together into a resonating vibration that strangely soothed his nerves.

Suddenly it was like musical popcorn. More and more and more marble slabs spun in ninety degrees all around him, changing colors as they did so, while a stunned, often dirty, sometimes injured person winked into existence on top. Sato finally quit trying to take it all in and instead focused on Mothball, then Rutger. Both of them were gawking at the strange sight around them, but Lisa was staring straight at him.

She raised her eyebrows in an unspoken question.

"You know I don't know what's going on," Sato said. "Let's just hope none of these people are maniacs bent on killing us."

"I just don't . . ." She trailed off, her eyes focusing on something past Sato's shoulder. They widened in surprise, then shock, then a huge smile wiped the anguish and confusion off her face.

"What?" he asked, already turning to see what she'd discovered.

Lisa shrieked with joy, brushing past him and sprinting toward a group of shorter people—compared to the Fifths, anyway—a heavyset man, a brown-haired woman, and a little girl.

It had to be Kayla. And Tick's parents, too.

Sato hurried after Lisa, feeling a rush of excitement at meeting Tick's family, somehow putting out of his mind that they were all standing in an impossible place with no explanation of how they'd gotten there.

Lisa reached her family and practically tackled Kayla, pulling her into a tight embrace and twirling her around. Their mom and dad soon joined in, a group of entwined arms, jumping up and down and laughing. It was one of the sweetest things Sato had ever seen.

When he reached them, he stopped, wondering if maybe he should've left them alone to their reunion.

Lisa saw him and broke apart from the vise of her dad's arms. "Mom, Dad—this is Tick's friend Sato." She reached out and grabbed his arm, pulling him closer for the introductions.

"I'm Edgar," her dad said, taking Sato's hand and shaking it vigorously. "I don't know where we are or how we got here, but I'm honored to meet one of my son's partners in crime."

"Nice . . . nice to meet you," Sato managed to mumble. Everything suddenly felt like a dream.

Tick's mom pulled Sato into a long hug, then looked at him as she squeezed his shoulders. "I'm Lorena, and it's an honor indeed. Atticus told us about your parents and what happened to them. I was so sorry to hear the news. Your mom and I were dear, dear friends for many years. But after I left the Realitants, I had no choice but to lose touch with her. It has been one of the biggest regrets of my life."

Sato raised his eyebrows. "Why'd you have to do that? Why couldn't you stay friends?"

Lorena looked at the ground for a second, a flash of fear on her face. But then she returned her gaze to him and her eyes were filled with resolve. "Because Jane said she'd kill me if I ever contacted a Realitant again. She was scared I'd tell them about the Thirteenth Reality before she was ready."

CHAPTER
29

THE ONLY HOPE

Tick spent a long minute simply staring at the shifting faces of the glowing Haunce. Their eyes stared back, full of scrutiny and concern, waiting to hear his reaction to the pronouncement that Tick was the only one who could save the Realities from ripping apart and ceasing to exist forever. No pressure, right?

He decided to show how much he'd grown up in the last year or so. "Okay. I'm not gonna sit here and waste time. It's hard for me to believe I could do anything to stop or reverse what Jane's done. But you obviously know what you're talking about—I mean, you're a billion ghosts crammed into the space of a water heater. That's a lot of brains. So what am I supposed to do?"

The Haunce laughed just as its face morphed into that of a young woman with dark eyes. The sound was like electronic music. When the face changed to an old man with a mustache, the Haunce began speaking again. "No brains here, Atticus. At least not physically. But our combined knowledge is here all the same, stored on countless imprints of soulikens. But there will be time for school lessons later. You are correct that we should not waste any more time. We must get to the heart of the matter, and quickly."

Tick nodded, half-fascinated and half-terrified of what he was about to hear.

The Haunce continued, the faces forever shifting. "Atticus, we have been observing the Realities for many years—living them, breathing them, *being* them. We exist in the boundaries and seams that keep the Realities together and apart, united but separate, all things balanced as they should be. At times, we have intervened, but only in extreme cases of need. Never before has the need been so great as it is now.

"The seams are splitting. Dark matter is consuming them, triggering chain reactions of heightened entropy and introducing fragmentation on a level never seen. We believe there is only one way to stop it."

"How does it involve me?" Tick asked.

The Haunce's current face—a boy, maybe only ten years old—frowned at the interruption, then the expression smoothed away like rippling water. "As we said, we have been observing the Realities for countless centuries. And in all that time, there have been only two people with a concentration of soulikens and Chi'karda levels similar to ours. You are one of those people, Atticus. And Mistress Jane is the other. We do not yet understand how the two of you came to possess this power or why you both came to exist in the same period of time. But it will take your combined powers to reverse what has happened today."

Tick had to bite his lip. He wanted to shout a million questions, refute the Haunce's words. If saving the Realities depended on him *and* Jane—depended on their cooperation—then the battle was over before it had begun.

The glowing orb of the Haunce flexed, as if taking a deep breath. "We must rebind the seams of the Realities and restore stability to the inner workings of quantum physics. To do so, we will need to harness an unprecedented amount of Chi'karda. And to do that, we will need four components."

The Haunce paused, and Tick felt the agony of each passing second.

"In all of the Realities of the Multiverse there is a place where the Chi'karda levels are exponentially higher than at any other place. So concentrated, in fact, it makes the Realitant headquarters in the Bermuda

Triangle look like a spark of static compared to a lightning storm. You and Mistress Jane must join us there."

"Is it the place in the desert?" Tick asked. "Where Jane had that black tree? The dark matter, the Blade of Shattered Hope?"

The Haunce—now showing the face of an older, homely woman—slowly shook its head. "No. Jane chose that spot because it best fit her needs for linking the different elements of the Blade. Because she had an Alterant of herself in the same place in all thirteen Realities, it was more a matter of the substance of the Blade than it was of Chi'karda."

"Then where do we have to go?" Tick was saving the biggest and most obvious question for last: How in the world would they get Jane to cooperate with them?

"There's a place in the Thirteenth Reality where . . ." The Haunce faltered. The face of an Indian woman, the red dot on her forehead looking almost black against the blue glow of her skin, wore a look of complete sadness. "It is a place of atrocities and horror. We are sorry; it is hard for us to talk about it." Another long pause.

Tick didn't know if he wanted to hear the answer. After millennia of observing the world and all the things humans had done—both good and bad—the Haunce was having difficulty talking about a place to which Tick had to go. The thought was terrifying.

The Haunce finally continued, the look of sadness now draped across the face of a young Asian man. "We do not know why evil things have always been drawn to this particular spot in the Thirteenth Reality. There have been thousands upon thousands of deaths there—perhaps millions. The Chi'karda levels created by those tragedies is unsurpassed."

Tick swallowed a big lump, then took a guess. "It's where Jane's castle is, isn't it?"

The eyes of a little girl met Tick's. "No. Not there. Somewhere much, much worse."

Tick waited.

"The place we must gather," the Haunce said, seeming to have recovered its composure a little, "and where you must bring Jane, is . . . the Factory."

"The Factory?" Tick repeated.

The Haunce nodded. "Yes. It is the place where Jane manufactures her creatures. Her abominations. It is a hideous, wretched place full of death and tortured souls. But also the site of massive amounts of Chi'karda."

"And what do we do once we get there?" Tick asked. He was trying not to think too much about what a creepy and horrible place the Factory must be. "Assuming that we somehow convince Jane to come with us and do what we ask, I mean."

The pulsing, silver-blue orb of the Haunce moved several feet across the floor and back again, as if pacing, deep in thought. "The task you and Jane must do is simple. Both of you need to concentrate and summon every ounce of Chi'karda you can. Gather as much as you can, and then you must channel to us. Our job will be to harness the power and combine it with the Chi'karda that already exists within the Factory."

The Haunce quit pacing and took another one of those deep breaths. "Once we have gathered enough power, we will bleed the Chi'karda through the cracks of space and time, binding the seals of the Realities that are currently rupturing. Quite honestly, the task could destroy us, but we believe we can save the Multiverse before that happens. Before we ourselves cease to exist."

Tick didn't know what to think. The whys and hows didn't matter so much at the moment, and he couldn't pretend to feel a pang of potential loss at hearing that the Haunce might die in the act. Especially if the Haunce's sacrifice would save thirteen entire worlds—and his family. But still, hearing it all poured out so short and sweet when so much was on the line was dizzying.

"Do you have anything to say?" the Haunce asked, now showing the face of a pretty girl about Tick's age.

"Not a thing," Tick responded. "I don't know what else I can do but trust you. If you say we can do this, then let's do it. I guess the first thing is to figure out how to get Jane to play along. I'm sure once we tell her what's about to happen, she'll have to. I mean, how could she want everything to disappear, including her? That'd be beyond stupid."

"We can only hope." The Haunce morphed into an old woman. "There is one final thing to say before we begin. You must know that a lull has occurred in the fragmentation of the Realities. For the moment, they are safe. And so is your family. But . . ."

Tick felt a thrilling rush of joy as he realized that somehow he'd known all along that his family was safe. The relief lasted only a second before being tempered. "But?" he repeated, thinking, *What now?*

The face of a small boy responded. "But we have only thirty hours until the fragmentation begins again. And when it does, it will not stop until all that we know ceases to exist."

PART
3
THE FIFTH
ARMY

CHAPTER
30

A BOWL OF DEBRIS

Sofia lay on her back, staring at the twilight sky of the desert, the deep blue just beginning its fade to purple. No clouds. A throbbing pain pulsed somewhere inside her skull—something had knocked her out. Something had hit her in the head during the chaos right after Tick disappeared.

Tick disappeared!

She forced herself into a sitting position, groaning at the thunder of pain it ignited. She coughed, a dry rasp that hurt her throat. She needed water. Badly. The natural rock formations of Jane's secret spot still surrounded them, though several chunks had broken off and tumbled to the dusty ground during the earthquake. The tables and screens and computers used by Jane's people lay scattered and smashed, strewn about like abandoned toys. The air smelled burnt.

Twisting her head around, she searched for signs of her friends. She felt a fleeting moment of panic when she didn't see them at first, but it quickly vanished when movement under a collapsed table caught her attention. Master George, his nice suit filthy and torn, was wiggling his way out from under the heavy slab of the table. Paul sat a few feet from him, his arms wrapped around his knees, staring into the distance with a blank expression.

"You guys okay?" Sofia asked.

"They all vanished," Paul said, not bothering to look at her. "Jane first, and then everyone else right after. Zip, zip, zip. Zippity gone, just like that. Left us here to die, I guess."

"I'm actually quite surprised." Master George grunted. He finally freed himself from the confining rubble and stood up, dusting himself off. "She went to all that trouble to kidnap us, and then she simply ran away? Odd."

Sofia disagreed. "I don't think it's that weird. Somehow Tick winked away, or someone took him, whatever. But without him, she didn't have what she needed anymore. It's *his* family she took, after all."

"It's not even that," Paul said in a subdued voice, still staring at the rock walls like he'd been hypnotized.

Sofia scooted a little closer to him. "What are you talking about?"

"Look at that." Paul finally blinked and pointed to the middle of the depression where the black tree—the Blade of Shattered Hope—had been. It was gone, replaced by a small crater. The ground was blackened and charred, some of the desert sand actually glistening where the heat had transformed it to glass. "I think something went wrong with what that freak Jane was trying to do. Really, really wrong. She doesn't care about us anymore. She ran away to try to fix whatever it is she messed up."

Sofia stared at the dark scar of a hole and slowly nodded as she thought about what he'd said. Paul was right. The earthquake had been horrible, and all of Jane's people had run around screaming, falling down, and crawling over each other as they looked for a way to escape. Things had obviously not gone according to plan.

"That certainly sounds reasonable," Master George said. "What I wouldn't give to know what exactly happened here today. All that nonsense about dark matter. Perhaps it wasn't quite rubbish after all."

"Dark matter," Paul muttered in disgust; Sofia shared the sentiment. "I don't give a patooty about any of that stuff right now. All I want is a chance to put my hands around Jane's neck and squeeze."

Sofia felt her eyebrows rise in surprise. "A little violent this evening, aren't we?"

Paul looked at her for the first time since she'd come to, and she couldn't help but lean back a couple of inches before stopping herself. His eyes were full of fury and hatred. There was no sign of the normally lighthearted, joking Paul.

Sofia felt a deep anger inside of her, too. "Just kidding. I'd like to do that myself."

Master George walked over to Paul and offered a hand. "All in due time, Master Paul. All in due time. For now, we need to find water—or we won't live long enough to put our hands around a sandwich, much less Mistress Jane."

Paul ignored the offer of help, but did stand up, his face still tensed in anger. Sofia pushed herself up as well, and the three of them began searching through the debris. Jane's people had to have brought plenty of food and water if they planned on being out here for any significant amount of time. It took only a few minutes to find the stash.

Several coolers with bread, meat, fruit, and big, glass bottles of water—most of which had been packed tightly enough that they hadn't broken in the chaos— had been wedged between a toppled table and some large computer equipment.

Sofia drank half a bottle of water, trickles of the liquid splashing down her cheeks and onto her clothes. Even though the water was warm, she was sure she'd never tasted anything so refreshing in her life.

They didn't dare eat the meat, but the bread and fruit seemed okay, and soon they were all sitting together in one of the few spots clear of wreckage, enjoying their odd little meal. The sun had sunk even further, the shadows from the towering rocks stretching all the way across the desert bowl. Full darkness would be upon them soon.

Sofia hated the thought of being in the middle of a desert in the Thirteenth Reality at nighttime. "Guys, this is great to eat and rest a little, but what're we gonna do next? It'll be totally dark soon."

"We'll probably get eaten alive by fangen," Paul said, neither his voice nor his face revealing any sign that he was kidding. "Jane's probably already sent some out here to hunt us."

Sofia wanted the old Paul back. "You're real great to have around when things get rough," she said. "You really know how to look on the bright side."

Paul shrugged and took a big bite of an apple, wiping the juice on his sleeve.

"There are much worse things than fangen," Master George said with a doomsday voice.

Sofia stared at him, surprised and curious. He returned her look, his eyes squinting despite the fading light. When he said nothing, she finally asked, "What makes you say that?"

Master George glanced at Paul, then looked away toward the western wall of the bowl, now draped in shadow. "Our spies have learned a lot about Jane's extracurricular activities these past months. She has a place called the Factory, located in one of the heaviest Chi'karda spots ever discovered. Word is she's created things far more hideous than her precious fangen. Far worse. More vicious by a long shot."

"What are they?" Paul asked.

Sofia found it hard to believe something could be worse than those flying, snarling, diseased, sharp-toothed monsters.

"She hasn't brought them out for full usage yet," Master George said. "We've caught only bare glimpses and heard rumors. But her work in using nature to create nature has gone beyond anything you or I could dare scrape up in a campfire tale. Evil, evil things. We think she is also working to isolate the soulikens of . . . very bad people from the past."

Soulikens. Sofia had heard the word before, but she'd never pursued its meaning because of countless other things that seemed more important. Master George continued before she could voice her question.

"I haven't told you much about soulikens, because I myself didn't know enough. But I've spent every spare second since we last said good-bye researching the phenomenon. It might be the most fascinating thing I've ever studied—everything from the fundamentals of natural electricity and its role within human biology to old tales and rumors of ghost stories."

"Well, what *is* it?" Paul asked in an impatient voice. "What's a souliken?"

The sun seemed to finally disappear for good in that moment, the sky darkening as if all the light had been frightened away. When Master George turned his gaze to Sofia, she almost gasped out loud at how creepy he looked with the angles of his face deep in shadow.

"Soulikens are your eternal stamp on reality," he said. "They are the means by which you'll haunt the world far after you've rotted to dust and bone."

And then, for some odd reason, the old man laughed.

CHAPTER
31
∽

MAKING PLANS

Thirty hours?" Tick asked, hating how that sounded both long and short at the same time. "We have only thirty hours to save the entire universe?"

The silver-blue glow of the Haunce flared a bit then subsided. "Thirty hours or thirty years—it would not make a difference. There is not much we can do to prepare, and it might even be worse if we did have the time to try. The problem will be convincing Mistress Jane to cooperate. Once you accomplish that, all that will be left is our attempt to rebind the Realities and reseal the barriers."

Tick felt a bubble in his stomach as he shook his head in disbelief. "Once *I* accomplish it? You really think Jane is gonna trust me for even one second? You'll have to talk to her, not me."

The face of an old man frowned back at him. "We are sorry, Atticus. Our ability to appear in this form is extremely difficult to maintain. Once we leave here, neither you nor anyone else will see us again until the moment we make our attempt. The task of having Jane join us is entirely up to you."

Tick didn't say anything for a minute, trying to process the new information and its potential ramifications. He felt an incredible amount of pressure draped across his shoulders like an iron shawl.

Finally, he said, "Okay, look. I don't know how I can possibly do that. I'm not even sure I understand what it is I'm supposed to do. But you said something about my family being safe. I need to hear about that right now. How do you know they're okay?"

A woman with a big nose responded. "As Jane was building her cache of dark matter and assembling her Blade of Shattered Hope, we watched carefully. We normally do not interfere with the realm of living humans. It is not our place. If Jane had destroyed the Fifth Reality, we would have been shocked and horrified, but we would not have stopped her. However, when the chain reactions that could end all existence were ignited, we no longer had a choice."

Tick groaned on the inside, doubly annoyed. Both

at the long non-answer about his family and the fact that the Haunce would sit back and let an entire world be destroyed. "What does this have to do with my family?" he asked.

An annoyed buzz sounded from the ghostly creature. "We hope your impatience will serve you well since we will have little time left together. No more interruptions. We will not be able to appear in this form much longer."

The glow changed into three faces before Tick finally nodded.

"Good," the Haunce continued. "When the barriers began to break and the seals began to split, we knew immediately what we must do. We winked you here to Reality Prime, where we would be able to discuss things in private. We also winked your family away from Jane's prison, as well as a number of people from the Fifth Reality who were located in the area of your Realitant friends—Mothball, Rutger, and Sato. They are together in a special holding place we created long ago—a sort of way station that exists in a quasi-Reality that only we know about."

"What about—" Tick stopped himself, not wanting to interrupt again.

"Your other friends?" the Haunce asked. "Sofia, Paul, and your Realitant leader, Master George?"

Tick nodded.

"They are in the Thirteenth Reality, where you last saw them."

Tick couldn't remain silent any more. "Why didn't you take them to the same place as my family?"

The face of the Haunce flowed from an ugly woman to a pretty one, then morphed into a man with beady eyes. "They remain in the Thirteenth, because that is where you are going. You will need their help. You will be together very soon, though you will not have much time for happy reunions."

"Okay, so what do I need to know?" Tick asked, surprised at how steady he felt. He was ready to have this whole mess done and over with.

No one had spoken since Master George's explanation of soulikens. Sofia continued to sit still, staring at the dark shadow of a wall standing a few dozen feet from her. The sounds of the desert were soft and faint—an insect here and there, the sigh of the wind, sand scratching across rock.

When Paul spoke up, it startled her. She hoped he hadn't noticed her jump.

"Soulikens," he said. "Basically you're telling us that throughout our lives we create these freaky electronic imprints on the world that never go away but hang around us like a fog, building and building until it kind of becomes our ghost. Is that what you're telling us? That ghosts are real?"

"If you could see on a quantum level," Master George responded, "you'd see an aura of energy around you and others that very much resemble exactly that. A ghost."

Sofia felt a little creeped out. "Then I don't wanna see on a quantum level. I hate scary movies, and I hate ghosts."

"Now who's the cheerful one?" Paul asked.

"You rubbed off on me."

"I love scary movies. Especially the ones where lots of people die."

Sofia couldn't help but feel happy that the old Paul was starting to come back. "Call me crazy, but I prefer my movies to have the slightest hint of intelligence."

"When all this is over," Paul said, "check out *Steve the Slashing Monkey* and tell me that movie doesn't *bleed* intelligence."

Sofia couldn't stop before a snort of laughter came out.

"I knew it!" Paul yelled, his voice echoing off the rock walls. "I knew I could make you laugh!"

"You two are driving me mad," Master George muttered. "I believe I'm quite ready to get some sleep."

"But what're we gonna do?" Paul asked him. "Can't

you get someone to wink us out of this stinkin' place?"

"Sorry, old chap. If someone hasn't winked us by now, then there's obviously been a break in communication. Jane brought us here, remember, and her shield must still be working. And I don't have my Barrier Wand. I assure you, Sally's doing his very best to find us."

Great, Sofia thought. They had to spend the night in the middle of the desert, with no telling how many creatures of Mistress Jane lurking about. *Just great.*

"Well," Paul said, "at least it's not cold. I bet we can find some soft sand to snuggle in, Sofia. You in?"

Sofia leaned closer to him and smacked him on the arm. It felt so wonderful that she did it again.

Paul jumped to his feet and ran away, snickering as he rubbed his sore spot. "Man, for a chick who's a scaredy-cat of scary movies, you sure do know how to punch."

"I was glad you'd gotten over your sour mood," Sofia responded as she started looking around for her own place to get some rest, feeling with her hands mostly. "But now that you're back to normal, I kind of miss the grumpy Paul after all."

"I love you too."

She'd just found a nice spot of open sand when a slight thump in the air sounded behind her. It was barely noticeable, and she almost felt it more than heard it. She whipped around to see what had happened.

A shadowy figure of a boy stood between her and

Paul, a hump of a backpack on his shoulders. When he turned and faced her, the starlight revealed his face just enough.

"Tick!" she cried, scrambling to her feet and running to him. Paul reached him just as she did, and they all joined in a group hug. When she finally pulled back, she said, "What happened? Where'd you go?"

"And how'd you get back here?" Paul added.

Master George joined them. "Atticus! Speak, man, speak!"

Tick laughed a little, though it didn't hold much humor. "Calm down, guys. It's a long story, and we don't have much time to talk. We have to get moving. I'll tell you everything on the go."

"Get moving?" Sofia asked, feeling a slight chill. "Where are we supposed to go?"

"Some place called the Factory," Tick answered. "It's full of Mistress Jane's little monster pets. But don't worry. We have a billion ghosts to help us out."

CHAPTER
32

REUNIONS

Tick didn't want to waste a single minute. When the Haunce outlined the plan for what they needed to do to stop the fragmenting of the Realities, one thing bled through all the others: they needed to hurry.

Tick had less than thirty hours to get to the Factory, convince Mistress Jane to help—after getting her there in the first place, of course—then summon all the Chi'karda he could to help the Haunce rebind the barriers of the Realities.

No problem. Then why did he have the terrible feeling that nothing would go right along the way?

Sofia, Paul, and Master George stood in front of him in the darkness. The starlight was not strong enough to reveal their faces, but Tick could imagine the looks of surprise and confusion.

"Seriously," he said. "We need to go. We're gonna be winked in five minutes."

"Whoa," Paul said, his upraised hands mere shafts of shadow. "I'm not takin' a single step till you elaborate on this whole ghost business."

"A *billion* ghosts," Sofia added. "What was that all about?"

Tick was about to answer when Master George made an unpleasant harrumphing sound.

"What?" Tick asked.

"You met the Haunce, didn't you?" the old man responded. Tick could barely see him shaking his head. "I've met it only once in my life, and if I ever do again, you can bet your bottoms I'm going to have a word or two with it about holding back vital information about soulikens and all that."

Tick felt a flutter of confusion, but Sofia spoke up before he could.

"The Haunce? What's that? And why would it know everything about soulikens?"

Tick's confusion increased. "You guys know about soulikens?"

"You mean *you* do?" Paul responded.

Tick nodded even though he doubted they could see him. "The Haunce told me about them."

"What is the Haunce?" Sofia shouted.

For some reason a chuckle burst out of Tick. "We sound like the dumbest people who've ever lived." He remembered the urgency of what they had to do. "But come on—we really need to go. The Haunce wants us to stand at the spot where the Blade of Shattered Hope tree thingy was."

"Why?" all three of them asked in unison.

"He—*it's* going to wink us closer to the Factory. We can sort things out once we get there. Come on— can you tell where the Blade used to be?"

"Over this way," Paul muttered. "Doesn't sound like a good time to start doubting Superman Atticus Higginbottom."

Paul's shadow moved past him and started walking toward the central area of the dark stone walls surrounding them. Tick followed and heard Sofia and Master George right behind him.

Tick tripped twice over debris and stepped on things that clanged and snapped. The place must've gotten really messed up after he'd been winked away.

Paul finally stopped in an open spot and turned to face the rest of the group. "Pretty sure it was right about here. But be careful—some of the sand turned into glass shards."

Tick felt the crunch under his shoes, smelled something burnt. When they were all standing in a circle, he reached out and took Sofia's hand, then Paul's. "The Haunce told me we need to hold hands. It's easier that way."

Tick was glad they didn't argue. Sofia took Master George's hand, and then the old man took Paul's. Standing there in the dark desert with the slight breeze sighing as it passed over the towering rocks, Tick felt a major case of the creeps, like they were about to begin a séance.

"Okay!" he shouted. "Wink us away, Haunce!" The words sounded incredibly stupid, but he wanted to get this part over with. He had no idea what to expect once they got to where they were going.

Before this last thought even fully formed in his mind, the tingle shot across his neck and down his spine.

~

It had been a strange hour for Sato.

There'd been the reunion of Tick's family—without Tick, unfortunately—as well as hearing more details about Mrs. Higginbottom (a.k.a. Lorena) and her brief stint as a Realitant. Sato had been amazed to learn that she and Mistress Jane had been partners of a sort in exploring and seeking out new Realities, and they'd been together when the Thirteenth was discovered. They'd realized that something was special about it right away, and how odd properties of Chi'karda ran rampant there.

It was the first time Jane had started to show the dual signs of her thirst for power and her edge of obsession with the idea of a Utopian Reality. When Jane threatened Lorena if she dared tell anyone about their discovery, that had been the last straw. Lorena decided to call it quits, realizing she wasn't cut out for that kind of life—namely being killed by a crazy woman.

Sato eventually drifted away from the Higginbottoms. He suspected they probably wanted some time to themselves to bask in the joy of being together again. And, he admitted to himself, it hurt to see such a thing. It painfully reminded him that he'd lost his own parents, and that such a get-together would be impossible for him. It hurt, and he left them before it became unbearable.

But that's when things had really gotten strange for him.

There were several hundred people from the Fifth Reality in the strange space, all of them winked in from the general location of where Mothball's parents lived. How that had happened was beyond anyone's guess, but they'd mostly gotten over their shock and just generally reveled in the fact that they were still alive.

Or, Sato figured, at least they hoped that was the case. The bizarre place to which they'd been sent didn't seem like anything in the normal world. Maybe they *had* died and been sent to an afterlife. Who knew? Sato didn't want to think about it until he absolutely had to.

Once all the people from the Fifth settled in, they began to notice him. They began to see the resemblance he had to their recently assassinated Grand Minister. His Alterant. And now they surrounded him completely, a huge crowd of giants, all of them staring at him, waiting for him to speak. But he refused, sitting cross-legged with his chin resting on his closed fists. Mothball had to get him out of this. She had to do something! If not her, then her parents.

But they seemed to be enjoying the spectacle, along with Rutger. The four of them sat outside the crowd somewhere—he'd lost sight of them a good half hour earlier.

Sato buried his face in his hands and groaned, hoping everyone heard the scream of frustration barely veiled within it.

⌒

The first thing Tick noticed was that the air was much cooler, laced with a wetness almost as thick as mist. Then he saw the tall, looming poles of shadow all around them—trees. Lots and lots of trees.

They were back in the Forest of Plague—the place they'd come a year ago on a mission to steal Mistress

Jane's Barrier Wand. This time they'd be going in the opposite direction; the Factory lay due east, according to the Haunce.

Tick felt the reassuring grip of Sofia's and Paul's hands in his own. "You guys okay?"

"Still in one piece," Master George answered from a few feet in front of him. Tick couldn't see his face very well. In fact, he couldn't see much except for the trees and the dark shapes of his fellow Realitants.

"Fine," Paul grumbled. "At least it's not hot here. My pits are in desperate need of some deodorant."

Sofia sighed. "Pleasant as always."

"Okay, so where are we?" Paul asked.

"Yes, Atticus," Master George added. "No more time for hasting about until you answer some questions. Where are we? What's behind all this?"

Tick felt surprisingly calm despite the clock winding down inside his mind; he didn't have the heart to look at his watch. He knew the calm wouldn't last long. He knew terrible things lay ahead.

"Tick?" Paul prodded. "Speak up—can't hear ya."

"All right, listen," Tick began. "I'll explain everything, but then we gotta get going. Jane screwed up the whole universe with her dark-matter tree—that stupid Blade of Shattered Hope. The barriers keeping the Realities whole and bound together are fragmenting, breaking apart. Right now there's a lull, but the

Haunce says in twenty-something hours from now, it'll all snap, blow up, disintegrate. In no time at all, everything will cease to exist. That's how the Haunce put it."

"I feared the worst," Master George whispered, a deathly rasp. "However, this is beyond even what I cooked up in my head. But if the Haunce told you as much, then it's true."

Tick nodded despite the darkness. "It thinks we can fix the problem somehow, but it'll take me, Mistress Jane, and the Haunce itself together in the biggest Chi'karda spot in all the Realities. Which is this Factory place a few miles to the east of here."

"Oh, goodness gracious me," Master George said. The others stayed silent, maybe too shocked for words.

"Anyway," Tick said, "we can talk more about the details, but the Haunce wants me to do a quick job first." Tick reached into his pocket and pulled out the short metal message tube Master George had given him earlier. "First, it wants me to send an important note to somebody—wink it, actually."

"Wink it?" Sofia repeated. "You mean . . ."

Tick held up the tube between his thumb and forefinger, barely able to see the silver shine of its smooth surface. "Yeah. The Haunce wants me to wink it with my so-called powers. Called it . . . *practice*."

CHAPTER
33

SENDING A MESSAGE

Tick finally remembered that he'd packed a flashlight before leaving his house. He swung his backpack off and pulled it out, then clicked it on. The light reflected off the silvery surface of the metal tube, making it look like a valuable piece of jewelry.

"Atticus," Master George said as he moved closer and put a hand on Tick's shoulder. "Listen to me carefully. I want you to describe what the Haunce looked like. Once I'm absolutely sure this all came from our strange and powerful friend, I promise I won't doubt another word you say."

Tick let the flashlight tip downward until it illuminated the leaf-strewn forest floor. "It was a big, silver-blue oval of pulsing light, with hundreds of faces replacing each other in the middle of it, their mouths forming the words as it talked to me. Creeped me out big time."

Master George nodded as his eyes focused on the ground. "Indeed. Indeed. It's hard to put into words what it means that the Haunce visited you, Atticus. There's no longer any doubt that there is something special about you, something extraordinary. Especially if the Haunce thinks you can wink this message away without the use of a Barrier Wand."

"Yeah, well, we'll see," Tick said. He shone the flashlight under his chin to make his face look scary. "You both can think I'm special all you want, but let's see if I can actually do it."

"You *are* special," Paul said, not bothering to hide his sarcasm. "You're so special."

"He *is*," Sofia snapped. "Be quiet and let him concentrate. Do it, Tick. Show him. Show us what you can do."

Paul snickered, evidently thinking his joke was hilarious. "I'm just playin', man. Sheesh. What's the note in there say, anyway? And who are you sending it to?"

"It's for Sally—" Master George began, but Tick cut him off.

"No, it's not."

"What do you mean? You changed it?"

Tick shone the light on the silver tube still clasped in his other hand. "Had to. The Haunce said we had no chance of getting all the Realitants together in time to help us. They're spread all over the place, dealing with the earthquakes and junk that happened when everything went wrong."

"Then who's it for?" Sofia asked.

"It's a note for someone who already has a bunch of people gathered, ready to fight the first bad thing that walks in front of them." Tick paused, needlessly adding drama to the revelation, just for kicks. "It's for Sato."

Sato ignored every word spoken to him and every tap on his shoulder until he heard the voice of Lisa.

"Sato?" she asked. "You okay?"

He looked up to see she'd maneuvered her way through the tightly packed crowd. She stood in front of him, leaning down with her hands on her knees, looking at him with concern creasing her pretty face. The fact that she cared one whit made him feel a little better.

"I guess so," he replied. He swept his eyes across the tall people of the Fifth who were packing in tighter and tighter around him, still gawking and pointing. "I just don't know what they want. I'm not who they think I am—they have to *know* that! What do they expect me to do? Pretend I'm their leader raised from the dead?"

Lisa knelt down, the movement causing her blonde curls to bounce on her shoulders. "We all thought it was kind of cute until you put your head down and ignored them. Why don't you come over and sit with my family? Maybe that'll make them leave you alone."

Sato shook his head slowly as he considered her offer. How stupid was this? These people fawning over him were the least of his worries. Where were they and how were they going to get out of there?

"Sato?" Lisa asked. "You want me to—"

"No, no, sorry," he said. "I was just thinking that we need to figure out what's going on around here. I need to talk to Rutger and Mothball. Figure out if we can get in touch with the other Realitants somehow."

Lisa nodded. "Okay, sounds good. Why don't you . . ." She paused, looked around quickly, then focused back on him. "Tell you what—I'll get their attention so you can sneak off or something."

"Get their attention? How're you gonna do that?"

Lisa straightened, rubbing her hands together as if planning something evil. "I can be a brat when I need to be—ask Tick. I'll think of something brilliant to make them leave you alone."

Sato stood to join her, wincing at the gasps of anticipation his action elicited from the crowd. "Okay, fine by me. Good luck with that." He started through the crowd of Fifth citizens standing between him and his Realitant friends.

"You people listen up!" he heard Lisa shout from behind him. "Sato will be right back. He has to, um, go use the bathroom."

Sato stopped for half a second, thinking, *That is the best she can come up with?* But then he pushed on, making his way toward Mothball and Rutger.

➤

Tick did his best to explain what the Haunce had said about Sato and the others being taken to some kind of way station anomaly in the Realities for safekeeping. But it was kind of hard when he didn't really understand it himself.

"What *is* this place?" Paul asked. "*Where* is it?"

"I don't know!" Tick practically shouted, though he toned it down to a rough whisper on the last word. They couldn't risk Jane's creations finding them yet. "All we care about is that they're all safe—including my family, thank goodness—and that the Haunce is gonna move them very soon. Which is why I need to hurry. As soon as I get this note winked, we'll have time to talk about stuff while we walk toward the Factory." Annoyed, Tick pointed the flashlight in Paul's face. "Okay?"

Paul reached out, flailing with his hands. "All right, dude, get on with it!"

"Yes, Atticus," Master George pitched in. "I'm very anxious to see what you're about to do. Quite anxious indeed. And when we're done, I'd love to hear more about this hideaway spot in the Realities you mentioned."

Sofia reached out and lightly punched Tick in the arm. "We'll leave you alone, now. Do your thing. I can't wait to see it."

Tick had a sudden rush of terror. He had no idea what he was about to do—or even where to begin. The Haunce had left him with some parting words of advice—mainly about envisioning a conduit between him and Sato and opening an imaginary slice through space and time. But mostly, he was supposed to sit back and let his power do its thing. He needed to believe in it and let the Chi'karda take his vision of need and manifest it for him.

His mind knew what it wanted. His heart did as well. He had all the power he needed, waiting for a spark to set it boiling. All the ingredients were there, even if he couldn't lay out the scientific formulas on any chalkboard no matter how many times he tried. It was all there. The need, the ability, the power.

He just had to set it in motion.

He just had to believe.

"Tick, you waitin' on something?" Paul asked.

Sofia shushed him. "Seriously, Paul, shut up!"

"Sorry," he whispered.

Tick barely heard the exchange, but realized he was standing completely still, staring at some dark point in the distant woods. Giving his head a little shake, he knelt down on the ground, feeling the prick of a twig. Then he heard it snap, along with the crunch of leaves. He placed the flashlight on the ground, still lit, and brought the silver tube up with both hands to look at it, turning the thing slowly between his fingers.

Now or never, he told himself.

Now or never.

He closed his eyes, took a deep breath, and urged a sea of calm to wash across his body. He thought back to his two main encounters with Chi'karda, the times when he'd actually been able to see it visually.

Sparkling, orange clouds of mist.

Heat.

Raging, burning heat.

Something flickered inside him. He'd found the spark. It grew, warming him from the inside out. Surprisingly, it didn't terrify him. It felt more like comfort.

He squeezed his eyes tighter and threw all of his concentration into his thoughts. In the amoebas of darkness swirling there, he tried to form a picture of Sato. Different images kept flashing in his mind, different faces. Tick tried harder. The face of his friend wavered, then held. Unbelievably clear, it was like a photo had been implanted in his brain. Tick almost opened his eyes in shock.

But he controlled himself, focusing on keeping the picture clear. Sato. He thought of the silver tube, clearly told . . . who?—himself? maybe the Chi'karda itself—that he wanted that tube to dissolve into the quantum realm, travel through spacetime, and reach his friend.

The heat increased, forcing beads of sweat to break out all over his skin. He didn't dare look, but he knew that misty swirls of orange were floating around his body, lighting the darkness of the forest with an eerie glow. He held on to that vision of Sato and on to the precise and clear thought of what he wanted to happen.

Then, not quite sure if he was doing the right thing, he formed words inside his mind.

The silver tube. To Sato. He waited. *Now.*

As a tingling wave sent goose bumps bursting out all over him, he felt the weight of the tube disappear from his hands. He heard Sofia and Paul gasp. Master George shrieked with excitement like an old woman. But Tick didn't truly believe it until he opened his eyes and saw for himself.

The tube was gone.

The message had been sent.

CHAPTER
34

THE WAY STATION

Sato never thought he'd be so happy to see Rutger. "Why, you look a little uncomfortable!" the short man shouted when Sato finally made it through the crowd to his Realitant friends and Mothball's parents. "I was, uh, just about to come out there and rescue you."

"Yeah, I'm sure you were," Sato muttered.

"They've all taken quite the likin' to you, they 'ave," Mothball said, an enormous grin revealing her big, yellow teeth.

Those two were enjoying this ridiculous scenario way too much, and it was really starting to annoy Sato. "What am I supposed to do? We've all been winked to this psycho place, and those people act like I'm gonna save them or something. Just because I look like their murdered leader. What am I supposed to do?"

Tollaseat and Windasill were holding hands, looking on with pinched up grimaces as if they were embarrassed by the whole affair. Tollaseat reached out—and down—to pat Sato on the shoulder. "There, there, little man. Don't take it the wrong way, and don't be feelin' any pressure 'cause of this lot. We're all a wee bit scared, and a familiar face gives a lift, it does. Even I'll admit you seem like the natural person to take charge 'round these parts."

Windasill laughed, a sound that held nothing but kindness—no hint of mockery or condescension. "Reckon I ruddy agree with me love on that one. Can't you just pretend to lead a bit? Give 'em all a good talkin' to? Bring 'em straight out of the doldrums, you would. I'd bet me own two ears on that."

Sato knew he had to quit whining. Their problems were piling up by the minute, and—

An object appeared in front of his face—instantly, one second not there, the next second there—a small, elongated stretch of shining silver. He barely had time to see it or register what it was before the tube of metal fell. He reached out to catch it, but he didn't move in time. The tube smacked onto the weird marble floor and bounced with a couple of clings and clangs before rolling several inches and coming to rest next to Rutger's foot.

No one moved for a couple of seconds. Sato could tell they were all staring at the mysterious—and magical—visitor just as he was. He finally gained his wits and leaned over to pick up the tube, turning it this way and that for the others to take a look.

Sato was about to ask what it was when Mothball blurted out, "That there's one of them fancy message tubes from Master George."

"Open it!" Rutger yelled, jumping up and down in excitement—maybe reaching a grand height of three millimeters off the ground. "I knew he'd find us! I knew it! Don't you worry, we'll be out of here . . ."

He trailed off, a troubled look coming over his face.

Sato had been relieved to get the tube, but now worry swept over him. "What's wrong?"

"Well, I just . . . It's . . . well." Rutger cleared his throat. "It's just that if he could send us this message, why didn't he just wink us out of here?"

"Got plenty of worries without lookin' for fresh ones," Mothball said. "Open the ruddy thing, Sato, and see what the old man has to say."

"How do you do it?" Sato asked. He knew George often sent message tubes like these out before, but Sato had never helped him with them or even seen one up close.

"Just pull the ends apart," Rutger said with an annoyed huff.

"Well, excuse me for not being a message-tube wizard," Sato griped. Shaking his head, he gripped the two rounded ends of the tube and pulled in opposite directions. A seam appeared and expanded until he held two separate pieces. A rolled up piece of paper slipped out and dropped to the floor.

He snatched it up and unrolled it, so eager his hands were shaking. The tightly coiled note sprung closed twice before he finally got it under control enough that he could open it and read its handwritten contents. He'd barely started before Rutger yelled at him to read it out loud.

"Okay," Sato said, surprisingly not annoyed at the interruption. He cleared his throat and started from the beginning. "'Dear Sato. This is Tick. Mistress Jane did something really bad, and every last Reality is going to roll over and die unless we do something about it. You were taken to that place you're in by, well, I can explain all that later. You're safe for now. But a few hours after you get this, you're gonna be winked to the Thirteenth Reality. All of you. I need you to convince everyone there to come help me.'"

Sato paused for a big breath and looked around at his friends, all of whom stared back with wide eyes.

"Keep going!" Rutger snapped.

Sato did. "'There's a place called the Factory. Mothball should know about it. It's where Jane creates her fangen and some new things that are worse. I'll be there in a little bit with Master George, Paul, and Sofia. With any luck, we'll be working with Jane to fix the Realities. Yeah, long story, but we'll need her help. Anyway, once we're done, there's no way Jane will let us go. That's where you guys come in.'"

Sato saw Mothball shake her head back and forth, but he chose to ignore her for now and kept reading. "'The people of the Fifth are known as warriors—even those who don't do it as a profession. Somehow you and Mothball need to organize them and convince them to come rescue us. The Haunce—don't ask—also says there are lots of children we'll need to save while we're at it. Sato, you have to come! Be ready so when the Haunce thinks the time is right, it can wink all of you to the Thirteenth.'"

Mothball was quietly groaning now—almost wailing—but the note only had a few more sentences. Sato finished up quickly. "'I know you have a ton of questions, but there's no way I can explain everything in a stupid note. I hope you can trust me. The Factory, Sato. The Factory. Come and get us. And just so you know it's me: remember how mad you were that I saved you twice? Well, it's payback time. Tick out.'"

Sato stared at those last couple of lines for a few seconds. A trickle of doubt had entered his mind upon first reading the note—anybody could've sent the note. But now he knew it really was Tick. The tone, the phrasing, the reference to their exchange after Sato had been freed from Chu's Dark Infinity device—it was Tick, all right.

Mothball let out a sound like a bear with its foot caught in a trap.

Sato looked at her and saw something awful and afraid in her expression. "What's *wrong* with you?" he asked.

"The Factory," she replied in a whisper. "Master Tick's spot-on when he says I should know all about it. Know far too much, I do. Sorry to be a pussycat, but if that's where we're goin', then I'm a might scared, that's all."

Rutger nodded, his face a full shade paler than it had been before Sato had read the note. "She's right. Our spies in the Thirteenth have told us all about that nightmare place. I can't imagine what Tick's gotten himself into, but if he really is headed for that place of horrors, then we have no choice but to go after him. Just like he asked for. Even though it terrifies me just as much as it does Mothball." He leaned back to look up at his friend, a ball tilting on a pivot. "In fact, I'm pretty sure I've never *seen* you scared before."

"Hogwash," she mumbled back.

Sato hadn't known her nearly as long as Rutger had, but he'd definitely never seen her so afraid—at least nothing even approaching the way she looked now, pallid and sweaty with dead eyes. "Well, what *is* the Factory?" he finally asked. "Why is it so awful?"

"Tell him, Mothball," Rutger said. "Tell him what they told us."

The tall Realitant's eyes flickered down to her friend, then to Sato. She stiffened her body and held her head a little higher, composing herself. "Well, there's the obvious bit Tick mentioned. Factory's full of Jane's hideous creations, guardin' every last inch of it. But that's not the worst part. Not worst by far, the way I reckon it. What chills me bones is to think of what we'll see if we get *inside* the ruddy place. Things unnatural and evil. Things that just might cure us of sleepin' till we drop dead of it."

"Like what?" Sato asked, his curiosity mixed with a chilling fear. "What are they doing in there?"

Mothball pulled her long, gangly arms behind her and clasped her hands as she stared down at her own feet. "They take animals and . . . meld them with other animals, usin' the mutated powers of the Thirteenth's Chi'karda. Meld 'em right together into things you wouldn't dare tell 'round a campfire."

Sato held his breath.

Mothball's head snapped up so she could look him square in the eyes. "But that ain't the whole of it. Learned somethin' brand-new few weeks back, we did.

Somethin' that'll make your heart shrivel and scream."

Sato swallowed. It felt like a dried clump of dirt went down his throat. "What?"

Tears leaked from both of Mothball's eyes. "Kiddies," she said, her voice cracking. "The animals only be tests. She's done captured a bunch of kiddies and plans on usin' 'em soon as she's good and ready."

CHAPTER
35

DARKNESS OF THE WAY

Tick couldn't believe what he'd done. Even after some time to think about it, his mind still couldn't accept it. He sat on the forest floor, absently ripping apart leaves from a nearby bush, surrounded by darkness and cool air.

He'd winked something away. All by himself. After all the strange episodes leading up to that moment—the reappearance of the letter Kayla had burned, winking his group from the Thirteenth back to Master George's head-quarters, the near-catastrophe in the Fourth Reality—he'd finally used Chi'karda on his own terms. He'd controlled it and used its power to wink—a thing the Realitants thought only a Barrier Wand could accomplish.

He'd done it all by himself.

"Told ya you were superhuman," Paul said from behind Tick, startling him.

He needed that jolt because he didn't have time to sit and contemplate. He looked down at his watch and clicked the little light—it'd been at least ten minutes since he sent the message to Sato. At least, he *hoped* he'd sent the message to Sato.

He pushed off the leafy bed of the ground and stood up, turning the flashlight back on as he did so. The others all stood closely together, examining him. Only Paul was smiling.

"What?" Tick asked. "I told you what I was going to do."

"Yeah, you did," Sofia said. "But . . . it was kind of spooky to watch. You're really weird, Tick."

He knew her well enough by now to recognize the compliment. But what did she mean about the spooky part? "Why? What happened? What did it look like when I did it?"

Sofia glanced at Master George—who nodded once, slowly, then at Paul—who let out a little burst of a laugh—then back at Tick. "Little streams of orange light spilled out of your eyes and ears and then swirled around the silver tube until it disappeared. You didn't see that? You were staring straight at the thing like you'd been possessed by forty demons."

Tick felt only a little bit of shock—not so n...
at the orange light but the fact that he hadn't noticed
it. "No, I didn't see it. Maybe I was concentrating too
much. But when Jane pulled the Chi'karda out of me
when we were under Chu's palace, that's what it looked
like. Orange light—kind of like a fog or mist."

"No, well, kind of, I guess," Sofia responded. "It
was more like ribbons of orange, something you'd see
twirling off a cheerleader's baton."

"Interesting that it's orange," Master George said.
"I wonder why we never see Chi'karda manifest itself
that way when we use a Barrier Wand. Something tells
me it's related to the souliken discovery—though I'm
far from understanding everything about that."

Tick's mind started processing what the Realitant
leader had said, thinking it through and analyzing. He'd
spent so much time the last few months studying science
that such thinking had become second nature. But he
forced himself to stop. They had to get moving—they
were already behind schedule!

"Man, what are we doing?" he said through a
groan. "We have to get going. Now. Come on." He
took a step, but then stopped, frowning. "Wait, any of
you guys know which way is east?"

Master George pointed over his right shoulder, but
Paul cut in. "Wait, man. You just did something crazy,
like magical. Shouldn't we talk about it, figure out

...nd all that, so next time you can do it ... even better?"

... tired of saying it, but he repeated himself ... ...'ll have to wait—we need to go. Now. Just tru...

"Fine," Paul said, turning toward the direction Master George had indicated. "But you promised to explain things as we walked. Start talking."

"Okay," Tick said. He shone the flashlight ahead of him, revealing an endless expanse of trees and brush, then walked forward, his every step crunching twigs and leaves. He moved past Master George, and the others followed right behind him. The strain from winking the tube away had worn off, and he felt the chill of the air like a sprinkle of fine mist. Being on the move again would feel good.

They'd gone about fifteen feet or so, and Tick figured now was as good a time to start talking as any. His friends deserved an explanation—even if Tick didn't understand everything himself.

"So, the Haunce is like this big sack of people's memories and personalities and thoughts," Tick said. "It told me that every time we have a significant event in our lives, it leaves an electronic stamp on Reality, and those moments collect and become attached to us. That's what a souliken is. Seems a lot easier to just call it a ghost."

"I think I like *souliken* better," Sofia said. "I'm not a big fan of ghosts."

"Wuss," Paul muttered. "Ow!"

Tick heard the punch on Paul's arm that he'd fully expected.

"Doesn't matter right now," Tick said. "What matters is that the Haunce is a collection of millions and millions of soulikens, and it acts like a guardian of the Realities. Sort of a gatekeeper or a watchman. Whatever. But we gotta trust it."

"Yes, indeed," Master George added, his voice already a little winded as they tramped through the forest. "The Haunce has the Realitants' highest respect— there's no doubt in this matter. What the Haunce says, we should do."

"Okay," Paul said. "So what is it we're gonna do?"

Tick walked around a huge oak then settled back in on the course his instincts marked as east. "Well, ultimately the Haunce, me, and Jane are going to link and use our . . . power"—how he hated using that word!— "to rebind the barriers of the Realities that are falling apart."

"Yeah, ultimately," Paul said, a major hint of doubt in his tone. "But something tells me we're not gonna like hearing what you keep avoiding—what we have to do to *get* to that point."

Tick winced. Paul had hit at the heart of the matter.

"Um, yeah, you're probably right on that one."

Tick felt Paul's hand grab his arm as Paul forced him to stop and turn around.

"What!" Tick shouted way too loudly. But then he remembered what the next stage of the plan was and that being quiet didn't quite play into it. Now that he had to tell them what the Haunce wanted, he was terrified of their reaction. They weren't going to be very happy.

"Come on, dude," Paul said, almost pleading. "Don't make me give the corny speech about how we're all part of a team. Tell us what's going on."

Tick shook Paul's hand off his arm, but then nodded. Paul was right. He had to tell them. "Sorry. Obviously I've been avoiding that part."

Paul folded his arms disapprovingly. "Yeah, obviously."

"Come on, Tick," Sofia said. "Just tell us real quick."

Master George put his hands on his knees to catch his breath, not seeming to care one way or the other.

Tick thought furiously for a second. It hadn't sounded so bad when the Haunce had told him about this part. But then again, they'd been tucked away safely in Tick's home at the time. He decided to just get it over with. "Jane has a new creation—something called a Sleek."

He expected everyone to repeat the word or start

asking questions before he could continue. Instead, they all just stared at him, waiting.

"Once she had the fangen all figured out and perfected, she moved on to other creatures. And from the sound of it, always nasty and terrifying creatures. No big surprise there. But she always works with a purpose. The Sleeks are what she created to guard the Factory. And, um, we're getting really close to the place where they'll be hunting through the woods."

Tick saw fear flash across his friends' faces, and seeing that made him feel even more scared. "The Sleeks sound really, really awful. The whole purpose of their existence is to hunt down anything that's not supposed to be in these forests. They're tall and thin when seen straight on, but most of the time they're impossible to see clearly. They have ten times the strength of a fangen, and they have almost magic abilities using Chi'karda. The Haunce said they're wispy and fast, almost like living smoke mixed with wind. And once they catch sight of you, forget escaping. No way, according to the Haunce. But don't worry—there *is* some good news."

"I'm having quite a hard time seeing the *good* news in any of this," Master George said.

Tick looked at him. "Well, there is. Kind of. The Sleeks aren't allowed to kill what they hunt down. Mistress Jane wants to interrogate any intruders."

"Oh, no," Sofia said. "Don't tell me . . ."

"You've gotta be kidding," Paul added.

Tick was relieved they'd gotten it before he had to say it, but he did so anyway. "You guessed it. The Haunce wants *us* to find *them*. We have to let the Sleeks capture us."

CHAPTER
36

THE SPEECH

Sato sat alone, his heart like a dying filament inside a lightbulb, about to burst and flame out at any second. What Mothball had said—about Jane planning to use human kids for her creations—horrified him like nothing ever had before. He knew a lot of bad things had happened in the history of the world, but this had to top it.

Killing was bad enough, but . . . what was the word Mothball had used? Melding. Jane was melding animals together . . .

He slammed the door on that thought. His mind had already slipped close to an edge overhanging a dark and awful abyss from which he didn't know if he could escape. He needed to keep it together. Hold on to the anger, sure. Let it fester and boil inside him until he had no choice but to go forward in a rage and do what he had to do to stop what the witch was doing. But he couldn't allow himself to sink back into that dark place which had once haunted him every day after seeing his parents murdered, burned alive by Jane herself.

He shook his head, slammed another door in his mind. Looking around, he saw that the people of the Fifth were gathering around him again, though a bit more timidly than before. They must have seen the anguish on his face, enough to scare them a little.

But that look of awe still clung to their expressions, their eyes filled with something he could only describe as hope. Which was good. Ever since reading the note from Tick—and *especially* since Mothball's revelation about the Factory—he'd been heading down a path toward a decision. He didn't even quite know if he consciously controlled this path, but every part of him walked along it.

He was going to do exactly what Tick asked. Somehow.

The tall people of the Fifth inched closer and closer, surrounding him on all sides. Sato craned his neck to look through the scant open spaces to where Lisa and the rest of Tick's family huddled far outside the crowd, still seeming to revel in their reunion and the good news that Tick was alive.

Mothball and Rutger had told them about the note—all of it. Now wasn't the time to hide anything from anybody. Sato knew that the Higginbottoms also had mixed feelings, and more reason than ever to worry over their son. Just another twist of the path Sato traveled. Just another reason to make things happen, no matter what.

"Excuse me, good sir," a soft female voice said close to his ear. Closer than he felt comfortable allowing— he wasn't ready yet!

He looked up, ready to snap at whoever had invaded his space. But it was an old woman, as tall as Mothball and just as gangly, leaning over him like a wind-broken tree. She had a gentle, pretty face, and Sato's anger quickly slipped away.

"I'm sorry," he said. "You all keep asking me the same thing, and I can't answer it any differently. I'm not the guy you think I am." He returned his chin to his fists, his eyes to the floor. How was he going to do this?

"We don't rightly think that anymore," the woman answered. "We're not a bunch of dumb lugs, ya know. But there's somethin' right special about you, there is. And we want to 'ear from ya, that's all. Not too much to be askin', now is it?"

Sato took a long, deep breath. He had to do something, get the ball rolling. Sitting there with all of them gawking like kids at a zoo would drive him crazy if it went on for another minute.

"Fine," he said, sighing as he forced himself to stand. The old woman smiled, her grin revealing that she only had about half her teeth, and those remaining were dark yellow. But still, she had a pretty face, despite its age and wear and tear. Somehow, she was keeping him polite and levelheaded.

"Give us a speech," she whispered to him, still leaning down considerably. "We could all use a bit of uppity-up, no matter the source. You've got the looks of one who can do that right nicely. You do, really." She winked at him then stood straight, a good foot taller than Sato.

Sato looked away from her and around at the crowd. Many had taken a seat—especially the ones closest to him. Those farther back stood, arms folded, staring at him expectantly. There had to be at least three or four hundred people packed all around him. He slowly turned in a circle, taking it all in as he tried to think of something to say. The whole lot of them grew quiet.

You can do this, he thought to himself.

"I know why you guys are so fascinated by me," he said, wondering if he could've possibly started his speech with anything more stupid. He doubted it. "I know I look a lot like the kid who was your ruler until those crazy Bug soldiers assassinated him."

This caused an uproar, people shouting and yelling things all at once, many of them throwing their arms up and shaking their clenched fists in anger.

"Boo to the Bugaboos!"

"Death for the Bugs!"

"Drown the clowns!"

"No rest till the pests' death!"

Sato didn't think it was possible, but he felt even more uncomfortable. He held his hands up, palms out, trying to shush them. Finally, they quieted. And he started talking; where the words came from, he had no idea.

"I'm not the same person as your leader who was killed. It's really hard to explain, but I'm from a different world—one that's a lot like yours but . . . different. Maybe it's not so hard to believe if you just look around at this weird place. But none of that matters. I know why you want me to be your Grand Minister. Everyone wants a leader, someone to look up to. But I don't know if I could ever really be that person."

A surge of complaints started to explode from the crowd, but Sato cut the noise off by swiping his hands back and forth. "Just listen to me! We all need something here, and I think we can help each other."

"What's that then?" the old woman asked, her right eyebrow cocked high. "What can we do for ya, lad?"

Sato was thinking on the fly, caught up in the moment. He was *feeling* it. "I know Mothball. I know her family. I know that the people of your world are fighters. You're warriors. Am I right?"

A hearty shout of cheers rang through the air, fists pumping toward the endless gray sky of nothingness above. A surge of heat and electric energy filled Sato's veins.

"The first thing we have to do is get out of this place. I have a very good friend who's in a lot of trouble, and if he dies, we all might die. I need your help to go after him, to help him, save him. We also need to stop something that a very evil person named Mistress Jane is doing—the sickest, most horrific thing I've ever heard of. We'll give you all the details soon enough—I think we have a little time yet. But if you do this—if you'll help me and . . . fight for me—I'll make a promise to each and every one of you."

Sato paused, scanning the crowd, in awe at how every eye was trained on him. Complete silence settled across the strange place. Even Mothball and Rutger stood rigid, mouths slightly agape, probably wondering who'd possessed Sato's body.

"If you'll go with me," Sato said, the rush of adrenaline inside sounding like an ocean's roar in his ears, "and fight to help my friend and stop Jane, then I promise to go back to your world with you and lead the war against the Bugs. The endgame of all endgames. We won't stop until we wipe them from existence. All of them! We will fight. And I swear, we will win!"

The roar that filled that impossible place made Sato want to take a step backward and cover his ears. He did neither.

He stood tall and yelled right along with the warriors from the Fifth Reality.

CHAPTER
37

SHIVERS

The sounds of the night-darkened forest were starting to get to Tick as he and his friends slowly made their way eastward.

Besides the normal buzz of insects going about their business, a wind had picked up, something that seemed impossible based on how many trees crowded their pathway. Limbs and branches swayed and scratched against each other; leaves rustled; small animals jumped and ran through the bushy ground cover. Eerie mating calls moaned through the air, and every once in a while a catlike thing screamed far in the distance. It all added up to give Tick a major case of the shivers.

He'd tried his best to show a brave face when telling the others about how the Haunce wanted them to be caught by the Sleeks. It had seemed a practical matter—the best way they could get into the Factory and possibly face-to-face with Jane. And the others had reluctantly agreed to the plan after wasting five minutes arguing about it. Master George had proven to be the voice of reason that cut through the obvious hesitancy to do something so scary.

But now, trampling their way through the spooky woods, his flashlight beam stabbing the darkness ahead, getting closer and closer to something that was created by and for evil, Tick felt a different kind of fear than he'd ever experienced before. A thick terror sprinkled his skin with chills and surged in his throat, like a balloon had been shoved down there. With every crick and crash of broken twigs and crushed leaves as his companions and he walked forward, he had to fight the urge to look around, searching for an enemy he knew was coming for him.

Instead he forced himself to look ahead, to keep walking and dodging his way through the tightly packed trees until the attack came. He held on to the fact that they wouldn't have to fight or run this time— they just had to give up and be taken prisoner.

"Tick," came a soft whisper from behind him. Sofia. "Have you seen or heard anything weird yet?"

Tick turned to look at her quickly before facing

forward again, not missing a step. "We don't really need to whisper," he called out, louder than he needed to. "It kind of defeats the purpose of what we're doing. And no, I haven't really noticed anything too weird yet."

"Nothing too weird?" Paul repeated. "Some demon cat is being eaten by Satan out in the woods, screaming its fool head off. I'd call that weird."

Tick had to suppress a snicker, a fleeting break from the fear that had been suffocating him. "It's probably just a deer or something that broke a leg."

"A deer? Never heard anything sound like that on *Bambi*."

Master George spoke up. "My guess would be that we're getting quite close to the area where these guardian creatures roam and hunt. Based on what I've learned from Mothball's, er, reports."

George cleared his throat in an embarrassed sort of way, and Tick's suspicions shot up enough to make him stop walking. He turned to face him. "You just said 'er' and cleared your throat. What aren't you telling us?"

Paul and Sofia stopped as well and faced Master George. Tick held the flashlight so that the beam pointed at the ground, but the glow was enough to show a tight look of worry on the man's face.

"Really should keep walking, don't you think?" he said, trying to smile but somehow making himself look even more uneasy. He feebly pointed toward the direction they were heading.

"What's wrong?" Sofia asked.

"Yeah," Paul added. "You look constipated all of a sudden."

Master George folded his hands together—they'd been twitching slightly at his sides. "Our Realitant spies have recently been providing Mothball with information on the Factory."

"And you didn't say anything?" Sofia shouted. The echo of her voice seemed to hang in the tops of the trees for a full five seconds.

"Calm yourself, goodness gracious me," Master George snapped back, Sofia's outburst having brought back some dignity to his face. "We need to go there no matter what I know, and I was merely waiting for the right time to speak on it. But, if you must hear it now, what I have to say will only make our reasons for going forward even stronger."

"*What?*" Tick asked, not bothering to hide the impatience that came out in his voice.

Master George kicked a bush near his feet. "Oh, how it angers me. This, more than anything she's ever done. Jane is stealing children from towns and cities across the Thirteenth Reality and keeping them in the Factory. We suspect she is planning to use them somehow to create her abominations at the Factory. She's currently using her powers of Chi'karda to deconstruct various animals on a quantum level and put them back together again to serve whatever purposes she's dreamed up with her evil mind. *Horror* is the only word I can think of to describe such a thing."

The Haunce had told Tick about this when discussing the overall plan, but the reality of it hadn't hit until he heard his boss explain it in such stark terms. An emptiness expanded inside Tick, a void that should've been filled with a long list of terrible emotions but instead felt numb.

"She can't be that sick," Paul said. "She can't be."

"I'm afraid our sources are very reliable," Master George said. "I believe what happened to Jane in the Fourth Reality"—he shot a nervous and quick glance at Tick—"has driven her past a point from which I can't imagine anyone could ever return. Her life has been consumed by hatred and evil, encompassed by a delusion that she can still find her Utopian Reality and bring an endless peace to the universe. Bah! She'll have every last one of us dead. The woman's insane, I tell you. Insane!"

Tick had a disturbing thought pop into his head. "Well, I guess if we can't stop the Realities from going kaboom, at least Jane won't be able to steal any more kids."

"Don't let your mind wander down that path," Master George said, stepping closer to Tick. He put a hand on his shoulder. "Instead, let's focus on accomplishing what the Haunce has sent you to do. Once done, we'll stop Jane's madness *and* free the children."

Tick looked at Sofia, then Paul. Both of them had stern faces, made all the harsher by the sharp shadows from the flashlight. "What do you guys think?"

"What do you mean?" Sofia asked, an edge to her voice. "What do you *think* we think?"

"No," Tick said. "I just . . . does this change anything? We knew we had to get in there and convince Jane to help us. After we do what the Haunce wants . . ." He didn't know how to finish. Despite what George had said, every potential pathway that flickered inside Tick's mind seemed to head for disaster.

"Dude," Paul said in his gimme-a-break tone. "This only makes it clearer. Crazy Jane can do all the hokey-pokey stuff she wants, but if she's messing with little kids now . . . we gotta get in there and stop it. Simple as that."

Sofia was breathing as if this latest news had pumped up her adrenaline. "And Sato will come—just like you asked him to in your note. We can do it, Tick. You'll save the universe with your fancy powers, then we'll get the kids out, then we'll burn the whole place to the ground. Let's go!"

She didn't wait for a response but marched off into the dark woods, toward the east. Paul stepped in line right behind her.

Tick looked at Master George. "Guess I'm not in the lead anymore."

"Well, I think they could use your flashlight. Let's go, Atticus. Lots to do."

Tick nodded and started walking, shining his light up ahead so his friends could see. As they made their way forward for the next few minutes, the shadows leaping with every movement and the eerie sounds of the forest haunting the cool air, Tick realized his earlier choking fear had disappeared. It had transformed into impatience, an eagerness, even.

Sofia stopped, holding her hand up to signal them to do the same. Paul almost bumped into her, letting a branch loose as he caught his balance. It hit Tick square in the nose, but Sofia cut off his cry of complaint before it got started.

"Quiet!" she snapped in a harsh whisper, finally lowering her hand as she looked back at them. "Something just . . . whisked across our path. Up ahead."

Ice began to fill Tick's chest again. He stepped to the side so he could shine the light forward without his friends being in the way. He saw gloomy, towering trees and thick bushes and ivy, all the greenness muted and pale. The shadows stretched and retracted as he swept the area, but nothing out of the ordinary came into view.

"Hear the silence?" Master George whispered from

behind Tick, startling him. His voice seemed louder than it should have, and Tick realized why. All those creepy sounds they'd been hearing earlier had cut off. Completely. The sudden quiet reminded Tick of being outside after a heavy snowstorm back home—all sound sucked in by the cold, white stuff.

Tick caught a glimpse of something flashing toward him from the right—a wispy trail of fog that he barely saw. He imagined he could see the faint image of a head and a long body, an outreaching hand, when sharp tingles pricked the skin along his forearm, making him suck in a breath.

There was a popping sound, and then the flashlight went out.

CHAPTER
38

SMOKY EMBRACE

The needle pricks vanished. Tick instinctively held up the flashlight to take a look, but the darkness was too complete; black engulfed everything. He flicked the switch back and forth. Nothing. Then he shook it.

Shards of loose glass tinkled together and fell to the ground. The lightbulb hadn't burned out; something had smashed it, making it useless.

"Tick, dude, what happened?" Paul whispered, though it sounded like anyone within a hundred miles could've heard him.

"I don't know." Tick looked around but couldn't see a thing. He remembered the ghostly image of what he'd seen from out of the corner of his eye. Those long, smoky fingers of fog reaching out . . .

Leaves crunched a couple of times where Sofia had been standing.

"Sofia!" Tick shouted, a boom in the silence that echoed off the tree branches.

"I'm fine," she whispered back harshly. "Sheesh. I'm just feeling my way toward you." Another couple of steps, more twigs breaking. "I heard glass break—how did you smash your flashlight?"

Tick could see the shadow of her figure right in front of him now. He reached out and found her shoulder. "Okay. So, I was standing there, and then I saw something to the right. Something like a trail of fog. But it was kind of shaped like a . . . like a stretched-out human with really long arms and fingers. Then it felt like a hundred needles stabbed my arm, and something popped, and the light went out. It's broken."

"Wait a second," Paul said as he also took a couple of tentative steps toward Tick and Sofia. "What did you see again?"

"I guess it must've been a Sleek. Kind of smoky and long, looked human-like. What do you think, Master George?"

Silence answered him. Chills swept over Tick. He looked in the direction where he'd last heard George's voice. His eyes were already adjusting to the darkness, but he saw nothing except the tall, dark shadows of trees and more trees.

"Master George!" he called out, wincing at the loudness of his voice. Again, no answer.

"Those creepy things took him," Paul said in a fierce whisper. "And we're next!"

Sofia shushed him then spoke in a quiet voice. "That's what we *want* to happen, remember? We just have to—"

A twig snapped to Tick's right, silencing Sofia. A few leaves rustled in the same spot. The swell of chilling panic crept up Tick's chest as he looked in that direction, straining his eyes to see.

Something stood there, a dozen or so feet away, its shadow splitting the space between two huge, towering trees. Thin but man-shaped, the thing had to be as tall as a basketball standard. The edges of the shadowy figure wavered like a reflection on water, ripples of darkness running up and down. The slightest glint of silver shone where its eyes would be, and something about the light—maybe the hue, maybe the angle—made the creature look very angry.

"Who—" Tick's voice caught in his throat. "Who are you? Are you a Sleek?"

The thing's silver eyes flared brighter for just a moment, but it was long enough to reveal more of its features. Streamers of dark smoke were packed tight and swirling through and across each other, compressed together to form the tall body that stood before them. Tick thought they looked almost like worms being held back by some invisible force until they could be unleashed to seek out food.

But the face was different. It didn't seem to be made of the smoky substance. It looked . . . human. Real skin, though misshapen and scarred. Every cell in Tick's brain screamed at him to run.

The light of the creature's eyes dulled again, throwing the tall figure back into shadow.

"Ask it again," Paul whispered.

Tick didn't know if he could bring himself to speak. Sofia saved him.

"What are you waiting for?" she yelled. "We know you're a Sleek, so get it over with! Quit standing there all spooky, you haunted-house wannabe!"

Tick looked over at her, wishing he could see her face. Sometimes her bravery completely stunned him.

A noise from the creature pulled Tick's attention away from Sofia. A whispery, raspy sound. Harsh and guttural. It continued on for several seconds, but if the thing was trying to communicate, Tick didn't understand a word of it. The metallic glow of those silver eyes seemed pinpointed on him.

The Sleek quit talking, leaving them all in an eerie stillness. The sounds of the forest remained silent, as

if every living creature had long since run away. Then everything changed in an instant.

A wind swept through the woods, sudden and violent. A torrent ripped at the trees, sending leaves shooting through the air like flaky bullets. Tick threw his arms up to protect his face, catching a glimpse of the Sleek's silver eyes flaring again before they disappeared altogether. Darkness took over, leaving the world black and consumed by the rushing sound of wind.

Sofia screamed, the screech of it barely begun before it whisked away into the distance, fading and gone. Something had taken her. Paul yelled several terror-filled words, but Tick only caught his name. Then a scream even higher-pitched than Sofia's rang out, followed by a thump and the crack of a broken tree branch. The sounds of a body being dragged quickly across the forest floor were soon swallowed by the overpowering wind.

Sofia—gone. Paul—gone. Master George—gone.

Leaves and small twigs pelted Tick's body. The howling wind ripped at his clothes and hair. He risked a peek, lowering the arm he held tightly across his upper face, but he saw only darkness in front of him. Flecks of debris hit him in the eyes, making him squeeze them shut. He rubbed at them with his other hand, then opened up again.

He let out a cry of terror when he saw two silver

lights right in front of him, looking out of a hideous, mangled face. With a swirl of black smoke, the Sleek grabbed him by both ankles and squeezed them like a metal rope cinched tight enough to break skin and crush bones. His feet flew out from under him as the Sleek pulled. Tick's back crashed to the ground. Then his whole body jerked forward, dragged across the rough forest floor.

Master George knew what was happening the instant the tingle first sprinkled across the back of his neck. Someone at headquarters had finally locked on to his nanolocator and was winking him back to the Bermuda Triangle station. Sally, probably, having likely broken a hundred things in the process before finally figuring out how to do it.

And Master George knew what he had to do.

As soon as the dark forest vanished, replaced by the inner workings of his cramped Control Room with its bright monitors and blinking instruments and metal piping, he threw his hands up and started shouting.

"Don't wink the others! Don't wink the others! Don't wink back Atticus or the rest of them!"

Big Sally—dressed in his usual plaid shirt and overalls—stood at the main computer, a Barrier Wand clasped in his huge hands. The look on his perplexed face was almost comical, and somewhat pitiful as well.

"I's waitin' on that brain a'yorn to figger it out any-hoo," the burly man said. "'Bout chicken-fried my nog-gin gettin' you here as it was!"

Master George finally felt a bit of calm. "Excellent work, Sally, excellent work! We mustn't wink the others back quite yet—they have a very important task to accomplish first. But we need to get to work straight-away." He walked past Sally and headed toward the door.

"What's on that mind a'yorn?" Sally asked as he set the Wand down and followed George.

Master George reached the door and entered the hallway. "We've got things to collect before we move out. As many weapons as possible . . . and nanolocator patches—we'll probably need hundreds of patches. We must hurry!"

"Where you reckon we're goin', then?"

"We're going to meet up with Sato at a place called the Factory. We have to rescue Sofia, Paul, and Atticus." Master George turned to face Sally. "Not to mention a lot of children."

CHAPTER
39

THE SURGE

The wind in the forest stopped suddenly, cut off like a giant door slamming shut. Tick could hear the scrape of his body against the leaves and scattered debris underneath him. Things poked and scratched. His shirt ran up to his shoulders, leaving his skin exposed and vulnerable. Pain lit through him. The Sleek's grip didn't loosen; if anything, it tightened as it pulled Tick along.

He tried to look at it, but saw nothing except the occasional glimmer of silver light reflecting off tree trunks. He tried to pull himself up, crunching his abs as he reached for his legs, his ankles, but the speed and roughness of the way was too much. He fell back, his head slamming against a fallen log just as he popped over it.

Scratches and scrapes, bumps and bruises. Tick felt the warmth of blood trickling in his hair, wetting his entire back. The sounds of crunching leaves and snapping twigs as his body was dragged across them filled his ears. Darkness surrounded him.

His instincts had him reaching for Chi'karda before his mind formed the thought. Wrapping his arms tightly around his body, he rolled to his side, trying to give his back a break and let his shoulder take some of the abuse. Then he forced himself to close his eyes, searching and probing for the heat of the power within him.

There. A spark.

He reached for it with mental hands and grabbed it, squeezed it, embraced it. Quicker than ever before, the Chi'karda burst through him, filling his body with a raging burn. It pulsed and throbbed. Tick felt like it was about to explode out of him, devouring first his flesh and then the forest in flames. Tick heard the woods around him shake, heard the same odd bee-buzz sound from months ago when he'd unwittingly unleashed his power in fear, wreaking havoc with molecular structures, melding trees and other things together. The same had happened in Chu's mountain building.

Tick knew he was losing control.

He screamed and opened his eyes.

The first thing he noticed was that he'd stopped

moving. An orange cloud of sparkling mist surrounded him, illuminating the forest. The Sleek had released his ankles and stood several feet away, its silver eyes wide and bright, maybe out of shock. Tick could see the thing's body clearly now—the seething tendrils of black smoke that coiled and wrapped together to form the elongated body, the hacked-up face, the wispy trails of its fingers.

Tick was trembling, his hands balled into fists. He didn't feel pain anymore, only the surge of Chi'karda threatening to scorch him and everything around him. His jaw clenched as if it had locked closed forever. He wanted to kill the Sleek. Chase down the others and kill them. Rescue his friends. Run away. He almost boiled with the desire.

With a scream of rage, he jumped up and pounced on the Sleek, grabbing it by the neck just as it tried to break apart and whisk away. Tick slammed the creature against the closest tree, knowing he shouldn't be able to do this, knowing that he was somehow using the Chi'karda to make the Sleek maintain its structure and solidity. The thin neck of coiled smoke felt like shifting sands under his fingers, churning and slipping but staying in one place.

Tick squeezed, feeling the neck crackle, as if it *were* sand and hardening to glass. That creepy, cackling whisper of a voice escaped the Sleek's mouth, saying things Tick couldn't understand. But it seemed desperate and terrified, the sound of it chilling.

The buzzing sound intensified above them. Chi'karda blazed inside Tick. The orange mist swirled around him like a tornado of fire. A wind picked up, seeming to blow from all directions at once, though it did nothing to the cloud of Chi'karda. Tick felt as if the entire world were about to melt into a pool of lava.

He squeezed the Sleek's neck even harder.

Something tried to click inside Tick's brain. Tried to tell him that he'd forgotten the whole point of what he'd come here for. That in the pain and terror of being dragged through the forest, he'd let his anger take over. That he'd lost it, completely lost it.

And yet . . . he was controlling the Chi'karda more than ever before. He was controlling it! Kind of . . .

"Tick!"

A voice. A girl. From somewhere to his right. He barely heard it. He didn't want to look, didn't have time to look. The Sleek was almost dead, and then he could go after the others. Maybe he could experiment with Chi'karda, see what he could do with it. Strike out with it somehow? Maybe shoot beams of fiery lasers? Yeah, that'd be awesome.

"Tick!"

The voice was too loud to ignore this time, despite the ripping wind and blazing heat inside him, the buzz of things disintegrating and re-forming above him. He knew he was doing things to the trees again, but he didn't care.

"Tick!"

He snapped out of his delirious daze and looked over to see Sofia standing close to him. The smoky tendrils of a Sleek's fingers were wrapped around *her* neck. Paul was next to her, also in the custody of a Sleek. The orange glow of Tick's power made the Sleek's silvery eyes look angry and red.

"Tick!" Sofia shouted. "You can't do this! Remember why we're here in the first place!"

Tick didn't quite feel like himself. He'd let the burning power of the Chi'karda consume him and take over his bad parts—the anger, the temper, the thirst for revenge—and part of him had liked it. "You're just saying that!" he yelled over the noise of the wind and the buzzing. "You don't want them to kill you, so you're trying to stop me! Well, *I* can stop *them!* Look at this!"

He let go of the Sleek and took a step back, gesturing with his arms like a magician. The orange cloud swirled around him and through his fingertips, around his arms and legs, curling, almost caressing. Fire raged inside him. He turned, pointing at the wooden formations surrounding them. Dozens of trees had been blown apart on a quantum level and put back together again like a series of haunting sculptures crafted by a lunatic.

Tick couldn't believe it. He was close to understanding how it all worked, close to *really* being able to control it. So close. And he had no idea how—it was just . . . instinct.

He turned back to face Sofia and Paul, their necks still ensnared by the cuffs of smoky fingers. "I know I'm a little bit weird right now," he said. "But check it out. If I can really do this—"

"Dude, you gotta save it," Paul said. "You're freakin' me out here, man. You've got the crazy eyes."

Sofia tried to step forward, but the Sleek yanked her back. She let out a choking cough then said, "Tick, he's right. Something's wrong—on a lot of levels. Just let it go and stick to the plan. Let the Sleeks take us to Mistress Jane. Okay, Tick?"

Tick dropped his eyes and held out his hands to look at the glowing orange mist of Chi'karda swirling around his arms and through his fingers. Hunger burned within him almost as strong as the power itself, a fierce desire to wreak havoc on Jane and the rest of his enemies. But somewhere in the nooks and crannies of his mind, he realized that something wasn't right about the way he felt. Something on the cusp of evil.

"Okay," he said, barely a whisper. Then louder, "Okay."

He closed his eyes and imagined the cloud of sparkles retracting, absorbing back into his body. He pulled it all inside, then let it go, releasing it to whatever place it lay dormant in the quantum realm, where it would wait for him to snatch it up again. When a refreshing coolness rushed through his body and filled the void left by the Chi'karda, he had the thought that he'd just extinguished himself.

He opened his eyes and noticed the stark silence and darkness of the forest. Sofia, Paul, and their spooky captors remained still, staring at him. He could just see the two sets of wide eyes and four pinpoints of silver.

"All right," he said, amazed at how incredibly thirsty he was. "We'll go with the Sleeks, nice and easy. But this time we're walking. Don't make me mad again."

CHAPTER
40

FRAZIER'S GOOD NEWS

Mistress Jane wasn't happy. Everything had gone horribly wrong today, and the only thing that could make her feel better was for someone to pay the consequences. Anyone. Whether or not they were actually at fault for the debacle was a minor point she didn't care too much about at the moment.

She sat at the window of her room in the Lemon Fortress, looking out at a land covered in night, no moon to break up the darkness. The earthquakes and shattering lightning storms had finally stopped, though the damage they'd caused would take months to repair and rebuild. It was a miracle the castle still stood at all. She wondered if it was foolish to be up here. Who knew what had happened to the foundations and inner structure—the whole thing could collapse at any moment.

Her foul, foul mood darkened to black.

What had gone wrong? After months of preparation, the tireless, tedious work required to retrieve and alter the dark matter into the form she needed, the time to find and secure every single one of her Alterants in the major Reality branches—after all the planning and sacrificing and risking . . .

It had all gone wrong in an instant. The Blade of Shattered Hope had failed her.

That was the worst part. The second worst part was the fact that she didn't really know *why* it had failed. The Higginbottom boy had done something—she knew that much. But her instincts told her that his meddling alone had not caused the catastrophic change in direction. His trickle of Chi'karda had not ruptured the connection of the Blade, causing its apocalyptic damage to explode from its course and spread throughout each and every Reality and the barriers between.

No, it wasn't just him. She'd . . . missed something, done something wrong.

There—she'd admitted it to herself. But it didn't make her feel any better. It made her feel worse. Angrier.

Maybe, just maybe, the Blade could've overcome this fault if the addition of Higginbottom's usage of power had not occurred. Yes, maybe.

And that was enough for her. She had a focal point on which to exact her vengeance. Not that she really needed anything to make her hate the boy any more than she already did, but still, it helped.

The knock she'd been expecting finally rapped at her door.

"Come in!" she yelled.

She heard a thump then a small scrape. The big door was stuck because of the shifting of stones from the earthquake. With barely a thought, Jane dissolved the wood particles into the air to allow Frazier to enter the room. Once he was inside, she put the door back together again.

"I have news," her most faithful servant said.

A fire roared in the brick hearth, a luxury Jane loved even as the coolness of winter faded into spring. She pulled a few sparks out with her power and lit the huge candles scattered throughout the room. The glow showed an eagerness on Frazier's face that lifted her hopes.

"Have a seat and tell me what you've learned." She pointed to the chair across from her. "I don't have to tell you how . . . disappointing further bad news would be at the moment." She let the expression on her mask turn to anger for a second before bringing it back to smooth calmness.

Frazier nodded, the barest hint of a smile flashing across his face as he walked over and sat down on the edge of the chair next to her. "I think you'll like what I have to say."

"Then get on with it."

"Yes, Mistress." He leaned forward, his elbows on knees, hands clasped. "Over the last few hours, we've sent people to all the Realities to gather as much data as possible. We, um, had to send out quite a few, because they kept dying in all the chaos. More than half, actually."

Jane's first instinct was to snap at Frazier for wasting time about such an unimportant detail, but she kept her cool. "Yes, a worthy sacrifice, I'm sure. Whatever it took to learn what we needed."

"Yes. Yes, of course. Anyway, the devastation we saw here was universal. Massive earthquakes, catastrophic storms, tornadoes, you name it—it all happened in each and every Reality. Lasted for a good hour or two. Killed, um, millions of people." His eyes flickered to the floor at this last part.

"Feel no shame, Frazier. Remember, we knew there would be collateral damage in our mission for Utopia. For Chi'karda's sake, if the Blade had worked today like it was supposed to, six *billion* people would've died! What's a few million? Keep your focus! We don't have time to mourn the losses along the way." In truth, she felt a constant, choking swell of guilt, but had learned to accept it and live with it.

Frazier composed himself and continued his report.

"We know the destruction was widespread throughout all the Realities. But it seems to have stopped, everywhere. Maybe we've avoided the complete meltdown you feared."

"'Meltdown'?" Jane repeated. "That seems too sweet a word. What worried me was that we'd set off a chain reaction that would wipe us all from existence. I still sense something wrong in the air, in the Chi'karda, like a bubble that's about to burst. Don't be too confident that we're in the clear just yet."

"At least it's calmed down for now. That first hour or so, I was ready to accept my fate and make my peace. I don't know—I feel like we're good now. I think we're going to be okay."

Jane scoffed at him. "You trust your instincts over mine? Not a smart way to go about things, Frazier. What you're feeling is just the natural relief after a close call. We are not safe yet—trust me on that. If you're going to be my right-hand man, I need you to stay pragmatic and sharp and not fall for whimsical feelings of comfort and safety." How she hated being mean to this man, but she could never restrain herself.

"I understand, Mistress. And I promise we haven't let down our guard in the least. Our people are winking back and forth, constantly giving updates. If anything bad starts up again, we'll know right away."

"Good. What else? I have a feeling that smile you

couldn't keep off your face walking in here wasn't for this alone."

Frazier grinned enough to show his teeth. "Observant as usual. You always know—"

"Get on with it."

"Yeah, sorry. Um, well, I think I have some news for you that none of us could've expected this soon."

Frazier paused, staring into the eyeholes of her mask like a lover. His confidence and courage shocked Jane. Surprisingly, it didn't anger her, only made her more eager to hear what he had to say.

"Word has come from the Sleeks guarding the forest at the Factory. They've captured three Realitants. They're not quite to the Factory yet, but one of the Sleeks rushed to get the news to us. The prisoners will be locked up and ready for you to interrogate by the time you arrive, I'm sure."

Jane felt a pleasant tingle wash across the severely damaged skin of her entire body—something she hadn't experienced since the Dark Infinity incident. She didn't know she still had the capability for such things—for pleasure.

Almost forgetting herself, she leaned forward like an eager schoolgirl wanting to hear about a boy she liked. "I know what you're going to say next. I know who they've captured, or you wouldn't be so excited. Tell me I'm right, Frazier."

He laughed, surprising her again. "You are. Higgin-bottom and two of his friends. We got 'em."

Jane leaned back in her chair, then realized her mask had transformed into a giant smile. She quickly erased it, but that's how she felt. When Atticus had disappeared back at the Blade tree, she'd had a thousand troubling thoughts flash through her mind. The worst one was that the Haunce had gotten involved, and if that had been the case, very bad things could have happened. But there had to be another explanation if the Sleeks had captured the boy again so soon, so easily.

So . . . easily.

Her brief elation vanished. "Frazier, why in the world would those people come to the Factory? Why come to the Thirteenth Reality at all? Something's wrong here."

Frazier's face so quickly melted into distraught panic that Jane felt sorry for him. "I . . . don't know, Mistress. I . . . but . . . if we have them, does it matter? We caught them. Whatever they were trying to do, we stopped them!"

Jane stood up. "It's too easy, too simple. Tell the Sleeks to guard them with every creature they can spare. I want every weapon on the grounds gathered—send more if necessary. Search the entire area. Something is wrong!" She pulled up the hem of her robe and started marching toward the door.

"What . . . where are you going?" Frazier called from behind her.

She swiveled sharply to look at him, her mask full of rage. "No more chances, no more mistakes. The boy must die—he's too dangerous! We'll have to be careful so as not to accidentally ignite the powers inside him. But I'm going to kill him till he's dead, dead, dead!"

She felt a trickle of insanity—and relished it.

CHAPTER
41

AN INTERESTING GATE

Tick's display of power must've made an impression on the tall, wispy Sleeks. They didn't make a sound as they moved through the forest, and they had even let go of their prisoners' necks, letting them walk freely as long as they stayed on course. And they came nowhere near Tick himself.

Dawn had finally hit the world, making everything in the forest look dull purple. While the extra light made the journey easier, it also reminded Tick of how long it had been since he'd last slept, and exhaustion weighed on him like soggy clothing. He knew they must be close to the Factory. He couldn't help but hope that once they got there, they'd throw them in a prison cell where he could get at least a little rest before Jane showed up and they had to do their magic tricks to save the universe.

He'd tried twice to speak to Paul or Sofia, but neither of them would respond, flickering their eyes at the Sleeks as if scared of the consequences. Tick guessed he could understand their hesitation, but he felt no fear of the creatures anymore. It was odd—their creepy look alone should've made him shudder with chills every time he looked at them, but his episode earlier with the surge of Chi'karda had pumped him full of confidence.

Those things weren't going to mess with him again. Right that second, he thought nothing in the world would ever mess with him again. His rational side tried to tell him that he was being stupid, but he pushed it away, wanting to enjoy this feeling of invincibility for a little while longer.

The air around them brightened suddenly, a combination of the trees thinning out and the sun rising higher by the second. Tick looked up and saw the sky for the first time in a while. A flat layer of bumpy clouds panned across most of it, the eastern edge outlined in fiery orange. Something smelled really awful, growing more pungent as he thought about it. He was pretty sure he'd never been around a rotting animal before, but for some reason that's exactly what the odor made him think of.

He shot a glance at Paul, wrinkling up his nose.

Paul returned the sour face, then waved his hand back and forth in front of his nose.

Tick returned his attention to the path ahead of him. The Sleeks refused to walk in front of him, instead pointing every once in a while with a rasping, hoarse croak. Tick just loved it—the things were scared of him. Scared of *him!*

Shut up, Tick, he told himself. *Something's wrong with you.*

He knew he didn't have time to worry about it, but he felt like he'd ingested rotten milk into his system. There was a taint of . . . evil coursing through his veins. Maybe using Chi'karda—and letting it consume him and take over his emotions, his anger—had a price to it.

He shook it off. Things were changing up ahead.

They stepped past a last bunch of trees into a wide open, muddy space, void of any vegetation. A hundred yards or so away stood a tall, jagged wall of lumber, the thick pieces thrown together as if by accident. The wall ran in both directions for at least a mile before curving out of sight. The only break was a large gate made of twenty or thirty black iron bars, the upper tips ending in spikes. Heads of fangen and other monsters had been impaled on each and every spike.

Tick shuddered. Weren't fangen and other creatures *created* here? Then it hit him. Just as you might see several auto models displayed in front of a car factory, so were the products being shown off here.

Tick continued walking without missing a beat, each footstep squishing in the mud, his eyes fixed on the heads on the gate. He wanted to remember them for later, for when he would need something to give him incentive to stop what was going on here. Everything about the Factory disgusted him, and for just a second, he felt a flare of Chi'karda ignite inside him. He put it down and kept moving.

He didn't break his gaze until they'd crossed about half the open area. He wanted to see what the Sleeks looked like in full light. They still walked right behind Paul and Sofia, their tightly wound coils of smoke looking blacker than ever. Their bodies were impossibly long and drawn out, little puffs of dark fog bleeding off them with every step. They wore no clothes and looked like nothing but a ragtag doll made of old, dirty rope. Their silver eyes were the only things that broke the monotony; they flared just as brightly during the daytime as they had in the night.

Tick caught Sofia's eyes, then Paul's, silently telling them that this was it, things were about to get interesting. As he swiveled his head back toward the approaching gate, he wondered about the Sleeks. What were they? Had they been created here in the Factory? Mistress Jane had used her powers to set this all up. Was it something

Tick could learn if he wanted to? Surprisingly, the question intrigued him and, for the briefest of moments, excited him. The thought chilled his heart.

Yeah, something's wrong with me, he thought. He caught a powerful whiff of something totally foul, making words like *rotten* and *decay* pop into his head. Pinching his nose shut with two fingers, he took the last few steps until they were standing just in front of the looming iron gate. Oddly, the only thing he could see through the bars of the gate was a grove of trees.

"All right, Sleeks," he said. "What now?"

One of the smoky creatures walked ahead of him, seeming to float along, then clasped its smoky fingers into fists and leaned forward as it screeched out a breathy series of harsh words, completely indecipherable.

"That guy needs a cough drop somethin' awful," Paul said, the first time he'd spoken in a good hour or two.

"How do we know Jane will come here to see us?" Sofia asked. "For all we know, she could just tell them to kill us and be done with it."

Tick winced at the thought, but he had confidence that wouldn't happen. "She'll want to know what I did to ruin her black tree thing. That, or she'll want to rub it in our faces before she slaughters us herself. She'll come, don't worry."

The Sleek moved to stand with its companion behind Tick and his friends. Tick turned his attention to the gate, feeling each breath draw in and out as he anxiously waited for the thing to swing open.

A low rumbling noise seemed to come from everywhere at once, like the sound of cranked-up machinery. The ground vibrated, then intensified to an outright shake, making Tick's feet almost bounce in the mud. He warily took a step backward, then a few more. Paul and Sofia did the same until they were about twenty feet from the iron bars. The gate remained closed. The sound of thrumming machinery grew louder.

"Seems like a lot of work just to open a stupid gate!" Paul yelled.

Tick nodded but didn't respond, his gaze riveted ahead, the anticipation making him feel waterlogged in his chest. His concentration was so focused on the gate itself that he didn't notice what was happening at their feet until Sofia shouted for them to look down.

A huge section of the muddy ground was shifting, the front edge right in front of the gate lowering, tilting on a fulcrum in the middle of the section. Tick and his companions rose as the other end sank like a giant seesaw. The angle steepened at an alarming rate, approaching forty-five degrees before anyone could react.

"Get—" Tick began, but couldn't finish, his feet slipping out from under him.

He fell on his butt and scrambled to hold on to

something, but his fingers found only wet, slippery mud. He looked up, frantic, and saw a big chunk of black smoke heading for his face. It hit him like a hard shot from a firm pillow, and then he was sliding toward the gaping hole that had opened at the foot of the gate.

He slipped through the slimy sludge, Paul and Sofia right next to him. Down, down, until they reached the edge and plummeted into dark, empty air.

CHAPTER
42

STRIPS OF FIRE

The fall lasted only ten feet or so, but it was the longest and worst second of Tick's life—a terrifying second when he felt like he'd either drop forever or be smashed to a bloody pulp far below. He barely had time to curl into a protective ball before he slammed into a dirt-packed floor. He felt the wind knock out of him and heard the grunts of his two friends. He only peripherally noticed the section of ground above them slam shut with a metallic clang, leaving them in complete darkness.

Groaning, he rolled over onto his side, knowing he'd been lucky to avoid a broken bone or worse—even though at the moment, his whole body hurt.

"You guys okay?" he called out.

"Fine," Sofia answered.

A few seconds passed, then Paul said, "I think I broke my spleen."

"What?" Tick forgot his aches and pains and sat up.

"I'm kidding, dude. I'm fine. I don't even know what a spleen is. Does *anybody* know what a spleen is?"

Tick spoke before he knew what he was saying. "It's a highly vascular lymphoid organ between your stomach and diaphragm." He paused. "Sorry. Been reading a lot of science books lately."

"I already knew that," Sofia said.

"Yeah," Paul replied. "I'm sure you did, Miss Italy. What do you think happened to Master George?"

Tick got to his feet, the jarring pain of the fall starting to fade for the most part. "He's probably being held somewhere else. This can't be the place they want to keep us. Why would they have a prison cell right below the gate?" He held his hands out, trying to feel for anything in the darkness.

"I bet it's a trap," Sofia said. "Ya know, for people who come here who aren't supposed to. Like us. Makes sense to have it below the spot they'd most likely come to if they wanted in."

Paul must've been exploring, too, because he bumped into Tick. "Oops, sorry." He patted Tick on the shoulder then walked in a different direction. "I don't know, Sofia. Maybe it's just a marker or something, and the way you actually get into the Factory is to come down here."

Before Tick could say anything, a loud clang filled the air, and a source of faint light made him look to his left. A huge door had swung open, and a dark figure stood in the widening crack, mostly in shadow because the glowing, orange light source was behind him. Or her. Or it. Tick couldn't quite tell yet.

The door opened all the way until it came to rest flush against the wall, their visitor standing alone in the doorframe. Something was odd about the thing, and when the light behind it flared brighter, as if someone had stoked a fire, Tick got a good look for the first time.

It was man-sized and man-shaped, but any other comparison to a human being ended there. The creature had no eyes, no nose, no mouth, no ears. Its arms were stumps without hands. Winding strips of what looked like thick cotton covered every inch of the thing's body, protruding from the skin, moving and swaying back and forth like flags in the wind. Each strip was about a foot long, and they shot out from the body as if charged with static electricity.

"What . . . who . . ." Sofia began but didn't finish.

Tick and Paul remained silent.

The creature turned its head, looking without eyes at each of them in turn, its odd strips whipping the air like they were trying to escape and fly away.

A rush of chills ran along Tick's arms and shoulders.

A female voice came from somewhere down the tunnel, echoing and bouncing its way to them like scurrying bats. The voice was strong, but whispery. Scratchy. Creepy. It said only two words.

"Firekelt, burn."

In that instant, Tick remembered the water monsters that had tried to kill his mom and dad. Jane had called them *waterkelts*. *Kelts* must be some term she used for her new creations. And if this one was a *firekelt*—

Bright, flaring light cut off Tick's thought.

Each strip of cloth on the creature's body from head to toe ignited into searing hot fire, like a thousand old-fashioned wicks soaked in oil. Flames licked out in every direction, the blazing ribbons whooshing and spitting and hissing so that the monster looked like Medusa with fiery snakes.

Intense heat radiated from the firekelt and washed over Tick in waves as he backed away, Sofia and Paul right by his side. Sweat beaded on Tick's forehead, dripping into his eyes.

The creature took one step toward them, sudden and quick. Then another. The strips continued licking at the air like tiny solar flares, raging with fire but not burning up in the least.

"What do we do?" Tick shouted.

"Got a bucket of water on ya?" Paul responded.

"It won't hurt you," said a voice from behind the flaming monster, that same scratchy voice that had instructed it to burn in the first place. Tick guessed it was Mistress Jane, and when she spoke again, he had no doubt. "Firekelt, extinguish."

A great swooshing rush of air swept through the door and swirled inside the big room. It intensified, seeming to come from all directions at once and gusting back and forth like a hurricane. Tick instinctively reached out and grabbed Paul for support, feeling as if he were about to be swept off his feet. Sofia joined them, and they huddled together in a strange group hug.

The wind tore at the firekelt, whipping its flames toward Tick and the others. The odd wicks flapped tightly, parallel to each other as they tried to tear loose from the body of the creature. The fires flared brighter at first, but then flickered and sputtered under the enormous pressure of the windstorm. Each flame traveled down the course of the strips until they reached the ends, holding on for dear life. The creature waved its arms in frustration, helpless. Then the final small blazes winked out, throwing the room back into relative darkness.

The wind stopped without warning. The sudden silence that descended almost popped Tick's ears. Hesitant, he let go of his friends. He looked at the firekelt, mostly in shadow again because of the faint orange light still coming from behind it.

The creature stood tall, defiant. Each flameless wick began to move about again as if a slight breeze still remained.

Mistress Jane spoke again, her raspy voice making Tick want to cough and clear his own throat. "The firekelts are mostly used for lighting purposes only. You'll have to pardon my desire to show them off—I'm quite proud of my creations. Now, feel no alarm when it lights up again. Firekelt, burn."

Sparse flames ignited on the tips of the wicks then worked themselves brighter and brighter, consuming the cloth-like tentacles for several seconds until they were fully on fire again. The light seemed even brighter this time; Tick finally had to look away, splotches of afterglow in his vision.

From the corner of his eye, he saw the firekelt turn away and walk out of the room, taking most of the light with it. Then the robed and hooded figure of Mistress Jane replaced the creature, standing in the doorway, the front of her completely in shadow. She clasped a tall staff made of wood in her heavily scarred right hand.

"Welcome to the Factory," she said, as sincerely as a tour guide. "I'm sorry our last meeting didn't go so well. I promise things are going to be different this time. Yes, things are going to be very, very different."

CHAPTER
43

THE FIFTH ARMY

Sato had finally asked all the people from Mothball's Reality to sit down, cross-legged, so he could actually see them as he spoke. Even then, the tops of their heads came to the middle of his chest, which made it all the more absurd that he was suddenly their leader. But there they were, rows of soldiers sitting on the checkered marble-like stone of this bizarre place, all eyes upon him.

After a long break, he'd reassembled the group. He had no clue how long it'd be before Tick—or whoever—winked them away. Or even if it was really going to happen.

No, he believed it. Tick's voice had been alive in that note, as had the urgency he felt. Something big was about to happen, and Sato had to get these people ready to help with it.

"You gonna stand there all day or talk to us?" said Rutger, sitting in the front row, just a few feet from Sato.

"Hold on! I'm thinking. If you wanna get up here and lead this army yourself, then do it!"

Instead of being taken aback, Rutger nodded, as if in approval. As if he were proud of his own son standing up here. This annoyed Sato greatly.

Next to Rutger were the Higginbottoms—Mom and Dad, Lisa and Kayla—the four of them having not separated an inch since being reunited. Of all the things that worried Sato about what was coming up, Tick's family was Number One. They obviously couldn't fight—not with Kayla to care for. They protested, of course, when Sato had pointed that out earlier, but even then it was halfhearted. Their first priority had to be keeping Kayla safe, and going off to battle wasn't the best way to do that. But Sato didn't know what else to do with them.

He realized he was staring at the family; Mr. Higginbottom tentatively waved at him. Sato shook his head slightly and tried to save himself by smiling. *Okay,* he thought, *I have to get on with this.*

He returned his attention to the waiting rows of Fifths. "I guess it's time for my big motivational speech. We could be winked away from here at any second to the Thirteenth Reality, where very dangerous stuff is going to happen. I hope you're all a little more aware of things like winking and other worlds by now—I know Mothball and her family have been around talking to you all about it. Well, none of that matters much. All we need to care about is that we're going to a bad place, and we need to save some good people and a lot of children."

He was relieved to hear a low rumble of positive responses—"Yeah," and "Let's get 'em," and "Ruddy ready, we are"—along with vigorous nods and shaking of fists. These really were a warrior people—Sato would never doubt it again. How the Bugaboos had lasted this long against them, he had no idea. Of course, they came from the same stock, he supposed . . .

"We've got no weapons!" someone shouted from the back, breaking into his thoughts. Then another person called out, "Don't even know who we're ruddy fighting! Or what!"

Instinct told Sato what he needed to say in response. If their confidence was going to be solidified, it needed to come from within. "Good questions! So, are you saying we should give up? Not even try? Throw in the towel?"

A chorus of angry denials thundered through the vast space, a deafening roar backed by red faces and pumping fists. Some even stood, looking as if they might charge Sato and wallop him for even suggesting such a thing.

"No, I didn't think so!" he yelled as loud as he possibly could. The Fifths quieted. "We'll fight with our hands and our feet, with sticks and stones! We'll fight with our elbows and knees! Whatever it takes!"

A shocked silence greeted this last part. Mothball finally said from her spot, "A bit much, but I like your spirit, I do." A few chuckles rose from the crowd.

Sato would have none of it. "I don't care if it's a *bit much*. If you guys wanna take this as a joke and treat me like a little kid, then fine! But we don't have weapons, so we have to be willing to *do* terrible things to *stop* the terrible things we're about to see! Are you willing or not?"

Impossibly, the chorus that greeted him was even stronger than before, piercing his eardrums with a needle of sharp pain. The roar went on and on, and this time every single Fifth stood up, arms raised to the sky, shouting and screaming. Sato let it go on, looking around with a stoic face, accepting their display of devotion.

When it started to die down naturally, he lit into them again. "When this is over, when we've gone to the Thirteenth and rescued our friends, when we've destroyed this unnatural and evil factory of creatures, we won't stop. We'll go back to your world, we'll gather more people—the greatest army the world has ever seen—and we'll wipe the Bugaboos from existence!"

More shouts, more cheers. Sato kept going, trying with all his might to increase the volume of his already strained voice.

"We are the Fifth Army! Say it with me! The Fifth Army!"

He raised a fist to the sky and screamed the words, ripping his throat to pieces. "The Fifth Army! The Fifth Army! The Fifth Army!" His soldiers shouted the words along with him, a sound so loud it seemed to shake the strange floor upon which they stood.

Sato stopped, knowing he'd need his voice in the hours to come. The others didn't quit, however, and kept chanting as if they never planned to stop.

Rutger stepped to Sato's side. "Nice work. Now what?"

"Now we wait for the call," Sato said. "It's coming, and when it does, we'll be ready."

Lisa watched the pep rally with mixed feelings—a whole barrage of them.

Her parents sat to either side of her, Kayla in her lap, the four present members of the Higginbottom clan clasped in an awkward but wonderful hug. Despite having everything in their world turned upside down, Lisa felt safe at the moment. But deep down she knew the feeling was fleeting, and there were a thousand and one things to worry about.

Sato's speech had really shocked her. He'd seemed quiet for one thing, and then to suddenly stand in front of this crowd of human giants and speak so loudly and convincingly was quite a thing to see. She thought his speech was a little bit on the cheesy side with a few roll-the-eye moments, but that's what you needed for something like this. Overall, very impressive.

But still.

What could they do? What could a few hundred people—even tall, gangly, gimme-some-blood warrior giants—do against this psycho lady Mistress Jane? And more importantly—personally, selfishly—what was going to happen to Lisa and her family? They couldn't go to this Thirteenth Reality place and fight. The idea was ridiculous. She almost laughed at the picture of herself running around like a chimpanzee trying to jump on bad guys and, what— bite their ears?

Plus, there was Kayla to think about. Lisa and her parents had already decided that the battles and the mysteries and the monsters should be left to the Realitants—including her own brother, Tick. For the rest of the Higginbottoms, staying away from danger and protecting Kayla was all that mattered. They couldn't do much else, anyway.

Could they?

Lisa hugged Kayla a little tighter to her chest.

The Haunce floated in eternity.

The Haunce floated in the spaces between the spaces, in the darkness between the light, the light between the darkness. It floated in the smallest of the small and the largest of the large. It was everywhere and nowhere, up and down, left and right, big and small.

The Haunce floated and watched, its countless soulikens observing and communicating on a scale no individual human could ever understand.

The lull in the catastrophe Jane had started was almost over. The slipping and cracking and shattering of the Barriers would resume soon. And then it wouldn't stop until all was lost.

Atticus had reached Jane. They were together in the Factory.

It was time.

The Haunce floated—and watched.

Then it acted.

First, remembering the most human of emotions—compassion—it sent the family of Atticus back to their home. There, they would be safe, as long as everything went according to plan.

Once done with that—a thing that took less than a nanosecond of time—the Haunce winked Sato and his makeshift army to the Thirteenth Reality.

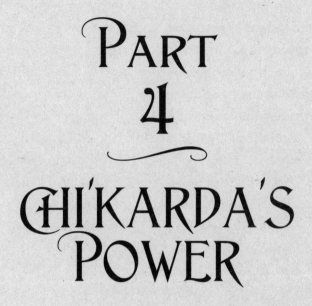

PART
4

CHI'KARDA'S
POWER

CHAPTER
44

TALKING WITH THE DEVIL

Tick and his two friends followed Mistress Jane down a long tunnel dug into the bedrock beneath ground, the hissing flames of the firekelt the only sound and light. No one spoke, no one asked questions, no one made any threats against anyone's life. Tick rattled his thoughts with each step, trying to come up with the best way to talk to Jane about what needed to happen and to convince her that they needed to put their heads and powers together to stop the Realities from imploding.

But he didn't know what to say or do. Was he supposed to wait for the Haunce to show up? He sure hoped so, because he didn't have the first clue how to go about things.

They turned a corner around a jagged edge of dark stone, Jane and her fiery creation a step ahead of them. But Tick stopped. He felt and heard the same womping sound he'd experienced back in the woods near his home, right before finding Jane in his basement. Right before this whole mess started.

Womp.

There it was again—a faint but definite pulse of energy, the vibration of horns and bees.

Womp.

Paul and Sofia took another couple of steps before noticing he'd quit walking.

"What's wrong?" Sofia asked.

Jane noticed as well, turning around to face them. She tilted her wooden staff forward as though about to strike him with some magical spell. The wavering splashes of light from the dancing firekelt flames turned her red mask the hue of wet blood.

Womp.

"Why have you stopped?" the robed tyrant asked in her painful, raspy voice. "Don't even think of trying anything—there's more Chi'karda coiled inside this Barrier Staff than you've seen in all your prior glimpses combined. I programmed it especially for you, Atticus Higginbottom. It's set to unleash its fury on you the second you even breathe a wisp of the power."

Womp.

Tick felt each and every energy pulse like a wall of water crashing over him. "I just . . . I just keep feeling surges of Chi'karda. Why?" He ignored her threat about her Barrier Staff; they had bigger problems to solve before he could worry about himself.

Jane hesitated, her mask void of expression, probably mulling over whether he was being sincere or trying to trick her. Finally, she said, "You and I are very sensitive to the ripples of energy triggered by Chi'karda, Atticus. I think it's something you picked up since growing more in tune with the power inside you. Get used to it, or it'll drive you crazy. Especially in the Factory, where it's constantly churning. Now come on—I want to show you something."

Womp. This time the pulse did feel a little more distant, like a constant breeze that he'd grown accustomed to. Or maybe more like breathing—you realize it's happening only when you think about it.

"Jane . . ." Tick began, wanting to bring up the subject of his mission and get it over with. But the words lodged somewhere down his throat.

"You will call me *Mistress* Jane," she said with a flare of anger on her mask. "After the horrible things you've done to me, I would think you could at least find a smattering of respect for your elders. For your superiors."

Tick didn't care about his pride anymore. He didn't even feel an ounce of fear for this woman. The only thing that mattered—that throbbed in his mind like a beating heart—was what the Haunce wanted him to do.

"I'm sorry. *Mistress Jane.* Whatever. We'll do whatever it is you want us to, and we'll see whatever it is you want us to see, but we need to talk first. Something really bad is about to happen, and I . . . we . . . need your help."

Jane's face melted into a slight frown, a look of curiosity on her mask. She took a few steps toward him. "I can tell you're not lying. What are you talking about?"

Her response surprised Tick, and something told him that the only reason she didn't fly off the handle was because she already suspected the truth. He played for that angle. "You have to know that things really went screwy when you tried to destroy the Fifth Reality with your dark matter Blade of Shattered Hope. Well, things are worse than you think. A lot worse. You made the Barriers unstable and ignited a whole bunch of bad stuff that's gonna end up wiping us all away. We have only a few hours until we'll all be dead—thanks to you."

Jane didn't answer for a long time, her eyes concentrating on Tick, her hand gripping the odd staff. Tick wondered if maybe it just looked like wood but was actually something else. She'd called it a *Barrier Staff* . . .

She finally spoke. "How could you know these things, Atticus? What kind of trick—"

"It's not a trick!" Tick yelled. "You're supposed to be the grown-up here! Act like it! The Haunce rescued me from you—and it told me all this stuff. Your Blade of Shattered Hope did something really bad to the Realities, and we have one chance to fix it."

Her red mask sharpened and tightened into a fit of rage; she visibly shook.

Tick knew he had to save himself, and quickly. "I'm sorry—just please listen to me! If I'm lying, you can do whatever you want to me, I swear. I promise I won't even touch Chi'karda. Just please listen."

Womp.

There it was again, the first time he'd noticed the energy pulse in several minutes. Jane had been right—he was getting used to it.

"You dare stand there," Jane said, "looking at me with that pathetic little innocent face of yours, and tell me this? That the Haunce visited you? Spoke to you? You expect me to believe such nonsense? You almost had me until you took it that far. Your capacity for evil was proven quite well back in the Fourth, but to lie like that . . . amazing. Do you even have a conscience?"

Tick sucked in a few dry breaths, frustrated into silence. He wouldn't have guessed she'd believe him right away, but her tone and arrogance made it seem as if she wouldn't even consider the truth. He finally snagged some words and forced them out.

"Seriously, Ja—Mistress Jane? You're seriously going to act like that and not even hear me out? Are you so full of yourself that you'd risk the whole universe?" He threw his arms up then slapped the sides of his legs. "Unbelievable. Fine—do what you want. The Haunce'll be coming here soon anyway. Maybe you'll believe it then."

Jane walked toward him again, not stopping until she stood only a foot or two away. Her yellow robe glowed in the firelight; her now-stoic mask shimmered and glistened. Her scarred, metal-pocked hand gripped the Staff tightly, the bones seemingly ready to burst through the taut skin.

"Look into my eyes, boy," she whispered, a sandy croak of sound.

"I already am," Tick replied, standing as straight as he could and holding on to the small amount of courage he'd scrounged up from within. "All I can see are little black holes with no life in 'em."

"You . . ." She made an odd squeak like someone holding back tears. "If it weren't for you, things would be so different. I could've stopped Chu and used his technology for good. I wouldn't be scarred and hideous from head to toe. Do you have any idea how hard it is to lead when people can't even glance at you? Do you have any idea how humiliating it is to look like a monster? And if it weren't for you, the Blade would've functioned perfectly, and we'd be on our way to a

Utopian Reality. But no, you've ruined everything. You've ruined my . . ."

She stopped and shook her head slightly. "No. I won't say that. You've made things difficult—no doubt about it. But you haven't ruined everything. You haven't ruined my life. Do you know why, Atticus? Because I won't give up. I'll overcome it all, and in the end, I . . . will . . . win. I promise you."

Tick momentarily lost every bit of hatred for the woman. Every bit of frustration and angst. The only thing he felt was pity. And the familiar pang of guilt for what he'd done to her.

"Mistress Jane," he said. "I'm sorry. I'm sorry for what I did in Chu's building. I promise I didn't mean to. I swear."

"You're sorry, you promise, you swear. Too little, too late, as they say." She started to turn from him.

Tick reached out and grabbed a fold of her robe. She spun and knocked his hand away, glaring at him. "Don't . . . touch . . . me!"

Tick stepped back, trying to shrink into the wall behind him. A spark of Chi'karda flared inside him, but he pushed it away. Something about that tall staff gripped in her hand terrified him. Plus, this was no time to battle her—he had to win her over.

"I'm sorry," he said again, trying to throw as much humility into his voice as possible.

Jane touched the top edge of her staff to Tick's head, then pulled it back. "I'm not a fool, Atticus. I'll listen to what you have to say. But first, you will come and see the Factory. I want you to see my gift to science. I want you to see me change the world."

And with that, she turned away and set off down the tunnel.

CHAPTER
45

SPLITTING UP

One second, Lisa had been sitting on the cold, hard floor of the magical nowhere place, Kayla gripped in her arms. The next, she felt a tingle shoot down her back, and their surroundings changed completely. From light to dark, from vast and open to close quarters. She sat on something soft. Kayla was still in her lap, Mom on her left, Dad on her right.

"We're home," her dad said, squirming to stand up. "We're home!"

Lisa knew he was right before he'd said it the second time. The faintest glimmer of dawn—or twilight?— shone through the curtains of their living room windows. She saw the worn-out armchair her mom always sat in to wait for them after school, the piano, the crooked arrangement of family photos on the wall.

Dad stood in the middle of the room, slowly turning with his arms outstretched like that lady in the wildflower-strewn mountain field in *The Sound of Music.* Though he looked a lot more ridiculous. Lisa laughed, which sent Kayla into a fit of giggles.

"I think we've officially had the strangest day in the history of our family," Mom said, leaning back on the sofa with her arms folded, smiling at Dad. "But I have to say, I'm a little offended that whoever is in charge doesn't think we could help out in this fight of theirs."

Dad toppled a bit, obviously having grown dizzy. He collapsed into the armchair, its springs groaning in complaint. "Come on, dear. We're not cut out for that stuff. Especially with Kayla and Lisa to think about. Let the Realitants do their job—and I'm sure Tick'll be home safe and sound before we know it."

Lisa agreed about Kayla, but felt a little swell of self-defense spring up inside her. "Hey, speak for yourself, Dad. I could've helped Sato. Put me in a room with this Mistress Jane witch, and I'll show her what bony knees and sharp nails I have."

Mom reached over and squeezed Lisa's knee. "That's my girl. Maybe old Master George will be knocking on our door for you once this is over." She looked down at the floor, her smile fading. Then she seemed to catch herself and brought it back, returning her gaze to Lisa.

"What, Mom?" Lisa said. "What's wrong?"

Her mom had a second of surprise on her face, probably chagrined that she'd been caught. "Oh, well, it's nothing really. I guess I just feel a little ashamed that I quit being a Realitant all those years ago."

Lisa thought long and hard about that. She gave Kayla a squeeze before gently pushing her over to sit with Dad, who took her into his arms while his eyes darted back and forth between Lisa and Mom.

"What's goin' on in those heads of yours?" he asked.

Lisa reached out and took her mom's hand, helping her stand up. "Dad, Mom and I are gonna play a big part in all this. Somehow. Aren't we, Mom?"

Mom stared at her with glistening eyes. "Why . . . yes, Lisa. Yes, I think we are."

"Good. Let's be ready when the time comes."

∼⌒⌒

Sato had known it was coming—hoped it was coming, anyway—but he still felt a thrill of shock when the winking tingle scooted across his neck and back. He instinctively started to yell at the people of the Fifth to get ready, but of course, by the time any words popped out of his mouth, they'd already arrived at their location.

They stood in a big field of drying mud. The morning

sun had just lifted over a forest to their left, its brilliance cutting through the last leaves and branches at the very top. To their right was a huge wall of stacked logs, stretching in both directions until they curved away and disappeared. The air smelled truly awful, like a rotting dump.

Sato had a few horrible seconds when self-doubt hit him as he looked back at his army. Most of them were gawking left and right at the place to which they'd come, many patting their chests and arms in disbelief at the seemingly magical experience of having been winked there. Sato didn't know what he'd been thinking—how could he lead an army? He had zero experience, zero training, zero confidence. What was he supposed to do? Yell "Charge!" and start rushing the fence? The whole idea seemed ridiculous all of a sudden.

The Fifths appeared to be gathering their wits a lot quicker than he was. Sato watched as they stood in rows, composed and standing at attention, waiting for him to give a command. They really were warriors. They really did consider him their leader.

Buck up, he told himself. *When this is all over, then you can sit down and have a good cry about it.*

"Okay, listen up!" he yelled. Rutger, Mothball, and her parents were standing right in front of him in the very first row. He exchanged glances with his two fellow Realitants, relieved to see there'd be no teasing. Time for business.

When the Fifths had quieted and all the attention turned to Sato, he continued. "We don't know what to expect, what kind of defenses they have, who's watching us—anything. Jane could send a whole pack of fangen or who-knows-what at us any second now, so we need to get moving. I want us to split into three groups: left, right, middle." He pointed as he spoke. "Middle group stays here, close to the fence. Rutger, you and I will stay with them."

The short man nodded, his face scrunched up as if considering whether he'd gotten a good assignment or a bad one.

Sato pointed to the left. "Left group, you guys go around the perimeter that way. Right group, go that way." He pointed in the opposite direction. "I want you to run as quickly as possible while still being able to keep a good lookout. With any luck, you'll make your way around that wall and meet up on the other side. Then come back here. We'll decide what to do based on what you learn."

As the Fifths separated into smaller groups, Sato started doubting his first major decision. What if they were attacked? What if, by splitting up, they'd weakened themselves too much? What if the groups never hooked back up again? What if . . . what if . . . what if?

He shook it off. He couldn't do anything until he knew what they were dealing with, and it seemed too dangerous to send individual spies out to scout the area. He was sticking with his decision, and that was that. He had nothing but his instinct.

"Okay, then! Go, already!" He shooed them like dogs, and immediately made a mental note that he probably shouldn't do that ever again.

But they didn't seem to mind. Mothball, her parents, and the rest of their group sprinted toward the right, heading for the fence. Once they were right next to it, they took off running alongside it. The left group did the same thing but in the opposite direction. Those ordered to stay put gathered tighter around Sato.

Rutger stood right next to him and reached up to poke him on the upper arm. "I'm proud of you, Sato. Have to admit, I didn't wake up this morning thinking I'd see General Sato by the end of the day, but here we are. Don't worry—worst thing that can happen is we all die."

Sato grumbled, not in the mood.

Rutger kept talking as if they were sitting down for a nice picnic. "I'm really happy about how it worked out. You need someone cranky to lead like this, and . . ."

Sato tuned him out, searching for signs of guards or visitors. He couldn't see very well over the tall Fifths, so he stepped out of the crowd, scanning the area with his eyes. The day was fully bright now, not a cloud in the sky.

A quick movement in the woods caught the corner of his eye, like someone had poked their head out to look around, then pulled back again, hiding. But when Sato focused his attention on the spot, he saw nothing but trees.

Sato pointed at three Fifths, one by one. "You, you, and you," he said, making another note to learn these peoples' names. "Come with me."

Rutger finally realized he wasn't being listened to. "Hey, what's going on?"

"Just be quiet," Sato replied. "Let's go."

He moved away from the rest of them with the three Fifths he'd chosen right on his heels. Keeping his eyes glued to the spot where he'd seen the movement, Sato ran for the forest. He'd made it about halfway to the tree when a figure darted out from behind it—an oddly shaped, wispy thing. It seemed to fly through the air like a ghost, quickly disappearing deeper into the dark woods.

Then other creatures did the same, darting out from behind at least a dozen other trees that lined the boundary between the field and the forest. They were all like living, flying shadows, gone before Sato got a better look.

He stopped and held up a hand. "Those had to be some kind of spies or guards. Now Jane or whoever's in charge of this place definitely knows we're here. I hope I didn't—"

A commotion from behind cut him off. He turned to see Rutger excitedly pointing toward the far bend of the wooden fence to the right, where the group of Fifths that had gone in that direction was already coming back, marching along through the slippery mud.

"Something's wrong," Sato half-whispered. "They shouldn't be back yet."

He headed in that direction, running as fast as he could, determined to meet up with them and see what was happening. He'd only gone about a hundred feet when he noticed several of the Fifths working together to carry large wooden boxes. Also, two newcomers were with them, looking very out of place. Sato almost fell down, already knowing what this meant and feeling like they'd won their first victory.

It was Master George—his Barrier Wand in tow—and Sally from headquarters.

More importantly, Sato was sure the boxes they carried had weapons inside them.

CHAPTER 46

A VERY BAD SMELL

Tick, man," Paul whispered to him as they followed Jane down the seemingly endless tunnels. "What's going on? Is she for real about that staff of hers? Is it some kind of Barrier Wand on steroids?"

Tick shrugged his shoulders. "I don't know. But I can't risk anything right now. We just need to stick with her and wait for the Haunce to come, I guess. Don't do anything to tick her off!"

"Tick her off," Sofia repeated through a half-hearted laugh. "That has meaning on so many levels, it's ridiculous."

Paul snickered. "I gare-on-tee you could take her, Superman. I'm not worried."

Tick rolled his eyes even though the others probably couldn't tell. He wasn't in the mood to talk to anyone, much less hear the junk about his powers. Despite what had happened so far, he felt no more like a superhero than he would a bird if someone glued wings on his back.

Jane reached a large shiny, metal door, big silver bolts lining the edges. It seemed almost too modern for the cavernous feel of the tunnels through which they'd been walking forever.

As they approached the door, Tick felt an increase in magnitude of the womps—the rhythmic pulses vibrating his teeth and skull.

Jane turned around to face them. The firekelt stood slightly ahead of her and to the left, and the light from its flames illuminated her perfectly. She spoke in her desert-sand voice.

"I don't know what you've heard about the Factory, but you're about to witness it firsthand. I'll admit that my pride has gotten the better part of me today. I desperately want to show this to the three of you—especially you, Atticus. Otherwise I wouldn't bother with the extra protection of my Barrier Staff and would've killed you already. Your lingering presence in the Realities is beginning to disturb me. Greatly."

"So you're gonna show us your evil factory and then kill us?" Paul asked, his tone full of the usual sarcasm.

"What is this, a bad James Bond movie?" Jane's mask didn't show any anger. Tick thought she probably didn't want to give Paul the satisfaction. "Please, boy. What you're about to see will be so above your mental capacity and intellect that even if you escaped, you'd barely be able to describe it, much less share any of my secrets. Just consider this a whim of mine. Nothing more."

"You said you'd hear me out," Tick said. "We don't have time for this!"

"Patience, Atticus. A short trip through my house of wonders, and then you can talk. Now, if you don't mind, I'll be the only one talking from this point on."

"Could you maybe drink some cough syrup first?" Paul asked.

This time Jane's mask did fill with rage as she pointed the upper tip of the Staff at Paul. An instant later, his entire body lifted up from the ground and slammed against the wall. He tried to scream, but nothing came out—only a slight gurgling in the bottom of his throat. His face turned purple with pain, and his hands squeezed into fists.

"Stop it, Jane!" Tick yelled, unable to stop the surge of Chi'karda that ignited inside him. "Leave him alone!"

Jane pointed the Staff at Tick; Paul dropped in a heap of arms and legs onto the floor. "Don't even think about it, Atticus. Pull your Chi'karda back, right now!"

Tick closed his eyes for a second, calming his heart. The spits of lava flaring in his chest puttered out, cooled. He still breathed heavily, though, as he looked at Jane once again. "You didn't have to do that to him."

Paul groaned and shifted his body. At least he seemed okay.

Jane's mask still held on to its anger. "I don't like him. He's a smart aleck. Tell him to keep his mouth shut." Her face melted back into the void as she turned toward the silver door once again.

Sofia immediately moved to help Paul to his feet, being more gentle than Tick had ever seen her before. Paul hunched over slightly, his face maybe forever locked into a grimace of pain, but, surprisingly, he said nothing.

Sofia looked at Tick and mouthed the words, "We're dead."

Tick shook his head adamantly but didn't say anything. Movement from Jane grabbed his attention.

She placed her right hand on the center of the silver door. Shocked, Tick watched as the metal seemed to liquefy at her touch. Jane's hand sank into the gray goop up to the wrist. A second later she pulled her hand back out again. Tick expected the metal surface to ripple like a pond, but it didn't, solidifying instantly instead.

Then, with a great rumbling sound, the entire door

slid to the right, disappearing into the rock and revealing a very modern-looking hallway ahead of them, with white tile floors, fluorescent lights on the ceiling, and glass windows on the walls.

"All the doors in the Factory have a Reality Echo," Jane explained. "That means it's actually a combination of matter taken from more than one Reality, visible in each place but absolutely impossible to open no matter what you do. Explosives, tanks, the strongest battering ram ever made—none of it would work. Only the pre-approved cellular structure of those previously recorded by my people can do it."

She looked at them over her shoulder, her mask alive with arrogance. "Even I wouldn't be able to use my powers to dissolve the material without an extraordinary amount of effort. The door is literally in different Realities simultaneously—therefore, nothing existing solely in this one could make it move. Reality Echo. Impressed?"

Tick nodded before he could stop himself. He was impressed.

Paul let out a low whistle, a small but telling sign to Tick that Jane hadn't killed his spirit completely, not yet—Tick hoped not ever.

"The door is nothing compared to what you're about to see," Jane said, a hint of giddiness in her voice. "Follow me."

She entered the brightly lit hallway, her shoes—hidden beneath the folds of her long robe—tapping on the tile floor. Tick hesitated a second before following, terrified of what horrors they might be about to see, not to mention the worry eating at him about the Haunce and what they were supposed to accomplish. His chest tight with every breath, he stepped through the doorway along with Paul and Sofia.

The first section consisted of offices—normal human people dressed in normal human clothes tapping away at computer keyboards with monitors, printers, and servers everywhere. Several odd-looking machines were also scattered about the desks, similar to the machines they'd seen back in the desert. But nothing too out of the ordinary. If Tick didn't know better, he would have thought it was an accounting business.

"This is where data is analyzed," Jane explained without turning around. She kept walking. "It's also where oversight of the melding processes takes place—a tricky operation that needs tight supervision."

Melding processes? Tick thought. She acted like she'd said *cereal production* or *car manufacturing*. How could she be so callous?

They came to another massive metal door exactly like the first one. Jane shoved her hand into the silver goop, and soon this one opened up as well. A rancid smell of decay surged through the door like an infested wind. Tick and his friends coughed and sputtered, covering their noses. Tick tried to breathe only through his mouth, but then he tasted the air, which was even worse.

"What is that?" Sofia managed to choke out.

"It's the smell of progress," Jane said as she entered the barely lit hallway on the other side.

Tick, despite the putrid smell, despite his queasiness, couldn't help but feel extremely curious. The surging, throbbing pulses of invisible power emanating from the open door pounded his senses.

He followed Jane into the stinky darkness.

CHAPTER
47

WEAPONS OF MASS
COOLNESS

Sato kept trying to dampen his emotions, stay levelheaded, but a new surge of confidence swelled inside him. For the first time, he felt like they were a real army with a real chance.

Now they had weapons.

The reunion with Master George and Sally had been thrilling but brief, exchanging barely a dozen words before they turned their full attention to the large wooden boxes. The Fifths looked like their eyes might pop, they were so excited and intrigued by what Mothball and Sally started pulling out of the crates, George explaining their uses in his very sophisticated voice, Rutger butting in now and then to say how cool this or that was.

The usual: boxes of Ragers—those little balls of compacted static electricity that exploded on impact in a display of destructive lightning. Some Shurrics—large guns of sonic power that devastated with sound waves.

A couple of new things as well: Squeezers, which were grenades full of tiny but extremely strong wires. When it exploded, the wires shot out and latched on to whatever was closest, then immediately retracted and curled up, no matter what the material. Very nasty results.

Finally, there was the Halter. A thin but sturdy plastic tube that ended in a cone, with a simple trigger on one end of the tube and a small cartridge on the other. Each cartridge equaled one shot: a spray of tiny darts spread out and injected its victims—potentially dozens if it hit a group—with a serum that immediately paralyzed them for hours. It was a variation of what Master George had created for Sofia to stop Tick's madness at Chu's headquarters. Very effective.

Ragers, Shurrics, Squeezers, Halters. Plenty to go around.

This could be fun.

The other group that had gone exploring returned about a half hour after Master George's arrival, saying they found nothing but a very long, encircling wooden fence, with only one exception—a gate of iron bars. The only thing they could see through it was a small grove of trees and nothing they did would open up the

gate or make someone appear. So they'd come back, relieved to see why they hadn't met up with the others on the far side.

Once the weapons had been passed out and the wooden boxes thrown into the forest to hide them—though they were probably being spied on anyway—the entire Fifth Army gathered around Sato. Time for business.

"Okay," Sato began, his voice raised. "Seems like we've got no choice but to climb over that stupid fence. It's probably about thirty feet high, but there are plenty of handholds and footholds, so it shouldn't be too hard. I'm just worried about what might be waiting for us when we pop our heads over the edge. Once we have a good, solid group of twenty or so right at the top, we'll throw volleys of Ragers and Squeezers to clear the way, and then we'll send the first group over to cover with Shurric fire while the rest of us enter. Sound good?"

Rutger tapped Sato on the arm. "What about me? Don't see myself rolling up the side of that fence very easily."

Sato had to hold in a laugh—he didn't want to embarrass his friend. "I think you, Sally, and Master George should use the Wand to go back to headquarters, monitor us, and wink us out when we're ready."

The look of relief that washed over Rutger before he quickly wiped it away made Sato like him more than ever. George stepped closer, pulling a yellow envelope from the inner pocket of his suit coat.

"Goodness gracious me," he said, ripping the envelope open. "I almost forgot the most important part." He pulled out a handful of square pieces of paper—no more than an inch on each side—then shook them on his flat palm for everyone to get a look.

"What are those?" Sato asked.

"Nanolocator patches." George poured the square pieces back into the envelope, then pulled a single one out and held it between his thumb and forefinger. "There are hundreds here, and all you need to do is slap this against the skin of any person. The microscopic nanolocator will immediately slide off the patch and onto the subject, at which point we can wink them away. If we're looking to rescue children from this miserable place, these patches will be our best shot."

Sato was amazed and thrilled. Solutions to his two biggest concerns had been opened up for him—how they'd fight without weapons, and how they'd herd a bunch of potentially injured, suffering children safely away while fighting Jane's monsters. Everything was in place.

"This is great," Sato said, ignoring that small part in his brain that said it all seemed too easy. Meeting whatever waited inside the Factory would probably cure him of that, and quickly. "You guys wink back to headquarters now. We'll take it from here."

George handed him the envelope. "Best of luck, then. There are plenty of those patches, so be sure to put them on everyone here first—except you and Mothball, of course. We already have you pegged. We'll have all the information we need back in the Control Room, and we'll be watching closely, I assure you. Sally will be at the Grand Canyon HQ with Priscilla Persephone from the Seventh to help with the children—we'll send them directly there."

"Just call me Papa Sally," the big man said. "Might even read dem squirts a story or two 'bout the old days on the chicken farm."

"Sounds good," Sato said. "Now you guys get out of here—time's wasting. I mean . . . please, whatever."

George hardly seemed to notice. He made a few adjustments to the Barrier Wand, had Rutger and Sally put their hands on it, and then the three of them disappeared. A few oohs and aahs escaped the Fifths.

Sato handed the envelope of nanolocator patches to Mothball. "Pass those out. We climb the wall in five minutes."

~~~~~

After sending Sally off to the Grand Canyon, Master George got straight to work at the Bermuda Triangle headquarters, walking around the mesh metal walkways of the confined and claustrophobic structure, pointing left and right.

"Rutger, I want every computer in this building set up in the Control Room. I want the Big Board lined up and ready to go with monitoring all those nanolocators. Put a call out to all Realitants—if they can make it here to help, so be it. With all the destruction, they may be needed elsewhere, but make them aware of our plans, anyway."

Rutger waddled to keep up, saying, "Okay," after every instruction.

"We need to help Sally and Priscilla set up a refugee camp at the Grand Canyon. They'll need beds and clothes and doctors and who knows what else! We also need to come up with a contingency plan—so many things could go wrong. And we—"

"Master George?" Rutger asked.

"Yes?"

"I got it."

"Good, then. Let's get moving!"

Rutger cleared his throat. "Could you, um, at least make me a sandwich while I'm doing all this work? I'm starving."

CHAPTER
48

THE FACTORY

The dark and smelly hallway, its walls made of black stone, wet and slimy, went about fifty feet before it came to its first window. Tick could see it just ahead of Mistress Jane when she stopped and turned to face them, but he couldn't tell what was behind the window. A sick anticipation poisoned his veins. The firekelt was behind them now, throwing their giant shadows along the floor like flat creatures of the night.

"What we do here," Jane began, "is the coordination of my lifetime's work in the fields of science with the special characteristics of the mutated Chi'karda in the Thirteenth Reality. We use bio-engineering, genetic restructuring and manipulation, and chemistry. But without the special touch of . . . shall we say magic? No, that's such a dirty word. It's all semantics, I guess. But without the special power of the Thirteenth's Chi'karda, all of this would suffer from a missing link."

She raised her arms, the robe fanning out like a fallen angel's wings. "But here, where I've put it all together to showcase the greatest scientific achievements of all human history—here is where the revolution of the Realities has begun. Here is where we begin our journey to a perfect place for all mankind. In a thousand years, they will look back and say it began with me. Now, watch and learn. Watch and let yourself feel wonder."

The mask on her face showed something like ecstasy, the black holes of her eyes actually widening for the first time Tick could remember seeing. She looked completely crazy.

"Amazing how humble you are," Sofia said. Tick was glad she spoke and not Paul, because he might not have survived the punishment a second time around. "If your intentions are so pure, then why do you care so much about taking all the credit? Sounds like a power trip to me."

Jane lowered her arms, her look of rapture melting into a glare. "Don't judge me, you spoiled, rich brat. Always had everything you wanted, always pampered, always safe. Always judging those less fortunate than you. Don't . . . judge . . . me." These last three words came out so enflamed that Sofia took a step backward and didn't respond.

"Now," Jane said in a much nicer voice, though laced with an icy insincerity. "The three of you will step up and look through the first observation window. You will say nothing, and you will not look away. You will not close your eyes. I, also, will remain silent, letting you get a good look before I explain what it is you're witnessing." She stepped to the far side, opposite the window, and gestured toward it with her Staff. "Now come."

Tick and his friends exchanged quick glances, then stepped forward until they stood together in front of the large glass square. Tick felt the struggle of each and every breath as he leaned forward, the window mere inches from his nose.

He looked. His mind jumped to full capacity trying to take in and understand all that he saw.

The room he observed was about forty feet square and dimly lit, mainly from four pale yellow panels on the ceiling. Three beds occupied the middle of the floor, lined up to form the edges of a triangle, the closest bed empty and parallel to the window. In the center of the triangle stood a hunched over monster of a man at least eight feet tall with his back to them. He wore black clothes and had no hair on his head. His massive back was covered in a tattered shirt, and the skin beneath the ripped clothing was wet with bloody gashes. The man didn't move anything but his arms, typing away at what Tick assumed was a computer on the other side of his gigantic body.

Tick turned his attention to the very different occupants of the other two beds, which lay at angles to either side of the workman. A large, odd-shaped tube, maybe ten inches in diameter, snaked from rafters in the ceiling and connected to the two bodies at the chest—right over the heart—linking them together. The left bed contained a large raven—black as oil and two feet tall. The bird barely moved; every few seconds its wings twitched, making Tick think it must be awake on some level and suffering horribly.

A good-sized black bear occupied the bed on the right side. It was bigger than the bed and looked underfed and abused, lying there as if asleep, its big paws occasionally twitching. The bear was also strapped down, that tube arching out of its chest to the rafter above before continuing across the ceiling and then back down to the bird.

Tick focused on that tube. It didn't seem to be made out of artificial material—it looked . . . alive. Like skin. Blue veins ran throughout the long object, just underneath the pale, translucent material, pulsing and changing shades from dark to light to dark again. The ends connected to the raven and the bear looked as if they had grown there like a natural extension. There was no sign of stitches or staples.

Two beds with two bodies. A bird and a bear. Connected by some kind of bio-engineered, monstrous-looking tube. The third bed was empty.

What did it all mean? What horrific thing was Jane doing to these poor creatures? Tick's hands shook; he reached out and pressed his fingers against the lower sill of the window to steady them. Out of the corner of his eye, he noticed that Paul and Sofia had actually clasped their hands together.

The third bed. What was the third bed for?

Jane spoke from behind them, her voice soft and low. Never before had it sounded so evil as it did then.

"What you see here—and more important, what you are about to see—is a miracle of science and technology that today's doctors and scientists can't even imagine, or wish for, or dream about. It's simply beyond their wildest spheres of possibility, beyond their capacity to comprehend. And even if they could, they'd never be able to make it happen. Not unless they were here and had a hundred years to figure it out."

"I think what you really mean," Tick said, throwing all the hatred he could into his voice, "is that they wouldn't be evil enough to do something like this. You're sick, Jane. Totally psycho. I don't feel bad for what I did to you anymore." He shouldn't have said it; he knew that. Not yet. Not until things with the Haunce were worked out. But he couldn't stop himself.

"I told you not to speak," Jane said in a completely calm voice, as if she hadn't heard his actual words. "Say one more word before I allow it, and I will hurt Paul. I promise."

Tick looked back at her. She stared at him, waiting for his response, practically begging him to call her bluff. He fumed, his breathing stilted. Luckily Paul didn't say anything. Finally, using all of his willpower to show restraint, Tick simply nodded. No more words. No more apologies.

"This first observation room is relatively early in the process," Jane said, in her tour guide voice, as if she hadn't just threatened bodily harm to Paul. "The genes and blood and cells haven't been consumed yet, haven't been . . . processed. The next room down the hall will show you what these two subjects will look like in about twenty-four hours. On we go."

She set off walking, her Staff tap-tap-tapping on the stone floor.

Tick followed, hating how she'd called the animals "subjects." Hating every single thing about this horrible woman.

When the next window came into view up ahead, Jane spoke again, over her shoulder. "I hope you haven't eaten in a while. What you're about to see is amazing and wonderful, but might be a bit disturbing."

CHAPTER
49

THE MIRACLE OF BIRTH

Sato had wanted to climb the wall himself, but Mothball made it clear that wasn't an option. She said they couldn't risk having their leader shot in the eyeball with an arrow to start things off. Sato grumbled, of course, but in the end he sent up a crew of six Fifths to peek over the top edge. He got back at Mothball by not letting her go, telling her she had to stay by his side as his second in command. When she grumbled as well, he had to hold in a laugh.

"Ready the Ragers and Squeezers!" he yelled when the six tall soldiers—Sato had decided to start calling them that—reached the point where all they had to do was pop their heads up to see the other side.

"Gotcha, Boss," Tollaseat said, his hands full of Ragers. His wife, Windasill, stood next to him, her hands full of the black, wire-filled grenades called Squeezers. Sato had told Mothball's parents they were supposed to stay near him as well, to be used for long-range action like this.

"You guys ready up there?" Sato called out.

Instead of speaking, the three men and three women above simply gave him the thumbs-up, a sign that was evidently universal.

"Okay. Tollaseat and Windasill will throw the cover weapons on my count of three. As soon as you hear the first round of explosions, pop over and climb down as quickly as possible. Start firing those Shurrics, and the rest of us will be right behind you."

Another round of thumbs-up.

"One. Two. Three!"

Mothball's parents brought their hands low then flung them toward the sky, letting go at the right moment to send the weapons flying up and well over the top of the wooden fence and the waiting Fifths. A few seconds later, the clatter of the weapons raining down on the other side was immediately followed by the ripping static thumps of the Ragers exploding. Then came the Squeezers' metallic clanging and sounds of wires whizzing through the air. All muted and distant, but loud enough to be heard clearly.

"Go!" Sato yelled. "Go now!"

The six soldiers were already on the move. They grabbed the very top of the fence and swung their legs over, the bulky Shurrics already gripped in one of their hands, ready to start firing. They disappeared from sight.

Sato started climbing the wall after them. "Go! Go! Come on!" He didn't need to say it—every last Fifth was already scaling the clunky wood face of the fence.

Just before Sato reached the top, a soldier's head suddenly popped back over, looking straight down at him. It was a woman, and she had a puzzled look creasing her skinny face.

"What's the matter?" Sato asked.

"You need to see this," was her response. She disappeared once again.

Sato clambered up the last few feet to look over the edge. He'd had ideas of what to expect inside—barracks, groups of creatures, large weapons ready to fire, a creepy hospital-looking thing that was the Factory. But he froze in confusion at what he saw below him.

Other than the grove of trees that grew close to the iron gate, there was nothing. Absolutely nothing.

From where he perched on the fence, looking left and right and forward all the way to the other side of the fence—barely visible in the distance—he saw nothing but dirt and mud and a few trees. Not one

building, not one creature, not one person other than the soldiers he'd sent over.

Dirt and mud and trees.

Sato turned to Mothball, who was right next to him and looking as bewildered as he felt. "Are we sure we came to the right place?"

~~~~~

Tick wanted to look away. Every single cell in his body wanted him to look away. Every notion of normalcy and human decency and right-and-wrong screamed at him to look away—that this wasn't something a boy like him should witness.

But he stared through the window in disbelief that Jane could really be this evil.

The room was identical to the first one—three beds lined up in a triangle, the odd, skin-like bio-tube, and a creepy man in the middle, his back turned, typing away at a computer. As before, the closest bed was empty and the left and right beds had occupants. But that's where the similarities ended and the true horrors began.

Another raven lay on the bed to the left—or what used to be a raven. The poor thing that lay there now barely resembled a living being. It looked like a corpse, its emaciated body sucked dry of fat and water, the feathers gone, yellowed skin clinging to its bones. The bio-tube still grew out of its dead chest toward the ceiling.

Tick turned his attention to the right bed, where a panting wolf lay clinging to life, the other end of the tube shaking with each desperate breath. Most of its black-gray fur had fallen out, littering the bed and the surrounding floor like some kind of haunted barber shop. Diseased skin stretched taut over the dying thing's bones.

And then there was that third bed. Empty. Waiting. For what?

When Jane spoke, Tick flinched, startled. "The needed materials have been fully exhumed from the subjects at this stage. They've been collected, filtered, sorted out, and reconfigured. All done with an intense heightening of the scientific process made possible by our special version of Chi'karda. The sweet sacrifice of these two noble creatures is about to conclude in an even greater achievement than their separate lives could ever have accomplished. And one day we'll be ready to use human subjects. I've already gathered many worthy candidates—children with the spark of Chi'karda strongly within them. Soon the possibilities will be endless."

Tick's hands compacted into tight fists. He felt like the skin might burst, he squeezed them so tightly. Trickles of Chi'karda burned within him. It took every bit of his willpower not to explode, do whatever it took to kill this insane, evil woman.

"Ah," she said with an intake of breath, a sick burst full of joy. "It's just about to happen. Keep watching, keep watching!"

Tick didn't want to. He wanted to run and hide. But some sense of duty made him stay where he stood, eyes focused, ready. He needed to know the truth—all of it—if he was ever going to stop Jane.

Movement at the top of the room caught his attention. He looked up to see a huge growth blossoming out of what he'd thought was a normal ceiling, but could now see was made up of the same material as the bio-tube. Bulky and bulbous, an orb grew out and downward, swelling until it was only a few feet above the tables, centered around the empty bed closest to Tick. Another growth shot out of the first one, a thick, squat tube that pulsed with life.

This second growth lowered down until it was directly above the empty mattress, then its end split open, pieces of material curling out and away like the petals of a flower. Gooey slime dripped out and sloshed across the white sheet, followed by a dark lump of a thing, squirming and kicking out its long legs. Before Tick could get a good look, the monster bounded off the bed and skittered across the floor, disappearing behind a large, boxy computer in the corner.

The man monitoring the situation from the middle of the room moved to chase the creature down, a nasty-looking instrument in his hands with metal rods and sparks of electricity shooting into the air.

Tick couldn't take it anymore. He turned around and leaned his back against the warm glass window, folding his arms. He pushed away the bubbling flames of Chi'karda in his chest.

"I know what you're thinking," Jane said, her mask set to something that looked like a teacher speaking to a student. "That I'm horrible. That I'm evil. That I'm a monster myself."

"Yeah, you witch," Paul said. "That's exactly what we're thinking."

Tick tensed, worried Jane would retaliate. But she kept talking. "However, you aren't blessed with the same perspective that I am blessed with. You don't share the vision of what the Realities will become. I need these creatures to carry out my orders, to help me defeat my enemies, to help me achieve my purposes. In the end, no one will disagree that it was worth the bumps along the road. That, as they say, the ends justify the means."

"Bumps along the road?" Tick asked, surprised at how tight his throat felt, how hard it was to get the words out. For now, he had to put aside the shock and disgust of what he'd just seen. "You're not even worth arguing with anymore. But you promised to hear me out about something. We need to talk, and we need to talk now. Things are gonna get really bad any second."

"Yes, I know," Jane said back in a whisper. "I've started to sense it. Something is wrong—"

She didn't finish because the entire tunnel seemed to jump three feet into the air then drop again, throwing the four of them to the ground. The whole place continued to shake, the groans and cracks of shifting rock thundering in the air. The glass of the window shattered, raining pieces down upon Tick, who knew in his gut what was happening.

The Haunce had predicted it: the final devastation and destruction before the Realities ripped apart and ceased to exist forever.

The end had begun.

CHAPTER
50
~

HOLES IN THE GROUND

Sato and the Fifths walked around the flat, muddy ground of the wooden fence's interior, kicking at occasional rocks and looking for anything that might give them a clue as to the purpose of the place.

"Why would they build a huge fence around dirt fields?" Sato asked Mothball, who walked beside him, mumbling about how time was a-wasting.

"Has to be a reason," she answered. "Whoever it is been winkin' us 'round like pinballs must know what they're doin'. We're in the right place, we are. I feel it in me bones. Just need to use them brains of ours."

Sato knelt down and dug in the mud, throwing handfuls to the side. "Maybe your dad was right. Maybe it's all underground, and there's an entrance somewhere in here."

"Can't imagine they'd have to dig their way in every ruddy time," Mothball said, but squatted down to help him. Soon they were a good two feet into the soft earth.

"I know a door wouldn't be under here," Sato said. "But if we hit a hard surface, at least we'll know there's a building underneath."

He glanced up to wipe the sweat from his forehead with his sleeve and stopped. The Fifth Army soldiers had spread out all over the place, following his example by digging in the ground. Sato rolled his eyes and got back to work. These people had gotten a little fanatical in their loyalty to him.

He was all the way to his elbows in greasy mud when the tips of his fingers finally brushed against a rough, hard surface. Spurred by adrenaline, he dug faster, throwing out huge chunks until he had cleared away several square inches of his discovery—a dark stone. Disappointed, he pulled out of the hole and sat back on his haunches.

"What's bitten your buns?" Mothball asked, looking up from her own pathetic excavation.

"I thought I'd found something," he muttered. "Something man-made. But it's just a big, buried rock."

"Must be a mighty big-un, then. Looks like I've found me own slice of it." She pointed toward the bottom of her hole.

Sato crawled over to her and looked down at the swath of bumpy, dark rock. His heartbeat picked up its pace. "You think maybe Jane's built something down there made out of this stone? Wouldn't surprise me, now that I think about it—her castle looks like it was made a thousand years ago. Why would her factory be any different?"

"Want us to keep diggin' around, do ya?" Mothball asked, eyebrows raised.

Sato got to his feet and cupped his hands around his mouth to shout the order, even though his people were already doing it. His first word didn't make it out of his mouth before the ground beneath him lurched, throwing him on his back. As he scrambled to regain his feet, the earth continued to shake, knocking him down again. Then again.

"Earthquake!" Mothball roared.

The ground moved and jostled and jumped. The world around Sato looked as if he was viewing it from a shaking camera, his vision blurry and bouncy. He concentrated on the ground directly below him, settling his feet into the mud so he could stand up and figure out what they should do. He balanced himself, holding his hands out as he slowly stood, swaying back and forth to avoid falling.

The soldiers of the Fifth appeared as if they were dancing, leaning to and fro, stumbling this way and that, falling into each other then away again. The quake increased in intensity, shaking everything. Sato couldn't think of one reasonable order or command to shout. What did you do against Mother Nature?

An earsplitting crack fractured the air, like the sound of an entire mountain shattering. A jagged piece of dark stone erupted from the mud about forty feet in front of Sato, thrusting up from the ground like a primitive knife. One of the Fifths had been standing on the spot, and he rose twice his height into the air before tumbling off, a bloody gash on his left leg.

To Sato's right, a huge gap in the ground opened up like the yawn of a sleeping giant; several soldiers screamed as they plummeted into the darkness below. More rocky pillars jutted up from the dirt, and more holes appeared out of nowhere, the crack of splitting stone like hammers on nails. All the while, the world shook and trembled. Still, Sato didn't know what to do. Everything had gone to complete chaos, and he had no idea how to gain back control.

He'd barely noticed Mothball sliding away from him when he felt the ground disappear beneath his own feet. He fell into an abyss, an embarrassing squeal escaping his throat when he landed on top of his tall friend ten feet below. He heard her grunt as she pushed him off. He rolled across dark, wet stone, barely lit by the sky peeking through the long, jagged hole in the roof above them.

Something furry and strong grabbed both of his arms.

He shrieked again as it dragged him into the deeper darkness until he could see no more.

⟨~⟩

The tunnel was breaking apart, splits and cracks and rocks falling. Everything shook.

Tick had fallen on top of Paul, who grunted and squirmed to push him off. Sofia lay just a few feet from them, not moving. Somehow Jane still stood upright, using her Staff as a brace in one hand. She had her other hand raised, fingers outspread, and Tick realized she was using her powers to create a shield around them, the larger pieces of debris disintegrating before they hit anyone.

"Sofia!" Tick yelled over the sounds of splintering stone. "Are you okay?"

She moved, filling him with relief. When she turned to look at him, trying to smile to show she was okay, he noticed she had a long gash on her forehead— the guilty rock lay right next to her. She must've been hit before Jane had created the shield.

"Come on," Tick said to Paul, grabbing him by the shirt. Losing balance with each movement, they managed to scoot their way to Sofia. Tick looked up at

Jane. "This is what I was talking about! The Haunce said we had to work together to stop it!"

They bounced in the tunnel like they'd been thrown down a steep mountainside. Jane's mask showed no expression.

"Jane!" Tick yelled. "We can't stay here. We have to get out of here and figure things out!"

"Call me *Mistress*," she said, but without conviction. Tick wouldn't have been able to understand the words if he hadn't heard her say them before. He couldn't believe she'd worry about such a stupid thing right then.

"Mistress Jane!" he screamed at her.

She seemed to snap out of whatever trance held her, her mask transforming into a look of concern. Her voice boomed as if she used a microphone. "We need to get above ground—to the dirt fields on top of us. Nothing to fall on us there."

"Then do it!" Tick called back. "How do—"

He cut off when she gripped the Barrier Staff in both hands and thrust it toward the cracked ceiling of the tunnel. Its upper tip slammed into the rock. A bright burst of white fire made Tick shut his eyes and look down. A new sound overwhelmed the cracking and splitting of rock around them: pounding ocean waves and the familiar shifting of sands. He'd heard that noise before—when his own powers had heightened entropy and dissolved matter.

When he sensed that the brilliant light had died down, he looked up. Jane had created a massive hole that led directly to open air and cloudy skies above them. The cavity was round and smooth, as if it had been carved by the strongest lasers in the world. Before he could fully process it, he saw her grip the Staff in both hands and hold it horizontally, like someone readying for a quarterstaff fight. Then all four of them suddenly shot up from the tunnel, an invisible force lifting them through the gaping hole and into the outside air.

Tick didn't have the time or energy to wonder about how she did it. They flew like the fangen he'd seen at her castle, out of the collapsing rubble underground, across fields of dirt and mud which had pillars and jagged triangles of rock jutting through the surface. She found a safe spot just outside the large wooden fence they'd approached from the forest an hour or so ago. They landed with a soft bump, and the magic ride was over.

"Whoa," Paul said. "We don't even have wings."

Tick thought it was a perfectly absurd thing to say at the moment.

CHAPTER
51

FLIES IN THE BISCUITS

Sato squirmed and kicked and twisted his body as the monstrous, furry thing dragged him across the rough stone floor. He couldn't see a single thing, the darkness complete. Scratches and burns lit up his skin like biting flames. Even with the movement, he could tell the place around him still shook from the never-ending earthquake.

He decided to still himself and save up his energy for one concentrated effort to escape from the creature. He calmed his body and legs, trying to relax despite the pain. The thing continued to pull him through the black, cool air. After several seconds, Sato went for it.

He thrust up with his pelvis, at the same time planting

both feet and pushing off. Tensing his arms, he twisted his body as violently as he could, trying to flip over onto his stomach. The last gasp effort worked—the creature lost its grip on him and Sato heard it trip and tumble across the stone.

Sato scrambled to his feet and ran toward the sound, knowing that he didn't have time to pull out any weapons, that he'd have only one chance to surprise the monster and attack it. His foot hit a soft lump of something, and Sato pounced, falling on top of the creature. He felt around with his hands, squeezing the thing's body between his legs as it thrashed around, trying to throw him off. Sato felt fur and sweat. Sharp claws grazed across his upper arm, his shoulder.

He found the neck, gripping it with both hands, and squeezed. Eventually, the thing slowed its attempts to escape. And then it stilled completely, one last gurgled gasp of a breath escaping, the smell of it awful and rotten.

Sato fell off the creature, scooting away frantically until his back found a hard wall. He pulled his legs up to his chest and wrapped his arms around his knees as the dark place continued to shake and rattle around him. Rocks and pebbles rained from the ceiling, pelting his head. A sudden urge to quit—to forget all about his army and his promises and all the horrible things that were happening—almost consumed him, almost made him decide to sit there and wait to die.

But he couldn't give in. He pushed his fear away and slammed that door closed.

Trembling, terrified, and blind, deafened by the sounds of cracking rock, Sato somehow got to his feet and started running.

⟍⟋

Master George had to stop every once in a while and force himself to take deep, pulling breaths. The Control Room was abuzz with alerts and flashing indicator lights. Sato and his army had somehow been scattered, seemingly running around—and, inexplicably, up and down—like hornets with a busted nest.

Rutger came running in from the other room where he was doing his best to monitor TV stations around the world. "It's all started up again! Earthquakes everywhere. Lightning storms in some places. I don't know how much longer the networks will be able to keep broadcasting."

"Dear me, dear me. It's begun, just like Atticus said it would. At least he and his friends are still together—though they just moved a great distance rather quickly. Not sure how that happened."

"We're going to have our own worries," Rutger said, looking down at the clipboard in his hand, charts and graphs filling the first page.

Master George groaned, not needing yet another fly in his biscuit. "What is it, Rutger?"

"All these quakes are gonna send a tidal wave right down on top of us."

The muddy ground rumbled and grumbled around Tick and his friends. The trees of the forest were only a hundred feet away and shook like grasses caught in a wind. Every few seconds a loud crack filled the air as the wooden fence split from the raging quake.

At least nothing was falling on them from above.

Tick got to his feet, wobbling back and forth. The deep mud around his shoes actually helped him keep an uneasy balance. Jane stood nearby, her face blank, swaying with the earth's movements as she grasped her Staff with both hands. Tick decided to get it all out in a rush, leaving her no time to talk back until he was finished.

"Ja—" He stopped himself. "*Mistress* Jane. The Haunce is supposed to come here any moment. Then we all have to work together to somehow fix whatever it is you did to the Realities. If we don't, everything's gonna be destroyed, and every single person in every single Reality is going to die. So we need to make a deal—we need to put aside our fight and do what the Haunce wants us to do."

She didn't respond, only stared at him with those black holes she called eyes.

"Are you even listening to me?" he yelled, unable to restrain himself. "*You* did this! Now we have to make it better, make it go away. What good is it to you if we all—"

"Don't insult me, you stupid child!" she screamed back at him, her face transforming to anger so quickly that Tick didn't see the usual flow of red metal. "I'm fully aware of what's going on. Of course I'm going to do whatever it takes to fix it. You think I'd be foolish enough to jeopardize my plans over something so . . . human as pride? Now stop your arrogant spouting, and let's get on with it. Where is the Haunce? Where are we supposed to meet that big cloud of electrical waste?"

Her insults and tone didn't faze Tick in the least. "I don't know. It just said I needed to come here and convince you to help. We had to meet here because for some reason, the Chi'karda is stronger here than anywhere else."

"Of course." A particularly strong bounce in the ground made her stumble backward. "That's why I built the Factory here. And why I'm able to do the miraculous things you just saw."

Tick just happened to look at Sofia as she rolled her eyes, then literally bit her lip to keep from saying something smart. As for him, he didn't know what to do. He'd come to the right place; he'd convinced Jane she needed to help. What now?

A few minutes passed. No one spoke, only observed the world shaking and cracking all around them. Tick didn't know when exactly he'd dropped to his knees on the ground, but having the lower half of his legs firmly entrenched in mud sure helped his balance. His thoughts drifted to his family, to his Reality, to what horrible things must be happening there and the terror the people he cared about must be feeling.

Before his heart completely melted into a pool of pity and anguish, he snapped his mind away from it all. None of it mattered. Nothing mattered unless he got the job done right here, right now.

A stiff wind picked up out of nowhere, blowing swirls all around them, pulling at their clothes and hair. Tick squinted his eyes against the flying grit. A few jagged streaks of electricity abruptly knifed through the air in a spot just a few yards away from the group. The thin lightning bolts fired back and forth, collapsing in on each other as if they were trapped inside an invisible sphere. Then it all collapsed into a blinding ball of whiteness, hovering above the ground.

Tick looked away, a big bright spot in his vision. He heard a loud thrum of energy combined with the snaps of popping static. Surges of that now-familiar womping Chi'karda washed over his body in waves of tingles and vibrations. When he finally blinked his vision back to normal and returned his gaze to the spot, the glowing silver-blue orb of the Haunce floated there, its many faces alternating rapidly.

It spoke in a deep and resonating voice, its face changing from an old, wrinkled woman to a young boy as it did so. "It is far worse than we feared. Millions are dead already. Come, hurry. In thirty minutes, the universe will no longer exist."

CHAPTER
52

CREATURES IN THE DARK

Screams up ahead. Some human, but most unnatural, almost demonic. Explosions. Thumps of sound more felt than heard. Ragers and Shurrics, most likely.

Encouraged, Sato moved toward it all, keeping his right shoulder close to the rock wall, doing his best not to fall down at every lurch of the earthquake. The air had brightened slightly, but he still could barely see. Here he was supposed to be leading a great army in their very first battle, and he'd somehow ended up all by himself, nowhere near the action. He would've felt guilty if he had the time or energy to worry about such things.

Rapid footsteps approached, accompanied by grunts

and gurgly breathing. It sounded like a whole pack of Jane's creations coming straight for him. Sato reached into his pockets and pulled out a Squeezer grenade in one hand, a Rager in the other. He crouched down and backed into a natural alcove in the stone, hoping not to have to use the weapons until the monsters were past him, hoping they wouldn't notice him.

His wish came true—mostly. At least thirty creatures ran by in a storm of heavy footfalls and flying sweat. Sato could see only their outlines: hunchbacked wolves walking on their hind legs. He shuddered and had to fight not to close his eyes and act like a little kid wishing they were just nightmares that would go away.

The last one of the group stopped as its companions kept moving. Sato held his breath and tried to shrink into the stone at his back. The odd creature sniffed several times and pivoted its muzzled head back and forth. Sniffed again. And again.

Sato didn't move, only tightened his fingers around the grenade, ready to throw it directly at the monster's chest and run if it came to that. The creature took a step toward him, then another. Sniffed again. Made a low, wet, rattling sound somewhere deep in its throat. Another sniff. Sato could see its outline plainly; it was just a few feet away. He could only hope the thing had poor eyesight or wasn't expecting something huddled near the ground.

It took another step toward him, sniffed, and let out its growl again.

A sharp barking sound rang out from where its companions had gone. The creature in front of Sato barked back—a horrible, horrible sound—before it turned in a slow circle, giving the area one last look, sniffing again and again. It took two slow steps away from Sato then turned and ran after the others.

When the monstrous thing had finally been swallowed by the inky gloom of the tunnel, Sato got back to his feet and threw the two projectiles as hard as he could after it. He didn't wait to see the result, but sprinted in the near-darkness in the opposite direction, toward the still-clanging sounds of battle. A few seconds passed before he heard the Squeezer's boom and the clatter of flying wires behind him, followed by the electric-tinged explosion of the Rager. Inhuman screams pierced the air, flying through the tunnel like a wind full of death.

Sato kept running.

❧

The Haunce obviously didn't think there was any time for manners.

"We need to get rid of the boy and girl. We do not need them." Its eyes—set in the face of a middle-aged man with a huge nose—darted at Paul and Sofia. "And if they stand too close to us when we begin, they will explode."

Nervous pangs, almost painful, bit and poked at Tick's insides. Luckily, his friends didn't seem to think they should argue the point.

"So what do we do?" Paul asked, kneeling on the ground on all fours struggling to keep his balance.

Tick had an idea. "Master George!" he yelled as loud as his sore throat would allow. "If you somehow made it back to headquarters, wink Paul and Sofia back!"

"Wait!" Sofia snapped. "We should stay here, go find Sato. Help him rescue all those—"

Too late. She and Paul disappeared.

❧

"—kids!" Sofia barely got the word out before she collapsed to the hard metal floor of Master George's headquarters in the Bermuda Triangle. Going from an earthquake to the steady surface totally threw her off balance.

"Whoa! Hey!" This from Paul. "How'd you do that so fast?"

She looked at him kneeling next to her, mud caked all over his pants, then up at a grinning Rutger. "Yeah, how did you know what Tick was saying?"

Rutger looked like a proud parent. "You kids still have a lot to learn. I was monitoring your nanolocators more closely than anyone else's, and we can pick up the vibrations in your larynx when you speak. How do you think we kept such good tabs on you when you were being recruited?"

"You guys seriously creep me out sometimes," Paul said. He got to his feet and wiped at the mud on his clothes. He held out his hands, a disgusted look on his face. "Don't you think we deserve some privacy?"

Rutger scoffed at him. "We only monitor in emergencies. Now quit your boo-hooing and come with me to see Master George in the Control Room. We have some serious problems."

Why didn't Sofia feel in the least bit surprised?

As soon as his friends vanished, Tick made his way closer to the Haunce, stumbling left and right through the mud. The cracks of the nearby wooden fence splitting and tumbling filled the air.

Jane lifted off the ground and floated the few feet over to their visitor, landing with a squish in the soft earth just as Tick reached a spot right next to her. They both turned their attention to the Haunce.

The ghostly creature showed the face of a young

Asian boy. "We know the two of you are bitter enemies. We have observed you both from afar with the utmost interest. Your base and childish actions have disappointed us many, many times. We know that in your hearts, you both want to kill the other." Its face morphed into a pretty lady as it paused.

Tick, shocked by this odd opening statement, looked at Jane, but she didn't return his gaze, her mask blank, her eyes focused on the Haunce. Tick glanced back at the silvery glowing face, now an old man. "Yeah, you pretty much nailed that one."

The Haunce's voice rose in volume, sounding almost excited. "It is time to put that aside. We cannot let trivial matters interfere with what we are about to do. Your hatred, your anger, your ill-fated desires— they must disappear. Now. Do you both understand?"

Tick nodded, though he couldn't imagine actually accomplishing such a thing. He hated the woman next to him more than he'd ever known it was possible to hate. But he did try to slide those thoughts and feelings behind the angst of what was now more important. He would do whatever the Haunce told him to do.

The Haunce's eyes focused on Jane, waiting. Tick noticed in his peripheral vision that she gave a very slow but obvious nod. Just once.

"We can only hope," the Haunce said through the lips of a hideously ugly man, "that after this experience—

if we succeed—you and the rest of the living will remember how close you came to never living again. That you will learn how to live appropriately. That you will learn to see life as the gift that it is."

Tick couldn't help but feel a deluge of impatience. Now didn't seem like the best time for a lecture from a big, fat ghost. They needed to get on with it!

The Haunce's current face trembled, its eyes narrowing as if it had realized the same thing and was refocusing on the task at hand. "The minutes are ticking away. It is time to begin. What you are about to experience will feel very . . . odd."

Tick swallowed the giant lump in his throat. He felt such a powerful swell of nervousness in his chest, he thought for sure his heart had been crushed. But then the Haunce turned into a face that looked so much like his mom he almost fell backward. The lady smiled, and the smallest trickle of peace washed through Tick's insides.

It didn't last long. A blinding white light came from everywhere at once, the mud and forest and fence and blue sky swallowed by its brilliance. A loud buzzing sound filled his ears.

And then he felt himself explode.

CHAPTER
53

ETERNITY

Sato was thankful for the growing light as he ran through the tunnels, sick of that terrified feeling of blindness in the dark. But it was greatly tempered by the increasing sounds of horror from up ahead. Screeches, mostly from creatures he knew couldn't be human. Cries of pain from those that were. Explosions and cracking rock.

When he turned a corner and saw the full spectrum of battle in front of him, he couldn't help but stop. He stared at the scene, having second thoughts about his self-imposed calling for the hundredth time that day.

A massive chamber that looked to have once been some sort of underground atrium for Jane's Factory now looked like a tornado had touched down. Chunks of earth and stone littered the floor, some taller than a grown man. Patches of open sky broke up what had once been a painted ceiling—murals of Bible stories and famous moments from history. In his quick scan he noticed half of Noah's ark and a scene of Abraham Lincoln sitting in the theater where he had been shot.

On the floor, dozens of Fifths fought a variety of Jane's creations, outnumbered twenty to one. At least. But the advanced weapons of the Realitants seemed to even the score. Still, he saw with a pang to his heart that several of the tall soldiers lay dying or dead.

Squeezer grenades exploded on the left and right, downing a whole slew of hairy, fanged beasts, all of whom fell to the ground squealing and squirming from the attacking wires. One of the Fifths shot her Halter tube, sending a spray of darts that immediately para-lyzed five or six four-legged things with wings flapping their way through one of the holes in the ceiling; they plummeted to the ground and crashed with a sicken-ing crunch. Thumps from Shurrics pummeled the air like the beating of silent drums. Every time a shot hit its mark, a creature went flying until it smashed into a wall.

Sato watched the battle with an odd mixture of feelings—guilt that he wasn't out there, an urge to run and join them, terror at the thought of doing so, pride that his little army fought so strongly and bravely—were maybe even winning. Mostly though, it reminded him of what horrible things Jane was doing here by using innocent animals to create those hideous beasts—and soon she would be using children.

He knew what he had to do. He knew his place. There'd be plenty of time in the days and years ahead to lead men and women into battle. But for now, he had to leave the very capable Fifth Army to the fight. He had to find those kids. He had to find them and save them.

He was about to turn around and start searching the complex when Mothball appeared out of the fray, running straight toward him. She pulled up, sucking in huge gulps of air. Then she patted a bulge in the side of her shirt.

"Been . . . waitin' on ya . . . I 'ave," she spit out between breaths. "Got a whole . . . mess of them . . . nanolocators in me pocket."

She didn't have to say another word. Sato was grateful for the help.

"Let's go," he said.

~

Tick floated in emptiness in a realm he didn't understand.

He hadn't felt any pain when his body erupted into billions of tiny parts. It had been more like a wash of tingles spreading across a warm, glowing sensation. Really pleasurable, actually. But now a sense of panic set in as his mind tried to comprehend the impossible thing that had just happened to him.

He could barely articulate within his own thoughts what his five senses were experiencing. He saw spinning lights, orange globes, streaks of blue and silver—all on a canvas of the deepest black he'd ever seen. It was like he floated in the depths of unexplored outer space. That same buzzing sound surrounded him, mixed with something that reminded him of waterfalls. The air had a slightly burnt odor to it. Without understanding how he knew, he realized that he didn't exist in his usual human form anymore. He had become . . . part of the things that he witnessed around him.

And yet he was still Tick. Still had the cognitive functions of his brain. Still kid enough to simultaneously think this was really cool and also really scary.

The Haunce spoke, and its booming voice made those peripheral sounds dampened and dull. Tick couldn't see the collection of ghosts—just heard it with ears he didn't have at the moment.

"Atticus. Jane. Nothing we could have said beforehand could have prepared you for what we have done to you. For that reason, we said nothing. With time running out, we must begin our attempt to rebind the barriers of the Realities, to seal up the cracking splits and seams, to make the universe whole again. In the end, we promise we will do everything in our power to return you to your prior forms."

Tick didn't like the sound of that. If they succeeded, there must be a chance he'd never make it back to what he'd had before. Maybe he'd have to float here for the rest of his life.

"Where are we?" he asked, though he had no idea how he did it with no tongue and no mouth, no audible words. It was more like he'd projected his thoughts. "And what did you do to us. What are we right now?"

"Yes." It was Jane's voice, but not her voice. "I think we deserve to know what we've volunteered for."

When the Haunce spoke again, Tick heard real emotion in its voice for the first time: impatience. "We have mere minutes, do you understand? It would take us a hundred lifetimes to explain the complexities of what and who and where you are right now. You are in the depths of space, in the smallest of smallest quantum realms, on the infinite path, in the past, present, and future. All at once. You are a trillion miles long and an atom's width short. You are here and there and everywhere. You are, quite simply, joined with eternity. One day you will understand. Perhaps. But for now, you must do what we say, or everyone and everything will die!"

Tick listened in awe, hoping Jane would shut up and do the same.

The Haunce continued, sounding a little nicer. "The true power of Chi'karda lies not in scientific formulas and complicated theorems and atomic mapping. No. It lies within the heart and mind and spirit. It lies in the power of the soulikens. The two of you have more Chi'karda concentrated within you than any two humans we have ever observed. Far more. We still do not understand why this is so with Jane. Atticus, you have it because every one of your Alterants has died, and their soulikens have transferred to you. Why that happened, we do not know for sure."

If Tick's face had existed, he would've scrunched it up in confusion. But he remained quiet.

Jane didn't. "I thought you said we had no time to waste."

"Silence! Every word we speak is vital. You need to know that the Chi'karda is magnificently potent and powerful within both of you. Almost violently so. You must know this so you will have the confidence that the task you are about to perform will indeed accomplish our mutual goal of saving the Realities. Do not try to understand how or why. The breakdown of the intricate and infinitely complex background of it is for us to worry about. The two of you will use your powers in a way that your minds best decide to present it to you symbolically."

The Haunce paused then, maybe to let its words sink

in. Tick didn't quite understand—not at all, actually—but he knew better than to resort to any childish antics when everything was on the line. He'd only move forward and do what he was asked to do.

"The two most powerful and effective things in the universe are the human mind and Chi'karda," the Haunce continued. "They will now work together within you to present what we need in a way you will best understand it. Trust your instincts and accomplish the task. That is all. By doing so, you will put the pieces in place to heal the breaches in the Barriers. No matter what, trust what you see. No matter what, do what is asked of you. No matter what. Do you both understand?"

Tick's first instinct was to nod, but nothing moved because there wasn't anything to move. So he verbalized again. "Yeah. Yes. I understand."

"Jane?"

She didn't answer until a few seconds passed, probably trying to save a little face, a little power. "Yes. I understand."

"Then let the process begin," the Haunce pronounced.

CHAPTER
54

WORDS ON A TREE

Again, Tick could never have explained to anyone what happened next. The swirling lights and glowing orbs and colored streaks suddenly twisted around him like a pyrotechnic tornado, spinning and spinning until he wished he could close his eyes or look away. Dizziness filled him, those pleasurable feelings of floating and tingles and warmth gone in an instant.

Everything blended into one bright, all-encompassing light around him, joined by a rushing sound of wind and roaring trains. Tick felt a pressure, small at first then building, as if his parts had been thrown into a compressor and were being squeezed back together. It had just started to hurt when it all stopped, instantly. The light, the sounds, the heavy force.

He felt nothing. He saw only darkness.

Then things began to change.

One by one, his senses picked up new impressions. He heard a soft wind blowing through the branches of trees. Cold prickled his skin as he suddenly felt that same cool breeze, felt the crisp air all around him. The strong smell of pine trees filled his nose as he pulled in a deep breath. He licked his lips, tasted salt. The bottom of his feet pressed against something—he was standing—and they were cold, too.

Wind. Nose. Lips. Feet.

Tick had been put back together. But why the darkness?

Idiot, he chastised himself. His eyes were closed.

He opened them and took in another burst of quick breath.

A forest surrounded him, a thick layer of freshly fallen snow making the whole place a winter wonderland. Huge trees—mostly pine—towered above him, their branches heavily laden with the puffy white stuff. Tick glanced down to see his feet buried clear up to the ankles. Some of the snow had melted, and his socks were wet, his toes beginning to freeze.

He looked around at the tightly packed trees that went on in every direction as far as he could see. He slowly turned in a circle, taking it all in. The place was beautiful and reminded him of the woods near his home in Washington, though this forest seemed even larger and more widespread.

He'd turned about ninety degrees when he noticed a piece of paper stapled to a thick oak tree just a few feet away. The paper didn't seem wet at all, which meant someone had to have put it there recently, and several lines had been written on its surface. Curious, he stepped forward, slogging through the snow until he reached the mysterious note, now only inches from his eyes.

He began to read but didn't get very far before he knew exactly what it was.

A riddle.

Mothball's flashlight unfurled a spooky path in front of them.

Sato felt like he'd been soldiering with her for years. They slunk their way through the still-shaking tunnels and hallways of the Factory like old pros, anticipating each other's movements as they tried to use their four eyeballs to look in every direction for potential enemies. So far it seemed as if all of Jane's creatures had congregated at the main battle.

Shurrics cocked and gripped in their hands, they

searched and searched. They had to find where these monsters kept the kids.

When they reached a T, Mothball shone her flashlight both directions.

Sato asked, "Left or right?"

She didn't answer, but instead held a finger up to her lips to shush him.

Sato nodded slightly and listened. The faintest sound floated through the cracking and roaring of shifting stone around them. He strained his ears to hear it, even closed his eyes for a second. A whimper. A cry. Moaning. Sobbing. After a few seconds, the sound cut off abruptly with a terror-filled shriek. Then silence.

Sato met Mothball's dark gaze. "That way for sure."

They went to the left.

Sofia sat next to Rutger, fascinated by all the blips and numbers and graphs and charts and squiggly lines on the computer screens. She didn't know what all of it meant yet, and Rutger didn't seem too keen on teaching her with everything that was going on.

"Okay," he said. "I hope this doesn't offend you, Sofia, but what I really need most from you is to run messages back and forth between me and Master George in the Control Room."

It took all of her power not to growl at him like a wolf. No time for wounded pride. "Why don't you have all this junk in the same place?"

Rutger snickered like she'd told a joke. "It used to fit," was all he said.

"At least tell me what you're doing and what he's doing."

Rutger waved his chubby little hand in the air; Sofia had no idea why.

"He's in charge of organizing the rescue of the kids at the Factory. The Barrier Wand's hooked in and set up to wink the nanolocators from the patches we gave Sato and his army. Sally, Priscilla, and a few other Realitants have set up shop in the Grand Canyon. That's where the kids will be winked to. Not enough room here."

"And your job?" she asked.

"Two main things. We're tracking Tick and Mothball and Sato and his army. I'm also tapped into the meteorological reports and ocean monitoring stations. I don't think there's any doubt—we're going to get hit by a massive tidal wave from one of these earthquakes. Not if, when."

Sofia had been studying the screens as he spoke, and her eyes finally focused in on something she should've noticed from the very first. Sato and Mothball and the others had lots of information scrolling and blinking beneath their names. But not Tick.

His screen was blank from top to bottom. Nothing but black space.

She pointed at it. "What's up with Tick?"

Rutger let out a long and dramatic sigh. "Well, Master George says he expected something like this, but it still makes my feet all itchy."

Sofia felt something shrivel inside her. "What do you mean? What's wrong?"

"According to this, Tick's nanolocator is dead."

Tick couldn't believe it. A riddle.

Now he understood what the Haunce had meant when it said that somehow the healing of the Barriers would be presented to each of them in a form that would seem familiar. Symbolically. Tick thought it was almost like a video game—solving the riddle would be like maneuvering the joystick and pushing buttons on the controller, the complex processes and codes and circuits translating those movements into what he saw on the TV screen.

A riddle.

If anything had defined his journey so far as a Realitant, it had to be riddles.

And here he had another one. A doozy.

Concentrating, he read through it one more time:

Look at the following most carefully, as every line counts:

Be gone in times of death's long passing.
Henry Atwood sliced his neck.
Hath reeds knocked against thee?
If our fathers knew, then winds, they blew.
The sixth of candles burned my eyes.
Horrors even among us.
Leigh tries to eat a stone.
The canine or the cat, it spat.
Pay attention to the ghoul that weeps.

Your number's up, and it is missing. Wary the word second.
Shout out your answer.

A new line suddenly appeared at the very bottom of the page, the space blank one second, then filled with several words the next:

The universe ends in 11:58

And then, as impossible at it seemed, the written time at the end of the sentence started changing, ticking down like a digital clock.

11:57
11:56
11:55
11:54

Tick already had the riddle memorized. He closed his eyes and started thinking.

CHAPTER
55

AN UNEARTHLY SHRIEK

Sato heard more of the chilling sound bites over the now all-too-present quaking noises as he and Mothball stumbled their way down the tunnel and closer to a light source up ahead. Sato heard whimpers and cries for help—all of them the high-pitched voices of children. Anger stirred within him, almost completely obliterating the fear and trepidation he'd been feeling. And all the while, the threat of the entire Factory collapsing on top of them loomed over their heads—literally.

They came to a stony bend where the light grew stronger. Mothball stopped and crouched on the shaky ground right at the edge, her head just a few inches below Sato's. He leaned against the wall beside her, his gut telling him they were on the cusp now of discovering the true horror of this place. He sensed the fear around the corner, as if the kids' tears and sweat evaporated into a noxious cloud that poured through the opening he couldn't see.

Mothball dared a peek. "Gotta be it," she whispered. "Monster or two just 'round the corner, guardin' a door. Lug a Squeezer, we should."

Sato reached into his pocket and pulled out one of the small grenades in answer. "I'll throw it. Soon as it pops, let's charge in shooting the Shurrics."

Mothball nodded then returned her attention forward, gripping the Shurric firmly, its business end pointed away, ready to shoot. Sato stepped away from the wall so he could have the right angle, then tossed the Squeezer around the corner.

It bounced off the far wall then hit the floor with a clang, disappearing from sight as it bounced forward. Seconds later it exploded, sending out a spray of small metal rods. Many of them clinked against the stone, but a few found their marks with a deadly thud. Two or three creatures howled an unearthly shriek.

"Go!" Sato yelled.

He moved to run around the corner, keeping Mothball to his right. He was about to pull the trigger of his Shurric when he saw two bear-like creatures sprawled on the ground, unmoving. A small lamp stood on a table, its glass broken in two places but still lit. Two chairs had toppled over, along with the guards.

Sato looked at the wooden door they'd been guarding. "A Rager ought to—"

Heavy thumps from Mothball's Shurric cut him off, like invisible lightning and soundless thunder—felt, more than heard. On her third shot, the door exploded with a spray of splinters, flying away from them several feet before falling into some kind of abyss. Sato waited and watched, but he never heard the wooden shards hit anything below.

He exchanged a puzzled look with Mothball then warily crept toward the gaping doorway—he didn't want a sudden uptick in the never-ending quake's strength to send him over the edge—his Shurric armed and ready. He reached the threshold of the door and saw that the other side had no floor, only a sheer drop-off with no bottom in sight as far as he could tell. He slowly leaned his head out to get a better look.

They'd reached a vast, round chamber, at least one hundred feet in diameter, that tunneled toward the depths below, narrowing into a hole of blackness far, far down. Along the walls of the chamber were countless rectangular compartments, alcoves set deeper into the stone and open-faced. Inside those compartments were filthy mattresses with thin, ratty blankets. And on top of those nasty beds lay the most terrified-looking children Sato had ever seen.

"Oh, no."

Rutger hadn't spoken in a while, and Sofia realized she'd kind of fallen into a daze, worried about Tick and what it meant that his nanolocator had died. And why Master George seemed to think that was okay, or at least expected.

"What's wrong?" she asked.

Rutger turned away from the busy computer screens, scratching his nose as he stared at the floor. "It's a big one. A really big one."

"What is?" Sofia insisted, almost reaching out and shaking his shoulders.

Rutger looked at her, the usual sparkle in his eyes gone. "A massive tidal wave. Bigger than anything I've ever heard of. It's completely destroyed several monitoring stations. And I know enough to see it's gonna hit us dead-on!"

Sofia choked on several attempts to ask the obvious questions, but finally managed to speak. "When? How long?"

"Thirty minutes."

7:32
7:31
7:30
7:29

Tick had given up on the closed-eyes thinking bit. It wasn't working. Not at all. The lines of the riddle didn't make any sense whatsoever. None.

Something told him there was a visual aspect to it. Something in the first and last line appeared to be instructional, not part of the riddle itself. He forced himself to pretend he didn't have it memorized and read it from beginning to end once again.

Look at the following most carefully, as every line counts:

Be gone in times of death's long passing.
Henry Atwood sliced his neck.
Hath reeds knocked against thee?
If our fathers knew, then winds, they blew.
The sixth of candles burned my eyes.
Horrors even among us.
Leigh tries to eat a stone.
The canine or the cat, it spat.
Pay attention to the ghoul that weeps.

Your number's up, and it is missing. Wary the word second.
Shout out your answer.

5:47
5:46
5:45
5:44

His mind continued churning, pressing, scrambling, processing. There was definitely something visual about the riddle.

Look carefully.

Every line counts.

Your number's up. It is missing. The word second.

Look. Line. Counts. Number. Missing. Second.

His thoughts honed in on those six words. Somehow he knew they meant everything.

~~~~~~

There were a lot of things Sato didn't understand as he stood on that dangerous ledge, staring at the curved walls of cubbyholes filled with children. He had questions aplenty. Like why they were kept in such an odd location, why there weren't any ladders, how the children were used in the first place, where they came from. Plenty of things to wonder and ponder and feel disgust over.

But with the whole Factory shaking and ready to collapse at any second, there was only one thing that mattered: getting the nanolocator patches on every kid in sight.

"Divvy them up," he told Mothball, holding out his hand. "We don't have much time."

"Got no ladders or steps," she replied as she put a huge handful of the patches into his hand. "Got no rope. Whatcha ruddy thinkin' we'll do, fly around like birdies to save 'em?"

Sato slipped the square pieces of paper into his pocket and gave her a glare so hard that she took a full step backward. He was instantly filled with shame, but he said what he felt anyway. "Yes, Mothball. We'll fly if that's what we have to do."

Without waiting for a response, he turned until his back was to the abyss behind him, his toes balanced on the former threshold of the door. He crouched down, then let himself slip over the edge.

CHAPTER
56

WHAT IS MISSING

Sato put his hands out, letting the pads of his fingers and palms scrape along the surface of the stone wall as he fell. He focused his concentration so he would be ready for the first opportunity to grab on to something. Fighting off the terrifying panic, he felt as if each nanosecond seemed to beat out a long rhythm.

Bumps and cracks and knobs of rock tore at his skin, but his attempts to grip them proved worthless. The dark surface of the wall suddenly lightened, and he found himself staring into one of the rectangle cubbyholes at a small boy curled up into a ball on his ragged mattress, shaking from the earthquake or bodily ills, or both.

Sato threw his arms forward, hitting the lower floor of the compartment with a terrible bite of pain. His downward movement slammed to a momentary stop, but then he was slipping again, desperately grasping with his fingers for anything to hold on to. A curl of loose blanket, a moist wrinkle of mattress—gone as soon as he touched them. He was just about to fall completely away when his right foot landed on a jutting outcrop of rock; a jolt shivered through every nerve.

Crying out from the pain and shock of his sudden stop, he was still able to take advantage of the moment and adjust his grip on the lower flat edge of stone with his arms. Breathing heavily, Sato couldn't help but pause to make sure it was really true—that he'd really stopped himself from plummeting to his death far below. Hanging there, he looked up to see Mothball looking down on him from twenty feet above.

"A might risky that was," she called out, though a huge smile draped her homely face. Before he could respond, she reared back and took a giant leap to the side, sliding down the stone face as he had done until she caught the next compartment over—with a lot more grace and fewer bruises and scratches, no doubt.

"You think we can do this?" Sato asked, climbing up into the inset hole. The chamber still shook around him, but he'd almost gotten used to it, his body adapting to its movements.

"Like ya said," Mothball responded. "We'll ruddy fly if we have to."

Sato scooted close to the boy sitting there, his arms wrapped around his knees, his eyes filled with a hope that almost broke Sato's heart. The boy wore a dirty shirt and shorts, his hair messed and greasy.

"You okay?" Sato asked. "We're here to take you away. Save you."

The boy didn't answer, but the slightest hint of a smile graced his face.

"This is gonna surprise you, but in a few seconds you'll be far away from here." Sato took one of the nanolocator patches out of his pocket and slapped it on the boy's bare leg.

An instant later, the kid disappeared.

1:45
1:44
1:43
1:42

Tick couldn't help but stare at the dwindling time as it ticked toward the annihilation of the entire universe. His mind wanted him to waste his brain power wondering how all of time and eternity could be dependent on him solving a stupid riddle. He pushed the question away again and again. Pushed away thoughts of what Jane and the Haunce were doing and whether his efforts would matter anyway.

1:21
1:20

"Stop it, Tick!" he yelled to the empty forest. "Think!"

The answer floated just outside his sphere of concentration. He was almost there.

Every line counts.

Counts.

Nine sentences that made no sense at all or seemed to be related to each other in any way.

Number's up.

Number.

0:46
0:45

Sweat soaked his forehead, his armpits, his hands. The cold air did nothing to help.

0:40
0:39

Wary the word second.
Second.
Second word.

0:31
0:30

It all came together so instantly, so unexpectedly, that he felt a lump explode in his throat, racking him with a coughing fit. As he hacked the air through his sore throat, he focused on the words of the riddle. His eyes played tricks, making the answer appear as if the letters themselves had magically changed to help him out. He finally quit coughing and couldn't believe now that he hadn't seen it all from the very beginning:

Look at the following most carefully, as every line counts:

Be <u>gone</u> in times of death's long passing.
Henry A<u>two</u>od sliced his neck.
Ha<u>th ree</u>ds knocked against thee?
If <u>our</u> fathers knew, then winds, they blew.
The <u>six</u>th of candles burned my eyes.
Horror<u>s even</u> among us.
L<u>eigh t</u>ries to eat a stone.
The ca<u>nine</u> or the cat, it spat.
Pay a<u>tten</u>tion to the ghoul that weeps.

Your number's up, and it is missing. Wary the word second. Shout out your answer.

0:10
0:09

The second word of each sentence contained at least part of the numbers he was supposed to look for. To count. And yes, a number was missing.

0:04
0:03

Tick sucked in a quick breath of air then screamed as loudly as possible.

"Five! The answer is five!"

The forest around him sucked away into blackness as once again he exploded into trillions of pieces.

CHAPTER
57

FROM BAD TO WORSE

Sofia followed Rutger into the main Control Room, where Master George was waving his arms like the conductor of the world's largest symphony. Despite all their troubles crashing down at once, a small snicker escaped Sofia. She quickly coughed to cover it up, but Paul—sitting nearby with worry on his face—noticed and broke a half-smile that looked more like a wince.

"George!" Rutger barked. "Most of the earthquakes have stopped, but it's too late for that wave. It's gonna be here in fifteen minutes!"

Their leader shot them a quick glance then returned his gaze to the rapidly blinking screens in front of him.

"My heart can barely stand this confounded predicament!"

"What's the latest with Sato?" Rutger asked as he and Sofia moved closer.

Master George pointed to a series of purple lines that kept appearing then disappearing. Unlike the indicators for Sato and Mothball above them, these had no names attached. "They're doing it. They're doing it! We've already winked ten children to the Grand Canyon, where Priscilla and Sally have several doctors on hand."

Rutger let out a sigh that sounded like he'd lost every ounce of hope. "We won't survive it," he said in a tight whisper.

"What's that?" Master George asked, finally giving his full attention to his partner.

"The wave. There's no way we can survive it. It's too big. We . . ." Rutger looked at the floor.

"What? Spit it out, man!"

"We have to leave. This location—and us with it—has zero chance of making it through the wave's power. It'll rip our cabling technology to shreds, then pick us up and slam us into shore. We have to leave."

Sofia felt that shrinking sensation in her gut again. She half-expected Master George to argue, to say it would be okay, maybe express disbelief or babble about how life's unfair. Instead, he accepted the truth and immediately moved to what needed to be done. Sofia was impressed.

"Then we can only hope they reach every child in time—we don't have things properly set up at the Grand Canyon to wink them in from that location. We'll wait here, monitoring the situation and managing the nanolocator patches. At least we have a bit of good news—if the earthquakes have stopped, then Atticus and Jane must've done their job."

Sofia's heart lifted, but then she remembered their own problem. "What about the wave?" she asked, her eyes meeting Paul's, sharing a look that said so much with no need for words.

Master George puffed his chest out and folded his hands on his belly. "The four of us will wink away the second before it hits. It's time for us to be very brave."

Tick found himself back in that outer-space-like void of lights and streaks and glowing, brilliant orbs. He couldn't feel his body, didn't understand what or where or anything else. But he knew they'd done it even before the Haunce spoke to them.

"Through your efforts and power, we have healed the Barriers of the Realities. We will send you back now. Your worlds are not destroyed, but they have

461

still seen great, great devastation. The healing of such things does not rest in our hands. We say farewell."

The universe spun. Everything changed, and Tick felt the pressure of crushing diamonds.

～～～

Sato put everything out of his mind. The fear. The soreness of his entire body. His hunger, his exhaustion. From somewhere deep in his cells and molecules and tissue, he sucked out the adrenaline he needed to keep moving.

From one inset compartment to the next, he jumped. They were about four feet apart side to side, a little less up and down. Each and every time, for one frightening second, he thought he wouldn't make it and instead would plummet to the unseen depths far below. But so far he'd landed each and every time, gripping and pushing and pulling, squirming his way to the children without falling to his death. Mothball was doing the same, working the other side of the stony, rounded chamber.

He spared a glance for the latest kid he'd found—a shaky, pale girl whose eyes were open and focused on his. "Don't worry," he said. "We're here to rescue you." He'd always wanted to say that to someone.

He slapped a nanolocator patch on her arm, no longer waiting to watch as the kids vanished from sight, winked away by Master George. Already on the move, he crouched on the far end, ready to leap for the next hole, when he noticed two things at the same time that made him pause.

One, the shaking and quaking had stopped completely.

And two, he heard the distant sounds of flapping wings and a chattering, cackling chorus of grunts and squeals coming from below. He looked down.

Several fangen—those horrible creations of Jane's they'd fought at her castle when George sent them to steal her Barrier Wand—were flying through the murky darkness, coming up toward him.

Sato jumped to the next compartment.

～⌒～

Tick blinked, dazzled by the light of the sun directly overhead. He stood in the mud just outside the broken and jumbled heap of wood that had once been the fence surrounding the Factory. Mistress Jane stood right in front of him, her expressionless red mask only inches from his face.

For the briefest of moments, he forgot that she was his bitter, bitter enemy.

"I can't believe we did it," he said, not ashamed of the childlike wonder in his voice. They had, after all, just saved the entire universe. "All I had to do was solve a riddle—seems crazy. What did the Haunce make you do?"

Jane's mask broke into a smile so full of genuine kindness that Tick wondered if the whole experience had maybe changed something inside her. "Isn't it wonderful, Atticus? What does it say about our species that you and I could put aside our hatred for each other and work for the greater good? We should both feel very proud."

Tick let out an uneasy laugh, not sure how he felt about the way she was acting. "It's definitely pretty cool. So . . . you didn't answer my question. What did you have to do? How did you do your part?"

Jane's mask kept smiling. "Ah, yes. It was quite an amazing thing. The Haunce had me work through my master plan for how to achieve the Utopian Reality I've always wanted. What an invigorating experience it was to focus my mind and faculties in such a heightened, rushed state of anxiety." She moved even closer to him, almost touching.

Tick didn't know what to think. Maybe she—

A burst of pain exploded in his stomach, a wrenching, twisting stab of fire and needles. He stumbled back two steps and looked down. The hilt of a large knife jutted from his abdomen, a dark red bloodstain soaking his shirt, spreading.

Choking and sputtering a cough, he raised his eyes to Jane, whose now-angry mask matched the color of the growing stain around the knife.

"My plan started with something just like that," she said.

CHAPTER
58

FAMILY

Tick fell to his knees, both hands gripped around the hilt of the knife, his hands wet with warm blood. He didn't dare pull it out. Clumpy fluid lodged in his throat, cutting off his breath along with the panic that choked him. He tried to suck down air through his nose, but it ended in a cough every time. Bugs of light swam in front of his eyes.

He couldn't speak. He didn't know what he'd say if he could.

Jane crouched down to the ground, the mud caking her robe. "Subtle. That's what I told Frazier. I knew I had to wait until the right moment when you weren't on guard and ready to strike back with your Chi'karda. A knife deep to the stomach—such a simple and beautiful thing. So old-fashioned. It's almost impossible to find help in time. You're dying, Atticus. Tick. Nothing can help you now."

Tick collapsed to the side, and a fresh, striking burst of pain burrowed through his entire body, as if the knife had sprouted steely vines that coursed through his insides. On the outer rim of his consciousness, he realized he'd never come close to understanding the fear of dying. Death had never truly seemed real. And now it was here, ready to drag him away like a stolen bag of gold.

Jane leaned over until the cool metal of her mask touched his ear. She whispered, "The rest of my plan is for the good of mankind and the Realities. Except for one thing, one item on the list—revenge, Atticus. Revenge. I want your last thought in life to be this: to know that I will hunt down each and every member of your family and kill them. Your friends as well. I'll kill them just like I did you. Good-bye."

She stood up, though Tick could barely see her. His vision blurred, dark specks swirling like a cloud of stinging gnats. He felt his life slipping away, a physical dwindling as if he were made of sand and it was slowly leaking out of a puncture in some outer skin. He thought of soulikens and how those small and permanent stamps of electric pulses and energy might be the very thing he felt seeping out of him into . . . wherever they went. His Alterants' soulikens had come to him, according to the Haunce. Maybe now they would go to that odd, ghostly creature of eternity.

Jane was walking away, stabbing her Staff into the mud.

Tick hated her.

Life was running away from him. He closed his eyes, wondering if he would ever open them again. What he saw appear out of the patchy darkness was Kayla. And Lisa. His parents. Paul and Sofia and Sato. He saw them as if he looked at a TV screen.

The Chi'karda exploded within him.

No build-up this time. No slow burn that escalated like stoked flames. It was an absolute detonation of power. His whole body became a conflagration, a perfect and consuming inferno of force and might. He didn't know he'd done it, but he was suddenly standing. A tornado of orange, fiery air swirled around him. He heard himself speak as if he were an outside observer.

"Jane, you're not going anywhere."

CHAPTER
59

FISTS OF CHI'KARDA

The fangen attacked Sato just as he landed on his twentieth compartment. Sharp claws dug into his shoulders and yanked him backward. Sato spun, swinging with a fist. He made contact, thumping the creature's face. With a horrible shriek, it let go and fell away, its thin, translucent wings flapping weakly.

Sato knew there were more fangen, that this would be a tricky task indeed. He quickly stuck a nanolocator patch on to the tiny boy shivering on the stone then moved to jump to the next rectangular hole. He was in midflight when a fangen swooped in and grabbed him, pulling his body out to the middle of the chamber, its legs wrapped around him as it tried to bite his neck.

Sato clutched the top of the creature's head by a tuft of diseased-looking hair and pushed its gaping mouth full of teeth away. Then he punched it, slipping around its body in that moment of weakness so he was on the thing's back. They hovered over the abyss.

"Take me back to that hole!" Sato screamed in its ear, pointing to the place he'd been going. "Take me now, or I'll snap your neck!" He wrapped his hands around the thin pole of the fangen's neck and started squeezing.

The creature had to have some instinct to survive, some will to live. Making sounds like a strangled banshee, it flew toward the place indicated. Sato jumped off and into the inset compartment as soon as he was close enough. He pivoted and kicked out, connecting with the fangen's stomach. It squawked and pulled back, choking and coughing.

Sato pulled out a patch and stuck it to the little girl next to him. He readied for the next one. Nothing about this was going to be very easy. He jumped.

❦

Womp. Womp. Womp.

Surging throbs of Chi'karda sent waves of energy thumping away from Tick. He could feel its vibrations in the air, in the ground, in the forest behind him, shaking the deepest parts of the wood in the trees. His senses had heightened, almost unbearably so; the smells of mud and pine, the feel of the breeze, every sound amplified tenfold, the crisp clarity of his vision. It all felt wonderful and terrible at the same time.

Jane had stopped when he told her she wasn't going anywhere, probably consumed by curiosity. And, Tick hoped, a little scared. She turned around to face him, standing about thirty yards away.

"You can't handle that much Chi'karda," she said; Tick heard each word as if she'd spoken it directly into his ear. "It'll burn you to a crisp if you don't let it go. Release it, Atticus. Or you'll kill countless others along with . . ."

She faltered, her mask shifting downward just slightly, but enough to show she was looking at Tick's stomach. His eyes fell to see what had caught her attention, and he almost cried out in shock.

The wooden hilt of the knife smoldered, slowly inching its way as if by magic out of his skin. The long blade followed, glowing a hot red. The whole area sizzled like a cooking steak, small wisps of smoke rising from the wound. The knife finally came all the way out and fell to the ground with a thump and another sizzle as it hit the wet mud. Tick watched in shock as the slice in his skin healed back together in a matter of seconds. He felt an intense burning where the wound had been, stronger even than the Chi'karda raging through his entire body.

His dad had once told him how he'd seemed to defy death several times as a kid. What it all meant, Tick didn't know. Maybe his ability over Chi'karda went way further than he ever dreamed or hoped.

He looked back at Jane, quickly wiping the look of surprise from his face. "I'm getting control of it!" he shouted. "And you know I'm more powerful than you are! Give up. Now. Or I'll blow you up along with everything else in the Factory."

Jane's fingers tightened around her Staff. "You're an idiot child, Atticus. I wanted to kill you with subtle ease and avoid the destruction you might inflict if you let loose your chaotic abilities. But I'll do it this way if I have to. I'll never sleep in my bed again until I know the Realities are rid of Atticus Higginbottom. You're about to die, boy. I hope you've enjoyed your short time alive."

Tick's anger built with every word she said, and he couldn't take it anymore. He collected his power by thinking it, imagined what he wanted in his mind, like gathering a mental snowball with mental hands. The Chi'karda burned and roiled inside him, resisting as he compacted it tighter and tighter, compressing it into a dangerous and unstable sphere of pure energy. He saw the fiery orange cloud seeping back into his skin, like smoke in reverse.

Straining with the effort, he spoke through his trembling concentration. "I think I'll keep living." With a terrible scream, he threw his coiled power—all of it—at Jane.

A boom like a thousand strikes of lightning shook the world around him. Mud and dirt exploded from the ground in a straight path to Jane, as if it were a crowded minefield and every last mine went off at once. A visible wave of orange-tinged air slammed against her body, throwing her twenty feet into the air. She flew backward until she landed far on the other side of the broken wooden fence, her Staff broken into several pieces.

Tick had no idea how he did what happened next. But he willed himself forward, wanting to be by her side instantly, faster than he could possibly run. He was out of patience and knew he had to finish her off. In a dizzying instant, he suddenly stood right next to her, looking down at her as she struggled to stand. With a distant thought, he realized that he'd just winked himself.

He reached down and grabbed Jane by the folds of her robe, communicating with his powers of Chi'karda without talking, almost without thinking. He easily lifted her up and held her over his head. Then he threw her at the forest. She sailed several hundred feet through the air, arms and legs flailing; a piercing shriek ripped from her lungs. Tick watched as she finally slammed into a large oak tree and crumpled to the ground below it. She didn't move, a twisted heap of arms and legs.

Tick drew in deep, ragged breaths as he looked around him. He saw the hole in the ground that Jane had created to pull them out of the underground Factory, as well as a much larger gap with broken and jagged edges that had probably been caused by the earthquakes. He winked to the edge of it and looked down to where people from the Fifth Reality were fighting Jane's creatures. Tick saw and heard the sights and sounds of battle, the clashes and the blood and the screams. He wanted to destroy the Factory, level it, crush it, disintegrate it.

"Master George!" he yelled, knowing the man was listening in somehow. "Get them out! Get them all out!"

CHAPTER
60

TEN KIDS

"Tick wants us to wink them out!" Rutger yelled.

Sofia watched as Master George's hands flew furiously to turn dials and flip switches, type on the keyboard, adjust his Barrier Wand. "How much time until the wave hits us?" he asked in a tight voice.

"Three minutes!"

"We'll hold out until the last second. We must save every child we can!"

Sofia looked down to see that Paul had grabbed her hand. She squeezed back, terrified and hating how helpless she felt.

"Winking away the Fifth Army now," Master George said, sweat flying off his ruddy, bald head as he worked. "But not Sato and Mothball. Not yet."

"Two and a half minutes," Rutger said, his voice loud but sad.

Tick saw the tall people of the Fifth Reality suddenly disappear, winked away. The creatures they'd been fighting looked around in shock, growling and spitting.

Thankful that Master George had heard him, Tick had to assume that everyone was gone now. He hoped that George had also saved the kids Jane planned to use in her horrific experiments. He had to destroy the Factory now, before any of those monsters escaped. Then he'd finish off Jane and end this nightmare forever.

He closed his eyes for a brief moment, mentally gathering the streams and coils of Chi'karda, pulling it all in.

Then he fell to his knees with a scream, throwing his arms forward as if he were flinging his powers at the scene below him. His Chi'karda unleashed itself on the Factory, destroying everything in its fiery, angry path.

Sato's entire body ached like never before. Worse than when he'd gone through the agony of having Chu's Dark Infinity plague and being bound with ropes by Master George. His arms and legs screamed with weariness and hurt, begging him to stop.

But he didn't. He kept jumping from compartment to compartment, slapping the nanolocator patches on kid after kid, moving on before he even saw them be winked away. All the while, he'd fought off the relentless fangen with punches and kicks. He'd even poked one in the eyeball and sent it screeching away.

Mothball did her part on the other side of the vast, round chamber, leaping with more ease than Sato because of her height advantage. They were almost done. Sato could see the last row of inset rectangles just below him.

He landed in the latest cubbyhole, pulling out a patch before he even settled. A pretty girl with red hair lay curled in a ball, eyes lit with fear. He stuck the patch on her and turned to move on. Just as he did, a great explosion sounded from above, and the entire chamber started shaking again. Huge chunks of rock and metal fell through the air, cracking and clinging as they hit the sides along the way.

It had all started again. What went wrong! He dared not pause to think about it.

He punched a fangen just as it appeared, kicking

it and punching again. The hideous thing backed off.

Sato jumped, ignoring the increased danger of debris and quaking. He landed in the next compartment and reached for a nanolocator patch.

~~~

The Bermuda Triangle headquarters building trembled and groaned.

"Thirty seconds!" Rutger yelled. Despite the terror and worry she felt herself, Sofia couldn't help but feel bad for the poor little man. With his face flushed and sweat pouring off his skin, he looked like he might drop dead any second. "It's already straining the cables to the max—they're going to snap! We have to go! We have to go!"

Master George continued his frantic, feverish work. "Blasted! They're still working hard. It must mean they haven't reached everyone yet."

"Time's up!" Rutger said, pounding his fist on the desk. "Or we'll all die with them!"

Sofia felt a storm of different feelings and emotions rip through her heart: fear for her life, fear for Sato's life, sorrow for the kids. She squeezed Paul's hand even tighter and waited, holding her breath. The building shook even harder now, groans of twisting metal hurting her ears.

Master George swore, something Sofia never thought she'd hear him do. Then, "Fine. Let's finish this thing."

He started tapping buttons.

⁓

The entire chamber was about to fall down around Sato. The shattering cracks and thunderous rumbles of crumbling stone had risen to a deafening roar. Just after placing a patch on the latest kid, he looked across the way at Mothball and saw her staring back at him through the rain of debris. Her eyes said it all.

They could die here if they didn't get winked out immediately—who knew when the shaking would stop, when things would settle. But then, almost at the exact same time, they both slowly nodded. They wouldn't leave—not until they'd saved every last prisoner.

Sato broke eye contact first and scooted to the edge of his current cubbyhole. He did a quick scan and counted. Ten kids. There were ten kids left. Five for him, five for Mothball.

He coiled for the jump, but just as he pushed off, he felt a quick and cold tingle shoot across his neck and down his spine.

"No!" he screamed. But it was too late. The chamber vanished around him.

Sofia barely had time to notice they'd winked into the Grand Canyon sitting room, barely had time to feel the relief of solid ground under her feet, when Sato and Mothball appeared right in front of her. The two of them looked like zombies, filthy and scratched and worn.

"No!" Sato yelled, twisting around on his feet, as if looking for something. "Send me back! There were ten more! Ten more!"

Master George appeared through a doorway, his face cramped with a tight smile. "The children should be down in the valley. Ah, Sato, Mothball, thank goodness you're—"

Sato ran to the man and grabbed him by the shirt. "Send me back! The whole place is falling down—they could die! There were ten more of them!"

Master George shook his head back and forth. "I'm . . . I'm terribly sorry, Sato. It's far too late—everything was set up back in the Bermuda Triangle station. I simply can't send you back from here. I'm very sorry."

"You have to!" Sato's arms shook with fury or exhaustion. Probably both. "You have to send me back! We didn't get them all!"

"It's impossible," Master George whispered sadly. "Quite impossible."

Sato slumped to the floor. Sofia looked over and saw Mothball had collapsed on a couch, her eyes closed, tears leaking out from beneath their lids. Paul moved to crouch beside Sato and put a hand on his back.

Sato shook it off. "We left ten kids! Ten!"

Sofia joined them, sitting on the other side of Sato. "But think of how many you saved. And the others might escape in all the chaos."

She and Paul pulled Sato into an awkward three-person hug. He resisted at first, but then finally collapsed into Sofia's arms, sobbing.

"Think of how many you saved," she repeated.

CHAPTER
61

COLLISION

Tick stumbled away from the collapsing Factory, sucking the power of Chi'karda back inside him. He felt the flaming heat of it burn his insides. It had taken only three waves of it to destroy the complex. The sounds of crunching and cracking and splintering filled the air as the ground sank, swirling like a whirlpool of mud. He'd begun the chain reactions of destructive entropy that would leave the place as nothing but sand within minutes.

The earth began to give beneath Tick. There was no way he could outrun the collapse. With a thought, he quickly winked back to the forest where he'd thrown Jane's body just minutes ago.

She still lay in a heap at the bottom of the oak tree, but her arms were moving, and Tick heard her groan. His heart sank. He'd hoped she would be dead from the collision, because he dreaded the prospect of having to do anything more to her. His initial anger and adrenaline had subsided, and the reality of the situation was hitting home. If he finished what he'd set out to do, it meant he would have to end it, right here, right now.

He had to do it, no matter what. Unchecked, she could and would murder millions and billions of people. She'd already proven that. Tick had to finish it.

He stepped toward her.

The ground exploded under Tick, a wave of invisible force lifting him off his feet and throwing him backward. Before he could gather his wits, his back slammed into the soft ground, knocking the air out of him. He pushed himself up onto his knees, gasping for breath. If the mud had been dried and hard, he could very well have broken his spine.

When a rush of air finally filled his lungs, he jumped to his feet. Jane stood a few yards away, both of her hands outstretched, palms facing him. Tick reached for the Chi'karda that still churned within him.

"Wait," she said. "Wait. If we keep at this something really bad will happen."

Tick didn't waste time with words. He pushed a surge of Chi'karda straight at her, hurling it like a volley

of sun flares. The power hit her, twisting her body up into the air and back down to the mud where she slid thirty feet and smacked into the base of a tall pine.

Tick switched gears, concentrating on the trees around her. Using his mind as commander, willing what he wanted to happen, he made a dozen trees around her dissolve, the wood bursting into a swirl of tiny particles. They flew around her in a brown tornado, encircling her like a swarm of muddy bees. Then he made them collapse, sealing the wood back together like he'd done before several times now, though unconsciously.

With a loud smacking sound, followed by cracks and groans, a large mass of twisted wood formed around Jane, trapping her inside. Crushing her.

Tick doubled over, his hands on his knees, pulling in rapid breaths. The mental effort of doing such a thing made him feel as though he'd run ten miles in a sprint. He glanced back up at the hideous structure of coiled tree parts. No way she survived that. No way.

The thought had barely formed when the entire formation exploded, chunks and chips of wood flying out in all directions. Tick fell to the ground and covered his head with both arms. He felt the prick of splinters, the whoosh of bigger pieces flying right over him. When it seemed as though the worst had passed, he looked up and saw Jane standing there, her arms once again outstretched.

"Atticus, we have to stop this!" she yelled.

Tick jumped to his feet. She was trying to trick him; he knew it. He threw another blast of Chi'karda at her; she blocked it with a visible bubble of solid air tinted orange. The concussion wave bounced back and knocked him to the ground, jolting the breath out of him once again. As he struggled for air, he clawed to gather another pool of his power, knowing she'd probably finish him off while he was down.

But when he staggered to his feet, she only stood there, her mask surprisingly showing concern, not anger.

"Atticus, stop," she said in her scratchy, painful voice. "Give me five minutes to explain!"

Tick felt a rush of anger just as he pulled in a long, blissful breath. "It's too late, Jane! I can't let you go one more day killing and hurting!"

A ball of power filled him, almost bursting his chest. He unleashed it, threw it all at Jane.

Her shield formed again, resisting his attack. Tick was ready for the rebound of force this time, and he leaned into it, fighting it with his own strength. He let all his fears and inhibitions fall away, all his caution. She seemed to be getting stronger, and he knew he had to go for it. Screaming, he searched and probed his inner mind and body for every last trickle of Chi'karda, channeling it and throwing it at Jane.

She fought back. A wind tore through the air as

the crackle of electricity and booms of thunder filled the world around them. Streaks of orange swirled and kicked; bursts of fire ignited here and there like ribbons of flame; the trees in the forest bent unnaturally away from them; mud and chunks of wood took flight, swirling like loose paper in a tornado. As Tick and Jane fought, their battling powers looked like two stars colliding, white and brilliant and blinding.

Tick hadn't stopped screaming. The world rushed and burned around him. He couldn't see. Life seemed to be draining out of his body. He didn't know how much longer he could last. A trickle of despair dented his heart. He pushed harder.

Somehow he heard Jane yell the words, "We have to stop!"

"No!" Tick shouted back in a ripped shriek that tore through his burning throat. He pushed harder, flinging his whole life at her.

A sound like the world splitting in two pierced his ears, his brain, his every nerve.

And then, in a sudden instant, everything stopped.

All light disappeared. Tick felt himself flying through a dark and silent wind.

Time stretched on, blank and quiet. Eventually, he felt nothing.

CHAPTER 62

THE DETOUR

I can't believe my own eyes."

Tick barely heard the words. A man. His voice was soft, but slightly . . . menacing, like small, sharp-nosed worms, slowly working their way into Tick's brain, needling and hurting. The world around Tick was still dark.

The stranger spoke again. "Atticus Higginbottom and Mistress Jane. Together, with me, at last."

Tick felt himself blinking, felt tears in his eyes, felt pain coursing through every inch of his body. But still nothing—blackness.

The man wouldn't be quiet, and every word throbbed in Tick's skull. "I have no idea how it happened, but I can't say I'm not pleased. It'll be nice to have some help.

I'm sure between the three of us, we can get out of here."

Tick kept blinking and finally saw a faint smudge of light against the darkness.

"Where . . . where are we?"

Jane. It was Jane. She sounded even worse than usual.

The man chuckled, a horribly unpleasant sound. "You're safe and sound, Mistress. No worries. Plenty to eat around here. Plenty of everything."

The light grew in Tick's vision. Increased its pace of brightening. Shapes began to form.

"I . . . warned him," Jane said, her voice filled with resignation, as if she'd just accepted a horrible truth. "I . . ." She didn't finish.

Something clicked, and suddenly Tick could see everything. Gasping, he sat up, ignoring the bolts of pain that shot through his body. He sat on a beach with a perfect blue sky hanging overhead and crystal-clear water lapping against the white sand. An enormous and endless ocean stretched to his right, a forest of palm trees to his left. Mistress Jane lay flat on the ground, several feet away, her mask cracked and tilted.

And sitting cross-legged next to Tick was Reginald Chu. The man who'd once ruled the Fourth Reality. The man who'd tried to rule all Thirteen with his Dark Infinity. The man who'd been sent to—

"Welcome to the Nonex, Atticus," Chu said. "I hope you're ready to help me get the heck out of here."

EPILOGUE

THE MISSION

Sofia sat between Paul and Sato on the couch, her arms folded, her foot tapping. Sally and Priscilla, both of whom had been in charge of collecting and helping the children rescued from the Factory, sat across from them, looking down and as quiet as everyone else. Mothball was on the floor, leaning against the bricks of the fireplace.

Master George and Rutger finally entered the room, their faces grave.

"I believe we finally have our report," Master George announced, looking down at a stack of papers clasped in his hands. "The members of Sato's Fifth Army are mostly safe and accounted for, having lost only"—he cleared his throat—"seventeen lives in battle. It looks like Sato and Mothball rescued ninety-seven children in all, and they are currently receiving the very best in treatment from Realitant doctors."

"We lost ten of them," Sato mumbled under his breath. It was the first thing he'd said since winking away from the Thirteenth.

"Why . . . yes, Sato. Yes, we did." Master George paused, his eyes showing so much love for Sato that Sofia felt tears moisten her eyes. "The damage from our latest affairs is quite catastrophic. Every single Reality has suffered, and the recovery will take years. The worst by far is the Thirteenth, where . . . the final conflict inflicted utter devastation. It will take some time to discover just how much."

Sofia spoke up. "What happened to Tick?"

"Yeah," Paul said. "Out with it."

Master George nodded uncomfortably. "Yes, yes, we're all very concerned about Master Atticus and what has become of him." His voice squeaked on the last three words; a tear spilled down his cheek. "I'm afraid we have quite troubling—and confusing—news."

Sofia's heart froze; her breath stopped.

"I can't say I understand it," he continued, fidgeting with his papers. "His nanolocator started working again once his business with the Haunce was complete. But then . . . it just . . . well, it reported back something we've never seen before. Rutger, you tell them. I can't bear to say another bloody word." He threw the papers on the floor and stomped out of the room.

Rutger took a moment before finally speaking.

"According to our system, Atticus Higginbottom has ceased to exist."

~~~~~

Lisa had just fallen asleep—after a long time of trying to do so—when she felt someone shaking her by the shoulders, gently. She opened her eyes, ready to scream out in panic, when the sight of her mom silenced it. The glow of the moon shining through the window lit up Lorena Higginbottom's face, making it look somehow kind and fiercely determined at the same time.

Lisa knew she was up to something. "What's going on?"

"Keep quiet and follow me," her mom whispered. "Don't make a peep—you know your dad will wake up at the sneeze of a mouse."

Confused but intrigued, Lisa shook her grogginess away and got up from bed. Then the two of them tiptoed out of her room, down the hall, then down the stairs, both keeping to the silent spots as best they could. Before long, Lisa's mom had led her all the way down to the basement.

After flicking on the light, Lisa repeated her earlier question. "What's going on?"

Her mom walked over to a dusty corner of the large room and dragged a couple of boxes away from the wall, then crouched down. "I know both you and I have been feeling like we want to help. To finally do our part in this whole mess. Especially now that my son"—she faltered, choked back the usual cry that had come so often since Master George had sent word that Tick was missing—"is nowhere to be found. I think it's time we took a little of our own action."

Lisa nodded, feeling the same swell of emotion, knowing she couldn't speak without cracking. But she agreed. Agreed wholeheartedly. She wanted to *do* something. She wanted to act.

Her mom gripped a panel of the unpainted wall, and to Lisa's surprise it came loose. She lifted out a large square and placed it on the ground. Swirls of dust puffed through the air. In the dark recess behind her, an object glinted.

"You've been hiding something down here?" Lisa asked.

"Yes. Though I never, never, never thought I'd have to use it again." She leaned over and reached into the secret compartment.

"What?" Lisa asked, moving closer to get a better look. "What is it?"

Her mom pulled out a long, golden tube with dials and switches running down its sides, then held it up. "It's a Barrier Wand, sweetie. It's gonna help us find my boy."

A GLOSSARY OF PEOPLE, PLACES, AND ALL THINGS IMPORTANT

Atticus Higginbottom—A Realitant from the state of Washington in Reality Prime.

Alterant—Different versions of the same person existing in different Realities. It is extremely dangerous for Alterants to meet one another.

Annika—A spy for the Realitants who was killed by a pack of fangen.

Barf Scarf—The red-and-black scarf that Tick used to wear at all times to hide the ugly birthmark on his neck.

Barrier Wand—The device used to wink people and things between Realities and between heavily concentrated places of Chi'karda within the same Reality. Works very easily with inanimate objects, and can place them almost anywhere. To transport humans, they must be in a place concentrated with Chi'karda (like a cemetery) and have a nanolocator that transmits their location to the Wand. The wand is useless without the Chi'karda Drive, which channels and magnifies the mysterious power.

Barrier Staff—A special Barrier Wand created by Mistress Jane.

Benson—A servant of Reginald Chu in the Fourth Reality.

Bermuda Triangle—The most concentrated area of Chi'karda in each Reality. Still unknown as to why.

Billy "The Goat" Cooper—Tick's biggest nemesis at Jackson Middle School.

Blade of Shattered Hope—A weapon created by Mistress Jane that allows her to harness the power of dark matter and utilize the linking of her Alterants to sever a Reality from existence.

Bryan Cannon—A fisherman in Reality Prime.

Bugaboo Soldiers—The nemeses of the Fifth Reality, these assassins are bent on taking over their world. Often dressed as clowns, they are very unstable.

Chi'karda—The mysterious force that controls Quantum Physics. It is the scientific embodiment of conviction and choice, which in reality rules the universe. Responsible for creating the different Realities.

Chi'karda Drive—The invention that revolutionized the universe by harnessing, magnifying, and controlling Chi'karda. It has long been believed that travel between Realities is impossible without it.

Chu Industries—The company that practically rules the world of the Fourth Reality. Known for countless inventions and technologies, including many that are malicious in nature.

Command Center—Master George's headquarters in the Bermuda Triangle, where Chi'karda levels are monitored and to where his many nanolocators report various types of information.

Darkin (Dark Infinity) Project—A menacing, giant device created by Reginald Chu of the Fourth Reality to manipulate others' minds. Destroyed by Tick.

Earwig Transponder—An insect-like device inserted into the ear that can scramble listening devices and help track its host.

Edgar Higginbottom—Tick's father.

Entropy—The law of nature that states all things move toward destruction. Related to fragmentation.

Factory, The—Located in the Thirteenth Reality, it is where Mistress Jane "manufactures" her abominable creations.

Fangen—A creature created by Mistress Jane utilizing the twisted and mutated version of Chi'karda found in the Thirteenth Reality. Formed from a variety of no fewer than twelve different animals, the short and stocky creatures are bred to kill first and ask questions later. They can also fly.

Fifth Army, The—Sato's fighting unit, made up of people from the Fifth Reality.

Firekelt—Creation of Mistress Jane. A monster covered in hundreds of cloth-like strips that ignite on demand.

Fragmentation—When a Reality begins losing Chi'karda levels on a vast scale, it can no longer maintain itself as a major alternate version of the world and will eventually disintegrate into nothing. Its cause is related to entropy.

Frazier Gunn—A loyal servant of Mistress Jane.

Frupey—Nickname for Fruppenschneiger, Sofia's butler.

Gnat Rat—A malicious invention of Chu Industries in the Fourth Reality. Releases dozens of mechanical hornets that are programmed to attack a certain individual based on a nanolocator, DNA, or blood type.

Grand Canyon—A satellite location of the Realitants. Second only to the Bermuda Triangle in Chi'karda levels. Still unknown as to why.

Grand Minister—Supreme ruler of the Fifth Reality.

Grinder Beast—An enormous, rhinoceros-like creature with dozens of legs in the Tenth Reality.

Halters—A weapon that shoots out tiny darts laced with a paralyzing serum.

Hans Schtiggenschlubberheimer—The man who started the Scientific Revolution in the Fourth Reality in the early nineteen hundreds. In a matter of decades, he helped catapult the Fourth far beyond the other Realities in terms of technology.

Haunce, The—A mysterious, ghostly, powerful being made up of billions upon billions of soulikens.

Henry—A boy from the Industrial Barrens in the Seventh Reality.

Hillenstat—A Realitant doctor from the Second Reality.

Jimmy "The Voice" Porter—A Realitant from the Twelfth Reality. Has no tongue.

Katrina Kay—A Realitant from the Ninth Reality.

Kayla Higginbottom—Tick's youngest sister.

Klink—Guard of the Execution Exit at the End of the Road Insane Asylum.

Kyoopy—Nickname used by the Realitants for Quantum Physics.

Ladies of Blood and Sorrow—A mysterious society of women loyal to Mistress Jane.

Lemon Fortress—Mistress Jane's castle in the Thirteenth Reality.

Lisa Higginbottom—Tick's older sister.

Lorena Higginbottom—Tick's mother.

Mabel Fredrickson—Tick's great-aunt. Lives in Alaska.

Master George—The current leader of the Realitants.

Metaspide—A vicious robotic creature from the Fourth Reality that resembles a spider.

Mistress Jane—A former Realitant and ruler of the Thirteenth Reality, she wields an uncanny power over Chi'karda. Since the accident in which she was "melded" with fragments of the Dark Infinity weapons, her power has increased tenfold.

Mothball—A Realitant from the Fifth Reality.

Ms. Sears—Tick's favorite librarian.

Muffintops—Master George's cat.

Multiverse—An old term used by Reality Prime scientists to explain the theory that Quantum Physics has created multiple versions of the universe.

Nancy Zeppelin—A Realitant from Wisconsin in Reality Prime.

Nanolocator—A microscopic electronic device that can crawl into a person's skin and forever provide information on their whereabouts, Chi'karda levels, etc.

Nonex—When Alterants meet, one disappears and enters the Nonex. A complete mystery to the Realitants.

Norbert McGillicuddy—A post office worker in Alaska who helped Tick and his dad escape an attack by Frazier Gunn.

Paul Rogers—A Realitant from Florida in Reality Prime.

Phillip—Owner and operator of the Stroke of Midnight Inn in the Sixth Reality.

Pick—Master George's nickname for a major decision in which Chi'karda levels spike considerably. Some Picks have been known to create or destroy entire Realities.

Priscilla Persiphone—A Realitant from the Seventh Reality.

Quantum Physics—The science that studies the physical world of the extremely small. Most scholars are baffled by its properties and at a loss to explain them. Theories abound. Only a few know the truth: that a completely different power rules this realm, which in turn rules the universe: Chi'karda.

Quinton Hallenhaffer—A Realitant from the Second Reality.

Ragers—An advanced weapon that harnesses extreme amounts of static electricity. When unleashed, it collects matter in a violent, earthen ball that can shatter whatever gets in its way.

Realitants—An organization sworn to discover and chart all known Realities. Founded in the 1970s by a group of scientists from the Fourth Reality, who then used Barrier Wands to recruit other quantum physicists from other Realities.

Reality—A separate and complete version of the world, of which there may be an infinite number. The most stable and strongest is called Reality Prime. So far, thirteen major branches off of Prime have been discovered. Realities are created and destroyed by enormous fluctuations in Chi'karda levels. Examples:

Fourth—Much more advanced technologically than the other Realities due to the remarkable vision and work of Hans Schtiggenschlubberheimer.

Fifth—Quirks in evolution led to a very tall human race.

Eighth—The world is covered in water due to much higher temperatures that were caused by a star fusion anomaly triggered in another galaxy by an alien race.

Eleventh—Quirks in evolution and diet led to a short and robust human race.

Thirteenth—Somehow a mutated and very powerful version of Chi'karda exists here.

Reality Echo—An object that literally exists in two Realities at once, making the object indestructible.

Reginald Chu—Tick's science teacher in Reality Prime. Also the person in the Fourth Reality who founded Chu Industries and turned it into a worldwide empire. They are Alterants of each other.

Renee—An inmate at the End of the Road Insane Asylum.

Ripple Quake—A violent geological disaster caused by a massive disturbance in Chi'karda.

Rutger—A Realitant from the Eleventh Reality.

Sally T. Jones—A Realitant from the Tenth Reality.

Sato—A Realitant from Japan in Reality Prime.

Sato Tadashi—Former Grand Minister of the Fifth Reality, killed by the Bugaboo soldiers. An Alterant of the Realitant Sato.

Shockpulse—An injection of highly concentrated electromagnetic nanobots that seek out and destroy the tiny components of a nanolocator, rendering it useless.

Shurric—Short for Sonic Hurricaner, this weapon is the more powerful version of the Sound Slicer. Shoots out a heavily concentrated force of sound waves, almost too low for the human ear to register but powerful enough to destroy just about anything in its direct path.

Sleeks—Creations of Mistress Jane. Wispy and strong, lightning fast. They guard the forest that surrounds the Factory.

Slinkbeast—A vicious creature that lives in the Mountains of Sorrow in the Twelfth Reality.

Snooper Bug—A hideous crossbreed of birds and insects created by the mutated power of the Chi'karda in the Thirteenth Reality. Can detect any known weapon or poison and can kill with one quick strike of its needle-nosed beak. Pets of Mistress Jane.

Sofia Pacini—A Realitant from Italy in Reality Prime.

Soulikens—An imprint or stamp on reality, created by natural energy and Chi'karda, that becomes a lingering piece of one's self that will never cease to exist.

Sound Slicer—A small weapon outdated by the much more powerful Shurric.

Spinner—A special device that shoots out a circular plane of laser light, displaying video images on its surface.

Squeezers—A grenade that shoots out strong wires that contract and curl up.

Tick—Nickname for Atticus Higginbottom.

Tingle Wraith—A collection of microscopic animals from the Second Reality, called spilphens, that can form together into a cloud while rubbing against each other to make a horrible sound called the Death Siren.

Tollaseat—Mothball's father, from the Fifth Reality.

Waterkelt—Creation of Mistress Jane. A monster made completely out of water.

William Schmidt—A Realitant from the Third Reality.

Windasill—Mothball's mother, from the Fifth Reality.

Windbike—An invention of Chu Industries, this vehicle is a motorcycle that can fly, consuming hydrogen out of the air for its fuel. Based on an extremely complex gravity-manipulation theorem first proposed by Reginald Chu.

Winking—The act of traveling between or within Realities by use of a Barrier Wand. Causes a slight tingle to the skin on one's shoulders and back.

DISCUSSION QUESTIONS

1. Tick has to deal with a lot of bad things happening to his family. Often he must weigh their safety against much bigger dangers that could result in enormous loss of life. What would you do in such a situation?

2. How do you feel about Mistress Jane after reading this book? Do you think she's purely evil? Is there any truth to her feeling that the ends justify the means? In other words, if the end result is her perfect Utopian Reality, is it okay for her to do anything, no matter how bad, to reach that point?

3. We learn a little more about Sofia and why she doesn't feel very welcome at home. How does that make you feel?

4. We find out that Tick is the only version of himself still alive throughout the known Realities. He has no surviving Alterants. What's your theory as to what this means? Do you think it has anything to do with his odd powers over Chi'karda?

5. What do you think of the Haunce? It seems distant and unwilling to interfere with human life until the entire universe is in jeopardy. And yet it obviously has strong powers. Should it help out more?

6. How do you feel about the progress Tick has made in controlling his powers? Is his power something you would wish for, or would it be too much pressure and too dangerous?

7. Sato is devastated that he wasn't able to save every child from the Factory before being winked out by Master George. Put yourself in that situation. How would you feel? Would you be able to focus on the ones you saved instead of being haunted by the ones you didn't?

8. Were you surprised that Tick ended up reunited with Mr. Chu and Mistress Jane in the Nonex? What do you think is in store for them in Book 4?

THE 13TH REALITY

BOOK 4

THE VOID OF MIST AND THUNDER . . .

The forest smelled of things dead, things rotting.

Jacob Gillian paid it no mind as he walked along the narrow path that threaded through the tall oaks and pines like a dried-out stream. Of course, the reason he paid it no mind was that he'd lost his sense of smell thirty years ago after an unfortunate encounter with an angry skunk. His grandson Chip had to tell him that the place stunk like a three-week-old dead rat stuck under the pipes.

The two of them had been hiking together for well over an hour, and they both knew full well that something horrible had happened deep within the dark woods. Jacob had heard the awful sound of ripping and shredding and booming. Chip had smelled the nose-wrinkling stench afterward. Those two things together spelled trouble. But exactly *what* had happened was still a mystery, and the reason they were out there.

Jacob and his grandson had moved to the boonies after Chip's parents had been killed in a train collision near Louisville. Ever since then, Jacob and Chip had learned to live with little and less, but loved the wild freedom and exhilaration of being smack-dab in the middle of nowhere. Their closest neighbor was a good thirty miles down the poorly maintained state road, and the nearest town was forty miles the other direction. But that's just how Jacob liked it, and the lifestyle had seemed to grow on Chip as well.

One day they'd return to civilization, start Chip learning the ways of society. But for now, there was time. Time to heal, time to grow, time to enjoy. Time to have time.

"I think I see something up ahead, Grandpa," Chip said, a little too enthusiastically—considering the circumstances that had brought them out there.

"What is it?" Old Jacob couldn't see much better than he could smell.

"There's a bright patch. Looks like it goes all the way up to the sky!" Chip grabbed Jacob's hand and started hurrying down the little ribbon of beaten leaves and undergrowth. "It's just to the right of the path. We're almost there!"

Jacob followed along, being as careful as he could despite the speed with which Chip dragged him along.

They'd just rounded a bend, skirting two mammoth pines that looked like brothers, when Chip suddenly pulled up short. Jacob ran right into him—almost knocking him over. Then Jacob saw what had stopped the kid, and all he could do was stand and stare. He felt Chip's hand slip out of his own, probably from the sweat that suddenly coated his palm.

Fifty yards ahead of them, a swath of the forest had been wiped from existence—replaced by a brushstroke of . . . something else. Starting deep in the ground and shooting all the way to the sky was a wide gash in reality, a window to another place. Jacob could see part of a beach, the deep blue waters of the ocean beside it, and a sun where there shouldn't *be* a sun. The time was hardly noon, and the *real* ball of fire was directly overhead. It was as if someone had cut out a section of reality of this world and replaced it with another.

"What in the great dickens are we lookin' at?" Jacob whispered.

"Grandpa?" was all Chip got out in reply. His voice shook with equal parts confusion and terror.

"I've been from one end of this world to the other," Jacob said, not sure if he was talking to himself or to his grandson. "And I've never seen a thing like this in my life."

"Let's go home."

"Home?" Jacob tore his eyes away from the spectacle and looked down at Chip. "Didn't you hear what I said? This is a once-in-a-lifetime opportunity! Let's go check it out."

Jacob took Chip's hand once again, and they started marching closer to the impossible vision of another world streaked across their own. They were only twenty feet away when a person appeared on the beach, stepping into the picture from the right edge of the . . . whatever it was.

The person was a woman, though Jacob could only tell that from the ratty, filthy dress she wore. A hood was pulled up over her head, and a red mask, seemingly made out of metal, covered her face. The expression on the mask was one of anger.

She saw them just as they saw her, and she stopped to stare, the features of the mask *shifting* into an expression of shock.

Jacob took a step backward before he realized what he was doing.

"Who are you?" the woman asked, her voice raw and scratchy, like it came out of a throat scarred with acid. "Do you know how this happened?"

Jacob's mouth had turned into a bucket of dust, and he couldn't remember how his tongue or voice box worked. He tried getting some words out but nothing came except the slightest hint of a croak.

Surprisingly, Chip spoke up. "We heard lots of bad sounds coming from over here, and the whole place is stinky. Me and my grandpa were just trying to see what happened."

Such bravery from the kid meant Jacob had to speak. He found his voice. "Where you from, miss? Um, if you don't mind me asking."

The lady's mask melted—literally, by the looks of it—into a frown. "I'm from the Thirteenth Reality."

Jacob swallowed a lump of confusion the size of his big toe. "Um . . . This is Kentucky—"

Before the lady could respond, her image and everything around her suddenly spun into a tornado of colors that quickly merged and transformed into a gray storm. It swirled and swirled, picking up speed and creating a wind that tore at Jacob's clothing. And then the sound of terrible thunder seemed to come from everywhere at once, shaking the forest and splintering Jacob's skull with pain.

When the spinning mass of gray mist expanded and took him, he had the strange thought that, although he certainly wasn't a cat, curiosity had killed him all the same.